The cockpit of the lead AH-1S Cobra chopper was suddenly invaded by a loud buzzing noise and flashing red light. The rate of climb had fallen precipitously in a downdraft; the craft's pod load of eight TOW, or tube-launched, optically tracked, wire-guided, antitank missiles, and two pods of nineteen 2.75-inch rockets for softer targets—should infantry be sighted—were abnormally buffeted. The pilot instantly altered the pitch, and the rotors responded quickly in the cold Siberian air, giving more lift than they would have in the warmer climes of Western Europe and Southeast Asia.

Suddenly the first tanks were in sight, either T-72s or 80s; it was difficult to tell because of the camouflage netting.

The pilot felt the adrenaline taking over as he shot off a TOW missile equipped with the latest warhead, upgraded to penetrate the layered reactive armor of the Siberian tanks, which could explode an incoming round and diffuse its impact. The pilot knew that for all its versatility in the air, his craft was, at a speed of plus or minus 150 miles per hour, a slow combatant in the modern world of high-subsonic and supersonic warfare, and low to the trees it was terribly vulnerable. . . .

Also by Ian Slater:

FIRESPILL
SEA GOLD
AIR GLOW RED
ORWELL: THE ROAD TO AIRSTRIP ONE
STORM
DEEP CHILL
FORBIDDEN ZONE*
WW III*
WW III: RAGE OF BATTLE*
WW III: WORLD IN FLAMES*

Published by Fawcett Books

WW III:
ARCTIC
FRONT

Ian Slater

FAWCETT GOLD MEDAL • NEW YORK

A Fawcett Gold Medal Book
Published by Ballantine Books
Copyright © 1992 by Bunyip Enterprises, Inc.

All rights reserved under International and Pan-American Copyright Conventions. Published in the United States by Ballantine Books, a division of Random House, Inc., New York, and simultaneously in Canada by Random House of Canada Limited, Toronto.

Library of Congress Catalog Card Number: 91-93156

ISBN 0-449-14756-8

Printed in Canada

First Edition: May 1992

For Marian, Serena, and Blair

ACKNOWLEDGMENTS

I would like to thank Professors Peter Petro and Charles Slonecker who are colleagues and friends of mine at the University of British Columbia. Most of all I am indebted to my wife, Marian, whose patience, typing, and editorial skills continue to give me invaluable support in my work.

PROLOGUE

"At least four republics have said they will leave the command structure of the Soviet Army and form their own armies."

The Economist, October 20, 1990

"Nowadays it is not only misleading but also wrong to view Russia and the Soviet Union as one political entity. . . . Districts like the Irkutsk regions of Siberia have adopted declarations of 'equality and independence.' "

Time magazine, November 12, 1990

"In July 1990, Col. Gen. Nikolai Chervov announced that the Soviet Army had 41,580 tanks in Europe. With the Conventional Forces in Europe Treaty signed in November 1990, there were hopes that a significant fraction of these tanks would be dismantled. Data released by the Soviets on 19 November 1990 indicate that there are now only 20,694 Soviet tanks in Europe. Where did all the other tanks go?

"After stonewalling the newly aggressive Soviet press for two months regarding the mystery, the Ministry of Defense Information Administration finally offered to clarify the situation for the paper *Sovetskaya Rossiya*. Officials claimed that in excess of 20,000 tanks were moved beyond the Urals prior to signing the treaty document. About 8,000 tanks from Europe were handed over to Soviet units in Asia, either to bring them up to strength or to replace old tanks. A further 8,392 tanks were placed into storage bases in Western Siberia or Central Asia."

Armed Forces Journal International,
March 1991

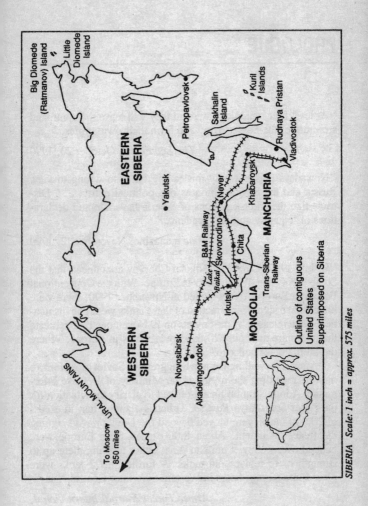

SIBERIA Scale: 1 inch = approx. 575 miles

CHAPTER ONE

GENERAL CHERNKO WAS a big man, his body hiding hers as he showed her the room. She had been chosen by Chernko's subaltern purely at random. Despite the severe rationing she had the kind of full figure, accentuated by the dark red dress she was wearing, that the major knew General Chernko liked: *kapitalnye titki*—"prominent breasts," as the general would say. "Something to hang onto."

"Don't undress," Chernko ordered her, and for a second the terror in the woman's eyes harbored a faint hope—dashed by his next words. "We'll have to hurry," he told her, as if she had any choice in the matter. "Soon the Americans'll be here." As he pulled the drapes closed she glimpsed the Kremlin directly across the square, still burning.

Even the goshawks, traditional guardians of the Kremlin's snow-capped towers, were fleeing the shell-pocked Citadel, leaving the Supreme Soviet to the crows—the Russian surrender to the legendary American general Douglas Freeman having been signed at Minsk by Marshal Kirov. Though the Allied troops had not yet reached Moscow proper, thousands of red fires, smoking sullenly amid the black-stained snow, marked the end for the city.

Chernko, chief of the Committee for Public Safety, the KGB, and now interim president of the USSR following President Suzlov's death, could smell the sickly sweet odor of cooked flesh and the acrid fumes of burning diesel rising from the gutted T-90s in the city's outer rings, the smoke bleeding darkly into the still, cold, blue air. Normally the sight of dead bodies didn't bother him—he'd had thousands of people executed in the course

1

of the war for un-Soviet activity and had carried out many of the executions himself—but now the sight of stiff, bloated bodies in the frigid dawn brought his own mortality closer. Had it been possible, he would have ordered the corpses buried in a mass grave, but the frozen ground was too hard for burial except in the craters left by the Allied bombing and the mass concentrated fire of the American 105-millimeter howitzers that had reduced much of the city to rubble.

It was 7:00 A.M., and Chernko knew it could not be long before Freeman's advance armored columns, with battle honors earned from Korea to Vietnam to the Iraqi desert, reached the inner city to occupy the Kremlin, which now lay smoldering across from his office in Dzerzhinsky Square. With President Suzlov dead, Chernko thought it possible the Allies might well use him as they'd used the Nazis in World War II to run the huge, complex government apparatus until they learned the ropes themselves. Or they might shoot him on the spot. He glanced impatiently at his watch.

It was 7:03. "Major, where's the car?" He was anxious to reach the new headquarters bunker in the outer ring. Communications here at the Dzerzhinsky Square offices were unreliable because of the artillery-severed underground cables. Any messages he wanted to send would have to be delivered by dispatch riders.

"Car's on its way, Comrade Director," replied the major, not yet used to calling Chernko "Mr. President." The Supreme Soviet Military Command—STAVKA—had backed Chernko when he had personally shot President Suzlov when the latter had issued the idiotic command to fight to the last Russian. But Chernko knew that while his action might have been supported by his Russian colleagues, it might not be so well received in the other republics. Everything was in flux.

"With all the debris," the major explained, "your car will probably have to make a detour around . . ."

The major's words were drowned out by a tremendous crash— the tower above the Kremlin's Spassky Gate telescoping into itself, crumbling amid flames shooting so high they threw the Citadel's rust-red walls into a stark, dancing relief. For Chernko the collapse of the tower was, ironically, like a shot of adrenaline, injecting him with an overwhelming urge to live. "Come here!" he ordered the woman.

She didn't utter a sound, didn't look away, for to anger him would mean death for her family as well as for herself. She had never seen Chernko before except in photographs. Already she was trembling, trying to be brave. At least, she thought, Beria, Stalin's KGB henchman, had gone out himself to prowl the streets for women. But Chernko no doubt considered himself above that. He sent underlings—his major.

She could smell the expensive cologne on Chernko, no doubt purchased at one of the Party's elite stores. In the end, Gorbachev and Yeltsin had changed nothing—the powerful were always the powerful. What could you do but submit?

He opened his greatcoat. "Take that scarf off," he commanded her. "You look like a peasant." He sat down, told her to kneel in front of him, and tore open her gray prison blouse, reaching forward, roughly pushing down her calico bra beneath her breasts. Now she was aware of another smell—his, mixed up with the cologne. "If you bite," he said matter-of-factly, sitting back in his doeskin recliner, "I'll kill you. Understand?" Before she could answer, he unzipped his trousers. "Slowly at first," he instructed her. "Go on!"

She did it as she and so many others had done so many other things for the chairman of the Committee of Public Safety and his thugs who called themselves the KGB. Soon Chernko was grunting like a pig, leaning forward on the edge of his chair, pulling and pushing her head until suddenly he seized her breasts so violently she gasped with pain. He shuddered, pushed her away, and then, backing up in the chair, its rollers going off the heavy, protective plastic mat onto the carpet, he shot her. Far enough away that no stains would get on his greatcoat, careful to use a U.S. nine-millimeter Parabellum load for his Makarov pistol in the unlikely event anyone would find her. Despite the physical release the woman had given him, Chernko was still anxious. He had learned from his agents in Novosibirsk that his name was on an official *Sibirskie predateli*—"Siberian traitors"—list for his part in Moscow's decision to surrender. He decided it was time to take out some insurance, but he was under no illusion. His down payment to the Siberians would have to be something spectacular—the biggest secret of all—an offer that, as American gangsters would say, the Siberians couldn't refuse. A plan that was certain to mollify Novosibirsk and protect him from the Siberian vengeance against those who had authorized the Russian surrender. A plan that would also wreak havoc with America.

It was at that moment that a dispatch rider, his arm bleeding, grimy uniform smudged with oil smoke, arrived and handed Chernko two messages from the new army HQ in the outer ring. The first message, from the Siberian capital city of Novosibirsk seventeen hundred miles to the east, beyond the natural barrier of the Ural Mountains, was short and to the point. If Moscow had surrendered, Siberia hadn't. Furthermore, it had no intention of doing so. Why should it? asked the Siberian Central Committee in Novosibirsk. Traditionally when Siberians speaking *podusham*—'from the heart''—spat out their contempt for "the West" they meant Moscow, which they distrusted as much as they did the U.S. Now the greatest collection of scientific minds in all the Russias, those of the Siberian *mozgovity*— "egghead"—city of Akademgorodok, just outside Novosibirsk, along with the Tartars and the twenty-nine other indigenous groups that made up the millions of *Siberyaka*, feared that with the mideast oil fields in a shambles from the war and still burning, the U.S., and particularly its resource-starved ally Japan, would take up where Moscow left off—sucking Siberia dry of her enormous natural wealth.

More than one and a half times the size of the entire United States (including Alaska and Hawaii), stretching for four thousand miles through nine time zones, from the Urals in the west through the space-launch stations on the steppes to the ICBM-studded granite fastness of Kamchatka Peninsula, Siberia's natural and industrial might—and now its own army—would be more than a match for the Allies. From its mountains, endless taiga, across its endless steppes to the deep gorges of its two-thousand-mile-long river systems, Siberia harbored vast reserves of oil, iron ore, gold, coal, timber, diamonds, and hosts of other strategic minerals, as well as the world's largest natural gas field at Novyy Urengoy adjacent to the Kara Sea.

The second message handed Chernko, from his KGB chief

in Novokuznetsk—a Siberian industrial center 180 miles east of Novosibirsk—was the one he'd been waiting for. It contained the details of a plan conceived by the directors of the city's giant Kuznetsky Metallurgical Kombinat, or KMK works. The conception was so daring, in Chernko's opinion he was sure he could trade it for a promise from Novosibirsk not only to protect him from Siberian extremists but to afford him, albeit secretly, a leading role in the Siberian wartime government and assure his future after the Siberian victory. The plan from the KMK was, Chernko confessed to the major, nothing less than *blestyashchiy*—"stunning." It would at first maul then consume the Americans if they dared attack Sibir.

CHAPTER TWO

To err is human.
To forgive is not First Army policy.

SO READ THE shingle above Gen. Douglas Freeman's headquarters in Minsk, which his aides were now in the process of taking down and packing for shipment back to the States. Freeman was a fighting general—of this the Pentagon, the president, and the Allied liaison commission in Washington had not the slightest doubt. At fifty-five he was the youngest four-star general in the U.S. Army—but not, as the State Department emphatically advised the White House, "diplomatic material." His abilities, Foggy Bottom pointed out, lay in action, "*not* in the delicate business of helping Russia back on its feet." The advisory memorandum from State quoted an interview that Freeman had, in State's view, ill-advisedly given the *Armed Forces Journal* four months before in Europe. Freeman had declared unequivocally that "nobody seems awake to the fact that even in Gorbachev's day the Soviet military had *expanded*, by getting rid of obsolete equipment and making it look as if it was reducing its forces"; that "in fact there were more mobile missile sites built during Gorbachev's tenure than by any other Soviet leader since the Russian Revolution." Which, Freeman had gone on to say just as unequivocally, "proves a sound military axiom, that you cannot trust any Commie son of a bitch as far as you can kick 'im!" And that "what the American people have to understand is that, when you get right down to it, regardless of changing civilian leaders, it's the Soviet military with which we will ultimately have to contend."

The Joint Chiefs of Staff, albeit reluctantly, agreed with State, yet they knew it would be unpopular in middle America to recall the general, and with such haste. It would be especially unpopular with the troops Freeman had led on his now-legendary nighttime airborne raid on Pyongyang in North Korea, whose leader he called "Kim Il Runt," and with those he'd led in an equally spectacular outflanking movement on Europe's northern plain, breaking out of the Dortmund-Bielefeld pocket—his armored columns racing ahead and breaching Moscow's defenses. He was, however, too brusque for Washington—a soldier's soldier—so that the Joint Chiefs of Staff felt they had no alternative than to agree with State in advising the president that it would be much "safer" for everyone to recall Freeman—to leave the peace to the experts.

At 7:14 A.M. the first car, a hand-tooled Zil limousine, weaved its way through the rubble-strewn snow and drew up in front of Dzerzhinsky Square, the two KGB door guards snapping to attention despite their weariness. A group of bleary-eyed and emaciated-looking army officers walking, or rather shuffling, up from the old Intourist Hotel through the ruins of Marx Prospect slowed to stare across the square. They managed to see two figures in civilian coats entering the Zil, the gray-uniformed chauffeur quickly checking the limousine's side mirror, and the car moving off quickly yet quietly in the snow. Several of the young army officers saluted but weren't sure whether it was the new president or not behind the black curtains. Seconds later a battered white Moskvich taxi, a four-door compact, swung into the curb and the officers across the square saw another figure, also in civilian garb, emerge from the old KGB building, the two guards coming to attention just as they had done for the Zil.

Inside the Zil, Chernko's aide tried to hide his surprise, having expected Chernko to wait and board the battered Moskvich decoy rather than following him into the highly visible Zil. The major said nothing, busying himself dialling the *"Patrul "*— "Flying Squad," the special motorcycle-and-car security unit that was to be less than a minute away from the director at all times. On occasion, however, particularly during the shelling, they'd taken as long as ten minutes. Immediate demotion followed. The major checked the squad's position against his watch the moment the unit answered his phone call. He glanced across at Chernko. "They're where they should be, Comrade Director. I mean, Mr. President." The KGB boss said nothing. The driver was busy finding his way through the body- and rubble-strewn Ordynika Street south through Red Square onto Gorky Street. A surprising amount of Soviet BMD armored personnel carriers were evident following the surrender, all strangely quiet on the hard-packed snow. Chernko pressed the driver intercom button on his plush leather armrest. "We'll go up Gertsen," he instructed the chauffeur, "around by the U.S.A./Canada Institute. What's left of it."

"Yes, sir," answered the chauffeur, and the limousine weaved through Manege Square past the alert military policeman, who had stopped all traffic the moment he'd seen the Zil in the outside VIP lane. The car turned right on Gertsen. The major was always tense at such moments. With Chernko you never knew. The director's passion for security verged on the paranoid—a reflection of the fact that he himself had sent so many assassins abroad to hunt others. And there had always been the danger of Siberian separatists long agitating for autonomy from Moscow to run their own federation. Never varying your routine, Chernko knew, was the biggest single mistake, hence his *proverki*—"spot checks," as he called them, on his flying squad. Despite the inconvenience it caused his own timetable, the major had to concede that such precautions were part of the reason Chernko was still alive to be chief of First and Second Directorate and now president.

An old *babushka*, a grandmother, head wrapped against the cold by the traditional black scarf, slipped on the icy sidewalk, the stroller she was pushing rolling out onto the road. The driver braked hard, and both Chernko and the major were jerked forward, restrained only by their seat belts. The driver instinctively slammed the car into a sliding reverse-turn. But it was too late. By then the Flying Squad had the road blocked behind and in front of the Zil—the gray figures of the squad emerging ghostlike, surrounding the limousine.

There were no harsh words from Chernko to the driver, but the latter immediately knew he would be punished—and at a time when he and his family would desperately need what few perks remained for the driver of the most powerful man in the Soviet Union.

The driver, normally a strong man, was reduced to a quivering jelly, looking back pleadingly, whey faced, at Chernko. He was crying. "I'm sorry, Comrade Director—Comrade President. I—"

"Vladimir," said Chernko, nodding at the two Flying Squad members holding the driver to release him, "it was only natural."

"But I should have known, Comrade. Remembered my training."

"Yes," said Chernko, sitting back in the plush Afghan leather, "you should have. It could have been a Siberian, eh?" The man wanted to speak again but couldn't find words. A small, bedraggled crowd of refugees was gathering; plainclothes KGB men quickly, brusquely, ordered them away.

Chernko knew news of the incident would spread quickly, as he intended it should, and then—for a while at least—everyone on security would be on special alert, and he would be safe long enough to make his deal—gain his insurance policy—with Novosibirsk.

"Full circle, eh?" he said to the major.

"I don't understand, Comrade President."

"*Insurance*, Major. Our KGB building in Dzerzhinsky Square was once an insurance building. Fitting, don't you think?"

As one of the security team took over as driver and the *babushka*, an agent in her early thirties, folded up the stroller, the Zil moved off back along the long, bedraggled line of people who, since the war had started, continued to line up day after day all the way down past the Alexander Garden toward Lenin's Mausoleum—not to pay homage to the founder of the revolution but to receive their daily ration of sawdust bread. Already fights were breaking out in the line, and Chernko sat grim-faced, staring ahead. The very idea, let alone the sight, of any disorder was deeply disturbing to him. Not only did it signify the end of the long reign of the Revolution, but if he could not protect himself he would lose all rank, all privilege, and be cast among them.

"Now, Major," Chernko said with renewed urgency. "To the new headquarters to transmit my proposal to Novosibirsk." He meant to the KGB shelter at their new HQ in the outer ring. "Before the Americans reach us."

"Comrade President, if I might mention something I heard at the officers'—"

"Yes?" Chernko said curtly.

"The plan you have to offer the Siberians . . ." The major hesitated. "Is it ex-War Minister Marchenko's plan you are . . . borrowing?"

"*Borrow?* I didn't borrow any such idea, Major."

"Of course," put in the major quickly. "I didn't mean to imply—"

"I *stole* it," said Chernko. *"Srazmakhom"*—"Holus-bolus." He turned, his steely blue eyes boring into his aide. "What does it matter where our strategy—where our tactics—come from? The trouble with you, Major, is you're a child of Gorbachev. In the revolution and now in this war there's no room for that sentimental bourgeois tripe about taking somebody else's idea— somebody else's *property*. We are 'the sword and shield of the State'—that is all that matters. The point is to deliver the blow wherever we see the opportunity present itself."

"A blow?" said the major, nonplussed. "When we have surrendered?"

"*We've* surrendered. Siberia has not. If Siberia were to defeat the Americans—" Chernko paused. "What is it the Americans say, Major? 'It's not over until it's over'?'' They were approaching the KGB bunker. "As soon as we arrive," Chernko instructed the major, "I want you to send up the file."

"Yes, sir." But the major sounded distinctly apprehensive.

"Don't worry," Chernko assured him, the president's mood now buoyant. "In a month we'll be watching news reports of the Americans reeling—while we're eating their rations. I call that sweet revenge, Major. And no matter what the Siberians think of us, they'll be grateful for the plan—the weapon I'm about to give them. They're not stupid. They'll want it spread around that anyone who helps them against the Americans will be rewarded. If my plan works, the Americans will be sent packing. For me it will mean full membership in Novosibirsk's Central Committee. You to full colonel—perhaps general—with all the benefits of rank in the postwar Siberian forces. Would that be satisfactory, Comrade?"

"Very," replied the major, knowing generalship would at the very least rate a chauffeur and access to the party's special stores. Chernko, of course, would probably get yet another dacha out of it—a few more and he could start a hotel chain after the war—after the American army had been chopped up piecemeal and swallowed by the vast winter that was called Siberia.

Gen. Douglas Freeman alighted from his military transport plane at Monterey Airport at 4:00 P.M., his impending arrival unannounced to the press by the Pentagon. In any event his departure from Washington had been deliberately delayed at the last minute by the Pentagon so that his arrival on the West Coast would be too late for the New York networks' evening news. This would minimize, the Pentagon hoped, any damage Freeman might do in an open press conference should he be asked any questions about the Russians.

Now that the brief if intense applause for him in the New York parade had died, the ticker tape swept away, Freeman didn't expect a hero's welcome on the West Coast. America was demobilizing much faster than it had mobilized, anxious to get on with enjoying the fruits of a hard-won victory, racing to put the war behind it.

As the general's car, pennant furled, headed south on Highway 1, the blood-streaked sun was sinking beneath the sharp black line of the sea. Freeman wondered aloud to his driver how quickly she thought the feats of First Army would be forgotten. The trim driver, blond hair swept back in a bun, was watching the road too intently to really think much about the general's question and said she didn't know. Normally the khaki Chevrolet would have been flanked by four MP outriders, but the general, ostentatious enough when it suited First Army's purposes, had set a frugal example throughout the war, insisting on stringent conservation measures regarding the use of gasoline now that the Middle East fields were once again in ruin. Freeman caught a glimpse of himself in the rearview mirror and was momentarily lost to the contemplation of whether or not he should stay in the army. At fifty-five he was hardly old, even in a modern, youth-oriented, high-tech military. Nevertheless, he and everyone else knew he was being put out to pasture. What made it worse was that he understood the Pentagon's decision. Damn them! They were right—he *was* a warrior. He had the spittle for battle but not for peace. He recalled the memo to the White House from the British liaison officer in Washington, Brigadier Soames, who had advised the president that London, like the U.S. State Department, considered Freeman "a tad too Hobbesian."

"Superior son of a bitch," muttered Freeman. Probably figured his memo wouldn't be understood by anyone who hadn't gone "up" to Oxford and "read philosophy."

"Well," Freeman had told his boss, General of the U.S. Army James Grey, "I've read my Hobbes and my Bugs Bunny. I know what that limey son of a bitch means, General. He's claiming I see man's natural condition as one of war."

"Now, Douglas," Grey had told him. "Don't go getting yourself all riled up."

"Well," Freeman had replied, pulling on his leather gloves tighter, flexing his fist. "Limey bastard's right. I do. Peace is war by other means, General. When you cut through the thin veneer of civilization, only thing that keeps the goddamn yahoos from running this world is strength of arms. Question is, whose arms? Ours or some Commie son of a bitch who'd take whatever freedom the IRS has left us? Lord—didn't we learn anything from what happened to Gorbachev? While every Tom, Dick, and Jane Fonda in the West were going ga-ga over *Gorby* all those Marxist-Leninist pals of his were just going along for the ride—till he fell '*ill*.' Then by God look what we got. Suzlov and now Chernko and his pals. Same old gang. Remember, General, we all wanted peace. The British lion sheathed her claws. The American eagle clipped talons and beak. And the Russian bear—why he was just so darned happy about it he hugged 'em both to death.''

"Go home, Douglas," Grey had told him. "Enjoy your ocean view. You've done yourself and First Army proud. The country's grateful. You ever doubt that, look at those rows of decorations you have—from every corner of the world. But you're smart enough to know that the peace—whether it's another form of war or not, Douglas—will be fought in board rooms and with diplomacy, God help us. The brigadier's right, Douglas, 'it's not your cup of tea.' "

Freeman grimaced. Even though he knew they were right the very thought of sitting in the bleachers while other players took the field and the glory was anathema to him. He knew it was pride—"pride *right through*," as he remembered Henry the Eighth had said of Cardinal Wolsey—but Douglas Freeman saw his pride as a God-given *hubris*—as natural as salt in the blood, as undeniable as the steel blue of his eyes and his graying hair. It was the fuel that drove his consuming ambition: to be the greatest commander in the history of the United States—in the history of the world—an ambition that had burned fiercely within him as a boy, long before his first glimpse of the plain at West Point. Intellectually, politically, he understood Washington was correct to recall him now the battle was over and peace secured; but in his heart the tunes of glory would always call, the snare drum's roll the sweetest music.

He remembered watching *Apocalypse Now*, at the armored school at Fort Hood, to which he and other officers had returned fresh from their victories in the Iraqi war. The gung-ho colonel in the film had confidently whipped away the yellow cravat of the Air Cavalry from his throat and, hands on hips, announced to a terrified subaltern, "I love the smell of napalm in the morning." Everyone in the theater had laughed derisively. Everyone except Freeman. He didn't like the smell of napalm in the morning or any other time—it plugged his sinuses—but he knew what that colonel had meant, what he felt. He, too, loved the smell, the sting of battle that shot adrenaline to his chest. Only then did he feel fully alive. Some men he knew were born with the same feeling and spent their lives hypocritically denying it in deference to the civilized world, but Freeman made no apology, believing his destiny, his responsibility, was to put it to good purpose, to preserve the civilized world—to defend his America against all those who sought to destroy her. Yet now, his career having finally rounded the corner, "heading into the straight," as his father would have said, the race was suddenly over, his purpose fulfilled in the clash of armor around Minsk and Moscow that had brought the Russian surrender. Suddenly he was adrift, his past glory flat as the twilight sea. Glory was like sex, he mused—having just had it you felt you'd never need it again. Then an hour later . . .

Outside his fog-shrouded house on the Monterey beachfront, a bungalow design with a six-foot-high, chocolate-brown fence running around it to ward off the encroaching dune grass, a crowd of well-wishers had gathered. One of the signs read "Welcome home, General Freeman"; another, "Freedom's Freeman!" Instead of her usual gradual braking, the corporal was forced to hit the brakes hard as the crowd surged forward unexpectedly, revealing a long, yellow tape, which at first she had thought was a yellow ribbon of remembrance. She now saw it ran clear around the house. Freeman could smell the fresh tang of the sea. Three army Humvees were parked about ten yards apart, right of the crowd by the curb, one of the vehicles sprouting its .50 caliber machine gun on a swivel mount immediately behind the six-man cabin. A California highway patrolman, in khaki cap and uniform, and one of the MPs from the Humvees looked as if they were arguing. Left of them a man in white shorts and T-shirt, his left hand on the lip of the curb which was overrun by dune grass, lay sprawled in the gutter. The white shorts were red with blood.

Now Freeman saw more policemen pushing the crowd back as the man was photographed from different angles. For a second the general thought he saw his wife, Doreen, in the crowd but it was difficult to tell with so many people, a hundred or more, milling and flowing about the house. A man in jeans and wildly colored Hawaiian shirt tried to duck under the yellow tape near the curb, holding up a newspaper with a picture of Freeman at the surrender ceremony at Minsk. A patrolman pushed him back behind the tape.

"So much for crowd control, Corporal," joked Freeman.

"Yes, sir."

Whether it was the sight of the army Humvees or the strange excitement of the crowd that tensed up his lumbar muscles Freeman didn't know, but it hurt like hell, and for a moment he was back in the Dortmund-Bielefeld pocket just after he'd given the order for the breakout, the "end run" that had outflanked the enemy and ultimately brought Chernko and his STAVKA to its knees. After leaving his headquarters near Munster the concussion from a 122-millimeter Soviet shell had knocked his Humvee right off the road, lifting the vehicle and flinging it into a ditch. His back took most of the impact against the Humvee's steering column and the driver's steel helmet.

The pain was still with him and bone deep. Determined not to show signs of what doctors insisted on calling "discomfort" to make themselves feel better, Freeman hauled himself quickly out of the Chevrolet, asking the corporal to answer the car's cellular phone that was bipping annoyingly in the back as Freeman alighted. It was a small detail, opening the door himself, but the kind that newspapers, hungry for copy, used to define what they called the "hands-on, no-nonsense Freeman style." The reporters didn't realize that the general opening the door for himself was more a sign of his impatience to get things done than it was disdain for ceremony.

As he emerged from the car the fog lifted, the sun's dying rays catching the edge of his decorations' strips, the blue-red-blue of his Silver Star vibrant in the fading light.

CHAPTER THREE

FOLLOWING THE KREMLIN'S surrender, President Mayne thought he had finished with the White House's subterranean "simulation room." Now, two floors below his oval office, he found himself once again walking past the Marine guards into the "bunker," its fluorescent light, oppressive as usual, illuminating the huge map stand with its clusters of blue and red pins showing the disposition of Allied and Russian forces at the moment of Moscow's unconditional capitulation. Glancing at the alert board, however, he saw there'd been a change. All Allied forces had been placed in DefCon II—"attack believed imminent." Press aide Trainor, who had been normally gung-ho even in the worst moments of the war, looked drained, as pale as the bluish white light. The silence among the Joint Chiefs of Staff and Allied liaison officers was deafening. Trainor handed the president the message. It was from SACEUR—Supreme Allied Commander Europe—Lieut. Gen. William Merton, and read:

Autonomous Siberian republic has disregarded Moscow's surrender. Novosibirsk has issued orders for all Siberian armies to resist "Anglo-American-European aggression against the 'Motherland.'" We are now facing forty Siberian divisions along Sino-Soviet border plus TVD air forces commanded out of Khabarovsk and entire Soviet Pacific Fleet egressing Vladivostok. Our forward units one hundred miles east of Moscow already under attack by elements of West Siberian Second and Fourth—

15

"Jesus Christ!" It was the first time Trainor had heard the president blaspheme, and despite Trainor's secularity it made him wince.

"Where's the rest of the message?" asked President Mayne, looking up at Trainor and the Joint Chiefs of Staff.

"Satellite communications were cut, Mr. President," answered Trainor. "Or rather jammed. By the Siberians."

"God Almighty!" said Mayne, looking down again at the message in disbelief. Brigadier Soames, Britain's European–U.S. liaison officer, cleared his throat politely. "London's received the same response, Mr. President," advised Soames. "Looks rather sticky, I'm afraid. But your chap Merton is in error regarding the Siberian divisions. There aren't forty."

"Well, thank God for that!" said the president. The brigadier looked around, untypically nonplussed, glancing for help at the Chiefs of Staff, but found he was on his own. "I'm sorry, Mr. President, but what I mean is that there aren't forty divisions. It's fifty-seven to be exact. With—ah—four Mongolian divisions in reserve around Lake Baikal."

President Mayne sat down, the message dangling from his left hand, his right unconsciously massaging his temple. "What the hell's happened? I mean, these divisions must be reservists?"

Army Chief of Staff Grey shook his head. "Afraid not, Mr. President. The Siberian divisions have a combat, Afghanistan-trained cadre of officers and NCOs. Crack divisions trained for a Sino-Soviet conflict. Moscow used to be more scared of China than NATO. Trouble is, it's not only the number of Siberian armies we're faced with—the place is so damn big. Westernmost border of Siberia doesn't even start till you get a thousand miles east beyond Moscow—then it goes on for more than three and a half thousand miles to the Pacific and, despite popular misconception, it has as varied a topography as the U.S. Far as the Siberians are concerned, Moscow's in another country."

Looking at the map, Mayne saw the Siberian divisions were stretched out from Siberia's East Cape then inland behind the mountainous Kamchatka Peninsula all the way down to Vladivostok and the Manchurian border, a dark red cluster showing enemy surface vessels and submarines off the coast around

Vladivostok and Nakhodka. "Thought we gave their Pacific Fleet a bloody nose off north Japan?" he asked Chief of Naval Operations Admiral Horton.

"*Elements* of the Pacific Fleet, yes, Mr. President," answered the CNO. "But the hemorrhaging stopped apparently."

"Their air forces?" Mayne asked Air Force Chief Allet.

"Fifteen hundred tactical aircraft, including MiG 29E fighters and Backfire bombers. The Fulcrums—MiG 29Es—are faster and more maneuverable than our F-18s. To qualify for Siberian station you have to have had combat experience in western Europe. Only the best, Mr. President." General Allet indicated airfields far to the northeast, near Siberia's East Cape. "They clearly don't intend letting us get across the Bering Strait from Alaska."

The president was shaking his head. The vastness of the new threat had descended like sheet lightning upon what, until only moments ago, had been the promising dawn of the Russian surrender. Blindsided by Siberia—the essence of the awful Allied blunder the assumption that all the Soviets would automatically follow Moscow's decree. It was so obvious now that Mayne wondered why they hadn't thought of it before. The only comparable miscalculation he could think of was the CIA's confident report, several months before the Shah of Iran's fall, that no such overthrow was in the offing. But then, the more he thought about it, the more he understood how the seed of the blunder had taken root; for he, too, had always lumped Soviets and Russians together. Oh yes, he'd known how dissident the Baltic republics were, and some of the Asian republics, but Siberia— so far from Moscow, a place where Moscow sent dissidents— had never been thought of as a separate entity. But now the full impact of the differences between the two Russian republics— the United Soviet Socialist Republics and the newly declared United Siberian Soviet Republics—hit him as the CIA overlay, each color representing a different ethnic group in the mix that was the Siberyaka, covered the huge expanse of Siberia which, in turn, overlaid the map of the Americas on the same scale, completely obscuring the U.S. The region of the Yakut alone was three times the size of Texas. The other Siberian regions— the Tartar, Kalmyk, Komi, Bashykur and the Karelian autonomous republic—were all united in their common determination with Novosibirsk not to surrender.

"Won't they deal?" asked the president.

"Why should they?" proffered the brigadier, realizing at once that he'd overstepped the line of deference accorded the president of the American republic. "With all due respect, Mr. President, our Allied forces in and around Moscow are, by all accounts, battle weary—quite simply worn out. Our supply lines through western Europe are overextended to say the least." Soames glanced at the American Joint Chiefs of Staff, their glum faces evidence enough that they agreed. Then he turned back to address Mayne. "Holding Moscow might seem a compelling victory to the general public in the West, sir, but—" He turned toward the map, his hand making a small arc across the expanse of Siberia. "Capturing Moscow, I'm afraid, is nothing geographically or strategically speaking. And now, it seems, not even politically. Our troops have, as General Grey pointed out, another thousand miles to go before they even reach the Urals, the western border of Siberia. Then there's the rest—almost four thousand miles of mountains, taiga, rivers and plains, deep in snow—thrown in for good measure. They've got the Ural Mountains on their western flank and the more mountainous Kamchatka Peninsula on the east. They could give away half of it and we'd still be in enormous difficulty. No, sir, I'm afraid the Siberian chiefs of staff in Novosibirsk have thought this one out rather carefully. It's a very sticky wicket indeed."

The president frowned, not because he didn't know what "sticky wicket" meant—the tone conveyed all the meaning he needed—but because the Englishman was right. What in hell could the Allies do?

"Sticky wicket means being between a rock and a hard—" began Trainor.

"I know what it means," snapped the president. "What I want someone to tell me is what in hell are we going to do about this mess?" He looked up at his CNO, the chief of naval operations, Admiral Horton. "Can we bracket them with our boomers, Dick?" He meant the Allies' ICBM submarines.

"Already have, sir. The Trident subs can drop an ICBM on them anywhere, but they can do the same to us even without their subs. Most of their ICBM sites are now in Siberia. Especially on the eastern flank down Kamchatka Peninsula. It would mean all-out nuclear war. And one thing the Russians—including the Siberians—were always ahead of us in, Mr. President, is civil defense for such an eventuality. We'd come out much worse than they would.''

"Yes, yes, I know that. A nuclear strike's no option.'' Next he turned to the army chief of staff.

"Sir,'' said General Grey, "Brigadier Soames is correct in his estimation. We've shot our wad for the time being in and around Moscow. It'd be another two months at the very least before we could muster enough men even to attack the Urals with any hope of breaking through. Best we can hope for there is to keep it at a stalemate.''

"What about their eastern flank?'' shot back the president.

"If we could get enough men across the Bering Strait fast. Perhaps. But there's still Kamchatka Peninsula further south. It's heavily garrisoned. And now it looks as if the whole coast—from the East Cape all the way south to Vladivostok—is also well protected. They've even got Soviet forces on the Kuril Islands running down from Kamchatka—case the Japanese move to reclaim the islands they lost in the Second World War. But either way we'd have to get men across the strait—take command of their East Cape airfields. Once we did that we could hit them further south without constantly worrying about their East Cape planes.''

"How about our air force?'' cut in the president. "General Allet, can you secure air cover over the Bering Strait so that we can get our boys across to their East Cape—secure a beachhead? What is it across there? Only fifty miles or so from Alaska?''

"Fifty-two miles, sir.''

"Well then?''

"Sir, before we could move anybody across there we'd have to have air supremacy. We'd have to take out the AA missile batteries, SAM sites, and the like on Big Diomede. It's shallow around there, some places no more than twenty fathoms—not deep enough for our subs.''

"Big Diomede?'' asked the president.

"Largest of two islands, sir. Little Diomede, ours, is the

smallest—on our side of the international date line. Big Dio-mede is theirs. High and solid rock. Locked in by ice and cov-ered in snow this time of year. It's a fortress—five miles long, one-and-a-half to two miles wide, with deeply recessed and super-hardened AA missile and AA gun battery defenses. They've also got half a dozen long-range naval guns in place that can shell Alaska's Cape Prince of Wales—our staging area for any invasion.''

''You telling me that they can shell us from over twenty miles away?''

Admiral Horton looked surprised that the president didn't know this. ''They've had the long-barrelled gun—got it from South Africa after that Canadian inventor Bull sold it to Iraq and—''

''Never mind the history lesson,'' cut in Mayne. ''I want to know what the hell we're going to do. If the air force can't guarantee it can take out this Big Diomede, can we try naval bombardment?''

''Too much ice for the battle wagons to get within range,'' said the CNO. ''But we can try carrier-borne aircraft from fur-ther south.''

''Then get ready to try, Dick, and while you're doing that I want you,'' he turned to General Grey, ''to send this to the Siberians and all Allied commands.'' As he began writing the message, he asked, ''Our K-16 satellite still operational?''

''Far as I know, Mr. President. But with all that snow in Siberia and the Siberians' camouflage, it's going to be difficult even for our satellite to pinpoint their positions.''

''Maybe so, General,'' said President Mayne, his writing hand moving with singular determination. ''But I have a hunch the Siberians might just be bluffing. I don't mean about what they've got to throw at us but whether this central committee or whatever it is in Novosibirsk has really been able to break free of Moscow's political arm.'' The president depressed the tip of his ballpoint, adroitly slipping it inside his suit jacket. ''Has it occurred to you gentlemen that we might be getting all steamed up for nothing? Anyway—'' He handed the message to General Grey. ''—this'll answer that.''

The president's message to the Novosibirsk central Siberian

command read, "You have twenty-four hours in which to surrender all your forces to Allied command. If you have not done
so by 0800 tomorrow Washington time, the Allied armies will
reengage with maximum force."

"Mr. President," asked General Grey, "you think there
might be some confusion about what we mean by 'maximum
force'?"

The president smiled. "Yes. That's for them to figure out,
Jimmy." He turned to Air Force General Allet. "Bill, I want
'covers off' at least a dozen. Midwest. And just in case the
Siberians aren't getting any satellite readings of their own, have
our K-16 photographs of our MX silos when their lids are off
beamed down to Siberian air space. Put them clearly in the
picture."

Brigadier Soames felt it his duty to voice his skepticism. "Mr.
President, I really don't think the Siberians would have gone on
the offensive against our troops in the Urals in the western sector
if they didn't think they could win this thing. And if we use
nuclear weapons no one wins. I don't think they're bluffing, Mr.
President. I didn't want to unduly depress anyone, but my aide
informs me that I'm also incorrect in my estimate of how many
divisions the Siberians have at hand. It is in fact in excess of
sixty-five. That's well over a million and a—"

"Yes, yes, I know, Brigadier, but threatening to use the MX
doesn't mean we have to. Our bluff could work. They might just
cave in when they see our determination."

"I beg to differ, sir. I think—"

"Well, let's give it the old college try, shall we, Brigadier?"

"By all means, sir. By all means."

Just as Press Secretary Trainor had never heard the president
take, as Mayne would have put it, "the Lord's name in vain,"
neither had he heard the president use "shall we?" before. The
president, he thought, had handled the brigadier—and thus in
effect the joint Allied high command's anticipated criticism—
rather well. "Shall we?" had just the right tone to it—one of
confident authority, unbowed by the frightening possibility of
having to confront more than sixty fresh, highly trained Siberian
divisions—twice the total number of U.S. divisions. Perhaps the
president *was* right. Maybe the Siberian colossus had not

shucked off the long political reach of Moscow and would think twice about it, seeing the missiles "standing proud"—that is, their warheads above the silo openings. Perhaps the Siberians *would* blink.

The president's message was transmitted in plain language so that all the Siberian forces would be aware of it. A smart move, Trainor acknowledged, in that there might have been some Siberian units reluctant to go along with Novosibirsk's decision to attack the Allied forces east of Moscow.

Though he didn't know it, Trainor was right. There *had* been such resistance, notably in the person of Vladimir Cherlak, the general commanding the Siberian Third Motorized Rifle Division at Tyumen, halfway between Novosibirsk and Moscow. Though no friend of President Chernko, Cherlak, like so many senior Russian officers, had attended the Frunze Military Academy. Using this tenuous connection with Chernko to maximum effect, Cherlak stated flatly that he had no intention of disobeying Moscow's directive to surrender.

Novosibirsk's Central Committee said it respected his loyalty to Moscow but appealed to Cherlak to place his responsibility to the United Siberian Soviet Republics above any personal loyalty to a defeated Moscow. Cherlak replied that his hesitancy to throw in his lot with Novosibirsk was not merely a matter of personal loyalty but one stemming from the oath he had taken to the Russian federation which Chernko now headed.

Novosibirsk decided there were only two ways of dealing with Cherlak: shoot him as an example to any other undecided officers or show him Chernko's plan. They sent an emissary to Tyumen. Cherlak was notoriously self-centered—some said he was so full of himself he must think himself a czar. But he knew when he had met his match, and upon seeing Chernko's plan was unabashedly awed.

"It's brilliant," he conceded. "Tell Novosibirsk the Third Motorized is with them."

CHAPTER FOUR

AS FREEMAN WALKED toward his house, the wind, cold for Monterey, carried with it the invigorating tang of sea air mixed with the oppressive smell of a high-sulfur-content oil, the lower grade of crude still being rationed for civilian use, while consumer and antipollution groups pressed hard for the less sulfurous grades previously reserved for the military to be released for the domestic market now that the war was over. Freeman saw that the man spread-eagled in the sand and dune grass was dead, his T-shirt dark cherry red, a Beethoven motif faintly visible in the clinging stain of blood. Freeman heard the sound of sirens in the distance; seemed to be one coming, one going. His battle-trained hearing was acute; he did not make the mistake of confusing the echo for its origin—a mistake that had proved fatal for those troops during the war who had come up against the five-truck platoons of forty multiple-layered BM-21 Katyushas—truck-mounted rockets—for the first time.

"General Freeman?"

"Yes?"

It was a young female police officer, short-cropped blond hair, sky-blue eyes, her khaki uniform smart, creases crisply ironed, green side piping without a wrinkle, the Smith and Wesson .38 high on her left side, he noticed. "My wife?" he said, the smile he'd had for the welcome-home crowd now gone. He could have been back at Minsk asking for SITREPS on unit deployment, his tone concerned, his control born in part from having witnessed what the Russians had called the *boynya*—"abattoir"—in Germany's Fulda Gap. There the Russian armored echelons had poured through in right and left hooks before being

23

stopped in the south by the American and Bundeswehr divisions, and in the north by the British Army of the Rhine—the choking dust literally dampened by blood as motorized infantry of both sides were torn apart in the shrapnel-filled air.

"Is she all right?" asked the general, a cheek muscle taut, his gloved right hand now a fist.

"Critical, sir, I'm afraid. She's en route to Peninsula Hospital."

"What happened?" A young boy, smiling, grasping a tiny stars and stripes, started beneath the ribbon toward the general. One of the MPs gently cut him off.

"We're not exactly sure, General," the female officer told him. "We got a 459 in progress—breaking and entering—about eighteen minutes ago. When we got here—" The officer turned, Freeman's gaze following her outstretched hand, her notebook obscuring the man's legs for a moment. "We found the front gate open. Back door was closed but not locked. Apparently he entered that way—round the back. We found some blood on the back pathway. It looks as if your wife fired two shots, but he made it to the sidewalk before he collapsed." She paused. "He's dead."

Freeman turned back toward the army car, its khaki/black/green wave camouflage paint dulled even further by moody stratus threatening the coast as far up as Santa Cruz. His driver was pale, waiting anxiously, the situation obviously beyond her experience.

"General, sir—" said the policewoman. "I know it's inconvenient, but could you identify the weapon your wife fired?"

"What?"

"The weapon your wife fired, sir. The man who broke in—well, he—he used a knife, General. We assume that Mrs. Freeman was the one who—"

Freeman seemed to be looking through the crowd, through the house, his right fist balling in his left. "Walther," he said. "Nine millimeter."

"This it, sir?" asked another police officer, holding up a Ziplock plastic bag containing a nine-millimeter automatic.

"Looks like it," said Freeman, glancing at the gun. "Serial number's in safety deposit." He was looking out to sea, eyes squinting in the metallic glare that was still present though the sun was covered with cloud. "First Savings and Loan," he told them. "Duplicate license at the base. Fort Ord."

"Registered in your name, General?"

"Yes. Look, I'd like to get to the hospital. If there are any more questions you can—"

A flashbulb popped. He froze—first rule for any combat soldier caught in a flare. Natural instinct was to dive, but movement was what the enemy was looking for. If you could steel yourself to stand perfectly still, chances were they either wouldn't see you or would mistake you for something else. It was only a second, but to the crowd outside his house it looked as if the general were momentarily transfixed with fright. Freeman sensed it and glowered furiously at the photographer.

Before Freeman arrived at the emergency ward at Peninsula Hospital there was a story on all the networks that the wife of General Douglas Freeman had been the victim of an attempted burglary gone wrong, was critically wounded, and that the general was—as the still photo accompanying the sound bite seemed to indicate—"visibly shaken." The photo was also picked up by Reuters and UPI, and the implicit suggestion, made explicitly in the tabloids of the La Roche chain, was that the reason Freeman had been recalled in such haste after the Moscow surrender was due to the "hard-to-disguise fact" that the general's nerves were already shot.

When Trainor handed the president the green file, a crimson diagonal stripe on its cover, containing the eight-by-ten blow-ups, he bent the gooseneck lamp down closer in the semidarkness of the working study with double steel reinforced walls in the south wing. Not far from the Oval Office, the smaller office was favored by the president not simply because it was more protected but because it had an older, comforting smell, reminiscent of his childhood—an air of old leather lounge chairs, of security, of how things used to be, of how he wished they could be again in the rapidly changing world. Also, here he could better work in the subdued light—a necessity, not a choice, when he was afflicted with the migraines that had plagued him ever since his Congressional days and which were as much a secret between Trainor, the president, and his secretary as were the codes for nuclear war in the possession of the air force officer who even now was sitting outside the study with the briefcase, or "football," containing the daily "Go" codes. The headaches didn't slow Mayne down; on the contrary, he held to Nietzsche's adage that that which doesn't kill you makes you stronger, and believed the will required to surmount the pain served him better than those whose faculties were not tried by any such ordeal. It was a constant reminder to him of what could be done, despite the obstacles, if you set your mind to it. He examined the photographs before him more closely, but the mountain range continued to puzzle him. Nebraska and Montana were as flat as a pancake—unless these MX sites he was looking at were smack up against the Big Horn Mountains or the Rockies of the Continental Divide that rose so dramatically from the prairie. "What was the name of that old Jimmy Stewart movie?" he mused aloud to Trainor. *"The Far Country?"*

"That's not the western states," answered Trainor, moving around to look over the president's shoulder. "It's supposed to be Kamchatka. Yeah—it is."

"No wonder I was—" began Mayne, feeling foolish, only now realizing what he was looking at—that the half-dozen black doughnuts, a white dot in the middle of each the size of a pinhead, were the *Siberian* ICBM sites set in the deep, V-shaped defiles of towering, glacier-hung granite. These were open missile silos in Kamchatka Peninsula. The next photo was of the ICBM complex at Petropavlovsk which, though difficult to get at with U.S. missiles because of the acute south-north turning angles required to hit a target in deep east-west axis defiles, could nevertheless very easily take out the U.S. Trident and Sea Wolf bases as far away as Washington State and San Diego.

"It's their answer, Mr. President," said Trainor solemnly. "They haven't blinked. You go nuclear. They go nuclear. Nobody wins."

Mayne, shoulders rounded, head bent like an accountant confronted by the overwhelming power of the IRS ranged against his client, reluctantly flipped over the other photographs. More black donuts in the Siberian snows. "Then it has to be all-out conventional," he said glumly to Trainor.

"Yes, Mr. President. But, as the Joint Chiefs point out, we'll have to neutralize the ICBM silos on Kamchatka sooner or later—can't afford to leave them there so they can pummel us anytime they like." Trainor pulled over a CIA report. "Siberian conventional ammunition reserves are sixty days. After that we'd risk them going nuclear."

Again Mayne was struck by the terrible irony of the nuclear age. You invented nuclear weapons, which supposedly made conventional arms obsolete but in order to make sure nuclear arms would never be used you had to fight modern wars with conventional forces and yet if supplies for the conventional weapons of one side ran out it might revert to nuclear anyway. So this meant you needed even *more* conventional weapons in the first place to take out the launch sites—to take out the nuclear possibility. It was an equation that the "Massachusetters," which was Mayne's term for all the doves, never understood, from George McGovern on down. But it was something with which every president, Democrat and Republican, had to contend once he sat in the Oval Office.

"Then," said Mayne, "looks like we're back in the war room."

"Yes, Mr. President."

"Damn!" With that Mayne got up and asked Trainor for a Tylenol 3 and an aspirin 222. Only the "double whammy" stood any chance of dulling the tightening steel band of pain around his head and the thick pain that had waylaid his trapezius and neck muscles so that they felt as hard as bridge cables. Trainor saw him wince on the way down, but once in the corridor leading to the room there was no sign that the president was in pain, and anyone noticing his drawn features, the bags beneath his eyes from lack of sleep, and the worry lines etched deep into his forehead saw these as the inevitable signs of the enormous responsibility shouldered by the commander in chief. And Trainor knew it was the truth, the strain taking its toll: more gray hair about the president's temples and a set about his jaw that came from him being a nighttime "grinder," the nightmare of a new war continuing to sabotage his already war-torn sleep.

* * *

It was not a very long meeting for the Joint Chiefs of Staff, the chief of naval operations, and the president's special national security adviser Harry Schuman. They were of one accord. As well as ordering the offensive on the western front reactivated, pushing from Moscow toward the Urals, U.S. forces, with Canadian air cover as an assist, would have to engage in an airland battle to attack Siberia's eastern flank and so establish a beachhead for Allied land operations against the United Siberian Soviet Republics.

"Cross Bering Strait?" proffered Mayne, seeking unanimous agreement.

"Yes, sir," replied the CNO. "But first the navy and air force planes'll have to knock out Big Diomede's early warning and AA as well as antiship missile batteries. No chance with a land force. Two Diomedes Islands'll be surrounded by a sea of jumbled drift ice." The CNO produced a photograph of the jagged expanse of pressure ridges created by wind and sea action, many of the ridges up to sixty feet in height and six feet thick. "Carrier-launched planes'll hit it from the south. Air force from the Alaskan peninsula."

"How about the Russian subs attacking our carrier?" put in Mayne.

"Our battle groups'll have usual guided missile destroyer and cruiser screen as well as helos and air cover—including fighter cover from the carrier itself and helos. Also we have several batteries of heavy guns on Little Diomede. Range to Big Diomede is less than three miles. Or five—depending on angle of fire."

"Can our batteries do much against granite?"

"Some. All depends how deep the Russians are dug in. But our big ordnance bombs should do the job." His right hand massaging his temple, Mayne said nothing, his mood of deep concentration inviting no comment. When he finally did speak, his tone was subdued. The confidence exuded by "big ordnance" men in the air force wasn't shared by him. They had never really learned the lesson of Vietnam or Iraq. In Vietnam they'd dropped more bombs on the network collectively known as the Ho Chi Minh Trail than they had in all of World War II, and they still hadn't beaten the North Vietnamese. In Iraq they'd hit Hussein's troops with over three thousand sorties within the first week, but at the end of the day the coalition had still needed the ground war to win. And Hussein's troops, though inferior to the Siberians, were dug in in sand, not granite. Also, the Siberians' morale was rock solid compared to the Iraqis'. No, Mayne wanted backup—just in case. "Freeman." It was more a question than a decision. After saying it he looked up at Trainor, the CNO, and the Joint Chiefs in turn as well as soliciting the wisdom of his special adviser Harry Schuman. Trainor heard the breath go out of General Grey, chief of the army.

The president shifted his gaze to the general. "What is it, Jimmy?"

"Sir. Douglas Freeman's a good man, but in his present condition, I don't think it'd be fair—either to the troops or to him."

Mayne was nonplussed. "You think he's too tired? Hell, General, we're *all* tired."

General Grey shot a glance of surprise in Trainor's direction then back at the president. "I thought you knew, sir. CIA report came in about an hour ago."

Trainor made no apologies. Reports were coming in all the time. There was a river of reports; you got buried in reports.

"What, about Freeman?"

"No, sir—his wife. In critical condition in Peninsula Hospital. Multiple stab wounds, they say."

Mayne tried to remember whether he'd ever met Mrs. Freeman—some reception or other for the Desert Storm veterans back from Iraq. A tall, good-looking woman, unpretentious, but the exact features of her face were lost amid a blur of official receptions.

"When did this happen?" asked Mayne, emotionally reassured by his own concern, that after a war that had claimed the lives of countless thousands he could still feel compassion for an individual. What was it Stalin had said? One death is a tragedy, and more is a statistic. It's something you had to guard against, particularly as president.

"Last night apparently," answered Trainor. "FBI was called in by the MPs at Fort Ord, Freeman's new HQ—because it had been called in on the police radio as a break and entry, possible burglary. But army intelligence figure it might be one of Chernko's boys."

"A SPETS attack?" asked Mayne, surprised. After all, Freeman was no longer a threat to the Russians.

The SPETS, short for SPETSNAZ or *Voiska Spetsialnogo Naznacheniya*, Special-Purpose Forces, were the highest trained, foreign-speaking, Russian commando elite who, among other things, had spread havoc when, dressed in American and British uniforms, they'd been dropped behind the Allied lines in the Dortmund-Bielefeld pocket. Under the command of GRU's, or Military Intelligence's, Second Chief Directorate, the twenty-five-thousand-man force was the most brutal and best trained of the Russian special forces. But an attack on General Freeman's wife? After all, hitting a commander's wife didn't stop a commander, and besides, Freeman was being recalled.

"It's to show, I suspect," put in the British brigadier, Soames, "that they can reach whomever they wish. A caution perhaps against us using Freeman. May not be Chernko of course—he's pledged his full assistance to us. It could be whoever is taking over his agents."

"It's Chernko's style all right," Trainor concurred. "He's been known to have his sleepers—agents already in place—target our nuclear sub captains while they're off base here as well as abroad. Two of them got it while they were on leave around Faslane in Scotland—near our Holy Lock sub pens. But the FBI doesn't figure he'd try that now, not after the surrender. Besides, our forward units are already in Moscow. What's in it for him?"

"Quite," said Soames.

"Problem is, gentlemen," Mayne reminded them, "that KGB or not, General Freeman's going to be too preoccupied with his wife's condition. We can't have him leading any mop-up operation after the bombardment on Big Diomede now." Mayne saw Trainor about to speak but carried on, "I know he's thoroughly professional, that he'd do it if we asked him, but the fact is he'll be too preoccupied with her condition. It's rotten luck. All other things considered he seemed the perfect man for a mop-up. But I don't want the life of one American—not one—endangered because of some minor detail overlooked by a man too over-wrought by family concerns back home. Once our naval battle group and air force take out Big Diomede I want it secured, and tightly, with no chance of them taking it back and cutting off our logistical supply between Alaska and Siberia. That'd be fatal. In any event, let's not worry about Freeman now. Hell, if your boys do a good enough job, Admiral—'' He was looking at Horton and then Air Force General Allet. ''—there won't *be* any garrison left to mop up.''

Mayne's confidence was bolstered by the plans of the naval battle group Admiral Horton was assembling out of San Diego, San Francisco, and Bangor, Washington. Even now orders were being issued for extra munitions to be rushed up to Little Diomede, for while its few guns on its more exposed western side couldn't hope to do any significant damage to the eastern cliffs of the Siberian island three miles from them, Little Diomede's gun emplacements would, along with the infamously changeable and hostile weather of the Bering Strait, run interference for the main naval battle group attack approaching from the Aleutians to the south and led in its center by the carrier USS *Salt Lake City*. Big Diomede was about to be subjected to a storm of firepower. While the island might withstand it, it was almost certain to destroy the will of the Siberian garrison so that Marines could be sent in and merely take it over. But all this wouldn't be necessary if Novosibirsk and all the space program brains of Akademgorodok failed to get the approval of the Soviet Pacific Fleet to go along with the Siberian decision. In any event, preparations were underway to reactivate an element of the joint American-British SAS—Special Air Service commandos—the Allied equivalent of the SPETS, based in Wales, whose main squadrons, of seventy-two men each, were in the process of being demobilized.

Mayne doubted they'd be used, but both he and the Joint Chiefs believed that the preparations would be another clear signal to the Siberians. If there was no Soviet naval attack in the next twenty-four hours, this would confirm quite clearly that the Soviet Navy, traditionally the most conservative of the Russian forces, *were not* in concert with Novosibirsk. The White House knew that if Novosibirsk lost its vital sea arm, it could not hope to prosecute any war for very long—let alone win one—and neither Freeman nor any other general would be needed.

CHAPTER FIVE

FREEMAN'S SISTER-IN-LAW, Marjorie Duchene, stood in silence by the general as he looked helplessly down in the intensive care unit of Monterey's Peninsula Hospital, watching the comatose figure of his wife, the array of blinking monitors, IV drips, and translucent green color of the oxygen mask transforming Doreen's appearance utterly. Here the general felt as useless as a conscript on his first day at boot camp—powerless to do anything but stand and take it. All he could do, as the chief resident informed him, was wait. For Freeman it might as well have been a prison sentence. The very idea of waiting, of being confronted by a problem he could not attack, do battle with, was anathema. He knew what he should be doing. He and Doreen had talked it over often enough, intending to empower each other to "pull the plug" if either of them was ever struck down by some such incontinent, paralyzed condition. But ironically the man who had been so thorough in his professional life—on more than one occasion astounding logistical officers with his attention to minor details of supply and combat support—was now faced by the fact that neither of them had actually got round to doing it—to making a "living will."

Back at the house the silence of the rooms was all the more oppressive because of the thunderous crashing of high tide and surf which, Freeman noted in his diary, were he an enemy commander offshore, would be disastrous for any amphibious operation. Pacing the rooms, flicking on the TV, seeing protesters against any impending war with Siberia, Freeman muttered an obscenity and switched it off. He was like a caged lion, spitting out his contempt for those whose selfishness was so profound that they would not fight for the very freedom that allowed them to protest. There was only one place for conscientious objectors—front-line stretcher bearers. That put their high principle to the test.

But it wasn't all anger with the protesters that was adding to his concern, or—dare he say it?—"anxiety" about Doreen, but rather guilt, a civilized luxury he rarely allowed himself. It was not the usual guilt of a military life—that he hadn't spent enough time with her; that now he had the time to give her, to make up for the long separations, she was probably not even aware that he was around. Rather it was the guilt he felt for being angry at her for being in a coma. It was bad enough he'd been put out to pasture but now, just as war threatened to reopen with the Siberian breakaway from Moscow, Washington would keep him out of it because of her. He knew it was selfish, but he knew that to command men in battle was what he had been born for, and he knew Doreen would be the first to understand. It was why he loved her. Yes, it was his duty as a husband to be with her, but if he couldn't do anything for her, what was the point of him staying around to—

"Thank God you're back home," said Marjorie in her bubbly God's-in-his-heaven-all's-right-with-the-world voice. "I'm sure Dory knows you're here, Douglas. It must be a comfort to her deep down. You know what they say about some stroke victims, that just knowing a loved one is nearby—"

"Yes, yes," said Freeman irritably.

"I'm sorry, Douglas," Marjorie said, mistaking his irritability for anxiety about Dory. "Why don't you go out to the pool, and I'll make some coffee and bring it out? Maybe you'd like to just sit awhile?"

Freeman gave in; it was the only damn thing you could do with relatives. Sit by the pool till she got so tired of her own goodness or the cold front locking in Monterey that she'd hightail it back to sunny Phoenix. She was one of those people who said God had planned it all. He believed the same thing in his own way, but whenever she said it she made it sound so pious and self-satisfied—leaving no room for the possibility of human intervention—that she sounded positively evangelical.

By the pool, Freeman fell silent, Marjorie patting him understandingly on the arm as she placed the coffee cups atop the bubbled plastic table. Again she'd completely mistaken his mood, his staring down at the pool an attempt to turn her off for a while, but she was as unrelenting as a Soviet artillery barrage, her vigor something he would have admired in any soldier. In her case it seemed nothing more than the energy of a certified airhead.

She was a good woman, doing the right thing, but by God he wished she'd go back to Phoenix. At heart her optimism was born of the same kind of deep-seated confidence that Freeman held in the face of life's vicissitudes, but something about *her* unquestioning conviction that "all is for the best" only moved him to seek the opposite view, if only for argument's sake, a perversity alien to his usual nature.

"My," she said, pouring the coffee in an irritating up-and-down motion that he saw no point to. "I was reading the other day about those Brentwood boys. Three heroes—all in one family. My, and the article said one of them was with you in Korea and the Dortmund-Bellfeld pocket."

"Bielefeld," grumped Douglas. "He wasn't with me there. He'd been dropped outside the pocket by mistake—smack into the Russian lines."

"You must be very proud of him," she continued, oblivious to the correction. "Medal of Honor winner and all."

"Proud of all my boys who—" He was about to say "are" instead of "were in my command." He pulled the coffee toward him. "Young David Brentwood. He's a good man. Wounded in Russia but back on his feet in no time."

For a moment that indicated to him that he'd been away from the front too long, Freeman almost found himself in violation of security—about to tell her that members of the Allied outfit in which Brentwood served, Britain's Special Air Service, were blood brothers with America's Delta Force.

"And the two other brothers," continued Marjorie. "The one on that *Roosevelt* boat."

"Submarine," Freeman corrected her.

"But that poor other brother—Ray—the one whose face was all burned on that other boat."

"Guided missile frigate," said Freeman, carelessly dropping in two sugar cubes as if they were dumb bombs.

"The miracles those surgeons did on him. My oh my. If ever I saw the hand of God at work, Douglas, that was it." A zephyr passed over the pool, wrinkling it, and he watched it like an omen before the surface was placid again. "And they have this special mask now—looks like one of those hockey goalies—to help the healing and . . ."

Freeman restrained himself, tempted to ask her where God's hand had been for the men who'd drowned in the attack on the USS *Blaine*—the first American warship to be hit in the war. But he didn't bother. He believed God's plan was a lot more complicated than that, that freedom meant the freedom to . . . But what the hell, he thought. Airheads like Marjorie also served Him—her task, no doubt, to talk the devil to death.

"Isn't it nice out here?" she said, taking a deep breath of the cool, salty air. "I always find the pool so calming. Don't you?"

Freeman grunted. Where Marjorie saw a translucent pool of ultramarine beneath the clearing sky—saw nature in harmony, insects happily skimming across the water's mirrored surface, Freeman saw an unending battle, one insect pursuing another— a fight to the finish. Which made him think again of amphibious operations. They were undoubtedly the riskiest of all military undertakings. There Murphy's Law was king.

No matter how much planning, how many rehearsals, disaster always lurked in the ever-changing sea. If the Siberian threat turned to war, the shortest distance was across the Bering Strait, which now would be a mass of ice floes. The moment he thought of ice he recalled two things simultaneously. The first was the English lord who, in the lounge of the *Titanic* as it struck the iceberg, had exclaimed imperturbably, "I sent for ice but this is ridiculous!" The second thing was the curious fact, filed away in his brain along with a thousand other apparently trivial yet vital pieces of logistical information, that at latitude sixty-five degrees, thirty minutes north the ice cakes forming in the dead of winter would be more dispersed, more loosely packed than in the warmer spring months when local currents and wind changed to shift ice northward—that is, packing it tighter together in spring than in the winter. It was precisely the opposite to what one would imagine, and this would make it much tougher for icebreakers or any other ship to negotiate. Also during the winter, unlike the spring and the fall, skies tended to be clearer, often with brilliant sunshine, bad news for close-support air cover when it would be possible for observers on Ratmanov, the Soviet name for Big Diomede, to see clear across the strait.

Anyway, you sure as hell couldn't launch a sea invasion of Siberia or Diomede if you had to contend with pack ice. There was something else about the ice that he could not recall—was it that there was no ice south of the Pribilof Islands? But hell, that was over 650 miles south of Ratmanov. No, it was something else, but it wouldn't come to him. Perhaps it was the note he'd made in his card index file—computer discs could be wiped clean by a big bomb's electromagnetic pulse—that unless a ship wanted to risk being locked in the ice, or forced to move so slowly it would be like a dinosaur as a target, it would have to stand off the southern, protective side of the Pribilofs to launch any cruise missiles at Ratmanov. No, that meant it was some other detail about the ice buzzing around in his head, but it wouldn't settle amid the constant patter of Marjorie's antiaircraft fire. He wondered if the Pentagon's contingency planners knew as much about the area as he did. He doubted it—not immodestly but from long experience. The trouble with the Pentagon was that there were too many desk jockeys—not enough people who had actually walked around and seen the places where they might have to fight a battle one day. Douglas Freeman had.

On his own money and time, he'd used every vacation and other time to visit every major battlefield in Europe before the war and had jotted down his observations on his three-by-five cards—operational plans for what he called potential "flash points." One such plan had been for the Kuwait-Iraqi border, another for the Dortmund-Bielefeld pocket. Freeman had also been to Alaska. He had trekked to see the lonely, windswept monument to Will Rogers eleven miles southwest of Barrow on the godforsaken tundra of Alaska's North Slope and had seen more than thirty bald eagles at once, on the banks of the Chilkat River, their white throat fur above the black body and white tails giving them a nobility among the winter-stripped cottonwoods that he would never forget. He had also been to Cape Prince of

Wales, where high up in the stunningly clear air at the western-most tip of Alaska's Seward Peninsula he had gazed out over the white strait, the cobalt blue line of Siberia on the horizon, and had seen the two specks that were the Diomede Islands. Perhaps it was there he had learned whatever it was about the ice that now he couldn't recall. He would have to go down to his base-ment, go through the rotary card file. "Excuse me," he told Marjorie. "Think I'll take a nap." He forced a smile. "Still not over my jet lag."

"Yes. You poor thing, Douglas. Thank the Lord I'm not af-fected."

"What—pardon?" asked Freeman as he stood up and pushed the chair back by the edge of the pool.

"Jet lag," said Marjorie serenely. "Thank the Lord I don't get it. I'm not affected."

"You wouldn't be," said Freeman under his breath.

"Pardon?"

"You're unaffected," said the general.

"Yes. To tell you the truth, Douglas, I think it's all in your head. If God had intended—"

Freeman wasn't listening, his attention drawn momentarily to the wind-ruffled pool, and knew instantly what it was about the winter ice floes in the strait. Not only were they looser than summer ice, but they were wind sculptured to heights of twenty-five feet above the frozen surface of the sea. He remembered them now—the purest white, glistening like mirrors in the sunny, clear air and then, as night came, turning to extraordinary hues of blue, a forest of jumbled sharp ice that would spell the death knell of any marine or army hovercraft invasion against Rat-manov, the ice too jagged to permit the necessary air cushion for the troop-carrying hovercrafts. They'd be torn to pieces.

Immediately he rang General Grey at the Pentagon, using his personal scrambler code to get a secure line.

"May I ask who's calling please?" said the secretary.

"General Douglas Freeman."

"Hold on please, General." Vivaldi's "Four Seasons" as-saulted him at full volume before the receptionist's voice came back on the line.

"Ah, Douglas," came General Grey's voice. "How's your wife?"

"The same, thank you. Look, Jimmy, with this Siberian thing looming I thought you could do with some advice from an old soldier out here." Freeman was waiting for a positive response but got none. He told Grey about the ice.

"Thanks, Douglas. Appreciate your interest. Really do. But to tell you the truth, we think this Novosibirsk thing is pretty much a bluff—to squeeze concessions out of us after the Moscow surrender. It'll blow over."

"What if it blows over Ratmanov?" asked Freeman.

"What?"

"Ratmanov. Big Diomede?"

"Oh—well, Douglas. CIA agrees with us that if we stand our ground, Novosibirsk'll back off. Besides, air force figures it can handle Big Diomede if it comes to that. And the navy, of course. But look—it's great to hear from you. You keep in touch, you hear? And Douglas—give my regards to your wife."

"Yes, sir."

Freeman put down the phone and cussed. He might be the commanding officer of Fort Ord, but he was effectively unemployed, out to pasture. The "No Help Wanted" sign up in Washington.

"Yoohoo! Douglas? Are you awake?"

"No," said Freeman, as he walked over and spun the globe, arresting the spin, turning it to him like the end of a football so he could see the Arctic Circle. Goddamn Diomedes were so small they weren't even marked. Like him, they were off the map. Get a goddamn grip on yourself, he muttered. Goddamn pity is for goddamn sissies. You a sniveller, Freeman? No. Then stop your goddamn whining.

"Yoohoo? Douglas?"

The general inhaled deeply, slowly, teeth gritted. Damn woman knew he was in his basement den. Why in hell did she have to—

"Yes? What is it?"

"It's visiting time. The hospital. You coming along?"

"Yes," said Freeman morosely. Then his conscience berated him, not only with what should have been concern for Doreen but because he'd caught himself at the shoreline of another sulk, the one thing he couldn't stand in anyone, least of all himself. "Yes," he said clearly, straightening up, grabbing his cap, "I'm coming." Surely the man who had handled the raid on Pyongyang and broken out of the Dortmund-Bielefeld pocket and pierced the famed Minsk-Moscow defenses could handle the barrage of inanities and clichés launched by his mobile sister-in-law.

"You see, Douglas?" she said as they walked out to the general's car.

"See what?" he asked as pleasantly as he could.

"How things work out for the best? I mean you coming home just when Dory needed you the most."

"Goddamn it, Marjorie—she's comatose!" said Douglas. "I can't do a thing to help her."

"But you're nearby. And just think—if you'd still been on active duty you might have got caught up in all this terrible Siberian business."

"Yes," said Douglas. "I probably would have, Marjorie."

"There, you see?" said Marjorie, slipping her arm through his and patting him. "It was meant to be."

Off Canada's west coast Captain Valery's *Saratov*, one of the Soviet Union's Pacific Fleet subs, out of radio contact with its home base of Vladivostok, was on silent running, listening on passive, rather than active, sonar. An active pulse, having to originate from the sub, would be too dangerous to use as the *Saratov* penetrated deeper into Allied ASW "microphoned" waters north of Vancouver Island. Sound from the ships it had been tracking for the last forty-eight hours was faint, yet discernible, the sound travelling at four times the speed it would in air, racing through the saline molecules of the sound layers.

Whether the contact was now fading because the ships his sub was shadowing had moved closer in to the coastline during the storm, further away from the *Saratov*, or whether they had in fact reduced speed, giving off less signature noise, Captain Valery couldn't tell, but with his sub at the end of its OSP— operational safety perimeter—he'd soon have to decide. "Take her up," he instructed the first officer. "Thirty meters."

"Up to thirty meters," confirmed the officer and planesman.
"Rising . . . angle ten . . . steady at thirty meters, sir."

"Up search scope."

Valery flipped the beak of his cap about, his eyes glued to the
column, and draped his arms on the scored grips, moving around
with the scope as if he were one with it. Now hopefully he would
see the actual shape of the ships his sub had been tracking so
far only by noise. What he saw through the infrared-penetrated
darkness puzzled him. In the grayish white circle of wave action,
obscured now and then in the night's dark curtain of spray, the
Canadian coastline, rather than being visible as a low blur before
the mountains, appeared to be missing. Only the sharp geom-
etry of the snow-capped coastal range beyond was visible, as if
the range rose straight out of the sea. He turned the scope another five degrees but still no trace of the coast. It was as if the
diameter of the periscope's gray infrared circle had been painted
black. Then he realized what he was looking at, why turning
the five degrees hadn't made any difference: two great slabs, the
two ships, had overlapped, obliterating the coastline. *"Gos-
podi!"*—"My God!" he called. *"Ya ikh vizhu! Pryamo peredo
mnoy!"*—"I have them dead ahead. Bearing?"

"Zero eight two," came the reply.

"Down scope!" ordered Valery. "Attack scope up."

"Down search scope. Up attack," confirmed the first officer.
Above the wheeze of the scope's column the tone signal of action
stations gonged urgently, though softly, in Control, the pulsating
red of the battle station's alarm bleeding pink into the red of
Control.

"Two of them," the captain informed the control crew as the
attack scope slid into position. "Both tankers. Enormous
brutes."

Eyes welded to the attack scope, Valery quickly picked the
ships up again on the same bearing. The attack scope, its field
of view not as wide as that of the search scope but higher,
allowed the sub to go deeper for a shoot. The scope's hair-
crossed circle was completely blocked by the massive walls that
were the tankers' sides, the bridge and crew housing astern of
one tanker etched silver in moonlight as the clouds broke and

two small blobs—tugs—could be seen bobbing up and down in the swells.

"Prevoskhodno"—"It couldn't be better," said Valery. Not only had he made the right decision by venturing in closer to the coastline—now he was no more than three miles from them—but at this angle of attack he would in effect not be firing at two separate hulls but at one long cliff of steel, over seven hundred meters—almost half a mile long. For safety's sake, the second tanker was sailing not directly behind the first where it could not hope to stop should anything happen to the tanker in front, but starboard aft of it in staggered convoy position. And the two tugs were all but obscured by the rising seas now. Even if they were armed with ASW depth bombs and sub-surface torpedoes Valery knew that they would be so busy with damage control if one or both tankers were hit that they would give him little cause for concern. In any event he ordered forward tubes two and four loaded with submarine simulator decoys of the kind that had been perfected after the cruiser *Yumashev* had been the victim of an American MOSS—a mobile submarine simulator—the cruiser dummied into positioning itself to be sunk by the U.S. nuclear sub *Roosevelt* in the early months of the war.

Now it was Valery's chance for revenge. But he would try to save the decoys for later use if possible. Hopefully he'd have complete surprise and wouldn't have to use them at all. He heard the officer of the deck confirming forward tubes one, three, five, and six were loaded with "live fish."

"Bearing?"

"Zero eight three."

"Mark!" Valery ordered. "Range?"

"Thirty-four hundred meters, sir."

Valery could feel a movement—energy transmitted by under-the-surface wave oscillation, a slight down pitch. "Hold her steady!" he said without unlocking his eyes from the scope. "Forward tubes one, three, five, and six. Set the up angle."

"Forward tubes one, three, five, and six—set up angle."

The confirmation came from torpedo control. "Up angle set."

The first officer was watching the relay screen showing the computerized, keyed-in angles that allowed for everything from the enemy's speed, variable friction caused by differing salinity, and water temperatures, to surface turbulence. Next he checked that the "decoy fish"—the simulators—were in forward tubes two and four.

"Bearing?"

"Zero eight four."

"Range?"

"Thirty-five hundred meters."

"Bearing?"

"Steady. Zero eight four."

"Shoot!" ordered Valery.

"Set," came the firing officer's reply.

"Fire one!"

"Fire one," confirmed the firing officer.

"Fire three," said Valery. A slight tremor passed through the sub as one was away and running.

"Fire three," came the confirmation.

"Fire five . . . fire six . . . down scope."

"Down scope, sir."

"Hold position."

The first officer was reading out the count from 120 seconds as the four twenty-one-foot-long torpedoes sped, without visible wakes, toward their target.

"Two apiece," announced the officer of the deck. Valery said nothing, his eyes on the computer clock. He knew he should hit both of them if all the computations were right, but with such a storm raging on the surface off the heavily timbered and logged coast there were bound to be deadheads, or floating logs, in the water. It would take only one torpedo to hit a piece of water-logged timber and the remaining three torpedoes could all be blown off track. *"Molis"*—"Pray," said Valery. "Sonar?"

"Sir?"

"Everything alright?"

"Humming, sir. Beautiful."

"Pipe it to the PA but low on the volume."

"Yes, sir."

Now everyone throughout the sub, as if equipped with steth-oscopes, could hear the fast, heavy heartbeats of the tankers and the steady hiss of the four torpedoes running for them.

"Get the book," said Valery. The officer of the deck passed over the enemy ship silhouette recognition binder. The moment they blew—if they blew—it was Valery's intention to surface for quick visual confirmation of type. Naval intelligence at Vladivostok would want to know. For a moment the surge of adrenaline in him stopped as he remembered the reason for HQ's insistence on getting all possible information including sea conditions during attack. The scuttlebutt going the rounds of Vladivostok was that apparently some Jews from the Jewish Autonomous Oblast, or region, around the Sino/Soviet border along the Amur River had been sabotaging munitions. Valery hoped it had only been air force and army munitions that had been tampered with and that when they found the saboteurs they hanged them—slowly. Shooting was too quick for saboteurs.

"Nine seconds to go," answered the first officer softly. Valery nodded, still leafing through the book, trying to identify the class of tankers he was attacking from the brief glimpse he'd had through the scope. He tried to suppress his excitement, but it was difficult. It was so easy—a dream of an attack. One thing he knew already—they were not VLCCs—very large crude carriers but *U*LCCs—ultra large crude carriers. "Ha," he exclaimed to the first officer. "Give it to the Americans—they always do things big, eh?" Even if only one was hit there'd be a hell of a spill; and if the crude's flash point was raised high enough and it started to burn, there would be no way the enemy crews could put it out. He could use the light to take his time on the second should any of the first four torpedoes miss.

On the first tanker, MV *Sitka*, captained by Jesus Llamos, assistant radio operator Sandra Thompson was taking her break. A shy, slim redhead, the subject of half the crew's on- and off-duty fantasies—despite the fact that she was married and in the early stages of pregnancy—she stood on the quiet, semidarkened bridge of the enormous tanker watching the amber island of light that was the Marconi anticollision radar. She found the phosphorescent dance of its hypnotic sweep comforting. Nothing was showing west of them. Eastward the coastline ran crooked, the radar trace a knotted, amber-colored snake flanked by the salt-and-pepper dots of offshore islands.

Glancing up from the radar for a moment, out through the darkness of the *Sitka*'s bridge, Sandra could see the moonlight bathing the sea's turbulence in a deceptively soft light, the great, sliding, gray metallic swells momentarily robbed of their violence. Something hit her, like a strong, hot wind. As she reached for the radar's console for support there was a flash from forward midships, an enormous crash, the ship shaking violently like a car at speed with a blowout, then a tremendous *whoomp* as the shock wave rebounded. In an ethereal moment of calm she saw Captain Llamos running toward the steering console, but his image shivered, and he looked as if he were moving in slow motion, hands outstretched for the auto-to-manual levers.

Then the ship listed to port. For a second Sandra thought the tanker had collided with one of the big tugs. The next moment the bridge shifted violently to port, and she was thrown hard in the darkness onto the cleated matting, glass shattering, its invisible hail all about her, alarm klaxons blaring, several lights on the wing tank monitor console blinking furiously, indicating at least five of the forward starboard wing tanks were ruptured, spilling their liquid cargo into the sea. Her face and hands soaking wet, she tried to get up, but the port list had increased to fifteen degrees, and she felt herself sliding down the incline. Suddenly lights came on.

"Put that damn switch off!" It was Llamos's voice shouting at the starboard lookout, Llamos hunched, hanging onto the steering console in the middle of the bridge.

"We're hit, aren't we?" the lookout yelled defiantly.

"You don't have to make it easier for them," Llamos shouted. "Keep the damn light off!" Sandra could see him dimly against the shattered bridge glass as he flicked on the intercom to the radio room, ordering the operator to send an SOS. There was no reply. He gave the order again. Still no reply. "Thompson?" he called out. "Sandra?"

"Yes, sir, I'm here."

"Go do it."

"Yes, sir." Pushing herself off the wet latticed decking she grabbed a flashlight from the port lookout's rack, making her way downhill to the radio room. Within seconds she was drenched, the sprinkler system going full bore. In the gossamer spray, cut cleanly by the beam of her flashlight, she saw blood streaming down her arms, only now realizing that her face had been lacerated by glass shards from the bridge. There was another flash of light; momentarily night became day. The second tanker was hit, one of her tanks immediately catching fire, an overwhelming explosion of crimson flame curling in the blackest smoke she'd ever seen, the flames now spiralling and joining. In the corner of the radio room she saw the operator trying to get up, holding his head. Instinctively moving to help, she checked herself and instead issued the SOS. As she went into the third repeat, giving the tanker's approximate position from the last fix, the computer readout dead, there was another sound like an enormous door creaking. The radio room began to move as if disembodied from the ship proper, and she knew that the *Sitka* was breaking, its spine snapped by either torpedoes or acoustic mines.

One of the Russian sub's torpedoes hadn't exploded. Valery entered it in the *Saratov*'s log as a possible dud, though he noted that given the sea's condition it might have gone off course because of a sudden thermocline. In any case, all Valery was concerned with now was that he had sunk two tankers—the first, though not on fire, was doomed, its funnel and aft crew sections, each half a quarter-mile long, drifting apart and in toward the wild coastline of British Columbia. Meanwhile the inferno on the second tanker was spreading over the sea in huge, fiery fingers, riding up and down the swells in the fast current. Because of the lack of surf between the protective offshore islands, the fiery spill, fed by its enormous tar balls and mousse blankets of crude, was already washing up on the pristine shoreline. Fanned by the gale-force winds, the huge flames were licking the dense shoreline forests, setting the timber here in the dry cold several hundred feet below the coastal range's snow line afire in what would be the biggest single blaze and ecological disaster since the oil spills and fires of the Iraqi war.

In the search scope Valery could easily identify the stricken tankers illuminated by the flames as ultra-large carriers of the Globtik Tokyo class, both in excess of three hundred thousand dead weight tons. "Even better than I had hoped," he informed the officer of the deck. "But I don't understand why the first tanker isn't burning."

"The fires were probably doused by the flooding," commented the OOD.

"Even so," rejoined Valery, "the tanker's own engine oil should—"

Suddenly Valery snapped the grips hard against the scope's stainless steel column. "Down scope. Dive to five hundred."

"Down scope . . . dive to five hundred!" repeated the OOD. The diving officer stood directly behind the two planesmen, hands gripping their two bucket seats, knuckles white as he watched the gauge of the sub. If they dove at too steep an angle, the sub's stern would come clear out of the water before they were fully submerged.

"Podgotovit' k vypusku torpedo—simyulator podvodnoy lodki. Zadnyaya truba."—"Prepare to fire submarine simulator torpedo. Stern tube."

As the torpedo officer confirmed the order, Valery explained the rush to the OOD. "A helicopter's coming off the second tanker. Most likely for crew rescue but could be ASW."

For a second Valery chastised himself for not having fired the submarine simulator before the attack, but it was an enormously expensive piece of equipment. Besides shooting out millions of rubles with each fish, its noise, while a decoy for any ASW aircraft or ship in the area, would have been picked up by the SOSUS, the underwater microphone arrays of the sound surveillance system, giving the sub's general "area position" away. With the depth needle approaching five hundred meters, Valery decided he'd made the right decision, saving the simulator till now. True, he'd glimpsed the helicopter on the tanker's deck for only a split second, but he was sure its rotors had been spinning, ready for takeoff, possibly with ASW munitions.

"Level at five hundred, sir."

"Fire decoy!"

"Decoy fired, sir."

"Silent running," ordered Valery.

"Silent running, sir."

From now on if any crew member made a mistake—dropped anything on the metal deck that might be picked up in the sound channel—it would cost the man three months' pay plus a "zebra"—a black-striped demotion entry on his blue service sheet.

But Valery himself had made a serious error. The Bell 212 twin-turboshaft chopper rising aft off the second tanker's stern housing pad was interested only in trying to rescue two crew members whose salt-activated vest lights were orange pinpoints in the raging cauldron about the stricken tankers. The spray-roiling beam that was the chopper's searchlight turned rust-red above the blankets of burning oil. In the beam's circle that was moving up and down the chaotic sea like an undulating sheet of blood, the two crewmen lay limp in the helo's harness, having suffocated in the oil after having been concussed by the explosions of the torpedoes. Likewise, scores of seabirds were already smothered in the bunker "C" crude.

Sandra Thompson, Llamos, and the starboard lookout struggled on the slippery incline of the stern deck of the first tanker. The ship's two halves continued drifting apart as the three survivors tossed over a white, drum-size Beaufort canister, its tether flying free of the ship like some long snake. The canister hit the water, instantly shedding its fiberglass shell and blossoming into a tent raft of vivid Day-Glo magenta highlighted by the fire on the second tanker aboard which small, toylike figures could be seen vainly manning a crisscross of hoses.

"Inflate your vest," Llamos shouted to the starboard lookout. "Hold your breath as long as you can and—" Llamos's voice was whipped away by the gale-force winds as he pointed toward the treacle-moated raft now about thirty feet away from the badly listing stern section. The lookout jumped.

Sandra pulled the CO_2 string on her life vest, heard the sudden hiss of air, felt the Mae West swelling above her bosom as she tightened the waist straps and bent down to inflate the vest of the injured radio man whom she and Llamos had dragged precariously from the bridge. Llamos had taken a turn about the operator's waist with a painter from one of the lifeboats to prevent the injured man from sliding down the deck that was now dangerously slick with the oil which had been blown skyward in towering black spumes before falling back on the tankers, drenching the four and

fuelling the fires with a driving black rain. The radio man
was so quiet, Sandra thought he was dead, but putting her
finger on his carotid artery she thought she felt a faint pulse.

"Go!" Llamos yelled out to her. "Jimmy and I'll look
after him. You need to reach the raft. Transmit our—" He
didn't finish, his voice drowned in a gush of superheated
steam, a boiler beneath them exploding, splitting the ship's
port after section, the stern heaving, the stack spewing boil-
ing water swept forward for hundreds of yards in the gale
force winds. The stern was now split and sliding back into
the sea, rolling, revealing the flanges of its enormous prop
blades. Llamos and the other three were toppling out of control down the cliff of the deck. A lifeboat wrenched from its
davits swung upward like a trapeze, smashing itself to splinters. The hissing roar of the stern was so loud it could be
heard above the gale by the few crewmen still battling the second tanker's fires. Unable to save Sandra or the others, the
two-man helo crew watched helplessly as the rear half of the
MV *Sitka* disappeared. Then they turned their attention to
the tiny frantic figures on the stern of the second tanker.

The chopper's pilot had ordered his assistant to jettison
the bodies of the two dead men they'd hauled up, lessening
the chopper's weight so the helo might try to pick up as many
survivors as possible from the twenty-five-man crew on the
second tanker and any others who, inconceivable as it appeared, might be alive on the forward section of the first
tanker. Though still afloat, it was certain to go under within
minutes.

The pilot shouted his instructions regarding excess weight
into the throat mike, and his assistant, after having grabbed
the auto-flash Canon and taking head shots of the two dead
men for later identification, pushed the bodies out. The chopper banked in the darkness toward the stern of the second
tanker, its fire now so fierce, there was no hope of the ship's
hoses extinguishing it. The hot air currents streaming up from
the blazing ship were so powerful that the pilot knew there
was no chance of getting anywhere close to the deck.

Cautiously he brought the chopper toward the stern, his
visibility now reduced to zero because of the continuing oil

smudge on his windscreen combining with the buildup of salt crust, a combination the wipers couldn't handle. His assistant saw a crimson streak several hundred yards away to the east— a flare—and in its flickering light the Day-Glo of a Beaufort "Teepee." Yelling at the pilot and gesturing eastward, the assistant guided them to the point seventy feet away. The chopper hovered above the raft and lowered the harness, swiveling in the C clip. But then seeing the raft was over-crowded with survivors from both tankers and that this could easily lead to a capsize should the chopper be suddenly caught in an updraft, the pilot shouted into the mike, "We're only a few miles from shore. Best leave 'em for Air Sea Rescue in the morning. Stand a better chance, I reckon."

"I dunno," yelled the assistant. "Could go belly-up any-way in the swells." During the second of hesitation the Bell 212, which could not fly on one engine unless traveling in excess of one hundred miles per hour, gave a shudder. An engine coughed, then the other cut out, its air filter jammed solid with soot from the oil fire. The chopper plunged, its rotors chopping into the loaded raft. Then, catching a swell, the blades cartwheeled the chopper several hundred feet, splashing into the mousse of bunker "C," parts of the main rotor whistling through the gale. Everyone aboard the tent raft was drowned, in effect suffocated by the oil, including Sandra Thompson and the two-month-old child she was car-rying.

General Grey had thought nothing of Freeman's call about the peculiar condition of winter ice in the Bering Strait. Surely the Pentagon planners would know this. Grey called down-stairs to make sure. They didn't know. This shocked Grey, but even so it wasn't Freeman's familiarity with the minutiae that now impressed him but rather the simple yet profound realization that for Freeman to think of such a detail in the midst of his wife's catastrophic injury meant that the soldier in Freeman was not only alive and well, but there was only the soldier—that Freeman was straining at the leash. With his genius for logistical detail as well as strategic thought he was unquestionably the man for the job. America had never fought a sustained Arctic war, but now, with the Mideast oil wells afire and the Siberians having answered President Mayne with the sinking of the two American tankers, which by itself constituted an immediate threat to the U.S. oil supply from the Alaskan North Slope, the U.S. had no option. It was war.

Grey lifted his Pentagon scrambler phone, got the Joint Chiefs' approval, including that of the CNO, Admiral Horton; then he rang the White House and suggested that General Douglas Freeman be appointed commander in chief, Operation Arctic Front, the moment he landed at Elmendorf Air Force Base Alaska. The president approved.

The call came through to Freeman in Monterey as Marjorie was watching a news flash cutting into "The Tonight Show" with Jay Leno announcing that America was at war.

"My glory—" began Marjorie, in a state of shock, one hand clasped before her mouth as the other worked the remote to bring in CBN. "You hear that, Douglas?" she called out. "Russian submarines have attacked two of our ships. We're at war again."

Freeman had put the phone down and was already doing up his necktie in an old-fashioned Windsor knot, so old that it was now said to be back in style. He had already called Fort Ord to make transport arrangements and issued a series of orders marshalling elements of the marines' rapid deployment force.

"My glory!" Marjorie repeated, slumped down in the recliner. "That's *terrible*."

"Yes," Freeman agreed. "Sure as hell is." It may have been the light of the TV flickering, but for a moment Marjorie could have sworn Douglas was smiling.

"Still, Marjorie," he added, "must have been meant to be." She suspected in a vague sort of way that it might be a jibe at her, but it was clear he also believed it.

"I hope it'll be quick," said Marjorie, "like Iraq."

Freeman's smile was devoid of condescension—one of those a parent gives when obliged to break a truth of life gently to his offspring, the truth that in life you couldn't hope for nonstop, easy victories. He took nothing away from the men who had fought in Desert Storm, in which he himself had led part of the Seventh Armored in the decisive outflanking movement north that caught the Republican Guard with their pants down. But the Iraqi war, for all its moments of undeniable American and Coalition bravery, had been, when all was said and done, a hundred-hour ground war. Even the dimmest private would see that Siberia was a far different situation, that any comparison to Desert Storm was naive to say the least.

He spoke quietly. "Marjorie—Iraq is desert. Some high country to the north, but in the main, a desert. Siberia has everything, by which I mean every natural land, water, and ice barrier on God's earth. And taiga—pine, birch, and fir forests—far as the eye can see. Wermacht used to talk of 'distance illness,' the endlessness of Russia. And Marjorie—'' He was looking in the mirror, straightening the khaki tie. "—the Krauts didn't even get to Siberia. They were in the *small* part of Russia." He buttoned up his coat, the rows of campaign ribbons and decorations attesting to the battles he had fought for America from Southeast Asia to Iraq to the Minsk-Moscow line, his reflection in the mirror at once eager for and awed by his responsibility. "There is," he said, pulling on his cap, "another minor detail."

"What?" Marjorie asked, though her attention was distracted by a CBN broadcaster. Somehow they'd got one of their cameras twenty-four miles across the strait from Alaska to Little Diomede Island and had it set up on the sloping but still steep western side of the small American outpost near the Eskimo village of Inalik. The CBN's camera was filling the TV screen with the ice-covered basalt that was the bottom half of Big Diomede or, as CBN was calling it, "Ratmanov Island."

Freeman shot a glance at the TV, and Marjorie had seldom seen such a look of outright contempt on his face as he watched the CBN announcer in a fur-lined Eskimo parka telling Americans how the U.S. Air Force were already assembling fighters and fighter bombers on the Alaskan Peninsula for what was "certain to be" an aerial bombardment of the 11.2-square-mile Ratmanov Island. The island was so heavily defended, the reporter continued, "that many military experts believe it to be *the* most heavily defended piece of real estate in the world whose troops, unlike the ill-supplied Republican Guard of the Iraqi war, are known to have months of supplies and ammunition deep within the granite fortress. Along with state-of-the-art air defenses that are bound to inflict heavy casualties upon the Americans if they try to take out the SAM sites on Ratmanov and which they must take out if they have any hope of . . ."

"It's *not* Ratmanov Island," shouted Freeman at the CBN announcer. "It's *Rat* Island, and we're going to exterminate the bastards! By the bushel!"

"Douglas!"

He flashed a winning smile. "Sorry, Marjorie."

"Aren't you going to tell me then?"

He looked at her, puzzled, a he unconsciously felt for what he called his "backup," his vest-holstered Hi-Vel .22 automatic beneath his tunic. "Tell you what?"

"You said there was one other thing about Siberia that made it so different. Oh, dear—you aren't going to tell me you expect it to be a long war, are you?"

"Yes," answered Freeman, slipping in a rubber-banded clutch of three-by-five index cards—"Arctic Ops"—into his pocket. "Siberia," he told her, "is twenty times the size of Iraq." Actually it was more than twenty-three times as big, but he knew civilians preferred round numbers. Suddenly Marjorie realized he'd been dressing with more ceremony than usual for duty at Fort Ord. "You're not going?" she charged.

"Ordered by the president, Marjorie," he said. "No choice." It was only the second lie he'd told since leaving Europe, the first during a news conference in Paris on his way home, in which he had apologized, under direct orders from General Grey, for having called his Russian counterparts a pack of "vodka-sucking sons of bitches." It was quite wrong of him, he said later, to have said anything against vodka—"Hell, I have it on good authority that you can run tanks on it."

"If I didn't know better, Douglas," said Marjorie, "I'd think you enjoyed it."

On the way to Fort Ord he heard on the radio that CBN was reporting that U.S. air strikes against Ratmanov from Elmendorf Air Force Base near Anchorage and from the bases further west on Cape Prince of Wales were imminent.

"That's right, you bastar—" He stopped short, old-fashioned about using rough language in front of women. "Wonder is," he told the blond chauffeur, "they don't tell the Siberians how many planes are involved."

"They're probably working on it, General."

CHAPTER SIX

WITH MOST OF the U.S.'s seventy-six F-117A Stealth fighters still in Europe, only five were immediately available to Alaskan command, the F-117A's primary role being radar avoidance attack, not defense. Led in by a Wild Weasel F-4G Phantom jamming Big Diomede's radars with white noise, the five Stealth fighters, despite their relatively low maneuverability—something not known by the public at large—thundered only four hundred feet above the white blur that was the eastern half of the Bering Strait.

Coming in at seven hundred miles per hour, executing both "high" and "over-the-shoulder" toss bomb release runs, they sent Paveway 2,300-pound laser-guided ordnance, along with twelve-foot-long, modular-glide bombs, sliding down the "ice-cream," or laser, cone toward the eastern cliff face that sprouted retractable Flat-Face, Squat-Eye, Spoon-Rest, and Low-Blow radar arrays that serviced batteries of four barreled eighteen-inch-diameter surface-to-air missiles. Seconds after the four nose canards behind each laser seeker-detector nose assembly whistled through the dry Arctic air, their explosions lit up the face of "Ratmanov," or Big Diomede, in crimson-curdled orange balls of fire. The thunder rolled between the two islands on the

clear night, jagged sea ice reflecting the light so that Big Diomede was lit up like some huge, black-veined massif that had
only suddenly burst through the frozen sea. It was an illusion
created by enormous slivers of ice sliding from the island's cliff
face from the heat and the concussion of the bombs crashing
into the sea ice below.

The following Aardvark, or F-111F fighter bombers, came in
on the deck at 570 miles per hour to deliver their "slide" beams
for more laser-guided bombs, pilots expecting to run into heavy
antiaircraft fire on the approach, weapons officers centering the
cross hairs on the infrared screens. Closing on the target, lasers
were activated to "lock on" and, seconds before the "slide"
bomb launch, the electronic warfare officers tensed, expecting
heavy AA fire. But there was none. On the second approach by
the F-111 fighter bombers, flying low to deliver more bombs,
the aircraft presumably radar safe in the "frying pan" static set
up by the F-4G Phantom Wild Weasels, Big Diomede suddenly
erupted, spewing streams of red and green tracer crisscrossing
the sky in deadly tattoo, the white noise now settling down so
that the F-111 pilots knew that either the Wild Weasels had
stopped their jamming or the Russians had outjammed the jam-
mers.

Whatever the cause, over forty batteries of ZSU Quad twenty-
three-millimeter cannon and Soviet SA-10 missiles filled the air
above the strait, each gun firing over ten thousand rounds a
second. The twenty-three-millimeter fire created a curtain of
red-hot metal in the narrow corridor that the Wild Weasels had
believed secure for a safe run in. Yet, despite the heavy AA fire,
only one of the F-111 fighter bombers and one Wild Weasel were
taken out, the F-111 going down, spitting flame then erupting
on the ice into a thousand fiery pieces, the Weasel crashing
because the intakes of its twin eighteen-thousand-pound-thrust
jet engines were fouled as the plane struck a mass of terrified,
glaucous-winged gulls. By now the F-111 fighter bombers had
delivered their loads against the cliff face in an effort to penetrate
the enclaves of the AA fire, but many of the heat-seeking missiles from the F-111s had been dummied by what photo reconnaissance later discovered were wired hot spots to sucker the
heat-seeking American missiles, the Siberians' ZSU twenty-

three-millimeter and SA-10 missiles coming from relatively cooler apertures from within the sixteen-hundred-foot-high cliff face of the eleven-square-mile island.

In most danger were the five Stealth fighters. Poorly maneuverable, compared to the F-111s and Wild Weasels, and slow, at seven hundred miles per hour, the Stealth's only superiority to the others lay in radar evasion. They sought the safety of flying practically on the deck, only two to three hundred feet above the jagged ice that was racing like an endless white runway beneath them. One, just off the northern end of Little Diomede less than two and a half miles from target, had ironically begun to climb for an over-the-shoulder toss when a wind shear created among the ice floes' jagged peaks sucked it down for a fraction of a second. At seven hundred miles an hour the Stealth could not rise in time, and the Siberian Quads' fire raked it from the ventral scanner below the pilot past the canopy actuator to the left-hand tail fin. It was as if a swallow's tail had been suddenly clipped; the plane's implosion on the ice and the detonation of the Paveway two-thousand-pounder blew a black hole in the ice, the giant eruption of flame from it illuminating the strait between the islands like some enormous charred skating rink. For an instant it was bright as day, the Siberian gunners pouring an enfilade of ZSU twenty-three millimeter fire toward it. It took a full burst, and the second Stealth was gone.

High above Big Diomede thousands more seabirds, screeching in panic, driven aloft by the shrapnel-filled night, cried even louder, some falling now, tumbling down toward the ice, either killed outright or stunned by the bombs' explosions and AA fire. Two Siberian SA-10 missiles—radar-identified by a high-stationed, rotodomed Boeing E-3—streaked toward two of the three remaining Stealths as they banked hard right, turning north, swinging still further to an eastward heading.

There were two winks of light from Cape Prince of Wales' Cape Mountain, and in less than five seconds two 20-foot-long, 2,200-pound U.S. Patriot land mobile surface-to-air missiles intercepted the two Soviet SA-10s, blowing them out of the sky. In the mobile command center of the Patriots in a bunker in Cape Prince of Wales the videos from the cameras of the first American wave were already being shown. The representatives from Raytheon Co. of Lexington and the Martin Marietta Corp. of Bethesda, Maryland, the prime and subcontractors for the 1.4-million-dollar-apiece Patriots, were well pleased, watching their companies being guaranteed future contracts for the 152-million-dollar Patriot's mobile five unit system.

They were also joining in the congratulations to those pilots who had "toggled" the laser-guided bombs, via the white cross of the TV image, smack onto their selected targets, the silent, soft white bursts of light on the videos showing the smart bombs exploding. But there had been very few secondary bursts within the initial explosions, meaning no ammunition or missile dumps.

But if the contractors were pleased, the CO of Alaskan Command wasn't. He had lost four multimillion dollar aircraft and six air crew, two each from the downed F-111 fighter bomber and the Phantom 4-G Wild Weasel, two from the Stealth fighters. And for what? If the high-frequency Russian radar hadn't picked them up because of the earlier jamming by the Wild Weasels, then low frequency, which had been known to work on the Stealths before, must have. In any case, what was the result? he pointedly asked the hitherto exhilarated pilots. The infrared videos showed nothing more than the cliff face splattered with black, sootlike marks and splotches like white paint, clumps of old guano that had accumulated against the sixteen-hundred-foot-high granite cliff now covered in ice and snow. Yes, the bombs had landed where they were supposed to, but there was no evidence of any real damage. Where the hell were the knocked-out ZSU quads? Never mind the absence of any real damage to the SA-10 and radar array sites.

"Probably all recessed," proffered one of the remaining F-111 weapons officers.

"Of course they're goddamn recessed," said the general. "They popped up long enough to get a fix on you, fired, and then they were gone, back in their holes like a bunch of prairie dogs."

"We must have hit a few ventilator shafts, sir—that led in from the cliff. They have to breathe."

"Hell, Captain, they could have ventilator shafts coming in from all over that island from the western side. Island's only three miles wide. We were firing at hot spots that the videos now show were just that—hot spots. Thermal patches, each one probably run by a goddamn flashlight battery. I don't know how the hell they're doing it, but we're wasting bombs, and we've just shot off five million bucks worth of ordnance in five seconds to shoot down missiles from sites we can't even see."

"Well, sir," continued one of the two remaining Stealth captains, "we're just going to have to get those satellite boys in Washington to get their magnifying glasses on. Has to be somewhere we can get ordnance into that sucker."

"*Time*, gentlemen," said the general urgently. "*Time!* The Joint Chiefs want this one taken out in a big hurry. We don't knock out Big Diomede, we can't cross the strait. We don't cross the strait, and the Siberians can move everything they've got to their eastern flank—fifty miles from us." The general was studying one of the video stills. "We'll have to go in with more infrared seekers—hope some of them can fix on RHPs." He meant residual heat patches, which theoretically should have been identified by thermal patch imaging sights even after the periscopelike radar antennae popped back down in their holes.

"Trouble is, sir, it's so cold, RHPs' signatures disappear on you almost immediately."

"I know, I know. I'll put the word out to our chief weapons officer—see whether he can crank the infrared sensors up a notch or two."

"I'm surprised we didn't run into any MiGs," said the captain in charge of the Stealths.

"Maybe they don't have any in their eastern TVD." He meant the Siberians' eastern theater.

"Right," said the Stealth captain cheekily, "and I'm Marilyn Monroe."

"Then come to bed, Marilyn," said one of the weapons officers. But no one felt like laughing. The exhilaration of the attack was wearing off with the realization that six of their buddies were no more. And in the two Stealths alone, Alaska Air Command had lost 250 million dollars of the taxpayers' money.

One thing was for damn sure, the general told his aide after the debriefing—he wasn't going to send any more pilots against that "hunk of rock" until he could loosen it up a bit by "other means." By which he meant that, despite NORAD's insistence that the attack on Ratmanov not siphon off any aircraft from the continent's vital North American defense line, he would request that a B-1 bomber be released from its blastproof shelter six hundred feet above sea level to launch air-to-ground 86-B cruise missiles at the rock.

Firing the three-thousand-pound, two-thousand-mile-range missile outside the Siberians' effective air-to-surface missile envelope from a distance of between forty and fifty miles would be like hitting the rock at point-blank range. If that didn't shake a few things loose, granite fortress and all, he didn't know what would. He could, of course, wait for more bombers to be released from Europe, but this was unlikely now that they had to contend with containing the Siberian west flank. And the air commander knew that if he couldn't shake up Big Diomede—and quickly—knocking out its radar, AA, and no doubt its surface-to-ship missile batteries, he would have to yield the job to the navy. He was right.

The Tomcats aboard USS *Salt Lake City* with their 14,500 pounds of ordnance on four underfuselage points and two wing hard points were even now taking their turn as squat, bright yellow mules—tractors—positioned them ready for the four waist and bow catapults. The Alaskan air commander was too much of a professional to let petty interservice rivalry with the navy stand in the way of an operation's success. Still . . .

In the backseat of the lead Tomcat, Frank Shirer's RIO, his radar intercept officer, Walter B. Anderson, a twenty-four-year-old from Wisconsin, raised his thumb, signalling the red-jacketed ordnance men that he had seen all the red-ribboned safety pins extracted from the bomb racks. Now through the white blaze of steam-curtained light, shadows of yellow- and green-jacketed men darted about the bow and waist cats and blast deflectors—the twin, bluish white cones of the Tomcat's Pratt and Whitney TF-30 engines going into the high scream of a forty-thousand-pound thrust. Shirer saw the yellow jacket drop, left knee on the deck, left hand tucked up behind his back, right arm fully extended. "Go!"

Shirer braced himself. There was an enormous hiss. Shirer felt himself slammed back into his seat, saw a blur of deck lights, felt a rush like a long feather pulling through his rectum, involuntarily ejaculated, and was hurled aloft at 180 miles per hour, the carrier deck a yellow postage stamp sliding away downhill into the darkness behind him.

Shirer was already feeling nostalgic for the Tomcat. After this he would be transferred to shore duty at Elmendorf, navy fighters being used to fill the NORAD gap. It would mean he'd have more opportunity to be with Lana, but he liked carriers—they kept moving. Now, however, all thoughts of Lana La Roche, née Brentwood, her beauty, her fear of her husband, Jay La Roche, a wife-beater and psychopath all rolled into one behind the respectable exterior, had to be put aside as Shirer, leader of the twelve Tomcats, headed toward Ratmanov Island, their offset aiming point the quarter-mile-high Fairway Rock twelve miles south of their target.

Shirer's F-14, coming in over the ice pack, led the attack, diving into the slot of the Bering Strait where the blip of Ratmanov was already on his target scope, magnified by the second. Then the Arctic night came alive with streams of red and green tracer, not shot higgledy-piggledy, Shirer noted, as in the Baghdad raids he'd been on, but carefully vectored toward the ten-plane arrowhead formation. His RIO, Anderson, reported that he had a cluster of Siberian Spoon-Rest radar masts on the eastern cliff of Ratmanov in the cross hairs of the green infrared screen. He switched on the laser designator beam and in less than a second informed Shirer they had a "lock-on"; in another second two-thousand-pound dumb bombs fitted with Paveway conversion kits, turning them into smart weapons, were sliding down the beam. At the same time six batteries of quad-mounted ZSU-23s opened up along the cliff, sending swarms of sixty-five-round-per-second, thirty-millimeter fire at the American jets. Faster eighteen-foot-long SA-10 missiles followed, the Siberian radar having got a radar fix.

"We've been painted," warned Anderson. The missiles, at over forty-two hundred miles an hour travelling faster than a rifle bullet, were streaking toward the American formation.

The F-14s began evasive measures, but Shirer's Tomcat was hit as it rose sharply before a dark cleft in the cliff erupting with massed machine-gun fire, the Tomcat's wings going into the swept position for more maneuver, its turbofans screaming on afterburner. Shirer felt a shudder. The tail actuators were severed.

"Eject! Eject!" he yelled. Anderson pulled the eject handle. There was a bang, the explosive bolts disengaging.

Knowing his RIO was out, Shirer pulled his eject and the next moment was shot out in the rocket-assisted Martin-Baker ejector seat. The freezing Arctic wind howled about him as he reached the apogee of the thrust. He began to fall, heard the snap of the chute opening, and in flickering flare light spotted Anderson below, off to his left, as they descended toward the snow-covered southern end of the high, rocky island.

They had been illuminated by the flare light for only a second or two, but it was enough for the six-man troop of the elite Russian SPETS commandos, who, unseen by the Americans, came up out of their deep, rock-roofed tunnel complex and, invisible because of their white winter overlays against the snow, ran with the controlled pace of top athletes. Despite their heavy weapon load, they continued sprinting toward the island's narrower, southern end.

Anderson, from the downed Tomcat, had barely finished wrapping up his chute when Shirer quickly released himself from the chute before it could drag him over the seventeen-hundred-foot-high edge of the cliff. The SPETS were almost upon them.

"Ne dvigat'sya!"—"Don't move!" Neither the pilot nor his RIO knew a word of Siberian, but they understood the lead commando's shouted command, and stood, hands raised.

The first two commandos knelt, covering them with their AK-74s. As per regulation, at least one of the elite SPETS troop, the tail-end Charlie, spoke English—and without a trace of an accent. "What airfield are you from?" he asked them both, his gaze settling on Shirer who, despite the fact that the Russian was only several feet away, couldn't make out the commando's face beneath the dark makeup and the hood of the white overlay.

"My name is Franklin G. Shirer. My rank is colonel in the U.S. Navy. My service number is—"

"Who's the senior officer?" snapped the Russian commando, his infrared goggles giving him a grotesque, bug-eyed, alien appearance.

"I am," Shirer told him.

"You!" said the commando, turning immediately to the RIO. "What airfield are you from?"

"My name is Captain Walter B.—"

"Vozmite ego!"—"Take him!" ordered the commando. Two of the other SPETS grabbed the captain. Shirer instinctively moved to help and felt himself lifted off the ground, the pain hitting a moment later, the blow to his stomach winding him so acutely that despite the howl of the wind moaning across the icy crust of the island, he could hear himself gasping hoarsely, his windpipe making a rasping sound as he struggled for breath. Amid the flashes of the Siberian ZSU-23 quads and streams of tracer gracefully arcing and climbing skyward he glimpsed his RIO at the edge of the cliff. "What airfield?" shouted one of the Russians holding him. Anderson wouldn't answer. The next second he was gone off the cliff, his screams quickly lost beneath the loud rattle of the Siberians' AA quads.

"Jesus!" shouted Shirer. "You bastards—" A SPETS hit him again, and he blacked out.

The navy's air attacks from the *Salt Lake City* were fierce, fearless, and ineffective. The only thing that they achieved was a pervasive sense among the Siberian tunnel garrison of the superiority of their "Saddam Bunker" defensive measures— lessons learned from the Iraqis' experience during the massive American and Allied bombing of '91.

Even if the *starye perduny*—"old farts"—in Russia's Frunze Military Academy had not absorbed the experiences relayed to them by their pupils, the Republican Guard survivors, the lesson of the logistical brilliance of the Americans had been duly recorded by the Soviets' *Liberation Army Daily*.

It was not so much the lesson of the U.S.'s "Smart" bombs, as, despite the propaganda spread about by what Novosibirsk called the unwitting dupes of the Western media, the Americans' laser-guided weapons constituted only 7 percent of the total bombs dropped, the remainder being World War II iron bombs, some of these turned into GBU—guided bomb units— with the Pave penny laser seeker conversion kits. No, it was the logistical capability, the "tooth to tail" supply lines feeding and in general maintaining over a quarter-million men and machines with everything they needed, from 5.56 rifle rounds, HEAT (high explosive antitank) rounds, Starlight infrared night vision goggles, condoms (to reduce the 14 percent VD casualty rate of most armies), and MRE (meals ready to eat) trays, warmed by body heat alone, to toothpaste and toilet paper.

This logistical capability of the Americans was, in the Siberians' eyes, the real victor of Desert Storm, as the Siberians believed that, man for man, their troops, raised, born, and trained in the Arctic, were far tougher than the American and British allies. The Americans were superb at organization and improvisation, the commanding officer, Lieutenant General Dracheev, pointed out to his two-thousand-man Ratmanov garrison, and the American capability was seared into the psyches of the entire garrison. The Siberians, in their "Saddam" tunnel complex, now moved with a well-oiled efficiency, as if some vast collective unconscious had risen from within the great rock to insulate them between Ratmanov and the Smart bomb attacks.

Only in two places, the northeastern end of the island and through a clutch of radar antennae, whose bases had become dislodged before they were able to be retracted far enough, did shrapnel from the Allied bombs permeate, killing eight men and wounding a score more. Even so, the integrity of the rock proved anew the fact, grudgingly conceded by the U.S. Air Force and the pilots of the navy Tomcats and the beloved Grumman A-6E Intruders, with their eighteen-thousand-pound bomb loads coming in from *Salt Lake City*, that aerial bombardment, though it might cause jaw-splitting headaches, *toshnota*—"nausea"— from "shock wave multiples," and blurring of one's vision, could not win against, or even dislodge, the deeply dug keepers in the oil-cushioned "Saddam" bunkers of Ratmanov Island.

Lieutenant General Dracheev, who knew that the sole reason for the Ratmanov garrison's existence was to remain an immovable threat and obstacle to the Americans, obviating the need for Novosibirsk to risk precious aircraft over the strait, felt secure in his control bunker. Halfway down the island, it had been dug one hundred feet into the solid rock, three hundred feet in from the eastern cliff face.

He peered at the night sky though his infrared periscope,

which could be used at either the level he was now standing, sixty feet below the surface of solid rock, or two levels further down in Control at the hundred-foot level. Seeing no sign of enemy activity and assured by his radar controllers that no air traffic could be detected in the local area of the Diomedes, Dracheev headed down toward his bunker from the first periscope level.

The concrete stairwell was watched over by a KPV Vladimirov heavy machine gun post, only part of its 135-centimeter-long barrel visible in the ball turret mounted in the door. At the machine gun the reinforced concrete stairwell took a downward-sloping U-turn to yet another closed door. Here, at the second of the three levels, another machine-gun inset had to be swung open to allow the commander and his aides into this eighty-foot level of the hundred-foot-deep bunker. The floor was a two-foot-thick antidetonator slab of reinforced concrete and high tensile steel. The next flight of stairs led to the air lock, in the event of chemical attack, outside the main command bunker at the one-hundred-foot level. All three levels were separated by at least ten feet of rock. The upper level contained a SPETS guard detachment, whose dormitories, canteen, and bunks were on the second level, which also contained all communications consoles, a conference room, and two bedrooms for Lieutenant General Dracheev and his aide, a SPETS colonel.

The lowest level was comprised of electricity generators, water tanks, along with air, water, and sewage filtration units. Other nuclear shelters like it had been built, but this command post had earned its name as a "Saddam" bunker because it had pressure-pumped, quick-setting, rubberized cement poured beneath it as well, filling every nook and cranny at the base of the enormous command center with what was effectively a hard, rubberized foundation four feet thick that even extended five to six feet outside the bunker to fill the gaps between the hewn-out rock shaft and man-made steel walls of the deep, rectangular bunker. This allowed it not only to withstand the shock waves of a nuclear burst but also to "move" on the rubberized foundation in the event of earthquakes and other natural realignments that radiated out from the inherently unstable Aleutian chain.

The Allies had heard rumors of such bunkers for years—ever

since the Iraqi war, when they had failed to get Saddam as he moved from bunker to bunker. The Allies were better acquainted with the layout of the Siberian bunkers for the troops. It was a fundamentally simple design, combining the best German engineering with the best British steel to create a series of interlocking H-shaped "pipe tunnel" garrison complexes drilled out of the basalt.

The complexes, one deep below the northern half of the island, the other beneath the southern half, consisted of a series of prefabricated high-tensile steel "sewer pipe" tubes or rooms leading off from a connecting cylindrical tunnel corridor to form an H. Each of the sewer-pipe-shaped chambers was a one-hundred-foot-long, ten-foot-diameter barracks containing at least one hundred troops, who slept on fold-down bunks at the ends of the tube. It was an astonishingly cost-effective and efficient design, borrowed from the Federation of Nuclear Shelter Consultants and Contractors. Each H unit was only one hundred and fifty feet from end to end and barely two hundred feet left to right. An extra twenty feet of concrete extended from either side as an added margin of protection for the tubular barracks. In twenty H barracks, ten north of his command bunker, ten south, Dracheev housed a thousand troops together with a sick bay and kitchen stacked with dried foods. The air vents were cleverly concealed at surface level in natural rock chimneys and fissures all equipped with chemical attack filters. Dracheev's command bunker, while midway between the two, was not connected by the usual ten-foot-diameter, tubular, bombproof corridor but a narrow two-and-a-half-foot-diameter crawl pipe so that in the event of the island's secure, buried land lines somehow being cut and radiotelephone links severed between the three elements, communications could be shuttled by the use of runners. The tunnel was only wide enough for one man at a time.

Though neither the British nor the Americans knew the extent of Ratmanov's subterranean defenses, Freeman, en route to Alaska, doubted that the Russians would have failed to make any garrison as bombproof as possible, so that even as the B-1 bomber with its short-range attack missiles taxied down Elmendorf runway, Freeman was addressing himself to the problem. "Dick—" From force of habit he looked behind him to speak to Colonel Dick Norton, who had served as his aide in Europe and whom he had requested for this operation, momentarily forgetting he was still en route from Europe. "Reach, isn't it?" he asked the young major who'd been appointed by the Pentagon as his interim aide.

"Ready and waiting, sir."

"I want Three Soc up here and deployed at Cape Prince of Wales, ready for disembarkation in twenty-four hours." Three Soc—Special Operations Capable—was the name for the twenty-two-hundred-man marine expeditionary unit, the smallest MAGTAF—Marine air-ground task force—unit out of Camp Smith, Hawaii, based on the Pacific Fleet's *Salt Lake City* carrier.

"Yes, sir," answered Reach, but even as he conveyed the order to one of the 727's console operators for encoding he wondered aloud to Freeman whether it wouldn't be better to collect the FMPac's Hawaii-based marine expeditionary brigade. It was a force of almost sixteen thousand: fifteen thousand marines and five hundred and fifty navy, medical, and support liaison staff, in turn supported by forty Marine A-V/8 Harrier fighter bomber jump jets, F-18s, forty-seven assorted amphibious vehicles, troop-carrying hovercraft, and a hundred helicopters.

"Hell—" said Freeman, watching their ETA for Elmendorf Air Force Base change on the computer screen due to strong polar winds. "We're not going ice skating." The general could see Reach still didn't get it.

"It won't be amphibious, Dick—ah, I mean Reach. Johnny, isn't it?"

"Yes, sir."

"Well, it won't be amphibious, John. I want airborne. And fast."

"Airborne!" said Reach. "A chopper assault?"

"What? Hell, no," responded Freeman. "Siberians'd pick 'em off those heavy assault Chinooks like flies with their SAMs. I mean HALO—high-altitude, low-opening chutes. Drop 'em right on that goddamn Rat Island before the Rats know what's hit 'em. Anyone drifts off target—they'll be all right. Wait on the ice until later. Marine choppers can pick 'em up after they've taken in the MEV to mop up.''

Major Reach was astonished by Freeman's plan, as was the British brigadier, now being apprised of Freeman's request for a seventy-man squadron of joint British/American troops from the SAS—Special Air Service—unit out of Hereford in Wales, the same unit in which David Brentwood, Lana Brentwood's younger brother, had so distinguished himself during the SAS's breaching of Moscow's innermost defenses.

"But General," protested Reach, "don't you think the hovercraft amphibians could launch an assault against the island? They have infrared, high-resolution optics—"

"No, I don't. Pressure ridges between the Alaskan mainland and Diomedes stretch the full twenty-five miles. That's no goddamned hockey rink out there, Reach. You ought to know that. It's pack ice—thirty feet thick and rougher'n Granny's tits. Up and down, movin' all about. Those hovercraft'd get a good run going on that air cushion, then bang! An ice ridge, big as a house. Besides, it'd be a turkey shoot for those Rat batteries. Might as well give 'em invitations to a ball. No, Major, I want the best parachute troops we've got.''

"Why don't we call Fort Campbell?'' suggested Reach. "Hundred and First Airborne. Get them and their 105 howitzers aboard those big C-141s. They could be up here within twenty-four hours. Or we could get the Eighty-Second Airborne's Ready Brigade out of Fort Bragg?''

Douglas Freeman looked sternly at Reach. The young major seemed amiable enough, but two things about him were bothering the general. The first was that Reach either didn't know or had forgotten that the Screaming Eagles of the 101st Airborne were now only air mobile, no longer a parachute-delivered force, despite the retention of their gung ho title. The second thing was that Reach didn't know the Eighty-Second Airborne were still in Europe, trying, along with the Brits and U.S. Ranger battalions, to penetrate the Ural Mountains on Siberia's west flank. In any event, the marine expeditionary unit wasn't to be a spearhead but would only go in after, *if* the SAS and any other special forces Freeman could dig up could first "unplug," in the general's words, "the Rat's maze" that was Big Diomede.

"Reach?"

"Sir?"

"You're fired! Don't know a goddamn thing about the ice, and you still think the Eighty-Second is in North Carolina. You also think the One-Oh-One uses chutes. Nothing personal, Major, but I can't afford to have you around. You don't do your homework. You get yourself back to G-2. Bury yourself in Siberiana, and if God's with you, you'll get a second chance with me. But not against Rat Island. Your ignorance is too damned dangerous, son."

In the silence between the Boeing's banks of electronic consoles all that could be heard was the Boeing itself, its four twenty-one-thousand-pound Pratt and Whitney engines in a steady roar as if endorsing the general's decision.

By the time the Royal Canadian Air Force F-18s from NORAD, released by headquarters in Cheyenne Mountain to escort the general's plane for the second half of his journey to Alaska, were high over the Rockies in Alberta, Major John Reach's unorthodox firing was known to everyone aboard the Boeing and among ground operators from Anchorage to Nome. Freeman hoped it would sweep right through Alaska Command, especially through the twenty-two hundred men of the MEU and to every pilot aboard the MEU's four Apache attack choppers and those who would be driving the sixteen CH-46 and CH-53 medium- and heavy-lift assault transport choppers, to every man and woman associated with Operation Arctic Front, that old Hardass Freeman was back. Besides, if he didn't take Rat Island, the Pentagon'd fire *him*. If he didn't take it, he'd fire himself.

Freeman called Fort Bragg to ask for two of the remaining one-hundred-man Delta Force companies, the best combination of demolition, radio, and hand-to-hand specialists who, with their blood brothers, the SAS, would go in first.

However, Delta Force command, even drafting instructors from its Shooting House—used for antiterrorist training at Bragg—could come up with only seventy men at most, only as many as the SAS would have, the remaining SAS and Delta

Force already in action trying to take out the Siberian prepo sites—giant ammunition and fuel dumps—believed hidden and well-camouflaged in the Urals. Most of these were American and British commandos from SAS and Delta Force who in '91 had been dropped behind the lines during the Iraqi war looking for the kind of upgraded Scuds that some Moslem fundamentalist groups were now threatening to use against the British and American southern command that was spread out between the Black and Caspian seas.

With SAS and Delta Force commandos combined Freeman would have only one hundred and fifty men at most to throw in on the HALO jump, but with what he had in mind—a quick, unexpected spearhead attack by the superbly trained British and American commandos—it might be enough. To bolster that confidence, he had personally requested that the survivors of the SAS raid into Moscow—especially young David Brentwood, who also had the experience of the Pyongyang raid behind him— be included in the attack.

Freeman also insisted Big Diomede be referred to as Rat Island because of the danger of mixing up Big Diomede and Little Diomede in the maze of radio transmits that would fill the air once the assault was underway, and that if the Siberians were stupid enough to risk sending troops across the ice to assault Little Diomede's Patriot antiballistic missile batteries, the batteries should be destroyed. The last thing Freeman said he wanted was casualties from "shorts" or AD—accidental discharge—that is, friendly fire. He knew better than most soldiers that up to 12 percent of all casualties would result from friendly fire anyway. After D-Day in July '44, the U.S. breakout from Rommel's beachhead defenses into the *bocage*—the open hedgerow country—had been seriously delayed because of "shorts." "Second Household Cavalry," he told his new interim aide, "suffered more casualties preparing for D-Day than they suffered in the first four months after D-Day. You believe that?"

"Ah—yes. I don't know, sir."

"It's true, all right," said Freeman.

"I'm sorry, sir. I didn't know," said the aide, still unnerved by Reach's dismissal.

"No reason you should, Captain," Freeman assured him.

"But just about every possibility in war has already been thought of. Trick is to think of it again." Freeman smiled. "You read your history, Captain. It's all in there." Freeman steadied himself against the buffeting of a wind shear that suddenly sucked the plane down in a gut-wrenching plunge. All the while his gaze remained fixed on the play-dough model of Ratmanov that he'd made up after ordering four loaves of bread from the gallery, squeezing the bread into the tooth shape of the island.

"Course," said Freeman, "there's always the surprise factor." Rule of thumb told him that for any assault on the island to stand a ghost of a chance he should have a five-to-one advantage, but then again that's just what the Siberians would expect from the Americans—a massive chopper-borne attack.

Everything came down to a matter of speed—the kind of speed the black-hooded SAS had used on May 6, 1980, "cleaning out" the Iranian Embassy, taking out all the terrorists, and rescuing the hostages in eleven minutes flat—with the kind of professionalism and hair-trigger expertise that young Brentwood and his SAS troop had penetrated the Kremlin's defenses. Suddenly Freeman was gripped by a bowel-chilling fear. He recalled the report of at least two navy flyers going down. They had ejected safely, but no ID flares appeared, though they would have shown up brilliantly against the snow if the flyers had had time to activate them. Which meant that the moment his SAS/Delta Force airborne troops landed, enemy troops might well be ready to swarm up and out like cockroaches, bringing the battle to the Allied force before any of the British or Americans had landed. "What we need against those rats," said Freeman, "is a big can of Raid! Get me Elmendorf—the air commander."

"Yes, sir."

As the young captain contacted Elmendorf he tried to figure out what the general was up to. You had to start figuring things out with Freeman; otherwise the hardass would come down on you like a ton of bricks. As he heard Freeman outlining his latest brain wave to Elmendorf, the captain couldn't help thinking there were a lot of guys who'd like to see Hardass on the end of the first chute.

After the call Freeman seemed more relaxed, even if preoccupied. His calm blue eyes now fixed on the dough model like a chess player, noting again how the island sloped steeply westward from the seventeen-hundred-foot-high eastern cliffs. You could go around the island—come in the back door—but the island was so small (five miles long and three miles at its widest) that it didn't matter where you landed a combined SAS/Delta team of a hundred and forty men, providing they didn't land too close to the cliff's edge. As the general stared at the cliffs of his makeshift model, he was no longer aboard the Boeing but back at Monte Casino, where the Nazi troops, reinforced by SS commandos, held off the attacking Allies for weeks. Weeks were something Freeman knew he couldn't afford. Every day lost was another day that the Siberians could use to reinforce their far eastern flank. It had to be a complete surprise after the air force had roughed up the Rat's nest with their cruise missiles.

Running his hand through a shock of graying hair, Freeman kept his gaze on the model, trying to think what the Siberian commander would do if the cruise missile attack didn't do the trick and if the Siberian anticipated an airborne invasion. Hopefully the missiles would knock out the island's main defenses from the sheer shock of the explosions. A piece of crust—part of the cliff's edge—was swelling as the cabin pressure altered during the Boeing's descent, then fell off.

"We should be so lucky, eh, General?" said the captain, handing him a coffee. "They say the SPETS are their upper crust, General."

"Yes," answered Freeman. He sounded morose. Suddenly feeling all eyes on him, as if every console operator on the Boeing had suddenly become unnerved by his tone, Freeman adopted an airy, friendly mood. "You know what the upper crust is, gentlemen?" he asked, immediately answering his own question. "Lot of crumbs stuck together with dough!"

A few laughs, some groans.

"You're right. It's awful. All right then—how about this? Guy comes home and his wife points to the light bulb and says, 'That bulb's been flickering on and off all day. It's not the bulb—it must be the wiring or something. Will you fix it?'

" 'Do I look like an electrician?' says the guy and flops down in front of the TV. 'Get an electrician.'

"Next day he comes home and she tells him the tap in the basement is dripping—driving her nuts. Will he fix it? 'Hey—do I look like a plumber?' he says and flops back down in front of the TV. Next night he comes home, the light's working fine—and no more dripping tap.

" 'You did it yourself!' he says.

" 'No,' she answers. 'That young guy down the lane out of work. He fixed them.'

" 'What'd he charge?'

" 'I asked him, and he said he didn't want any money. Either I could go to bed with him or bake him a cake.'

" 'Geez!' says the husband. 'Hope you baked him a cake!' and she says, 'Do I look like Betty Crocker?' "

Laughter was mixed with the whine of the undercarriage going down. Buckling up, Freeman turned to his interim aide. "You know what causes the largest percentage of pre-invasion casualties, son?"

"Airborne, sir?"

"If you like."

"Practice jumps, sir. Chutes that don't open," replied the captain. "Friendly fire."

"Vehicle accidents," said Freeman. "Most of our young Turks are under twenty-four, Captain. Drive like maniacs. Any man convicted on a speed or reckless-driving offense answers to me—personally—and his CO pays the fine: five hundred dollars. Got it?"

"Five *hundred* dollars, General?"

"First offense. A grand for the second."

"Yes, sir."

"How old are you, son?"

"Twenty-one, sir."

Freeman nodded.

"Now when we reach Cape Prince of Wales, Dick Norton, my aide from Europe, will take over your job in my HQ. I want you to understand there's nothing personal in this. It's just that we've got very little time to spring this thing, and Dick and I've worked before. Planned the SAS Moscow raid. Understand?"

"Yes, sir. No problem."

The young captain was enormously relieved. Rumor was that

when you worked for Freeman it was a steam bath: twenty-four hours a day, seven days a week, on call every second, and God help you if you screwed up. Only man that worked harder than Freeman's aide, they said, was Freeman himself.

"But—" continued Freeman, "to stress that I've full confidence in you, son, you're invited along for the jump." In a rush—like the feeling when he'd slithered down the bannister when he was a boy—cold-bowel fear struck the captain. Freeman was going to take the airborne in *himself*! Given his reputation in the Pyongyang raid and the fact that the general had led the Allies' armored breakout from the Dortmund-Bielefeld pocket, it shouldn't have been a surprise, but it was.

"Dick Norton," said Freeman happily, "is gonna have a pup! Goddamn, he hates flying. Course," said Freeman confidently, "I'll need him to stay behind to coordinate the MEU follow-up. He'll come in after in the choppers. But I'll kid him a bit. You watch his face, Captain. Go white as flour—sort of like yours." He slapped the captain heartily. "Just kidding, son. No one's going in who hasn't had HALO training. You come in with the choppers, too." The captain's legs felt weak.

As the wheels hit then grabbed the tarmac, Freeman saw the drops of condensation on his window, wind-driven into long tears. "Just hope to Christ that that Siberian son of a bitch isn't anticipating an airborne assault. Course it won't be necessary if that big bird from Elmendorf does its job."

CHAPTER SEVEN

IN ALASKA, HIGH above the Yankee River's winding ribbon of gray ice that cut through the predawn darkness of the Seward Peninsula's mountains, the four crewmen aboard the Rockwell

B-1B, its four thirty-thousand-pound GE-F 102 turbofans on afterburner, could see the two white dots of the Diomedes jutting up westward through the white ice pack as the bomber rose to "stand off" position.

In a direct line eighty miles from Big Diomede, the B-1's wings were now fully extended for greater stability as it fired off ten million dollars in the form of eight SRAM AGM-69Bs— short range attack missiles—each with a one hundred mile range. They streaked in eight white contrails from the bomber's "revolver chamber" rotary launcher. The B-1's EWO ignored the missiles the moment the launch was over, alert now only to the Eaton defensive avionics system; another crewman kept a close eye on the Singer-Kearfott inertial navigation system. The sound of the earsplitting explosions as the three-thousand-pound warheads hit Big Diomede's eastern cliffs was heard almost instantaneously in Inalik village on Little Diomede, followed seconds later by the shock wave. The latter started loose ice and rock falling; it crashed a quarter mile north of the village in a dirty spill of unearthed boulders and rubble that spilled onto the ice-fringed shore. The multiple cracks on the thick ice floes sounded to the villagers like the splitting noise of stiff sealskins drying in the bitterly cold wind.

Meanwhile the commander of Little Diomede's Patriots was primarily concerned about possible Soviet air strikes against his hydraulic-legged canisters, which for quick action against any incoming missiles bound for Alaska needed to be on the surface and ready to go. So far he could only conclude that the Soviet MiGs were not being used against Little Diomede because they were being saved to deter any possible American invasion force across the fifty-two-mile-wide strait, a force that Big Diomede's radar would give the Siberians ample warning of.

Most depressing of all to the Patriot commander this minute was the information that he reluctantly had to convey to the general in charge of Alaskan Air Command. Although the eight SRAMs had all hit Big Diomede, sending boulder-size ice and rock fragments flying over a thousand feet into the air before they rained down on the ice floes—a few hitting Little Diomede—there was no apparent "in depth" damage done to the Siberians' radar-guided ZSU-23s. For while the enemy cliff face, as seen through his infrared goggles, was badly scarred—the SRAMs' explosions had sheared off great sheets of ice that fell crashing down onto the frozen strait over sixteen hundred feet below—the impact of the SRAMs had done nothing to silence the deeply revetted missile batteries.

The enormous and foreboding cliffs of Big Diomede were impervious, it seemed, to any attack but that of an atomic bomb, a course of action that once initiated would set off a nuclear chain that would destroy both sides. For the young captain on Little Diomede in charge of the Patriot defense unit, Big Diomede had grown in menace over the preceding months. Its summit was often obscured by clouds so sharply, it was as if someone had drawn a line with a rule along its five-mile length. But this morning, as changing pressure ridges from the ice reflected the pale winter sun, and the previously downed American aircraft wreckage flickered harmlessly here and there at its base, the enemy island seemed more brooding and threatening than ever.

CHAPTER EIGHT

DAVID BRENTWOOD WAS tossing in his sleep, willing the snow to stop, but the white storm that kept up during the Moscow raid wouldn't abate. He could smell it—the cold, fresh tang of the blizzard, shot through with the reek of burning armor. And through it all the warm, metallic whiff of blood from those SAS who lay dead in the Cathedral of the Assumption, the latter's strangely beautiful gold baroque columns dimly visible in the creeping dawn light as the Russians closed the net in the counterattack about the blazing hulk of a T-80 which Choir Williams had stopped with a round from the "little genie," a light and disposable French Arpac anti-tank launcher/missile pack. David felt the heavy weight of the squad automatic weapon weighing him down, every muscle aching from the fatigue of the jump and the fierce fighting in and around the cathedral across from the Council of Ministers. He knew the spell in the counterattack couldn't last for long once the enemy grader tank that was rumbling up pushed aside the burning T-80 blocking the remainder of the Russian column. Down to the last three magazines for the SAW, David selected semiautomatic fire and waited, Choir Williams and a few remaining SAS troops having made good their escape covered by David, who had ordered them to do so. Now, with only Captain Cheek-Dawson, the leader of Troop C, whose job it had been to secure the perimeter against the Kremlin guards streaming out of the Armory, David readied for the Russians to attack again. Cheek-Dawson, having propped himself awkwardly against one of the cathedral's columns, his leg shattered to the bone, told David to leave him with the SAW and the last of the grenades so that he could do a "spot of bowling." The grader came, but a counterattack was halted because of Chernko's surrender at Minsk. But as Cheek-Dawson would have said, it had been a "near-run thing," as vivid and as immediate as . . .

"David! . . . David!" It was a soft, urgent voice. He could smell it, too—roses, yellow summer roses, but it was still snowing heavily, and he was perspiring, sitting up, mouth dry as parchment though he was lathered in sweat. Only then, as he became fully awake, the outside view not Moscow—the snow-capped church spire he could see devoid of the onion domes of the Kremlin's inner sanctuary—did he realize that he was looking at the small church at Laugharne. And the snow that was falling was disappearing—into Carmarthen Bay, the outflow of the River Taft. And in the distance there was the open sea, indistinct, the defeated rays of the sun rising over Llanrhidian Sands smothered by sudden bad weather that had swept all the way down from the Brecon Beacons in southeastern Wales, where the SAS trained—down over West Glamorgan county, to Swansea and the mouth of the Bristol Channel.

"Poor boy, you have been in a state!"

David was catching his breath, embarrassed that Georgina should have seen him experiencing the recurring nightmare.

"Following in my brother's footsteps," he had happily put it when he had written home, telling his folks of visiting the Spences in Surrey during Robert's last leave in England before Robert had been recalled from the U.S. sub base at Holy Loch in Scotland to command the USS *Reagan*. In Surrey he'd not only met his older brother's new wife, the former Rosemary Spence, but her younger sister, Georgina. The "smart" money in the family, meaning that of David's father, retired admiral John Brentwood, predicted from his eldest son's letters home that Georgina wasn't young David's type. His skepticism was fueled, though he didn't know the details, by the failure of his daughter's marriage to Jay La Roche.

"What type's that?" David's mother had asked her husband. "Robert says she's pretty, very well educated—London School of Economics and Political—"

"A lefty!" declared the admiral, who had definite views on everything from LSE graduates to the conviction that battleships were "totally obsolete," that if the navy had any sense it would build more fast guided-missile frigates like the *Blaine* in which his middle son, Ray, had served, instead of spending millions refurbishing old battle wagons, like the *Wisconsin* and *Missouri*, purely "for sentimental reasons."

"How can you say that?" asked his wife Catherine. "Build more boats like the *Blaine*. That boat nearly killed him."

"It was not a *boat*, Catherine—it's a *ship*. I regret what happened to Ray as much as anyone. It was—but all that medical 'stuff' is over, Catherine. He's a distinguished skipper of—"

"It was horrible," said Catherine. The "stuff" John Brentwood was referring to was the other side of a theory about fast, light, modern ships that, like the HMS *Sheffield*, were so badly gored in the Falklands. One hit and they burst into flames, the fire reaching temperatures unknown in earlier warships. With the aluminum superstructures white hot within minutes, many of the crew would die not from the intense heat of the conflagration but from the overwhelming toxic gases given off by everything from synthetic carpeting in the officers' mess to the resins and plastics used in the high-tech electronic consoles.

When the *Blaine* had been hit off Korea it sent the first of what the medical establishment euphemistically referred to as "unprecedented burn cases" to San Diego's Veterans' Burn Center. Many had died, and it took more than a dozen sessions under general anesthesia and the most intricate plastic surgery before Ray Brentwood's face had regained even the faintest resemblance to his former self. Admiral John Brentwood, more afraid, in fact, than Catherine of facing the horror, had tried his best to rise above it. It sounded noble, but in the long, dark nights he suspected it was not so much an act of bravery as of escape.

"Anyway," he told Catherine, "we were talking about this Georgina Spence. David's not the intellectual type."

"You mean he isn't smart."

"Of course he's smart, but she sounds a bit hoity-toity to me. Degree in political science and . . ."

"You may know a lot about boats, John, but you've a lot to learn about women. David's probably attracted to her *because* she's got brains. Lord, you don't want an airhead for a daughter-in-law, do you? Besides, you didn't mind Robert marrying her sister, and she's a school teacher."

"That's different," proclaimed the admiral. "More, well—now they've got the young one coming along. This Georgina, on the other hand, doesn't seem the marrying type."

"Then you've got nothing to worry about."

"It's this shacking-up business," retorted John Brentwood.

"Oh, so that's it. You think she might be 'preggers,' as the English say?"

"Well—aren't you concerned?"

"Fiddlesticks! I gave up worrying about that a long time ago. After Ray. I didn't think he'd live through that ordeal, and I vowed to God that if he did—if Beth, their children, that family came through together, I'd quit worrying about things that don't matter."

"Don't matter! You tell me pregnant doesn't matter??"

"Of course it does. But David's a grown man, John. You still think of him as a little boy."

"Yes," he said, and paused. "I do."

"John, your sons have been decorated by the president of the United States. And if young David has survived that maelstrom in Europe, don't you think he can take care of himself in bed?"

"Not the same."

"I should hope not. I'm glad he's not in combat."

"He might be if he marries too soon. By God, Catherine, I've seen domestic situations in the services. Make your hair stand on end. Like sailing into a typhoon. Husband's away at sea for months at a time . . . you can't expect—"

"Well, we've stayed together haven't we? Anyway, David isn't in the navy, and for another thing he's about to be demobilized."

The admiral, normally tight-lipped about such matters, decided that it was time to enlighten Catherine about something that normally wasn't discussed, even between husband and wife. "Catherine, David's in the army, yes, but he volunteered for SAS."

"I know that."

"But you only know that because those blabbermouths on TV have no regard for military security. If I'd had my way, I wouldn't have allowed anything to be printed about the raid on Moscow. For my money every damn blabbermouth on those networks would—"

"John, don't go on about what you'd do to Peter Arnett. Besides, I don't think it's anatomically possible with a cannon."

The admiral scowled, Catherine patting his arm. "What were you going to say about David?"

"He's on the SAS/Delta Force list. They're on twenty-four-hour call, Catherine—especially during crises like this."

"Like what?"

"Good God, Catherine. Siberia's decision to—"

"Oh, that. I'm sure they're bluffing."

"*Bluffing?* Woman, haven't you been watching the news?"

"You told me I shouldn't watch TV."

"I didn't say you shouldn't *watch* it. I said you shouldn't *believe* any of the goddamn—"

"Then why watch it? And don't swear. It makes you sound like a 'lefty.' "

While Admiral Brentwood was fuming, his youngest son was calm, made so by Georgina Spence's attentions; but there was nothing inactive about his serenity, the blood pumping through him with every caress. The old stone cottage turned motel was a favorite among SAS because it was no more than fifty miles from Brecon Beacons, the three-thousand-foot-high twin peaks east of Carmarthen Bay that marked the site of the most gruelling commando courses in the world. He'd chosen the cottage carefully for he could be back in Hereford, SAS HQ, in a matter of hours should the call ever come.

But here, in Laugharne, he and Georgina were away from it all, in the world of *Under Milk Wood*, not twenty minutes from the tiny, rough-and-ready room, with the copy of Van Gogh's "Bedroom" tacked on the worn white wall, where the drunken genius of Dylan Thomas had poured forth its heart. For Georgina, despite what her father had earlier referred to as her "somewhat radical" politics, or perhaps because of them, the room had quite unexpectedly become a shrine when her cool reason happened upon the banal yet arresting truth of the heart that the "heart hath reasons that reason cannot know."

Georgina snuggled close to him, holding him. The panic-filled disorientation of the nightmare drained from him as she gently nibbled a lobe of his ear, the nails of her trailing, sensuous touch stroking him until all thoughts of the Moscow raid were replaced by visions of her astride him, gently rocking back and forth, her hair softly whipping his chest, her lips against his. But for now Georgina hadn't moved from where she was. But he knew she would stop stroking him soon, taking off the engagement ring, and he would moan, "Oh, God, no." Which meant "Yes, but tease me a little longer." Then slowly she would rise from the bed, fending him off, and walk about the room wearing his khaki drill shirt, slipping on, pulling up her panties, slowly swaying like a tart in front of him and then, holding onto the two bedstead knobs at the end of the bed, gently pushing herself, thrusting, against the brass bars, moving sideways against them.

"No more!" he begged.

She pretended not to hear him; then suddenly she pulled the cord of the overhead light and all was in darkness. He would have to find her. When he did she switched the light on. "I love you," she said, and enjoyed watching him watch her. "We'll do it," she told him. "*Any way, every way*—until you're sore."

He moaned, his arms outstretched, feeling for her hair.

"Love you," he said. In answer her tongue slid down on him, her lips tight about him, sliding back and forth with a furious intensity.

CHAPTER NINE

DEEP IN RATMANOV'S control bunker, Lieutenant General Dracheev was stressing the importance of a quick response to his Special-Purpose Forces, or SPETS—emphasizing how the moment any enemy paratroopers were detected or even suspected of being dropped on the island fortress, the SPETS teams must go out and engage. *"Pomnite Antverpen"*—"Remember Antwerp," Dracheev reminded them. "Cut them to pieces before they even touched ground."

As General Douglas Freeman stepped out of his plane onto the rain-polished tarmac at Elmendorf, and a push of reporters, some in anoraks, their hoods up against the pelting rain, crowded about him, he was handed an urgent message from the White House. It read:

UNDER NO CONDITION ARE YOU TO PERSONALLY LEAD AIRBORNE ASSAULT. GENERAL J. GREY, JCS.

Freeman's first order upon arriving at Cape Prince of Wales was that the CBN reporter was to get off Little Diomede—"posthaste." Another CBN reporter who challenged him on this order had a follow-up question. "Is it true, General, that you've referred to the Siberians as rats?"

"Well, they sure as hell aren't family," retorted Freeman.

Some of the British reporters from ITN thought this was rather good, but the CBN reporter was determinedly grim-faced. "Is it true, General, that you said, 'We'll pound them so hard'—" He consulted his notes. "—'they'll have to pipe in sunlight'?"

"I did not—wish I had!"

The CBN lead story, flashed around the world, was that General Freeman called the Siberians "vermin." As this was being received by enemy troops as well as those at home, the CBN reporter, in what he said would probably be his last broadcast from Little Diomede because of the general's "extraordinary" order that no newsmen were to remain on the island, asked the general via the satellite linkup whether he was conscious of the "extremely delicate ecological system of the Arctic," and did he have any information on "what adverse effects would be produced on the environment because of the imminent bombing of Ratmanov Island?"

"Well, sir," answered Freeman looking at the video hookup of the CBN reporter on the forlorn western side of Little Diomede, the same bitter Arctic wind tearing at the gaggle of microphones thrust before Freeman's face and flapping the Eskimo-style hood of the CBN man. "Seems you're a lot less worried than I am about the environment."

"What do you mean, General?" asked the reporter, somewhat nonplussed by the unexpected retort. All the reporters at the conference were now looking at the linkup picture of the CBN reporter on Little Diomede.

"That blue fur collar on your hood," said Freeman. "Arctic fox, isn't it?"

The reporter's face was turning red. "I—don't know, General."

Freeman looked grim. "I respectfully suggest, sir, that you find out. Blue Arctic fox is on the endangered species list. One of the most beautiful animals on God's earth. Crying shame to be butchering them just to keep us warm. You should know—" The general turned to all of the reporters clustered about him, some of them wearing identical parkas. "—that it is strict Defense Department policy not to use animal fur in deference to our concern for the environment. Synthetics only—and that goes for everything from gloves to full winter uniform."

* * *

"That true?" asked Colonel Dick Norton, the general's aide.

"Yes it is, Dick. My God, did you see that Greenpeace fella? Thought he'd have a goddamn stroke right on the spot. That'll break up their marriage with the media for a while I'll tell you." Stopping, pulling on his gloves tightly, he told the general of Alaska Air Command, "I want that CBN joker off Little Diomede. Now!"

"And if he doesn't go?" enquired a brassy CBN news crew chief out of Anchorage.

Freeman ignored the newsman's question. He had learned his lesson in Iraq. To give them a deadline by which they had to remove the reporter from the island might be to let slip an approximate ETA for the new wave of U.S. bombers he was asking Alaska Air Command to send over Ratmanov. Instead, Freeman told the news chief that Little Diomede would undoubtedly be suspected by the Russians of being a laser indicator—bouncing lasers off suspected Soviet SAM and radar sites to provide slide cones down which laser-guided bombs could plummet to their targets with pinpoint accuracy. In fact, no such plan was afoot. The laser designators would be the attacking aircraft themselves.

Freeman entered his mobile trailer, which was dug deep in the Alaskan tundra on Cape Prince of Wales, and gave his second order for Alaska Air Command to undertake another bombing run against Ratmanov. If it was effective, it would give the enemy commander a surprise Freeman doubted he could anticipate.

Kneeling beside his cot, Freeman prayed that he would be proven wrong—that Rat Island might be neutralized quickly and effectively. As he made his supplication he could hear the sonic booms racing across the tundra only fifty miles away from the enormity that was Siberia.

It was only a few pinpricks of light on the amber screen at first, and the Siberian operator on the eight-to-midnight watch deep in Ratmanov control dismissed it as possibly a burst of white noise caused by the notoriously changeable Arctic atmosphere. But the next second the top third of the screen was a haze of tiny lights, and he knew what it was. He called the officer of the watch. *"Khlam"*—"Chaff," he told the lieutenant—strips of foil cut to various wavelengths to clutter the radar, overloading it with incoming signals, as a cover for another air attack. The only good thing about the chaff was that it meant the Americans couldn't use laser slides—the chaff would cut the beam.

"Outboard personnel stand up!" It was the sergeant aboard the C-130 transport high above the chaff, finishing his air safety check. "Hookup! Check static line!"

"Aw, shit!" responded the air force corporal, not seeing any humor in the sergeant sticking to normal jump procedure and wanting to get the hell out of Rat air space before "white tails"— Siberian surface-to-air missiles—began streaming up through the darkness. "Push 'em out, Sarge. Let's get the fuck outta here!"

Outside in the black void the stars were so bright the corporal felt he could reach out and grab them, but below the thundering roar of the airplane the blackness was absolute; the dark camouflage mushrooms of the T-10 static line were quickly disappearing into the swirling clouds of Arctic air—so cold that even with full thermal issue the corporal's throat felt a hot burn of the freezing Arctic air. The fifteen-foot yellow static lines fluttered now like ribbons above the swirling, chaff-riven night.

In Ratmanov's complexes one and two, north and south, the guttural Klaxons sounded, like submarines diving, as smudge-faced SPETS zipped up white overlays, snatched weapons from the rack, and raced for the spiral exit shafts that wound one hundred feet through the rock up to the wind-swept surface of the barren, snow-roofed island, ready to engage the enemy before they even touched ground. Five minutes later two Stealth F-117As swept in low at 690 miles an hour on a south/north run. Even at this subsonic speed they were over the five-mile-long island in twenty-seven seconds. Most of the chaff had now dissipated, and Siberian radar picked up one of the Stealths via ultra-low frequency radar and fired an SA-10 but missed.

Even though the SPETS were already out and had closed the triple-armor manhole covers of the exits, the infrared video taken by the Stealths in their twenty-seven-second overflight revealed the exits, the latter's HE, or heat emission, spots distinct against the snow—showing up on the video film like white, overexposed blurs on a negative. The moment he was awakened and given the information—ten exits, five north, five south of the island's midpoint—Freeman ordered them CMR'd—computer map referenced. It was done in less than five minutes. While his staff was exultant with the way he had dropped weighted chutes, duping the Ratmanov commander into sending out his troops and so revealing the exit/entrance positions, Freeman was too busy to celebrate.

"Alright, Jim," he told his air commander. "Tell your boys we're going to give 'em the can of Raid—make up for what those cruise missiles of yours failed to do. Get them to drop three laser-guided babies on each of those exits. Two-thousand pounders. Mightn't do the trick, but it's better'n dropping dumb proximity iron bombs."

The whooping continued in the revetted mobile home that was Freeman's Prince of Wales HQ. "You suckered 'em, General!"

Freeman told everyone to quiet down. It was true he had tricked the Siberians—a bunch of hotshot SPETS now running across the snow shooting at dummies or whatever the air force could put on the end of a chute to simulate an airborne attack on the Russian radar. But if the laser-guided bombs didn't blow up the exits, penetrate and spit some fire down the seams between the exit plates and rock, then he'd have to go in with the airborne after all. "Just pray those bombs do the job, gentlemen," Freeman told them. Someone who'd lost a buddy in one of the F-11s mumbled that so far God hadn't been listening.

CHAPTER TEN

ACROSS THE DARK blue of Dutch Harbor on Unalaska Island, the first big island near Alaska in the Aleutian Chain, Lana La Roche, née Brentwood, and Elizabeth Ryan, a black nurse from Boston, could see the bobbing lights of the fishing boats that normally plied the seas north of the Aleutian arc south of the ice pack. The harbor this evening was fairly glistening with the dipping lights of the small but powerful deep-sea trawlers that had run for cover in the harbor before a clump of Arctic fronts that were en route from the Pole with 150-kilometer-per-hour winds in the offing.

"I thought," said Lana easily, "there was supposed to be a blackout in progress?"

"You know what those fishermen are like, honey," said Elizabeth, who had done her nurse's training with Lana on the East Coast at a joint U.S./Canadian navy hospital in Halifax and from which Lana had been officially "transferred"—in effect exiled for having given a young, dying British seaman a woman's caring touch aboard an Allied hospital ship.

The head nurse at the hospital and on board the ship, Matron "Scud," so-called because it was said that you never knew where she and her broomstick would land, had been outraged by Lana's unprofessional conduct. So had Lana—for about five seconds. Then she realized she had only been guilty of being a woman who had given a dying man sexual release, something that, because of his youth and his very proper middle-class British upbringing, he'd hitherto not experienced. Besides, it wasn't as if they'd actually been in the bed together. But it made no difference to Matron, and so Lana had been sent to "America's Siberia''—the Aleutians. Yet, despite the fact that she didn't like her posting in Dutch Harbor, that she always felt cold, she never regretted doing what she had done for the young Englishman. Look at what had ensued from it. His personal effects had been returned to his parents in England by Lana's eldest brother, Robert, a submariner, when he had taken leave from Holy Loch in Scotland. Robert had met Rosemary Spence, the boy's eldest sister, and ended up marrying her.

"Till it hits them like a williwaw they'll keep the lights blazing," said Elizabeth. A williwaw was the hundred-mile-an-hour wind that, along with fog and rain and sunshine, which could all occur within half an hour, made the climate of the Bering Sea one of the most unpredictable and harshest on earth. It was one of the reasons Lana was so deeply touched by Elizabeth having voluntarily transferred to Dutch Harbor to be with her.

"I hope they're right," responded Lana, "that it doesn't get this far south. The fighting, I mean."

"You heard from your sweetie pie?" asked Elizabeth as they headed for the bridge that led over to the clutter of buildings and what little night life there was in the harbor.

"No," sighed Lana, her hands folded, sending a piece of ice skittering across the road as they made for the dirty shoulder of salt and snow to allow an army truck to pass. They were heading for "Stormy's" restaurant, their big adventure for the week, to try some Greek chicken—one of the house specialties. Such outings from the naval base were rare now that the hospital, like so many other bases from Fort Ord to Faslane in Scotland, were reopening after only recently being closed down because of the Russian surrender at Minsk. The hospital staff found themselves short-handed. Everyone was working extra shifts, preparing for what they all hoped would never happen: massive casualties coming in from the battles on and across the Bering Sea.

She hadn't heard from Frank for a month or so but knew it wouldn't be long before he was mainland bound, to the naval air base at Elmendorf with two war tours in the Pacific behind him, during one of which he had shot down the MiG-29 Fulcrum state-of-the-art fighter flown by Soviet ace Sergei Marchenko as they'd mixed it up over the Yalu River in Korea. Though Shirer's radio intercept officer in the Tomcat hadn't seen a chute, and they'd both seen a pinhead-sized blossom that must have been the Fulcrum crashing into the frozen wastes of Manchuria, there had grown in Shirer's mind a nagging doubt about whether the Russian had gone down with his plane. Meanwhile the twenty-seven-year-old Shirer had been celebrated, except in the La Roche papers, for having shattered the myth of the Marchenko invincibility among Allied pilots.

"Where's he going to?" asked Elizabeth.

"Elmendorf," said Lana. "He might already be there."

"Uh-huh," murmured Elizabeth. Scuttlebutt was rife around any base in any war. They'd all been told that, and how rumors were sometimes spread by the enemy just to eat away at morale. So no way Elizabeth was going to tell Lana that there was a rumor floating around that *Salt Lake City* was in the thick of it, launching air strikes against some Russian island up in the strait, that some planes had been shot down. Anyway, maybe Lana was right, and her man was safe and sound at Elmendorf.

"You know something, Elizabeth?" Lana asked, stopping.

Elizabeth kept walking, glancing back. "Honey, you'll freeze your ass off you don't keep on truckin'!"

"*Elizabeth.* What've you heard?"

Elizabeth stopped and turned around. "All right. I heard that no-good husband of yours—*Mister* La Roche—has been living pretty high off the hog. I mean girls, lots of 'em. Papers are full of it, they say."

Lana shrugged. "It wouldn't be in the papers if he didn't want it known. He likes to show off. Big shot. Big kid. They don't print the rest of it." Elizabeth was starting off again, Lana catching up, their thick-tread winter boots cracking the brittle ice, their breaths clouds of steam above their anoraks, the ice-crystalline air so clear, the moon looked like a huge communion wafer.

"You want to talk about it, honey?" said Elizabeth, ever the willing ear to her friends.

"No," said Lana. "You wouldn't believe it."

"Honey. Nuthin'—I mean *nuthin'*—fazes 'Lizabeth Ryan. I've seen them all."

No, you haven't, thought Lana, but she said nothing, trying not to think of Jay La Roche, trying to ignore the fact he wouldn't give her a divorce. He loved power and wouldn't let go of anything. It wasn't enough that he owned the huge chemical/arms La Roche multinationals, from New York to Shanghai to Paris. He had to control everyone and everything in his world. Lack of control spelled not only humiliation for Jay La Roche but the secret fear of madness. Yet the great irony, she knew, was that he was already mad—clinically certifiable—but his power was a moat around his castle keep that normal society could not cross. His tabloids would smear anyone who tried. His lawyers would do the rest.

"Hey," said Elizabeth, "isn't it your birthday next month?"

"You know my blood type, too?" said Lana, smiling, trying harder now to forget Jay La Roche, how one night—the last terrible night, in Shanghai, before she'd left or, more accurately, escaped—in one of his drinking bouts, he'd poured whiskey on it and pushed it into her mouth, telling her if she didn't suck it "dry . . . I'll bash your fucking head in!" And if she threatened to take him to court, he'd use his tabloids, not on her but to smear "shit all over your lovey-dovey Ma and Pa—the big fucking admiral and Mrs. Fucking Admiral!" And then later, in the gray of the China dawn, he'd come in to her like a whipped spaniel, stale, boozy breath, telling her he was sorry, that he loved her. And the most awful part of it was her knowing he meant it—that he couldn't control his other self, the one beneath the public persona, beneath the lean, suave, rich-industrialist smile, the one that turned every act of love into a depraved ritual, obsessive and obscene.

"He's a survivor," said Elizabeth, and for a moment Lana thought she meant Jay.

"He's probably got his feet up in Elmendorf," said Elizabeth heartily, "chewing the fat with some other hotshot pilot. Probably writing you a letter this minute. Oh Lordy, will you look at that now!" It was a Marine sergeant, stepping out of a Humvee, the driver making a U-turn so the vehicle was facing back toward the town as the sergeant driver approached the two nurses.

"My," said Elizabeth huskily. "I'd sure like to mother him."

"*Elizabeth!*" said Lana as the sergeant kept walking toward them.

"Yes, ma'am," Elizabeth continued, unabashed. "He could

'spect my plumbin' any day. Mind you, he'd have to say, 'Please, ma'am—pretty please.' ''

"Hussy!" said Lana.

"That's me—Boston Boobs. You lookin' for me, Sergeant?"

"Ah—ah yes, ma'am. You Lieutenant Brentwood?"

"I am," said Lana.

"Ma'am," said the sergeant, snapping a salute. "They said you were heading over to Stormy's."

"Yes."

There was an awkward silence, and all Lana could hear was the spitting of the Humvee's exhaust, its long, bluish white curl trailing up behind the truck then suddenly disappearing in the pristine night air.

"Ma'am . . ." The sergeant saluted again and gave her the brown-widow envelope. It was stiff with cold. She couldn't open it with her mittens, and Elizabeth did it for her but didn't read it. Despite her almost legendary self-control Lana was crying, the tears freezing her cheeks.

"Can we give you a lift, ma'am?"

Lana looked at Elizabeth. She needed help. Elizabeth told the sergeant to forget Stormy's, to return them to the base. Then halfway back she thought perhaps they should have gone to Stormy's after all. Do something. Anything. She didn't know. They returned to the base.

"Thank you, Sergeant," said Elizabeth, noting the man's name patch: Dukowski. Ah.

Inside the Quonset hut, Lana was collecting herself, surprised at how poorly she'd handled it. "Good grief," she sobbed to Elizabeth, "I deal with this every week on the wards. I mean I used to—"

Elizabeth handed her a mug of coffee that Lana held between her knees for warmth. She began rocking gently back and forth like an old woman, and it bothered Elizabeth more than when Lana had first read the fax. "Hell, honey," Elizabeth tried to assure her, "never the same till it hits you."

"No," said Lana. "No, it isn't."

"Now you listen to me, Lana. That dumb old fax says 'MIA.' That doesn't mean . . . Well, if he's MIA, he could be on the ice pack up there. Better'n in the drink." Elizabeth looked up at the curved ceiling of the Quonset hut. No matter that it wasn't a ward—everything smelled of antiseptic. "Man, I never thought I'd be thanking God it was winter."

"I—don't understand," said Lana.

"Well, summertime they'd be in the water. Freezin' water. They stand a better chance out there on the ice."

"They?" Lana was confused.

"Two guys in a Tomcat, Lana."

"Oh."

"I know all about Tomcats, honey," said Elizabeth smiling. "I *like* 'em!"

Lana tried to be cheerful in kind but everything about her, the darkness about the Quonset hut, the smells of the hospital, of fresh coffee brewing, oppressed her—the very air suddenly too heavy and the forlorn howl of the Arctic wind soul-crushing. Other nurses—nurses who had lost loved ones—said it was the not knowing that was the worst, not knowing for sure whether they were alive or dead, but Lana felt no such yearning for a definite answer. So long as they weren't certain definite knowns there was hope that Frank had been rescued—or, as Elizabeth had said, was on the ice waiting to be rescued.

What frightened her most was that now, when she wanted desperately to remember every detail of her and Frank's intimacy, of his strength and gentleness when they made love, she couldn't see him clearly in her mind's eye. It had happened before, at moments when it seemed that she had wanted him too much. Jay La Roche's face, on the other hand, was so clear, his jealousy and hate so palpable, it was as if he were a presence in the room, with his contemptuous smile of victory, his eyes coke-sniffing bright and alive.

CHAPTER ELEVEN

NOT ONE OF the two thousand men in the two ANGES—Alaska National Guard Eskimo Scouts—believed that the four-foot-diameter, eight-hundred-mile-long pipeline that snaked its way from Prudhoe Bay on Alaska's North Slope through the majestic Brooks Mountains, over the Yukon River and down to Valdez on Alaska's south coast, could be adequately protected. Neither did Joe Mell.

Joe wasn't in the Eskimo Scouts, and Mell wasn't his real name, but white men could never get Athabascan names right, so he called himself "Mell." "Fucking Eskimo," was what one of the whites had called him. Joe never forgot it, along with all the other insults. "All right," he said, taking another suck of Southern Comfort, looking down morosely at his snowshoes—he'd made them the traditional way, from birch, and used caribou rawhide for the lacing—so the pink noses thought he was a dumb Eskimo. All they saw was a native with no teeth left and a rubbery smile.

He took another drag at the Southern Comfort. What did they know? Pink nose big shots from the oil companies down south, coming up with their prefabricated houses to give to all the natives. "No problem, pops!" they'd said. "You just stick 'em together." Yeah—well the pink noses didn't think he knew about Bethel town, far to the southwest, where the Kuskokwim River flows into the Bering Sea. The big shots had guys put all the prefabricated huts up in the summer, but come the winter they all started to crack and buckle. Joe took another belt of the Southern Comfort, swallowed, and grinned. Sod houses were still the best—had a soul. They knew the Arctic winds and ice.

Sod houses didn't fight the weather like the white man. Sod houses let their earth give a little here and there, and the wind understood. No crazy stiff doors either—only sealskin storm entrances that started way back from the house in the earth and angled up to keep out the snow. All white men weren't bad, though. Or stupid. One, from the other side of the ice bridge— the other big country—had paid him in the Cold War. A lot of money and booze, with a promise of much more if the Hot War broke out. Joe was to break the long silver snake. It wasn't a big pipe. All you had to do was wait for the next blizzard so there'd be no tracks found after and wrap a belt of hide about the four-foot-diameter pipe with the white package attached to the belt. You pushed the white button and you had five minutes—plenty of time to get away, even in deep snow, the man said. Then the rest of the money—U.S. dollars—would come. And whose country was it anyway? When some pink noses bought Alaska, the rest of the pink noses booed them, said it wasn't worth anything. So how come the pink noses had come up in the thousands? It sure didn't belong to the native people anymore. The pink noses from across the strait weren't much better. They stopped the Eskimo people from walking across the ice to meet their cousins and took everybody off the big island because some big pink nose secret had been going on there. One of the pink noses from across the strait said one of their sailors, called "Bering," discovered Alaska. Joe had known it was there all the time. Another thing he knew: the pipeline didn't belong here. It was like a scar on the land, as if a beautiful *chukchee* woman had taken her *ulu*—blubber knife—and slashed it across her face. It was a desecration. But if you put the strap on the silver snake, would the fire despoil the land?

"No," the Russian pink nose had told him. "Not at all. The fire will only burn the oil." Then Joe knew the white men sucking the oil from the North Slope would have to stop. Those who had insulted his Athabascan forebears with filthy talk about Eskimos wouldn't try to scar the land again—they'd know what could happen.

Joe heard the wounded cry of the land in the Arctic storm and knew it would not end until he had placated its soul, healed its hurt. Unhurriedly he put on his *kamleika*, the gut raincoat that once belonged to his father, and taking the hide strap and its package he crawled out through the sealskin storm trap and called the dogs, now like white lumps of sugar in the swirling snow. From his sod house through the village to the stretch of pipeline that bent in a long, gentle curve in the frozen valley of the Dietrich River on to the southern side of the mighty Brooks Range—the pink noses even gave *their* names to the sacred places—would take only half an hour. The silver snake would now be caked in an icy sheet, running alongside the wide gravel trail from Fairbanks in the center of Alaska to Prudhoe Bay on the Beaufort Sea. The pink noses called it the Dalton Highway. He took another swig from the bottle. Worst of all, some of his people had been traitors, had gone into the pink nose courts and palavered for money to allow the silver snake to despoil the land.

Joe looked intently at the dogs. Only the lead husky had turned and paid him any mind. They were tired and he was tired and he took another suck at the bottle then murmured to the dogs in the dialect of his parents, who had come from Galena far to the west. But the dogs didn't know his parents' dialect, as he only used it when he was drunk. Throwing the empty bottle away, he reverted to the dialect again, shouting into the wind, the words meaning "To hell with it. I'll use the Ski-Doo!"

Unsteadily he pulled the starter cord at least a dozen times and fell over once before the Ski-Doo gave forth its crackling roar. It backfired several times before settling into its high-pitched whine. He told himself the Greenpeace noses would be as happy as he was, because they were the only pink noses who understood about desecrating mother nature. The Ski-Doo plowed into heavy drift, but Joe gave the throttle sleeve more twist, and the steering skis went straight through it. Dogs were scattering in the village as he whooped at them—an old man shouting at Joe, telling him that he must show more respect for the dogs. But Joe was already through the hamlet, snow-curtained birch slipping by him on either side of the trail he knew like the back of his hand. The irony of the whole situation was that Joe Mell was considered by the Siberian Military Intelligence "canvasser" as one of the least reliable of the half-dozen natives they had suborned and the least likely to succeed in the mission.

On Ratmanov Island more than two hundred SPETS commandos streaming out of the exits fired at the descending shapes as they became visible only a few meters from the ground. Had they been paratroopers coming down it would have been a massacre; the SPETS' marksmanship with the AK-74s was highly accurate. They hit everything that had been used to weigh the chutes down. It took the white-uniformed SPETS, all but invisible against the snow, only two or three minutes to realize they'd been *obmanuty*—"had"—and, fearing an air attack, they quickly retreated to the exit/entrances like ants being vacuumed back into their deep hive, leaving the dozens of American chutes buffeted by wind and rain mixed with snow in the swirling blizzard now blanketing the island.

"Make sure the engineers have double-checked the exit/entrance seals," ordered Dracheev.

"They're already doing it, Comrade General."

"Good! The Americans are obviously going to use their Smart bombs. They have deceived us into betraying our exit points. The chaff must have covered the approach of a reconnaissance aircraft."

"Their Smart bombs cannot take out the Saddam entrances," said his aide, but his voice betrayed more hope than conviction. The general asked his radar chief if there were any signs of another American air attack on its way. There were none. His aides crowded around him, the smell of sweat mixing with the oily odor of the tunnel complexes' gun emplacements on rails behind sealed doors at the cliff face. General Dracheev was biting his bottom lip as he bent over the table's map trace, computer consoles giving immediate zoom blowups on the screen whenever he touched any part of the island map. He was worried. The whole point of having made Ratmanov self-contained, self-sufficient, was so that it could survive without Novosibirsk having to risk vitally needed aircraft over the narrow strait. But now the American Freeman would know where the exits were, and he was bound to send in air strikes, though the heavy snowfall would work in Dracheev's favor, effectively cutting the

American flyers' laser beams. Even so, the only exits Dracheev could now use with any reliability were the two emergency exits—R1, a quarter mile from complex one, at the midpoint of the northern half of the island, and R2, above complex two on the southern end of the island, the same distance from Dracheev's control bunker. Two exits for up to two thousand SPETS.

It had the makings of a disaster. Dracheev knew that if he failed to hold the Americans until Novosibirsk HQ had time to reinforce the Siberian coastal defenses, it would be best if he stayed on the island rather than make a run for it aboard his chopper to the mainland, for he would almost certainly be shot for his failure. But then he had what he called his *osenivshaya ideya*—"brain wave"—born of the fear of what would happen if he didn't hold the island—and from the deep anger he had experienced at being duped by the American Freeman's fake paratroopers, a humiliation made worse for Dracheev by the fact that in addition to his regular troops manning the island's underground AA network, he was answerable for the effective use of the SPETS, Siberia's elite force.

"We don't have much time," he quickly told his aides in Ratmanov control. "We'll use two emergency exits. Exit one for complex one, exit two for complex two."

"Eto originalno"—"That's original," murmured one of the SPETS, but Dracheev did not demand an apology. He had made a serious mistake sending out the SPETS before he had visual confirmation that they were really Allied paratroopers descending and not dummies, and the SPETS had every right to expect him to correct it. "I'm confident," he told them, "that the Smart bombs, while they may take out one or two of the exits the Americans have discovered, will not—"

"Samolyoty vraga priblizhayutsya!"—"Hostile aircraft approaching! Rising from Seward Peninsula."

"All second-level plates are to be sealed!" Dracheev ordered. He meant each exit's number two hatch, slotted in at the sixty-foot level in every one-hundred-foot spiral stair exit, had to be sealed like the hatches of a diving submarine, just in case any of the Smart bombs' high-explosive charges were, despite the lack of laser beam accuracy, lucky enough to blow out the top Saddam seal.

Within minutes the bombs started to fall. The lights in Control flickered momentarily as circuits were broken and auxiliary generators kicked in. General Dracheev, his legs shaking involuntarily from the Smart weapons' bombardment, turned anxiously and angrily to his aide. "The American flyer we captured. Do you think he knows what Freeman's strategy is?"

"He hasn't talked yet, General. He's a tough customer. We've tried to . . ."

"Then try again!" snapped Dracheev. The aide nodded to one of the two SPETS nearby. "Anyone can be made to talk!"

"With pleasure," said the SPETS who, on his way down the corridor, announced matter-of-factly to his colleague, "The general's right. Everyone has their breaking point."

"Even you?" asked the other SPETS challengingly.

"Yes. Of course. I couldn't withstand what I'm about to do to that American bastard. You'll see."

Electronic monitors were telling General Dracheev that four of the manhole covers had been breached and that the other six should not have their secondary hatches opened, even after the air raid had ended, for fear of red-hot debris raining down the shaft.

"Then that's decided it," General Dracheev told his SPETS commando leader. "We only use the two emergency exits. Your men'll have to move swiftly to get out in time—"

"To do what?" asked the SPETS commander. Red lights were blinking all over at the control center's console, indicating that rock flour, thick in the air from the bombs, had choked off some of the air filters, overheating them.

Soon the red lights faded, the backup filters holding, and the duty officer informed him that all electronic indications were that the six exits he had decided not to use might be usable after all. Dracheev, however, would not be deterred from his plan. He never doubted for a second that an Allied airborne assault would now follow, but to use the six exits would be suicidal. They were almost certainly pinpointed by the Americans and would be among the first targets should another bombardment precede the Allied troop drop. Only this time, Dracheev told them, they'd outwit the Americans. To this end he called a hasty radio conference of the ten company commanders of the two

SPETS battalions. He told the commanders, "The Allies'll realize they cannot bomb us out, that no matter how many bombs they drop, ultimately they will have to use troops. In this, gentlemen, we have the overwhelming advantage, for when they try to dig us out they can't be dropping bombs on their own men." He turned to the SPETS commander, his tone crisp with confidence.

The SPETS commander, a full colonel, soon understood the reason for the general's rush of confidence. Dracheev was good on his feet—a commander who didn't need hours to ponder a problem and used the American general's initiative as a spur to his own. The SPETS commander heartily endorsed the plan; it was brilliant and would cut the Americans to pieces. The colonel also knew that a citation from General Dracheev for the Ratmanov victory would slash his waiting time for an apartment in half. He told his battalion's political officer, the *Zampolit*, that he almost felt sorry for the enemy.

Dracheev's assumption was that the American general would attack soon after the bombing had shot its wad—and attack quickly. The American would know that every hour he failed to breach Ratmanov's defenses was that much more time for the Far Eastern TVD to build up Siberia's eastern flank. Some of the *chukchee* members of the SPETS—men chosen for their special knowledge of the area—didn't like General Dracheev, as he was a Yakut from central Siberia. But even so they, like the SPETS commander, had to admit—grudgingly—that he was making it easier for them. It would be nothing more than a seal hunt: all you'd have to do after is go out and club them. American cigarettes, gold teeth, watches. Burial would be the hardest job of course; the American dead would be frozen solid. No good covering them up with the snow; come spring the stench would keep even walrus away. Best thing, the Yakuts believed, would be to burn them, but General Dracheev probably wouldn't allow that, fuel consumption being one of his priorities. So in the end the corpses would be left to the blue foxes and the murres. The birds'd clean them to the bone come spring. And there were the golden eagles from Alaska. A feast. For the SPETS the idea of American eagles eating American dead was appealing and spawned many a joke as they waited for Freeman to take the bait.

Freeman, standing in his blast-protected mobile-home HQ, was dwarfed by the wall map of the Bering Sea. He donned his reading glasses and contemplated the Diomedes halfway across the funnel, showing up on the aerial recon photos as white fists thrusting up through the ice. "I'm glad you're here, Dick," he said, turning to welcome Colonel Richard Norton, a solidly built, amiable, at times intensely serious, five-foot-eight logistics officer and New Yorker who'd been with Freeman in Europe. But there was no time to talk over old times. Freeman told the colonel that the Siberian commander wouldn't be caught "with his pants down" twice. "Other problem, Dick, is half these jokers don't know a damn thing about Arctic warfare. Like those poor bastards Washington sent up to the Aleutians in forty-two in *summer uniform*. No wonder the Japs were all over them. I told the quartermaster this evening to make everything ready for an airborne attack on Ratmanov, jump time an hour before civil twilight. Hell, he thought I was talking about some dame called 'Sybil.' Then he thought it was the *end* of the day. So I told him, first light—"

"Eleven oh six hours," said Norton, taking his cap off, running his fingers through hair as gray as Freeman's. "Sunset around seventeen forty-one?"

"Correct. Now, Dick, I go in with the airborne at civil and exactly one hour later—earlier if we radio or fire red flares—*you* come in with the marine choppers." Freeman put the glasses back on, tearing off an incoming meteorological report on the fax. Looking down over his reading glasses at Norton he said, "Didn't think you'd be too keen on a HALO."

Dick Norton had a flashback to the time he'd been ordered by Freeman to fly in the back seat of an F-16B from Krefeld to Brest to hurry up air resupply from the French port for the beleaguered Fifth and Seventh American Corps and the British Army of the Rhine in the Dortmund-Bielefeld pocket. To this day Norton could actually feel nauseated just thinking about the terrifying night flight in the supersonic fighter. Hurtling through space and you couldn't see a damn thing and it wasn't nearly as smooth as it appeared from the ground. Everything shook. "I'm not too keen on any kind of jump, General," Norton replied. "You clear this with Washington?"

"The mission? Of course."

"No, sir," said Norton, looking at the map's order of battle clustered around Galena Field from where the marines would take off. "I mean *you* leading the drop personally?"

"Dick," said Freeman, turning to the map, tapping the map, using his glasses as a pointer, "main problem is going to be the palletized drops—we're going to need hundred and five millimeters. Now Rat Island's big enough, but our guys are going to be spread all over it, jamming C-4 plastique in every goddamn crack we find. We'll have to smoke 'em out, same way we did with the Japs on Iwo Jima. Same situation here—they're dug in deep. And Siberians haven't surrendered a fight in—"

"Except for the weather," interjected Norton.

"What?"

"Same as Iwo Jima—except for the weather."

"Minor detail," said Freeman, grinning.

"You know, General, it's minus twenty degrees over that ice pack."

"How do you know that?" asked Freeman, not disputing Norton's assertion but intrigued as to how he knew the specific temperature on the pack. "I can read upside-down type, General. Remember?" Norton indicated the fax Freeman was holding. "Anchorage says the satellite cloud cover indicates twenty-mile-an-hour winds. That drops the temperature to minus forty-six."

"Chilly," said Freeman. Before Norton could object further, Freeman slapped his arm on Norton's shoulder. "Dick. You see? By God, you're the right man for the job. No one else in this godforsaken peninsula knows that—windchill factor." Except every Eskimo, thought Norton. "*Details*, Dick. You and I know that's what wins wars."

"And strategy, General."

"That's my department, Dick," said Freeman, turning to the map, slipping his reading glasses back on. "And God's." There wasn't a trace of insincerity. His right hand swept across the Bering Strait. "*Speed*, Dick! That's what we need. Now we know where all those rat holes are. I'm personally going to see every one of those blown up—then you know what I'm going to do? I'm going to drop high explosives down those rat holes. It'll be surrender or die for them, Dick. White flag or beef jerky!''

"If there are SPETS on that island, General—and Intelligence suspects there are—there'll be no surrender."

"I know, Dick," said Freeman, pausing solemnly. "I know. We won't butcher them. I'm not a butcher. My SAS-Delta team'll give them fair warning." For several moments there was silence, broken only by the howling of the Arctic wind outside. " 'Bout two seconds. I've thought it through, Dick. I've tried to think of every damn detail, but I know it's still a gamble." He turned to look straight at Norton. "Ultimately all great victories are. Time's against us, but I say, 'Go!' "

Norton nodded, which meant that though he saw the general's logic and the military necessity as clearly as he'd seen the giant bergs on the way over from Europe—glinting like glass castles beneath the Arctic moon—he couldn't share in Freeman's enthusiasm. Never had. Freeman was a warrior to the bone: brave and unapologetic in his quest for glory. All Dick Norton hoped for was that he would be alive after the war, when he would be quite happy to retire, mind and body intact. He had fought in the snows of Minsk by Freeman's side and did not doubt the general's determination, and SAS and Delta were the best—trained to jump from high altitudes and make pinpoint landings. Even so he wondered how many would end up on the ice flow, and how they might be the lucky ones. The normal ratio, one that Freeman well knew, dictated that an attacking force must outnumber the dug-in defenders by at least five to one. But denied the luxury of waiting, the need for speed disposed Freeman to go in now with what he had—the 140-man SAS/Delta Force team. The Pentagon boys were saying Ratmanov Island was more than an ancient wrecker of ships—it was a career disaster waiting to happen.

In the predawn darkness of a blizzard, two long lines of SAS/Delta troopers, seventy in each line, made their way along the tarmac at Galena air base on Alaska's Seward Peninsula toward the gaping hold of the C-141 Starlifter.

"Bloody lovely!" said Aussie, one of the seventy-man SAS squad. The column to his left was made up of men from the American Delta Force.

"What are you whining about now?" asked "Choir" Williams, a fellow veteran with Aussie and David Brentwood, the leader of the SAS force, most of whose troop of twenty men had been wiped out in the Moscow raid.

"Last week you were getting right tired of Wales," said Choir Williams. "So the president and the prime minister say, 'What can we do now to placate Aussie?' and 'ere we are!"

"Very bloody funny," said Aussie. "*Wales* in Alaska. Should've known better. All set to go 'ome. Back to Sydney—up to King's Cross. Give those sheilas a bit of the old in-out. And where are we? Freezin' our bum off in another bloody Wales. I'm cursed with bloody Wales."

"Ah," replied Choir Williams, his deep Welsh baritone barely audible now as the noise of the C-141's pitch climbed. "You volunteered, laddie."

"Musta been bloody drunk!" said Aussie.

"Anyway," advised Williams who, like Aussie and the rest of the men lining up for the C-141, had qualified in the most gruelling Allied commando courses in the world, "you don't want to go back to Sydney. All those girls. You wouldn't know what to do with them."

"Yes, he would," called out another Welshman. "Aussie'll screw anything that moves, 'e will."

"You oughta know, Jones," responded Aussie.

"Yeah?" asked Muldoon. "What's Jonesy like, Aussie?"

"Very nice," said Aussie. "But too tight."

"Watch it!" barked the SAS sergeant major. "Officer on parade. The man himself."

A few turned to see Freeman, helmet down against the roar of the C-141 engines, and young David Brentwood, at five eight looking decidedly smaller than the general with whom he'd served on the Pyongyang raid.

One of the men in the Delta Force line noted that Freeman and Brentwood looked like father and son together, but it was an illusion created by the close attention Brentwood was giving his superior as they went over last-minute details. The other illusion was that Freeman was going to jump with them. He was certainly dressed for it, in full jump suit and helmet, wrist altimeter, and oxygen mask. But if Freeman, through ordering the decoding of a scrambled message from the president requesting him not to jump, had been successful in sidestepping Mayne's directive, he had failed to avoid an outright order from Army Chief of Staff Grey who, like Schwarzkopf's superiors in the Iran war, viewed Freeman as being infinitely more valuable directing strategy on the ground rather than risking his neck in combat. But Grey's instruction notwithstanding, Freeman was determined to at least go up with the SAS/D force and stoke morale before the jump. Going over the additional infrared shots from satellite pictures taken before the onset of the blizzard, Freeman and David Brentwood had ringed each of the "rat holes" that Freeman had suckered Dracheev's SPETS into revealing.

"Starting to snow again," said Freeman. "Goddamn it! Well, we can't wait, Brentwood. Another hour damn things'll be all covered in fresh snow. Be one big white blanket over that island. Cover up the bomb scabs. Anyway, the moment we take off, *Salt Lake City*'s going to hit the holes with a final F-14 strike. Lasers'll be chopped up by the snow, but they should get bombs near enough the exits to re-mark 'em for us." Freeman looked at his watch. "Tomcats should be halfway over the ice pack now. Remember: SAS out first, top half of Rat Island. Delta'll take the southern half. Now our PVS-Fives—" The general meant the night vision goggles powered by a twelve-hour, three-volt lithium battery. "—are much better than anything the Siberians have, but they'll be able to pick us up in civil twilight even if the snow keeps falling—"

"I know, sir," acknowledged Brentwood, not meaning to butt in, but his adrenaline was up for the jump. "I've told everyone in SAS/Delta. Diamond glow recognition." It was the foot-long Velcro diamond pattern that, like the inverted V of the Allied forces in the Iraq war, would distinguish friend from foe.

"Good!" said Freeman. "Then we're all set."

By now most of the troops in the two long columns, the first men in being the last men out during the jump, were inside the cavernous interior of the Starlifter. Last man in was Brentwood.

Freeman was already walking up the center of the deck, nodding cheerily as the 140 men took their seats facing one another and began to buckle up. The plane's engines reached fever pitch as it began its lumbering run down the tarmac. It was to take off and head eastward, away from the strait, to give the big C-141 time to gain sufficient height before it turned for the high-altitude, low-opening drop. The higher altitude would give the jumpers more time to steer themselves to the assembly points on the island, the PED—palletized equipment drops—scheduled to take place ten to twenty minutes after drop zone perimeters had been secured.

"You ready?" asked Freeman on the bullhorn.

There was a roar that for a second could be heard above that of the plane.

"Dumb question. Right?" hollered Freeman.

"Right!"

Freeman was walking down the center of the deck, holding onto the webbing net. "No need to tell you," he told the paratroopers over the bullhorn, "how important this is. Those F-14s from *Salt Lake City*'ll keep the bastards' heads down. Then we go in and whip their ass. I can assure you, gentlemen, that will send Novosibirsk a very clear message: 'Back off! Before you all lose your ass!' "

There was a chorus of approval and the stamping of para boots, which annoyed the air force jumpmaster intensely. The stomping was creating a minor dust storm inside the Starlifter.

"Well, Brentwood, we'll have snow to contend with but least we won't have the press. They aren't gonna Vietnam me, Captain. All those goddamn liberal lap dogs in the press running around saying they didn't lose us Vietnam—that the army did. Goddamn it, no one seems to realize we could have ended that war in half an hour. Two A-bombs on Hanoi would have done it. But we didn't. We get any marks for that restraint? Not on your life. You know what would have happened, though, if those squealing bastards had been taken prisoner by the Commies. They would have wanted the U.S. Air Force to turn that place into a parking lot. Well, they're not going to be allowed to do a Baghdad Pete on us. I've told the CO of that Patriot battery on Little Diomede to send that CBN son-of-a-bitch reporter and his Arctic fox headgear packing back to the mainland. They can all get pissed in Anchorage while we're setting these Commie bastards straight.''

''Yes, sir,'' said David Brentwood, remembering how a reporter once asked him, a thrice-decorated soldier, how he got used to it. You never did. The first moments of a battle were always as bowel chilling as the first time. Yes, you learned certain things, sensed when a firefight was more concentrated and more dangerous in one instance than in another, when there was twice as much noise as accuracy; you learned to husband your strength, ration it and not blow it all in the first few minutes; but you never got used to it.

''Vse gotovy?''—''All done?'' asked General Dracheev.
''Da!''

''Kharasho!''—''Good! A little surprise for the Americans, eh?''

''Sir?'' It was the air defense duty officer. ''Bandits. Looks like F-14s. Coming fast from the south. No more than a thousand feet. Trying for the exits one more time.''

''Neuzheli?''—''Oh really?'' commented Dracheev, with ill-conceived sarcasm. ''I thought they'd be bringing the mail.'' This got a good laugh from the SPETS commander. So even with the snow making it difficult for the F-14s to use their Smart bombs with their normal accuracy, the Americans would chop up the snow a little—maybe even buckle a few of the superhardened steel plates around the exits.

''They're not stupid,'' said the air defense officer, trying to regain his bruised dignity. ''I mean this Freeman. He will realize that some of the exits have probably not been used. That the pilots won't see them.''

''So?'' said Dracheev. ''He'll send his men looking for them.'' With that the Siberian general looked up from the dull red light of Ratmanov Control—a hundred feet of solid rock above him. ''All the better then.''

The air defense officer was even more offended, resentment growing by the second. Dracheev had obviously confided his plan only to the SPETS. Although this was normal procedure— SPETS always insisted their operations be kept as secret as possible—it still rubbed the wrong way. "Who in hell do they think they are?" the air defense officer asked his subaltern.

"The elite."

In his sod house in Little Diomede's Inalik village, the hunter, the high cheekbones of his Eskimo forebears catching the light of the golden hurricane lamp, civil twilight, before daybreak, still an hour away, puffed heavily on his walrus-bone pipe. "It's a lot of trouble."

"It's a lot of money," countered the CBN reporter.

The hunter took another pull of salmon jerky. The silence was broken only by the unsettling groaning of the pack ice off frozen Lopp Lagoon, north of Cape Prince of Wales. They could see the navigation light right on the point—the westernmost point of the cape, the wind coming straight off the flat ice of the lagoon in a soulful wail.

"Well?" said the reporter impatiently, holding his hands over the Sanyo kerosene radiator, its heat waves rising like a mirage in the hunter's sod hut. "I haven't got all day."

"Cash?" said the hunter.

"Hey, you think I carry that kind of money round with me?"

"Yes," said the hunter.

A professional smile creased the reporter's face. "How'd you know?"

"I can smell it."

"Shit you can."

"Yes, I smell shit. But I smell money, too. Up here you don't smell right, you die. What you see is important, too. When the—"

"Hey," interjected the reporter impatiently. "Time's racing, Jack. Have we got a deal or not? Five grand now. Five when we get back."

The hunter was thinking. It had been a bad year. The walrus had come south in a heavy fog and gone past the islands before they knew it, so they hadn't got the usual number to cut up and store with the murre birds—for flavor—in the frozen earth.

"You won't be able to show any light," said the hunter. "Those guys in the Patriot bunkers—they could pick you up on infrared." He thought for a moment. "Course there'll still be a lot of heat coming up from the rest of the huts after they evacuate us. So you'd be all right in here for a while anyways."

"They wouldn't be able to see me moving about in this snow-fall," said the reporter. "Cuts down the infrared signature."

"Maybe," said the hunter, caught out.

"There's another way," said the reporter.

"No," said the hunter.

"What? You don't even know the fucking question."

"Yes I do. You want to know if we could hike across to Big Diomede."

"It's only two and a half, three miles," said the reporter.

"We could get killed."

"Everybody gets killed. You ever do it?" asked the reporter, fixing the hunter with a challenging stare.

"Sure. Used to do it a lot after Gorbachev—for a while."

"So?"

"It's not a walk on an ice rink," said the hunter. "Pressure ridges push up against one another." He used his hands, push-ing hard against one another, to demonstrate. "Ice as big as buildings."

"Yeah, and it can be flat, too."

"And how about the infrared?"

"I told you—not if we go when it's snowing, Jack."

"It's not a hike, you know. You can get—"

"You scared. That it?"

"Yes."

"So am I," said the reporter, pulling out a wad of hundreds. "I'd bury this stuff here if I were you." He started counting. "How long will it take us—not right up on the island but off the ice floe—close enough in so we can hunker down—close enough to get some zoom shots of the airborne going in off the southern tip?"

"Four to five hours."

"That long? It's only two and a half miles, for Christ's sakes."

The hunter smiled. Here was an ignorant man. What did he think it was, a walk in some park? "Hey," he said to the re-porter, "you the guy who was in Baghdad?"

"Nope. But I'm gonna be just as famous, Jack."

"How you gonna send your stuff?"

"This little baby," said the reporter, patting a four-wire, direct satellite-link phone. "Even if I can't get a video because of the friggin' snow, I'll be in by voice. Live. Let's go!"

The hunter agreed because he doubted that the white man could hack it, even with all the special thermal gear. Out there on the ice—with the wind it would be in the minus fifties.

"If the ice gets too jumbled—we get a sheer cliff—we'll have to turn back. I get half—five grand!"

"All right," said the reporter. "All right. Let's get there before it's fucking over."

"How do you know there'll be an airborne attack?" asked the hunter, pulling on his sealskin boots.

"Hey, Jack, look at the map. Doesn't take a friggin' genius to work that out.'Sides, Freeman's the gung-ho type. Know what I mean?"

"Impatient."

"Yeah. That's right."

"Like you."

As the C-141 turned north then westward, having gained HALO height, the men made final weapon checks. The 12.8-inch-long Heckler and Koch MP5K submachine guns were coveted by the SAS. With its nine-hundred-round-per-minute, nine-millimeter Parabellum bullets, the gun was referred to by the troopers as a "room broom"—ideally suited for the anticipated tunnel fighting. The weapon was also capable of a high, eighty-yard line-of-sight accuracy if used in the open. For the men of Delta Force, the weapon of choice was the M3A1 Colt .45 caliber submachine gun, some of its mass-produced parts honed down or replaced by hand-tooled mechanisms for greater accuracy. As a general rule, Freeman told Brentwood, he didn't like the idea of two different ammunition sizes, preferring one that could be used by both SAS or Delta Force weapons.

"That's why the Brits lost Crete," Freeman told him above the steady thunder of the C-141. "Freyberg had troops from five different countries running around with everything from point three oh three to nine millimeter. Quartermaster's nightmare. A lot of troops—Aussies and New Zealanders—ran out of ammo. Hand-to-hand fighting, a lot of it. Could see the Nazis floating down. Sky was black with enemy chutes. Clear blue sky. Damn! What a waste of fine paratroopers. Even with the ammo screwup it was a near thing. A turkey shoot—lot of Germans dead before they hit the ground. Germans almost lost it—until Maleme was taken. Convinced the German HQ never to put their money on an airborne offensive.''

"Christ!" said Aussie, picking up the general's comment and turning to Choir Williams. "What the fuck are we doing here, then?"

"Ah!" said Choir with more bravado than he actually felt. "Not to worry, laddie. Rat Island's not Crete is it? Siberians are hiding—dug in.''

"Oh, that's bloody nice. Thanks for reminding me. I'd almost forgotten." And then, before the Aussie's fear could, like most of the men, force him to bear the rest of the flight in silence, he was seized by the habit that had made him famous throughout the SAS—and after the Moscow raid, throughout the entire British army. "Odds on," he announced loudly, "that SAS'll be first in!"

"In where?" came a voice shouting above the ear-drumming noise.

"In the fucking tunnels, you twit!"

"Ahead of *us*?" challenged a Delta Force sergeant from Brooklyn. "Gimme a break. We'll have coffee on 'fore you even find your hole."

"Aussie knows where his hole is," shouted an SAS.

"Don't be so fucking rude," said Aussie. "Welsh bastards! Come on, you lot!" He was looking across at Delta Force. "Where's your fuckin' esprit de corps? How about it, boys? As you Yanks say, 'Pay up or shut up.' Two to one we're down first."

"On the drop?" asked Brooklyn.

"No. In the fucking tunnels!"

"You're on, Aussie." Aussie whipped a stubbly indelible pencil from under his helmet and began taking the bets on a palm-sized notebook. "Right, mate. That's the ticket."

"Pounds?" asked Choir Williams.

"Pounds, dollars—U.S., not Canadian—yen, deutsche marks, but—" And now Aussie, watched by Freeman, adopted a Mexican drawl, showing his teeth. "—I don' wan' no stinking rubles!" There was a patter of laughter, quickly lost in the plane's huge interior, the jumpmaster landing his boot with a thud on the decking to get everyone's attention as he stood up and announced, "Get ready!" Automatically every paratrooper, despite his heavy pack, slid forward, seemingly effortlessly, to the edge of the folded metal seats, some making last-minute adjustments to their chin straps.

"Who is that joker?" Freeman asked Brentwood, nodding toward Aussie.

"Australian called Lewis," Brentwood answered. "He'd make book on the sun not rising. Took a lot of bets before the Moscow raid. Before the target was known we were doing practice jumps over Scotland. Aussie was convinced we were rehearsing for Korea, not Europe."

"Must have lost a bundle," said Freeman.

"No."

"How come?" asked Freeman, realizing the moment he'd asked the question what the answer was. After the Moscow raid there'd been hardly anyone left to collect.

Across from Brentwood the Delta Force commander was looking down his line. Though the SAS stick would be first out, he was making sure that every sixth man, assigned the 5.56mm M-249 squad automatic weapon, was strapping it tightly to the equipment pack. The SAWs would be fed by the new transparent plastic magazines of two hundred rounds so the shooter could see at a glance how much ammunition remained. In addition, several of the Delta Force men carried M-203 dual purpose rifle/grenade launchers with FETS—flare, explosives, tear gas, and smoke grenade packs.

Normally the jumpers would have been wearing the tried and trusted T-10 general-purpose drop chute, but the big twenty-eight-foot-diameter umbrella chutes couldn't be maneuvered as well as the arching, rectangular MC1-1B chutes. The latter could be steered by pulling down the left-right riser bars above the jumper's head, causing more air to spill on one side than the other, allowing the jumper to shoot forward at over four meters a second. In all the MC1-1Bs would make it aerodynamically a much more controllable drop, of the kind made by sports jumpers. The latter, however, as SAS/D instructors frequently pointed out, were unencumbered by 70- to 120-pound battle packs.

The red light was on. "Stand up!" yelled the jumpmaster.

"Stand up!" came the shouted response followed by a sound like a herd of elephants rising with planking strapped to their flanks. Normally, with the 120-pound pack, it would have been a lot louder but even with the QAP—quick attack pack—of 70 pounds, mostly ammunition, emergency rations, radio and grenades, it was still an effort for the 140 paratroopers.

"Hook up!"

There was sudden, tension-splitting laughter punctuated with a few catcalls. The huge rear ramp went down, and had it not been for the dimly lit interior, the jumpmaster's face would have appeared as bright as a Day-Glo buoy. So used to the massed jumps of the 101st Airborne and the static line used during most drops, he had forgotten for a split second that it was a HALO jump—free fall. Each paratrooper would dive head first, falling at 130 feet per second until, no more than two and a half minutes from jump-off, each man would pull a rip cord at two and half thousand feet above the island, steering the double-ply nylon air foil canopy to the snow-covered target.

The green light was on.

"Go!"

The shock of the cold hit Brentwood's face with the force of a body blow, and for a split second it was déjà vu, going down over Moscow, only this time the scream of the wind was louder, the cold already penetrating the double thermal suit, the oxygen mask fogging the infrared goggles momentarily. His arms were hard against his sides, his feet up behind him, forcing his head down to counter the tendency to spin. The air screamed like a banshee around the bulbous headgear. It was a third larger than the usual helmet in order to accommodate the starlight goggles, creating more resistance than usual. Now he was pulling his left arm and leg in unison, in tighter to his center line, the maneuver giving him left drift.

Far below him he spotted a flash of light through the goggles, light which he took to be the last of the Tomcat's bombs, and used it as an aiming point. Several seconds later he felt the shock wave of the explosion hitting him. A fierce crackling invaded the echo chamber of his helmet as radio silence was broken by the C-141, General Freeman shouting, "Mission aborted . . . mission aborted . . . field . . ." The rest was a surge of static. What the hell? Brentwood knew that by now most of the SAS stick would be out of the plane, possibly even one or two of the Delta force. He looked at the altimeter, couldn't make it out for a second, then saw he was less than a minute away from two and a half thousand feet. Then he glimpsed a bluish white dot, two of them, flitting by a thousand feet below him like tiny fireflies, and guessed, correctly, that it was one of the twin-engined Tomcats, probably on afterburner. It was split-second timing by the navy but cutting it a bit fine all the same.

Then the unfinished part of the message he'd received from the C-141 made sense, hitting him with the force of a high explosive shock wave as he saw orange pinpoints of light, like flashlights switching quickly on and off beneath the dim blanket of snow, racing up at him from the northern part of the island. The "field" in the radio transmit must be "minefield," set off by the Tomcat's bombs. The C-141 had broken radio silence to tell Brentwood and the other SAS already speeding down toward the island that Ratmanov had been seeded with mines. The whole island was a minefield. More splotches of light, white swellings on the infrared's green background, confirmed it. Worse—by now the snow would have covered any footprints, giving no clue to the pattern of mines laid—if there was any—nor indicating the positions of the rat holes. The Siberians had had at least an hour to—

There was another surge of static in his helmet from the C-141. But now all he could pick up was ". . . abort . . . abort . . ." and all he could see was the snow field becoming wider and wider as he neared touchdown. Had the mines been scattered willy-nilly, or were they, in SPETS fashion, laid so as to funnel attackers into deadly triangulated COF—"cones of fire"? But no matter how the mines had been laid, David knew the Allied paratroopers—mostly, if not all, SAS—would find themselves unable to move, forced to fight and die where they landed.

For a split second David thought of increasing the leftward drift and heading out over the cliffs for the relative safety of the ice floe. He'd save himself, but he'd be no use to anyone else.

The altimeter showed he was at three thousand feet, two thousand nine hundred . . . In three and a half seconds he'd be at twenty-five hundred. Pull the cord or drift eastward, away from the island?

He pulled the rip cord, heard the snap, felt the sudden deceleration, and tugged hard on the right toggle, feeling that side of the chute curl and brake as he went into a tight, controlled spiral, the sky around him alive now with lazy arcs of red and white tracer, the air exploding with the rattle and bang of AA fire, the screams as men died in the harness and the pop of flares adding to the cacophony of sound. Suddenly all was bright. A moment of civil twilight; then the flare dropped away from him. He could hear bursts of machine-gun fire like paper tearing. Quickly he paid out the fifteen-foot-long tether line attached to his equipment bundle, evening the pull on both toggles, his heart threatening to burst out of his chest. Below he could see long, black shadows piercing a white, flare-lit circle of snow.

CHAPTER TWELVE

THE FAX TRAFFIC, preferred by many MVD offices over the regular military channels, was informing Novosibirsk HQ that at this very moment, at 10:03 A.M. Thursday morning—that is, 11:03 A.M. Wednesday on little Diomede, only two and a half miles across the date/boundary line between the U.S. and USSR—with a half hour to go before the Bering Strait passed out of utter darkness into civil twilight, an Allied airborne attack was underway against Ratmanov Island.

Another fax, classified as *tayna*—"secret"—but momentarily considered less important to Novosibirsk HQ than the American general's attack on Ratmanov, came through with the

information that the submarine that had attacked the two super-
tankers off America's northwest coast had reported that one of
the torpedoes it had fired had not exploded, a common-enough
complaint from the Far Eastern TVD HQ at Khabarovsk. Normally this would merely have been entered as a *nerazorvav-
shiysya snaryad*—"dud"—but it was seen by an alert
intelligence officer at Novosibirsk who realized that it was opening up an old sore for Khabarovsk TVD HQ—the suspected
sabotage of munitions by Jews living in one of the YAOs, or
Jewish autonomous regions—in this case a lamb chop–shaped
Jewish enclave, 120 miles at its widest, around Birobidzhan. A
hundred and fifteen miles west of Khabarovsk, the Jewish region
was near the Manchurian border.

In Khabarovsk, KGB chief Colonel Nefski had just returned
from the Bear Restaurant having downed an enormous plate of
pig's feet, fresh bread, and wine served by an elderly waiter
whose atrocious French lent an air of sophistication whenever
Nefski and other senior officers patronized the restaurant. But if
Nefski could be fooled by pretensions of French cuisine, there
wasn't much anyone could tell him about the best way to deal
with suspected saboteurs. Gorbachev, of course, had *vsyo is-
portil*—"ballsed everything up"—so that even after he had gone
and things started to return to something like normal around
Khabarovsk there were still idiosyncratic pockets of bureau-
cracy so that, for example, before he could have "absolute"
authority to deal with the Jews it was necessary to get Novosibirsk's approval. No one would have questioned him had he
gone ahead with his own plan, but Nefski knew how pieces of
paper not obtained could be used later against one by unscrupulous political opponents. Gorbachev and that other fool, Yeltsin—God rot them—had actually encouraged the Jews for a time
to believe they had the same rights as any other Soviet citizen.

As Nefski waited impatiently by the window of his third-floor
office for confirmation that his fax had gotten through to Novosibirsk, he took another Sobraine from his cigarette tin and
lit it, pouring the acrid, bluish-gray smoke against the frosted
windows through which he could faintly see the red-and-yellow
tram cars making their way in the blizzard along Khabarovsk's

wide avenues. One's position, he ruminated to his subaltern, was all a matter of distance from the capital. First, Moscow. Now, Novosibirsk. Like the Americans who lived in Alaska and the American Northwest who were never understood by Washington's bureaucrats, Nefski had ample evidence that Novosibirsk never understood the tyranny of distance, never fully appreciated the enormous implications of the fact that the lifeline of the Trans-Siberian Railway passed barely fifty miles from the Chinese border out here.

Should the Americans, now that they held Korea, decide to cross the Yalu River that separated China's Manchurian provinces from Korea then wheel westward onto the Great Northern Plain of China, the Jews would seize their chance and cut the rail line, thus effectively cutting off Khabarovsk and Vladivostok farther south on the coast. Disaster would follow. Khabarovsk and Vladivostok were the linchpins of the entire Siberian offensive against the Americans on the eastern flank.

This was true not only for the entire Far Eastern TVD in the war against the Americans but for any air war against Japan, should the Japanese, less than two hundred miles east of the coast, decide to attack as a military down payment on the oil they would have to get from the American North Slope if their industry was not to grind to a halt.

Personally, Nefski confided to his subaltern, a KGB lieutenant, he doubted the Americans would risk incurring the wrath of the Chinese by striking through North Korea, but with Korea in their possession, it was a temptation: a left hook from Najin in North Korea northeastward, less than two hundred miles around the coast on the Sea of Japan to attack Vladivostok. The military consequences of Vladivostok being cut off were too horrendous to contemplate, but it was precisely that that Nefski had to think about. Losing the ice-free port would mean the entire Soviet Pacific fleet would be cast adrift—with no home base, no supplies.

And if this wasn't enough to fire Nefski's determination to root out the Jewish saboteurs whom he believed were responsible for the local attacks on the Trans-Siberian Railway link, then his humiliation during the short-lived Minsk Treaty was. He and other KGB officers had been "required" to make public apologies to the Jews for certain "irregularities" during the war. Indeed, Nefski and his aide had been imprisoned for forty-eight hours by the Jewish underground, destined to face charges in what the Jews called "open court." Open court! Well, everything had changed very suddenly with Novosibirsk's rejection of Chernko's cowardly Minsk Treaty. The following day the Jews had fought sporadic actions along the rail line 160 kilometers between Khavarovsk and Birobidzhan, cutting it in several places; but with Siberia's decision to continue throwing its vast resources and armies against the Allies, and military reinforcements being rushed out from western Siberia, the Jews were on the run again—the hunted, not the hunter.

"Kings for a day, eh?" Nefski remarked to his subaltern, without taking his eyes off the tram cars that had fascinated him ever since he was a child and afforded him the warm, secure feeling of someone safe looking out at a hostile world. Then Nefski, with a full stomach to stoke his confidence, explained to his subaltern that even if Ratmanov fell, which he doubted, an attack by aircraft from American carrier-based fleets that might steam toward the Sea of Japan from the Americans' Aleutian bases was highly unlikely. First there would be the blizzard facing them as well as the *zhelezny zanaves*—"iron curtain"— of antiaircraft missiles and gunfire that would be thrown up at them by the formidable defense network of the Kuril Island screen, four hundred miles off the coast. And even if they got past the Kuril Islands, the Americans would then be met by swarms of Soviet fighters rising to meet them north of Japan from bases dotted along the six-hundred-mile-long shield of Sakhalin Island just off the Soviet coast. And this quite apart from the *koltsa*—"rings"—of AA missile and gun emplacements around Vladivostok and inland around Khabarovsk itself.

Nefski glanced at his watch, frowned, and pushed the button for "cells." "What are they doing down there?" he asked sharply, the sour stench of his *kumiss*, the fermented mare's milk so beloved by the Yakuts, filling the overheated, stuffy KGB office. His subaltern tried to hold his breath as Nefski spoke, surmising that the colonel's breath was so foul that if they could pipe it down the narrow, winding, stone staircase to the cells four stories below, the Jews would agree instantly to tell Nefski whatever he wanted to know about who was who in the Jewish resistance.

"They had some trouble with the woman," the subaltern explained, pulling a file. "After we brought her and those three brothers of hers in." He was reminding Nefski of the time they had pretended to shoot the youngest to get her to talk. "She apparently went bonkers when we picked her up again after Novosibirsk rejected the Minsk treaty." He laughed. "They all thought they were about to be liberated when Chernko signed at Minsk. 'Next year in Jerusalem.' "

"If she's crazy," said Nefski, "she's no use to us. This time we won't be generous—to her or her gangster brothers. No more blanks to frighten them. This time we'll use—"

"No, sir," interjected the subaltern, "I don't mean crazy mad, sir. I mean violent."

"Then for God's sake give her an injection."

"That's what they're doing, sir," answered the subaltern, trying to hide his anxiety. He prayed nothing had gone wrong downstairs. If he helped Nefski break the Jews, it would mean a promotion from lieutenant to captain.

Nefski lit another Sobraine off the first, the lieutenant grateful for the infusion of the thick tobacco smoke to counter the foul smell of sour cheese. Nefski had completely misunderstood his subaltern's anxiety about the woman, mistakenly interpreting it as concern. "If you're going to be an old woman about this, Ilya, I don't want you here. These vermin pose as great a threat to our supply line as did the Czechs."

Nefski was referring to the bizarre incident of the Czech legion in World War I who, ironically, on their way home and fed up with delays, had held most of the Trans-Siberian Railway during the bloody civil war between the Reds and the Whites. Canadian and U.S. forces in Murmansk were trying even then to hamper the Revolution.

The lieutenant didn't comment, the analogy between a few score of *zhidy*—"yids"—and the Czech legion being a monstrous exaggeration. Still, he knew Nefski had a point. Despite the fact that they would not know what part of the line was under infrared surveillance hidden in the birch taiga or monitored by the vibration meters of the kind perfected by the Americans in

Vietnam to detect even foot traffic along the Ho Chi Minh Trail, a rail line could be uprooted by a child with a fistful of plastique and the guts to try. Anyway, with or without the dangers posed by the Jews, the subaltern was certainly not an old woman. Didn't feel squeamish at all. In fact, and this he did not mention or even hint at to Nefski, the prospect of torturing the Jewess, Alexsandra Malof, a pretty, dark-eyed, and well-endowed nineteen-year-old, excited him. Compared with the usual run of ugly, stodgy peasants they had to deal with it would be a pleasant change. Sometimes Nefski let his men do an ''Iraqi''—which meant the most diligent and loyal interrogators were given an hour or so alone with the woman in the cell.

The thought of the Jewess naked, tied to the bare birch bunk, breasts rising quickly up and down with her fear, thrilled him long before he heard them dragging her up the narrow staircase. He had an erection and so busied himself by the records cabinet, going over her file so that his back was turned to Nefski who, if he saw the subaltern's condition, would make a great joke of it. Turning his head slightly to look out at the top of the stairwell, he glimpsed her and saw that after only several days of solitary she'd lost weight. But starvation initially gave some prisoners a more determined, alive look, separating them, as Comrade Nefski often said, into the ''quick and the dead,'' and made the ones who wanted to live more exciting. Yet their stubbornness was in the end a death sentence. When you took them back to cells after the initial interrogation and held out food as a reward, there was almost nothing they wouldn't do.

As they hauled her through the door, he turned, holding the file low in front of him. He heard a high, buzzing sound and saw the fax light come on. Nefski was standing by the window, gazing out—his usual ''disinterested'' ploy—and so the lieutenant tore off the fax as the two guards pushed her into the chair. She was one of those women whose long, dark hair looked beautiful no matter what you did to them. He glanced down at the fax. It would make Nefski very happy: Novosibirsk ''fully concurred'' with Comrade Nefski's ''assessment of the Jewish problem.'' Indeed, Novosibirsk HQ pointed out, it was partly because of sabotage in the Baltic states that many Russian gunners had found themselves firing dud rounds during the battle for Minsk. Comrade Nefski was instructed to "take all measures necessary for the solution of this problem in your sector of the TVD."

She wasn't wearing a bra. This was normal procedure, of course—some of the Jews had even tried to use shoelaces tied together to hang themselves rather than face KGB interrogation. And because she had done nothing to help the guards on the way up, resisting them as they dragged her full weight over every step, she was perspiring heavily; the faded, thin blue cotton prison tunic was clinging to her body like a wet sheet.

Nefski didn't bother turning from the window as he spoke. Ilya grinned, the colonel always pulling this *lidery*—"bigshot"—bullshit, not deigning to look at the prisoner. That was fine. It gave Ilya more time to look at her. Already she'd responded by not responding, her lucid brown eyes focussing on some distant point beyond him—Jerusalem perhaps? He could feel the resistance in her like electricity in the air. He knew she wasn't going to cooperate—not yet. This was a waste of time. Still, they always did this part by the book, and he opened the file, moving to the left of Nefski's brutish, wooden desk to take notes. But now Nefski unexpectedly turned and shook his head. No notes. Ilya slipped the file away and closed the drawer with a satisfying click. No record of the interrogation; it was a good sign. They'd have a bit of fun with her. After all, Novosibirsk had given them carte blanche.

CHAPTER THIRTEEN

THE "SNICK" DAVID Brentwood heard off to his right about twenty yards was no file cabinet shutting but a SPETS AKMS butt stock unfolding, extending the 7.62-millimeter submachine gun's length from twenty-eight to thirty-five inches. Not as heavy as the AK-47, the Kalashnikov 74 didn't have the heavier hitting power of the AK-47 but with less recoil gained greater accuracy.

The burst hit an SAS trooper before he touched ground, and although Brentwood couldn't see the barrel flashes, he heard the heavy thump of the SPETS burst hitting the man, his body dangling, its radiant heat a shiver in David's Starlight goggles in which green snow enveloped the man as he fell dead into the soft powder. The trooper's chute, its flapping audible, still invisible to David, was dragging the man along through the snow in a tug of war with the anchor of his equipment pack.

Fifty yards away Brentwood landed softly, shucked off his chute, and within seconds was crawling, sweat turning to ice about his collar, using his boot knife to quickly probe the snowy ground in front of him for mines. He saw then heard a ragged series of orange flashes off to his left, the air reeking of cordite. A "Bouncing Betty," a Siberian M-16A1 antipersonnel mine, had jumped, disintegrating five feet above the orange-flickering snow, the mine's shrapnel whistling through the snow-curtained air. He heard an agonized scream somewhere behind him and saw a flare illuminating another chute coming down, the SAS soldier kicking frantically in pain, hands clutching raspberry-colored goo that had been his face. In the same light Brentwood glimpsed SPETS—three of them—forming a defensive triangle no more than twenty yards away at ten o'clock. Mentally he marked the spot but could do nothing for now until he reached his pack and unhitched the nine-millimeter MP5K submachine gun. In any case it wouldn't be any good until he knew which way he could roll to avoid the return bursts. Feeling the ice-cold outline of the gun in its plastic wrap and its thirty-round "banana" magazine, he flicked the safety on the left-hand side to the three-round burst position.

A machine gun's rip sounded left of him, grenades exploded, and there was a steady, low "bump-bump-bump" as SPETS triangles continued to pour deadly fire through flare light into the white forest of descending SAS troops farther behind Brentwood. He could see at least two troopers dead in their chutes and another torso, the white blur in Brentwood's infrared goggles the man's blood bubbling from the headless body. "Jesus—

Jesus—'' Brentwood said. Two others hit mines as they landed, snow erupting, covering the troopers like icing sugar, deeper granular snow peppering the collapsing chutes like hail.

Brentwood saw the black blob of a grenade coming his way, followed by an obscenity, but it crashed ten feet beyond him, and he lay deathly still as the uprooted snow peppered him, the grenade's purplish-blue flash a jagged cross that lit up one of the SPETS it killed, giving Brentwood a start that he was so close to them. Another two were momentarily visible in the flash, and he fired two bursts. One SPETS flew backward like a puppet jerked off his feet, taking the full shock of the burst in his chest; the other man managed to get off a wild burst as he slipped on the snow that had instantaneously turned to ice in the heat of the explosion. Now another trooper, his body sagged in harness, hit the snow, the chute collapsing around him, when suddenly, having faked it, the trooper came alive, announcing his arrival with a long burst that ended with ''. . . fucker!'' in an Australian accent.

Figuring the dead SPETS must be within a safety moat around a rat hole—they'd hardly put themselves in the middle of a minefield but rather would have ''sown'' the area around the rat holes—David made a split-second decision: if SAS had screwed up, not bringing any MIC LICs—the 330-foot-long mine-clearing line or ''hose'' charges, cables packed with explosive charges to clear an eight-yard-wide swath through minefields during an infantry advance—then he'd just have to improvise.

Taking off his gloves he quickly reeled in the tether line that had been attached to the equipment pack. He froze as a chute flare popped high to his right; it wasn't shapes they'd be looking for as much as movement. As the light waned, the flare drifting east over the high cliffs only a hundred yards or so in front of him, David lined up the six HE grenades. The first three had seven-second fuses, the other three, designated for ''room service'' by the SAS, only three-second ones. He waited for the next SPETS flare—they'd been coming at fairly regular intervals near where he and Aussie had hit ground. But now that David wanted to see one none came, and he realized that his and Aussie's drop, and possibly a few others, marked the southern extremity of the drop over the northern half of the island.

Then a flare mushroomed a quarter mile north of them, its fierce incandescent light macabrely beautiful, the snow acting like a million tiny strobe mirrors, turning night to bluish white day, the dazzling effect belying the life-and-death struggle most of the SAS stick further north were now engaged in, having bailed out only seconds before the abort command from Freeman. David knew he'd have to make, as calmly and accurately as he could, six throws in as many seconds before the first grenade exploded. Six arcs, each shorter than the one before it, using his seventy-pound pack as a shield for the one that should explode nearest him, the overpressure from its V-shaped detonation, as well as its shrapnel, hopefully setting off any antipersonnel mines. It occurred to him he might not even be in a minefield at all but in a mine-free zone used by the SPETS as they'd back-walked to the rat hole entrances after having sown the mines. But if he was in a minefield and took one step forward . . .

He slipped off his gloves, flexing his fingers quickly to keep the circulation up long enough. Ten yards or so back of him, Aussie Lewis picked up a rush of movement on his goggles' green background. His trigger finger slipped off the guard at the same instant that he saw the top of a diamond—another SAS trooper—at one o'clock, thirty feet away. Ten to one, he told himself, it was Brentwood—no clear image to go by, of course, just the infrared blur of helmet and white thermal jump suit, but Brentwood, as leader of the seventy-man SAS stick, had been the first out of the C-141. "You beaut! You little—" Aussie whispered, his voice drowned by an earsplitting roar and earth-shattering "crump" of heavy 120-millimeter Soviet mortars.

David Brentwood took a deep breath, exhaled half of it, held the rest and tossed the grenades—one, two, three, four, five, the fifth one going off as he let go of the sixth, dropping to the snow and pulling his equipment pack against his helmet as cascades of powder snow and fragments of rock pebbles fell on him and a sliver of white-hot metal passed through the thermal suit, gashing his right thigh. A second later he felt a burning sensation on his back—hot or freezing cold he couldn't tell. It was lumps of snow, now ice, fused by the grenade's heat.

Using the pack as a rest he fired two long bursts, tattooing the ground along the twenty-to-thirty-yard line of the grenades' explosion. Only one more mine went off, with an almost disappointing "pop," but it was loud enough for Aussie who, though further back, had his face pockmarked by splinters, his goggles scratched so badly they were no longer of any use to him. David clipped on a fresh magazine and was up and running straight into the rough canal-like fissure cleared through the snow by the grenades, firing from the hip, Aussie covering him, two SPETS rising out of "fucking nowhere," as Aussie would later recount, off to their left, the telltale stutter and flame of their two AK-47s silenced in a long, angry burst from the Australian. The Siberian commandos fell face first "while fucking Brentwood—no fucking apology for my face—does a fucking Babe Ruth for the home plate. Lucky bastard's first one to see a ventilator shaft, then a sealed-off rat hole. Crafty buggers had it protected under an overhanging rock ledge."

It wasn't as easy as Aussie made out, the truth being that when David tried to fire into the ventilation mesh, a ricochet from the titanium-hardened grate, its apertures too small for a bullet to pass through, almost took off his knee. While Aussie covered him, David ran ahead, snatched two grenades from the dead SPETS he'd cut down, their faces so black with camouflage paint that he could only make out their eyes, put the grenades against the mesh, and then shoved one of the SPETS hard up against the grenades and ventilator grate before he pulled the pins. The concertinaed explosion blew a grapefruit-sized hole in the mesh and had one of the SPETS' carotid arteries spurting blood like a hose, making it slippery on the now snow-free rock.

"Thanks for shovelling my driveway, mate," said Aussie as he and David dropped two tear gas grenades into the ventilator shaft.

It was of no use, for the exit had been sealed off at the sixty-foot level, besides which the ventilator shafts, being of Saddam design and built in the halcyon days of Gorbachev/German friendship, had no difficulty filtering out the tear gas. Aussie and Brentwood looked around for the rest of the SAS stick, but there weren't any. At least fifty-six of the seventy had landed farther north of them in another minefield into which SPETS were pouring machine-gun and mortar fire from rocky enclaves

on high ground. The SPETS were calling it the *boynya*—
"butcher shop." And it was still dark. Come civil twilight in
another fifteen minutes the SPETS would have an even easier
time of it, no longer inhibited by inferior night-vision goggles.

Surrounded by mines, the SAS would systematically be cut
to pieces, as they were too near the SPETS for any close air
support to help. Any strafing or bombing run would kill them
as well as the SPETS. The terrible irony was that those SAS
dropped farther north than Aussie, Brentwood, and a few others
had made a textbook descent right on target, having been guided
by the heat-emission patterns seen through their PVS-7s. But of
those fifty-six-odd SAS troopers there were now only thirty-
seven.

They were no more than two hundred yards from an exit, one
of the two hitherto unseen by Allied reconnaissance and designated by Dracheev as R1 and R2. But with the minefield between them and the SPETS they might as well have been two
hundred miles away. A few had tried Brentwood's method and
had cleared a path, but here the SPETS heavy Vladimirov 14.5-
millimeter fire was so concentrated and overwhelming, coming
from over two hundred SPETS, that it seemed come civil twilight the SAS, and thus the Allied offensive on Ratmanov Island,
was doomed.

South of the main body of SAS, Aussie, Brentwood, and two
other troopers began placing C-4 charges about the double-
armored cover of the sealed-off rat hole. With only ten minutes
till civil twilight they knew their only chance of survival, let
alone of doing any damage to the SPETS, was to penetrate the
tunnel system. To make matters worse, the tear gas, albeit in
weakened form after having been processed by the subterranean
filter system, was being vented through the snow around them,
adding to the eeriness of the place. For in the bitter, windswept
blue of the cold, predawn light, it seemed as if sulfurous fu-
maroles were leaching up poisons from the earth's violent interior.

Aboard the C-141 General Douglas Freeman was about to
make one of the toughest decisions of his or any other military
career. Twelve minutes to the first rays of civil twilight and

Freeman didn't hesitate, but the Pentagon and the president *had*, "advising" him to call the Ratmanov operation off but craftily leaving the final decision to him as "the man on the ground." He wasn't on the ground, but he knew what they meant: "You decide—you take the rap."

The press, specifically CBN—how the hell did they know? Freeman wondered—had somehow gotten wind of the minefield catastrophe, and sniffing disaster in the air, reporters were collecting like jackals around the carcass of the White House, its authority bleak-looking beneath the low, leaden sky, its rose bushes forlornly naked but for traces of snow on the thorn. Press Secretary Trainor was swearing to get whomever was responsible for the "minefield" leak "by the balls"; he wanted a list of everyone who knew, from the White House ops room to C in C Alaska air command. Had anyone used plain language instead of the scrambler for God's sake?

"No," he was told—some CBN bastard was doing a "Baghdad Pete" on them.

"You mean he's actually on Big Diomede?"

"Either that or close enough. Maybe Little Diomede."

"I thought Freeman ordered that son of a bitch off?"

The aide, a bright young masters degree from Princeton's International Relations program, was red-faced. "Ah, bit of a screwup there, Mr. Trainor."

"Spill it, Simpson, spill it!"

"Ah—one of the Eskimos that came out on Little Diomede's Evac chopper—" Simpson was looking down at some hurriedly scribbled notes. "Couple of hours before the attack. Well, far as we can tell so far, someone apparently saw the press credentials hanging around someone's neck and figured it was the CBN guy."

"But it wasn't!" snapped Trainor.

"Doesn't look like it, sir. Uh, all rigged up in winter gear, snow flying everywhere around the chopper, they said—hard to see I guess."

"Jesus! Jesus! Jesus! *Who* said?"

"Uh, Nome control."

"Is it hard to count?" barked Trainor. "Why didn't the son of a bitch in charge count the fuckers?"

"Maybe they did, Mr. Trainor. Guess no one was sure exactly how many were in Inalik."

"In-a-what?"

"Inalik village. West side of Little Diomede. They'd already moved everyone down from the village on Little Diomede's northern—"

Trainor was so upset, pacing back and forth in the operations room, young Simpson thought he'd have a stroke right then and there in the basement beneath the map of Siberia and the strait. Trainor raised his left hand in a fist, flattened it as if to strike the map, then suddenly pulled back, quietly fuming, holding his hand over his eyes like a tennis shade. "All right. So this son of a bitch is close enough to know Freeman fucked up. Close enough to see the minefields. How's he getting the info out?"

"By phone, Mr. Trainor. A four-wire direct satellite hookup. Portable pocket-sized dish—unfolds to umbrella size apparently." The aide paused, gulped, and continued. "We're only getting sound bites. No pics."

"Oh, that's terrific, Simpson. That's a big help. Whole friggin' world's hearing we screwed up—*Freeman* screwed up—but no pics. Beautiful. It's worse with radio. People's imaginations run riot. Think we've already lost it."

Simpson had always been told by Trainor that you couldn't hold back the truth if you had any hope of effective damage control. So he put it on the line. "Well, we have lost it, haven't we?"

"The island, yes, but not the whole shebang. I mean—" Trainor, for the first time in the White House, was at a loss for words. Young Simpson's truth, like poisoned air, was quickly filling the whole room. Young Princeton had it right. If they'd lost Rat Island—the first game—the whole series could be lost.

Aboard the C-141—three Siberian SAMs had been taken out by the Patriots as they'd raced toward the big transport—General of the Army Douglas Freeman had other ideas, but he had only ten minutes till civil twilight—till, in the undressed phrase of Dick Norton, "slaughter time." It was to be the most controversial decision in American military history: the kind of controversy that had followed his career from the night drop on

Pyongyang to take out, in Freeman's words, "Kim Il Suck!" to the Minsk front where he'd insulted the entire Soviet high command by insisting that they salute the Stars and Stripes before negotiations could begin. "Give me Alaska Air Command!" he shouted above the combined thunder of the C-141's engines. "General Riley!"

Riley's voice was crackling with static; even the most sophisticated electronics were prey to the vicissitudes of solar flare–driven northern atmospherics. "Riley here, General."

"Colin. I want immediate FAE strikes. Coordinates one six niner zero three . . ." As Freeman was speaking, the mauvish brown screen display in the NORAD regional combat command at Elmendorf was flashing the status of all aircraft aloft in Alaska Command; the smaller green grids to the right listed, in descending order, weapon status, fighter, reconnaissance, and airlift mission schedules. In front of Riley the duty officer was bringing up the buffer zone signified by the map grids covering the Bering Strait from latitude sixty-six north to sixty-five south. On the five magnification Riley saw the position Freeman had given them for the FAE strike was on a midline running across Ratmanov Island near the eastern cliffs.

"That's too close to our own men," he told Freeman.

"Whole island's too close to our own men, General. I want FAE strikes now. You've got—nine minutes."

"I don't know whether any—"

"I'm taking full responsibility."

Riley had to gather spittle to talk, the terrible risk having made his mouth dry. "I know you are, Douglas. What I mean is that it'll take five minutes or so to load up FAEs. We've got nothing up there carrying—"

"Then don't waste time. Start loading, damn it! I want those air strikes, Colin. Now!"

Freeman was off the air and relaying orders to Maj. Harold E. Morgan, leader of the Delta Force stick. "Goddamn it! Even from subsonic from Galena it's less than a minute to Rat Island. What the hell's the matter with him? All right, now listen, Harry. We're going to keep circling in this big bird till we see the FAEs. Soon as the flames die down—which won't be long in this blizzard—you boys go. Don't bother looking for SAS, they'll link up with you soon as they can. Go for that exit the Tomcats've reported." He pointed to the circled position on the map. "It wasn't on the photo recon. Must be one they had up their sleeve."

"Yes, sir," said Morgan, knowing what the general had meant by not "looking for SAS." It wouldn't only be a waste of time; there might not be many left if the fuel air explosive—the deadlier cousin of napalm—spewed out anywhere near them. In any case, Morgan wasn't about to judge Freeman for using the tremendously high overpressure created by an FAE to detonate mines so close to his own men. The court of public opinion would put him in the dock soon enough.

"Sir," said the Starlifter's pilot, calling out to Freeman. "Elmendorf's reporting Bogeys rising from East Cape." It was the Siberian side. "Look like Fulcrums." The Mikoyan-Gurevich 29-Fs were the pièce de résistance of the Siberian air arm. As Major Frank Shirer, now held prisoner by the SPETS, had found out over the Aleutians, the eighteen-thousand-pound thrust of the twin Tumansky R-33Ds–powered Mach 2.8 fighter could put the Fulcrum into a near-vertical climb position, attain a hammerhead stall/tail slide, evade enemy radar, and come out of nowhere with six deadly pylon-mounted Alamo air-to-air missiles and a drum-fed thirty-millimeter machine gun sheathed beneath the left wing.

"Then by God," said Freeman, "Novosibirsk must be worried to risk their air force. Is Galena intercepting?" Freeman asked the pilot.

"Affirmative. F-18s. And Tomcats—'fingers four' from *Salt Lake City*. They've been refueled midair—flying protective screen for the carrier."

"Good," commented Freeman.

The Starlifter's engineer didn't agree. "Gonna be like the Fourth of July up here."

No one answered. He was right. And there was the danger of collision with everyone flying on instruments in the bad weather and on radio silence as much as possible; the chances of slamming into someone else were high. Even so, it was nothing compared to the risk the SAS on the ground faced if the pilots, dropping the FAEs, weren't on the ball.

"You reached anybody down there yet?" shouted Freeman.

"No, sir," replied the copilot. "Siberians are jamming everything. You'd need land lines to evade that lot."

Freeman said nothing; he didn't have to. If the SAS weren't informed of the impending FAE drops the risk to them was even higher. If the FAEs missed them and he secured the island with Delta Force he'd be a hero, but he knew that while victory would have many parents, defeat would be an orphan—his. The president and the Chiefs of Staff were right—it was his responsibility. It came with a general's pay.

The SPETS were no longer interested in Shirer. Any information he could give them now was null and void with the SAS trapped and about to be wiped out in the dawn's early light. Nevertheless, the SPETS resented the American's stubbornness in refusing to tell them anything but name, rank, and serial number. It transcended all common sense. Everyone broke sooner or later, and if you didn't, then you outraged your captors' assumption of omnipotence. The SPETS had orders from Dracheev not to kill the American ace Shirer, and they saw the sense in this, for when the Allied commandos failed to take Ratmanov, Shirer, whose nickname in the Western press was "One-Eyed Jack," might be useful in a prisoner exchange. Americans were soft—always willing to trade five of yours for one of theirs.

"Last chance," the SPETS corporal told Shirer, who was tied to a metal chair near the base of one of the ventilator shafts. "Why do they call you a one-eyed Jack?" The corporal's English was impeccable.

The other SPETS looked at the corporal, switching to Russian. "Why are you asking him that? You know he used to be one of their Air Force One pilots. They wear the black patch on one eye so if there's a nuclear airburst and everybody else on the plane is blinded, the pilot still has one good eye to fly the instruments. We know that—what the hell are you wasting time for?"

"I didn't know," the corporal answered him in Russian. "Bastards think they're tougher than we are. Need a lesson."

"So give it to him. But let's hurry, eh? It'll soon be twilight. I don't want to miss out on the fun."

"You won't. Here, hold him steady!"

The corporal unslung his AK-47, rested it against the far side of the ventilator, and pinned Shirer's arms even tighter against the chair.

"That's it," said the other SPETS, and took Shirer by the hair, pushing his head back hard on the top of the chair so that Shirer was forced to look up at the heavy, steel-reinforced roof of the ventilator tunnel.

"Look at me!" he commanded Shirer. Shirer, his face contorted by his previous beating and bruised from the scrape against the canopy when he'd ejected, glanced defiantly at the SPETS. He wasn't going to tell them squat about Air Force One. In one quick movement the SPETS slipped the ballpoint pen from his pocket and drove it into Shirer's eye.

Shirer was screaming, but the SPETS' voice was louder, reverberating around the ventilator shaft. "That's why you're called one-eyed Jacks." Grinning, the SPETS looked across at the corporal, who was slinging on the Kalashnikov. "His flying days are over, Comrade."

"C'mon!" said the corporal impatiently. "You'll miss the party."

The "party" had already started in the blizzard over Ratmanov Island as F-18s, their Litton inertial navigation system and Martin Marietta AN/ASQ-173 laser spot tracker and forward-looking infrared giving the Hornets the edge above the blizzard level where the Fulcrums had to pursue them if they wanted to engage. Below, in the blizzard itself, F-15C Eagles on afterburner went into the furball as other MiGs tried to take out the big Starlifter, which was now opening its ramp once more. Freeman, the first man in the Delta Force stick, cinched the straps holding the Winchester 1200 modified riot gun to his pack, its perforated heat shield already frosting under the plastic. Freeman quickly wrapped another layer of waterproof camouflage sheet about it to prevent the four fléchette cartridges and the slugging shell in the chamber from getting too cold. If the FAEs did the job properly, he wouldn't need the fléchettes until he got inside the tunnels, but a slugging shell, which could go through an engine block at three hundred yards, might come in handy on the already bomb-rattled rat hole covers.

"General," Harry Morgan advised him, the major's voice whipped away by the slipstream, "you're not supposed to be leading, General."

"You have any objections, Harry?" Freeman shouted, one hand on the webbing net by the door as they hit unstable air, the other hand busy tightening the oxygen mask before the helmet came down.

"Hell, no, General, glad to have you along. But Dick Norton told me that I should remind you that General Grey—"

"General Grey ordered me not to lead the drop!" Freeman shouted against the wind and roaring crescendo of the Starlifter. "Now did I lead the drop, Harry?"

"Well, not technically I guess. The SAS—"

"Right. Major Brentwood led the drop. Hell, I'm just followin' up the rear. Besides, what kind of commander would I be, sending men down into that without going myself?"

"Yeah," a Delta Force corporal told his buddy down the line. "But he won't be the one at the fucking barbecue!"

"Don't worry," his buddy told him. "Jumpmaster tells me Tomcats are coming in with those FAEs. They can land on an angled deck in the middle of the fucking night, man. They can drop those FAE babies just where they want 'em. Like in Iraq."

"Iraq! Those mothers were dug in miles from us. These fuckers are only a coupla hundred yards from those limeys."

"Don't worry. Our carrier guys are used to putting those birds down on a postage stamp. They're not gonna screw up."

The Tomcats *didn't* screw up. Coming in low, wings fully extended for maximum stability, they risked lower speed and more vulnerability to the Siberians' missile and gun AA fire. The snow was now falling only lightly, and the predawn darkness above the island was filled with what seemed to be the crazed patterns of contrails from wing tips and missile stabilizers in a cacophony of sound that made it all but impossible for the Tomcats' RIOs and pilots to hear one another. Though lighter, the snow still segmented laser designator beams so that the Paveway conversion nose assemblies attached to the FAE pods of jellied fuel could not be taken advantage of. The pilots had to rely as best they could on wind-vector corrections to aid the computer in making the low-level drop. Wind shears, always unpredictable around carriers as much as above airports, were especially so around the island, where constantly shifting pressure ridges changed gusting north winds by the millisecond. The first two FAE pods tumbled, textbook perfect, close to the cliffs, the great, rolling vomit of black-edged flame consuming at least half-a-dozen SPETS' heavy machine-gun positions, roughly twenty-five men in all, and drowning several elevator shafts in a river of flame. Dracheev's northern complex could no longer be garrisoned. More than five hundred SPETS beneath were now directed south to the midline where most of the SAS had landed and were now in imminent danger of being wiped out by SPETS clustered in the rocky enclaves about the hitherto unknown R1 exit.

Despite increasing, almost hysterical AA fire, the second Tomcat released its single 12,573-pound "Big Blue 82" fuel air explosive mixture of gelled ammonium nitrate, aluminum powder, and polystyrene soap. The canards afforded it some stability in the fierce wind gusting about the cliff tops, but not much. A hundred feet above the minefields, its cloud detonators released, allowing the slurry of gelled explosive to blow out of the casing; it became a vast aerosol, or chemical mist, over the snow.

At twenty-three feet above the ground the cloud detonators ignited the now lethal explosive/air mix, wind gusts having pushed it sharply westward. The vast "in-curling" flame, over two hundred yards long and over a hundred yards wide, immediately killed over forty of the fifty-six SAS.

It was not the FAE's ferocious heat or terrible overpressure or the detonation of all the mines in the area in one cataclysmic upwelling of black, rock-streaked snow that killed the SAS commandos, but asphyxiation. The flames instantly consumed all oxygen in the area, and in the process sucked every last bit of air from the trapped men's lungs. Over seventy-three SPETS suffered the same fate, the heat and shock wave felt through the canopy of the following Tomcat that, dropping its Big Blue, killed another eleven SAS troopers, leaving only sixteen scat-

tered further inland and several, like Brentwood and Aussie, to
the south.

The second FAE did not kill any more SPETS but flooded
ventilator shafts with fire, so that now more than a thousand
SPETS were assembling beneath the R1 shaft. Their imminent
exit was due not only to the befouled ventilation system but to
their desire to combat the troops that were certain to be aboard
the more than one hundred specks now showing up on Ratmanov radar—Apache gunships preceding a larger armada of over
150 Chinook CH-47 troop transport choppers. Dracheev was in
a rage; not only had this Freeman had the courage to call in
FAEs near his own men, so destroying SPETS minefields, but
had used the FAEs to clear landing space for a helicopter assault.
Well, it wasn't over yet.

"Flames still visible," reported the Starlifter's copilot.

"Okay," acknowledged the pilot. "We go around again. Tell
Freeman."

"Roger." There was an explosion at two o'clock high—either
a Fulcrum or an Eagle, it was impossible to tell.

The next time around the flames had abated, partially because
of the snow and the arrival of a bevy of rain-heavy squalls coming in over the pressure ridges in excess of a hundred miles an
hour. Freeman was first out, diving toward the now-blackened
drop zone. The rest of the Delta stick came behind him, hoping
that the squalls would pass well over the island; otherwise they'd
have one hell of a job steering into the cleared area. Two Delta
men were already dead, one sucked into the starboard engine of
a MiG-29 going down, the other man struck seconds later by
the same plane's canopy, his skull crumpling the cockpit's Per-
spex, momentarily turning it cherry red before the froth of brain
was consumed by the blizzard. Another MiG-29, having broken
radar silence in the final moments of his attack, and frustrated
by not having found the big Starlifter, glimpsed the unmistakable wing sweep of a Tomcat. But the Tomcat vanished before
he could fire an Alamo or Apex.

Freeman was pulling hard, lowering the left toggle, going
into a spiral. The drop point he had picked up in the eerie blue

of civil twilight held three charred bodies—SAS or SPETS he didn't know, but at least it would be clear of mines. There were several bright orange flashes a mile or so east of the cliffs and then a roll of explosions echoing off the cliff face: three Chinook choppers hit by Rat AA fire.

Freeman's landing was softer than he'd braced for. His right foot passed through the black crackle of one of the corpses. The only solids left by the blaze were bone, ammunition clips—their rounds set off by the fire—a partially melted Kevlar helmet that told him it had been a Special Air Service trooper, and a Heckler and Koch submachine gun nearby. The air was pungent with the sickening-sweet odor of burnt flesh. Freeman saw his equipment pack in a black, oily pool where SAS and others—he guessed SPETS—lay charred beyond recognition, one tightly stretched, leatherlike face staring eyeless at the sky.

Already Freeman was under fire, the pyrotechnics of inter-cutting red and white tracer against the Prussian blue of a now spectacularly clear Arctic morning mixing with orange streaks from the marine expeditionary unit's assault Apache as 2.75-inch-diameter rockets, fired in salvos, exploded against the high, dug-in cliff guns, followed by the skittering orange/red detona-tions of the ninety-five-pound anti-radar Hellfire missiles. In the distance writhing, smoking, umbilical trails of red-hot spent casings spun down from the Apaches' 750-round-a-minute, belly-mounted Hughes gun, adding to the deadly kaleidoscope of colors passing through and blending with one another against the vast bluish-white tumble of the ice-bound strait—the thin squiggle of Siberia's mountainous coast just visible twenty-five miles westward.

The CBN reporter on the southern tip of the island, two miles south of where the FAEs had scoured out a safe landing zone for Delta Force, was on a high, getting pics now as well as the clearest sound bites he'd ever heard, better than anything he'd gotten in the Iraqi war.

A wounded SPETS snapped off a burst in Freeman and Mor-gan's direction. Having shucked his chute, Freeman instinc-tively went on his belly, reaching in the black ashes of one of the corpses for the dead man's MP5K. The gun fired, and the SPETS rolled into Morgan's burst, shuddered, and lay dead even before the white flecks of his overlay, torn out by the nine-millimeter Parabellum, had fallen to the ground.

Freeman, the MP5K cradled in his elbows, began a fast belly crawl toward his pack ten yards in front of him when he saw two SPETS, one hauling a light machine gun, its bipod swinging, momentarily silhouetted against the azure sky at the cliff's edge, the latter's sharp black thrust of rock clearly visible now the snow had been melted by the FAE's explosion. Freeman fired again; now Morgan was close in beside him.

The SPETS made it across the gap in the rock, splinters of basalt flying high, catching the sun. Freeman patted the MP5K he'd dug out from the ashes. "By God those Krauts make 'em good, Harry." But now the gun's magazine, he knew, was nearly empty, and only a yard or two from the pack he used the tether line to bump it over a pile of shale, tearing out the Winchester 1200. Knowing he had the lead slug in the spout, he told Morgan to lead. The submachine gun was better able to sweep the SPETS' position than Freeman's lead slug, which was intended for steel doors and the like. The Delta major clipped in a new mag.

Having seen the Delta Force landing, Brentwood and Aussie and two other SAS had intended to join them, but with a sprawling half mile of snow, no doubt mined, between them and the Delta drop zone, the best the three SAS men could do was to try to work their way up along the line of the cliff where there were no mines but plenty of SPETS.

The idea was quickly abandoned, however, upon their sighting the MEU's choppers coming straight for the cliffs, albeit on a vector a hundred feet or so below the top of the seventeen-hundred-foot-high cliffs. Once they saw the choppers—AH-64 Apaches out front, the cliff taking a lot of hits, much of the shrapnel whizzing above them—the SAS men knew the chopper force, despite all the best intentions in the world, could not avoid overshoots of friendly fire. The choppers were forcing the SPETS aboveground to keep their heads down—likewise the few survivors of the SAS, the air now literally singing with warhead fragments. The whole idea had been for Norton and the marines to come in and secure the island *after* the SAS-Delta Force had "cleared the rats' nest," in Freeman's happy phrase.

"Little ahead of schedule," said Aussie wryly, keeping his head well down, waiting for the marines to sweep in. "Hope to Christ those leathernecks don't blast away at us."

Aussie wasn't alone in his estimation of the operation. A quarter-mile north in Freeman's drop zone, Brooklyn, another trooper, declared the operation "FUBAR"—fucked up beyond all recognition—as he hunkered down by an ice-veined rock a hundred yards from the R1 exit that Freeman and Morgan were now moving toward, Morgan calmly ejecting one mag and inserting the other in a smooth, three-second change that would have done any drill instructor proud.

The approaching choppers were no longer the size of gnats but football-sized as they began to rise for the final "hop stop" over the jagged lip of the cliff tops into the big FAE-cleared strip now occupied by Delta and being fiercely contested by SPETS who were oozing out of the R1 exit at an alarming rate. In fact, thanks to the FAE's ancillary benefit of having overwhelmed the ventilator filters, there were still over a thousand SPETS filling the tunnels leading to the bottom of the R1 shaft, eager to join their comrades above.

But the SPETS heading for R1 were now the victims of their own ingenuity, for to use R2 would be to split their forces, the southern contingent boxed in by the minefields they had sown on the lower half of the island to help trap the enemy paratroops. General Dracheev, although surprised by Freeman's cold-blooded daring in ordering the FAE drops though it risked the lives of his own men, now almost wished that Freeman had ordered in more FAE strikes to the south to clear a wider defense area for his own men now that R1 was so overcrowded. SPETS were pouring out into the thirty-foot-diameter rock basin that bulged protectively from the exit on the landward side of the cliff.

A Delta Force spotter, fifty yards to Freeman's left and on slightly higher ground, saw the SPETS come streaming out and tried to get a radio man to tell Freeman he'd seen at least thirty of the enemy exit in just over a minute. The spotter killed three of them before he'd been forced back from higher ground by fire from an RPK 7.62-millimeter light machine gun, too far away to toss his grenades. But the SPETS jamming was still effective, and the radio man couldn't get the message through to Freeman. Instead, a runner was dispatched—and cut down before he'd gone five paces.

The frustration of the seventy-plus SAS/Delta Force survivors, of men trained for lightning-fast IKO—in-kill-out—action, but who, because of the minefields, had been bottled up, forced into open-ground warfare without the assist of heavy mortars and the like, manifested itself in Freeman. He now saw the choppers getting smaller, Norton having presumably seen that despite all the noise and thunder of ordnance being thrown at the cliff face, most of the dug-in AA batteries were still intact, putting up a wall of lead that had already created seven gaping holes in the chopper line of attack. Norton had obviously decided that to take the marines in would have been nothing less than suicidal. It was a call he'd have to square with Freeman, if Freeman survived, but it was his call.

"Two oh three!" yelled Freeman, his shout immediately attracting AK-47 fire, albeit inaccurate, the SPETS probably on the move deploying a defensive line. Morgan and others responded to their fire immediately in an enfilade of semiautomatic fire erupting from the C-shaped Delta Force line, whose northern and southern arcs spread out left and right of Freeman. This time the sustained firing of Delta Force successfully covered the ten-yard dash by one of the two Delta men equipped with an M-203, in effect an eleven-pound M-16A2 rifle with a circular-ribbed, forty-millimeter-diameter grenade launcher—a replacement for the old M-16A1's forestock—with the 5.56-millimeter mag serving as the handgrip when pulling the trigger of the launcher. "You figure that basin of theirs is about thirty, fifty yards from here?" Freeman asked the commando.

"Split the difference, General—forty."

"Suits me, son. Lob six of those babies right in there. Start with HE and alternate with smoke and tear gas canisters. One after the other, son, quick as you can and we'll have a fuckin' rat trap sooner'n you can fart!" Freeman turned to Morgan, who was firing another burst on the other side of the M-203. "Henry, get your flank ready. Hand signals. Gas masks on. We go on ten."

"Go on ten. Got it." A loud bang stunned Freeman, the

SPETS bracketing them with heavy mortar, and even as he was signalling the crescent of Delta men on his right to ready for an attack on ten, he couldn't hear anything but buzzing in his ears, as if they were covered by a mass of wasps. Then he lost sight of his men, a thick cloud of tear gas enveloping both Delta flanks—from where he couldn't tell. Through the buzz he heard the crash of the first grenade in the basin, said, ''Good shooting!'' but couldn't hear himself, and was struck by the terrible thought that the SPETS, many of whom he knew were trained in English, might have picked up his shouted commands. Whether the tear gas fired at them had been a coincidence or was their own, backblasted by a change in the wind, he couldn't tell. Either way he knew he had no choice. He heard a second explosion, this one clanging, the HE grenade shrapnel ringing in the rock basin. There were screams of men hit, his or theirs he couldn't tell. Another grenade went off, then more—coming from the SPETS. He tried to look through the smoke but could see nothing. Next moment it cleared. Morgan fired, and there was a soft, red explosion—blood—no more than twenty feet away. The SPETS shooter slumped, not making a sound, his nose and right cheek missing. Freeman brought his wristwatch close to his face: nine seconds. Grasping the Winchester tightly he yelled, ''Go!'', the sound of his voice coming to him as if in the distance, through a long pipe.

La Bataille du Bassin—The Battle of the Basin, as the French papers were later to describe it—was not, as the headline suggested, some vast, sprawling engagement in the Arctic but it *was* fierce and unyielding to the seventy-plus Delta/SAS men who charged, following Freeman, through the tear gas screen to engage the enemy in a swirling, smoke-filled cauldron of firefights. The sounds of the battle reverberated off the rocky amphitheater as Americans, British, and Siberians closed hand-to-hand after exhausting their magazines and when the attacking Delta/SAS Force was so near the Siberians that further fire endangered their own men.

Morgan and Freeman were side by side as they reached the rocky basin's rim. Freeman had no option but to fire the lead slug, a metal projectile punching through three SPETS in the congested basin, blowing holes the size of sledgehammers and sending flesh and bone flying as if they themselves had exploded. Before the third SPETS fell, Freeman, a formidable sight coming through the haze of battle with his shotgun, had already pumped—Delta hands eschewing semi-automatic shotguns because of their proneness to jam—one of the four fléchette cartridges into the barrel and fired, then another, then another—in all, sending out 180 grek- or polyethylene-bedded steel darts in an expanding cone that killed at least six SPETS outright, injuring another half dozen or more.

Seven Delta Force fell under sustained AK-47 fire from the SPETS who, a moment before Freeman fired, had been a compact mass about the R1 exit. A shouted order from among the SPETS preceded the closing, or rather the attempted closing, of the R1 manhole. But by now another Delta commando had fired his lead-slug-loaded shotgun from only ten feet away and with a deafening ring, akin to the sound of some enormous bell being hammered, the steel manhole cover, once cold and therefore undetected and untouched by the Allied infrared guided aerial bombardment, was now billowing smoke like some fumarole.

The warmer air of the hundred-foot-deep tunnels streaming through the ragged, baseball-sized perforation blown out by the Winchester's slug immediately created a fog as it hit the Arctic air, adding to the confusion of the smoke-filled basin. Freeman went down, the victim of a SPETS stun grenade concussion, the Winchester clattering on the R1 cover. Brentwood's small band of SAS survivors breached the basin's rim to the right.

"Medic!" Morgan shouted, and then died, lungs pulped to a pink mass by an AK-74 burst at near–point-blank range. Brentwood evened the score, emptying a mag into the SPETS, punching him back into other comrades falling about him. Not pausing for a second Brentwood popped one, two, three grenades down through the hole in the R1 cover, the thumps and clanging of the explosions sending ricocheting metal zinging about amid the screaming and choking tear gas, adding to the general confusion and making it impossible to know friend from foe for at least seven seconds.

It was a relative silence in the roar of noise, and noticed only by the final group of four SAS and one Delta paratrooper who, like Brentwood and Aussie before them, had had to work more slowly than Freeman's "cavalry" through a grenade-shovelled path in the minefield in order to reach the basin.

No one except Dracheev, in his Saddam bunker a hundred feet down and a mile away, realized what the immediate implications of the Allied grenade attack in the shaft were. One moment the Siberian commander had been watching his men moving toward the R1 shaft, the next they stopped. Within seconds he could detect the unmistakable reek of cordite and throat-searing whiffs of tear gas streaming back through the tunnels. He knew immediately that the top section of R1 must now be penetrated. In fact, the whole of R1 had been penetrated insofar as the sheer mass of bodies—some barely alive—writhing in the hellish cauldron of the top fifty feet of the R1 shaft was preventing the steel trapdoor hatch at the sixty-foot level from being closed, thus risking the integrity of the entire system, the shaft jammed with dead and dying.

At the top of the shaft David Brentwood was yelling, "Half with me, half stay topside. Watch the other exits!" Brentwood knew that most of these rat holes would already be warped, even if they'd not been actually penetrated by the air strikes, and would therefore be effectively unopenable by the SPETS. Still, the Siberians would need only one or two exits to enable them to swarm up again. Even now the ten-man Delta squad deployed on the rim were readying to stave off any counterattack by ad hoc teams of SPETS who, having made their way along the cliff tops north and south of the rocky depression, were now attempting to head back to try and retake the R1 basin.

In the basin a medic, readying to give Freeman a shot of antitetanus, almost finished what the Siberians had begun, barely seeing Freeman's tetanus allergy bracelet in time as the general groggily regained consciousness long enough to give Brentwood an order.

"Yes, sir!" responded Brentwood, looking around, yelling, "Radio!" He had to call again before he saw a whip aerial swinging wildly like a fishing rod through the clearing smoke and fumes that were still issuing from R1. "They still have us jammed?" he asked the radio operator.

"Yes, sir. All static."

"All right. Get to the cliff top. Aussie, you cover him. Take two more with you." Brentwood turned to the radio man. "Use your lamp if you can't get a frequency. Signal Little Diomede for the MEU to come in. They'll pass it on. Four Apaches attacking first, the transports to follow fifteen minutes later, coming down on the other exits. But no spreading out—just secure the exits. There are still minefields on our flanks." Brentwood tossed down two more three-second SAS "specials"—stun grenades of the kind SAS had used to clear the Iranian Embassy in London of terrorists in 1980. Stepping back quickly from the cover, he heard Aussie telling him, "Cliff AAs are still active. They'll blow the MEU Apaches to pieces."

"Do what I tell you!" shouted Brentwood. "Take another two men with you." Within seconds two more Delta commandos were moving with Aussie up toward the rim to cover the rear right and left flanks of the signal operator, whose lamp was blinking eastward where anyone but the Siberians could see it. Dick Norton's scopes on Cape Prince of Wales spotted it the second it began winking—the radio relay from Little Diomede's Patriot battery not needed.

As the four AH-64s were taking off and heading out over the jagged twenty-five-mile ice flow toward Ratmanov, their Hughes gunbelts fully loaded and rocket pods resupplied, Delta Force and SAS were in their element, doing what they had trained months, in some cases years, to do. Every man of them was highly trained in a cross section of skills, and every one was in top physical shape. Eighteen headed north of the basin to carry out Freeman's order; twenty-seven headed south, where the AA fire from the recessed, rail-mounted batteries had been heaviest. Map references from the fighter aircrafts' largely futile attacks on the recessed AA positions were of some help, but the references couldn't be relied upon to any high degree.

"Clever bastard!" quipped Aussie to the radio man, but the latter didn't answer, his concentration eastward, lips moving with his Morse message. When he'd received the acknowledgment blink from across the pristine air of the strait he noticed shadows, scattered clouds sliding ominously across the ice pack. "Who's a clever bastard?" he asked Aussie. Aussie fired a long burst at a SPETS who, looking the worse for wear, was dodging between rocky outcrops thirty yards down from the basin's rim. The SPETS stopped then fell, twisting about, trying to reach his backpack. He slithered down into a pocket of dirty ice, streaked by FAE detritus.

"Who's a clever bastard?" repeated the radio man. "Brentwood?"

"What? Oh, yeah, him too. But I meant the old man."

"Von Freeman," grunted one of the Delta men, who'd lost two of his best buddies when the general had called in the FAE strike.

"Okay," said Aussie. "He's a rough customer, but this is a smart move, boyo!"

"You hope."

Aussie thought he saw the SPETS move in the snow—or was it a sense of movement created by passing cloud? "Five to one on it works," he whispered, clipping in another mag, not taking his eyes off the SPETS but not wanting to waste ammunition either.

"You mean what he told Brentwood?" said the Delta man.

"Yeah."

"What's five to one on?" asked the American to his right.

"He means," said the radio man, "you bet ten bucks to win one."

"Fuck *you*," said the other Delta man matter-of-factly.

"Hey, hey," said Aussie, adopting a quiet yet schoolmasterish tone, still not taking his eyes off the SPETS. "Watch your language. Three to one on."

"Done."

There was an explosion so violent that it shook ice from the cliff top, sending it on a sheer fall sixteen hundred feet straight down, where it shattered like glass on the floe.

"Christ, what was that?" said Aussie. There was a towering pall of smoke above R1 seventy yards behind them and the stink of human ordure.

"C-four," the radio man said quietly, his dull monotone suppressing his fear, so determined not to overreact he hardly seemed to react at all. "Brentwood must have dropped a whole—" He stopped, and the others knew why, for it might well have been a

SPETS-induced explosion. Taking his eyes off the SPETS, Aussie glanced back toward the middle of the basin, the towering black column of smoke now hundreds of feet in the air.

Because Joe Mell's Skidoo conked out—he'd had to clean the plugs and tinker with the carburetor to get it going again—it was civil twilight when he reached the snake. Mumbling that he should have "used the dogs" instead, he cinched the belt charge securely about the four-foot-diameter pipe, took another swig of Southern Comfort, and pushed the button.

They found bits of him as far as two hundred yards away, untouched by the inferno that followed the explosion: the charge had not ignited the oil until it raised the temperature of the crude gushing out of the pipe to its flash point. Forensic analysis of the molecular structure of dime-sized pieces from the charge's casing recovered by disc metal detectors confirmed what Anchorage FBI had been quick to surmise—namely that the material was of Soviet manufacture and that there had been no timer, a guarantee that Joe Mell, identified by dental records, would never be able to identify Chernko's Alaskan sleeper.

Only twelve minutes elapsed between Joe Mell's attack and the two other points of sabotage—one on the North Slope itself, the third at Valdez depot, where the crude was now afire and fouling the pristine beauty of Prince William Sound, huge globular tarballs of unrefined "mousse" crude suffocating every sea creature in their path. The fire at the spill's periphery was so fierce that it split the ice-cold fir trees lining the sound, their sharp "cracks" heard for miles along the frozen shore.

The environmental catastrophe that was fouling the waters and killing thousands of animals, from seabirds who had become trapped upon landing in the sludge to marmots hibernating in the Brooks Range, enraged environmentalists from Nome to Washington. What would cause the lights of Congress to burn late into the winter night, however, was the stunning realization that the United States—its consumption of fuel in the war five times normal usage—now had its vital oil artery cut.

The pipeline could be mended within a week, but with the Middle East wells afire, the awful vulnerability of the pipeline and of the tankers shipping the oil from Valdez meant that most of the Pacific Fleet's submarines would have to be deployed to protect the 1,900-mile-long tanker route from Valdez to Cherry Point, Washington to Point Conception in California. This meant drastically reducing the number of submarines available to the Pacific Fleet for action in and about the Aleutians and in America's ability to interdict the Siberian resupply routes from Vladivostok, Sakhalin, and the Kuril Island bases.

The only positive thing about the situation as far as the Pentagon was concerned was that the few peace protesters around the White House now dried to a trickle. Even those who advocated the United States should let the Siberians have their way could not stomach what the Siberians had done to the pipeline. You could kill a marine, but not a marmot.

Commander in Chief Pacific immediately requested Alaska Air Command to increase chopper patrols over the pipeline and ordered all available subs from Bangor, Washington, to the testing range at Beck Island in Behm Canal, twenty-four miles north of Ketchikan on the Alaskan Panhandle. They were to make ready for increased patrols up and down the West Coast, the chief of naval operations now convinced that with the pipeline under tighter surveillance, the weak points in the vital supply link would be the natural attack lanes between the offshore islands all down the coast, particularly those from Valdez to Vancouver Island in British Columbia to the San Juans off Washington State.

CINCPAC's orders sent another of the Brentwood brothers— Robert, the eldest—into action. His dual purpose ICBM/attack sub, a Sea Wolf II, the USS *Reagan*, slipped her moorings at Bangor, Washington, within hours of the Alaska pipeline having been severed. Heading out for another seventy-day war patrol off the West Coast of North America, her "blue" crew was not happy. Being submariners—men who, in order to accommodate all the gadgetry of modern warfare, were forced to live in confined spaces that would have driven landlubbers into a neurotic frenzy in two weeks—they were not whiners. But during their refit and testing runs on the range, they had been within a week of being relieved by the sub's "gold" crew. The nuclear reactor of the *Reagan* produced so much power, so much fresh water,

that the overflow had to be jettisoned every day. It was the men
who wore out first, not ship's supplies.

One deck below the control room, the missile warfare officer
was moving slowly through the red light of "Blood Alley,"
batteries of computers on either side of him winking green, red,
and amber in response to his testing, his earphones trailing cord
as he and Petty Officer Patrick went through a dry run. The
captain, like most of his Annapolis-bred ilk, was wont to give
orders for a launch any time during the long night of a patrol.
You never knew, the officer informed the newcomer Patrick,
whether it was for real or not until the last thirty seconds.

"Keeps us on our toes," said the MWO. The petty officer
had another phrase for it, but he was a petty officer because,
along with his efficiency, he knew when to keep quiet in the
silent service. Besides, he had learned that Brentwood was considered a fair man by the crew—the quiet, shy type—though lord
help the crewman who screwed up. In the world of the Soviet
Alfa II, not as quiet but faster than the Sea Wolf, a split second
either way meant life or death.

The cliff face erupted in gun and surface-to-air missile fire.
The Apaches flew in zigzagging attack pattern, but it didn't help
them. Two-thirds of the way across the twenty-five-mile floe,
one of them erupted in flame then disintegrated. The SAM-10
on the retractable launcher took only thirty seconds to slide to
the cliff opening—a pinhole from where the choppers were—
and unleash the missile that even the nimble firefly-evasive tactics of the Apaches couldn't shake. But the rolling smoke from
the cliff base, as Freeman had anticipated in his order to David
Brentwood, told the men whom Brentwood had deployed south
and north of R1 along the cliff face precisely where the SAM
opening was, as well as that of the medley of other AA weapons
whose assorted fire the remaining three Apaches were drawing.

David Brentwood and Aussie Lewis strapped their ice cleats
onto their vapor barrier boots, preparing to "visit," in the SAS
lexicon, the AA position nearest R1. A SAM "hole" had surprised Aussie and the Delta radio man when it opened up, seemingly only yards away but in fact a hundred feet almost directly
below them. Aussie quickly staked the piton for his white nylon

ply line, took the strain in his left hand glove, and abseiled in a controlled hop/fall down the wall of the cliff, another Delta man having taken his place to guard the radio man from any landward attack by the SPETS.

For a moment Brentwood was worried that his ice cleats would be heard cutting into the cliff face but just as quickly forgot about it as he went over the lip into the sustained roar of the Siberians' ZSU—quads—throwing out their tracer and the din of the SAM's flashback in its man-made cave. Aussie was abseiling down the cliff on the other side of the SAM hole, thirty feet from Brentwood.

From his vantage point on the island's southernmost end, the CBN reporter could see the dots of the three Apache helicopters and the cliff coming alive through the smoke, but because there was so much smoke, particularly the exhausts from the SAMs, whose breath immediately turned the frigid air to fog, the zoom on his Sony 5000 video camera was useless. "We've got to get closer," he told the hunter urgently.

"Through minefields? No way. You'd better signal a chopper ride if those troop whirlybirds make it back again."

"You've got an SOS flare haven't you?" shot back the newsman.

"So? That's for emergencies."

"What the hell do you call this? Moment you see those troop Chinooks going in, you pull that tab."

"You divert a chopper just so you can get pictures, man, you're gonna be in a lot of shit."

"I'll take the rap. It's worth another grand."

"Okay," agreed the hunter, "I'll fire the flare, but I'm staying here. I don't like those whirlybirds. I'd rather walk back to—"

"All right, all right," said the CBN reporter, anxiously looking through the eyepiece again. "Damn that smoke!" Now and then he could see white dots moving against the black cliff where one of the earlier and unsuccessful air attacks had blasted the ice off, exposing the black basalt beneath.

Had it not been for the smoke the reporter would have seen at least twenty dots: seven two-man teams and six individuals abseiling down the cliff face. Apache fire killed half a dozen of the Delta/SAS commandos as shrapnel ricocheted across the face. It killed two commandos outright; others lost their footing or had their lines severed and fell down on the floe. Aussie, Brentwood, and the other teams ignored everything else, focusing only on the particular rat hole below them on the cliff face.

At ninety-five feet, which had taken them less than a minute to reach, Brentwood and Aussie were above the SAM site, either side of it. None of the twenty commandos had used grenades but rather lumps of C-4 plastique with three-second detonator/fuses. They didn't want to simply snuff out the operating crews but knock the AA batteries and SAM transoms right off their rails, hopefully bringing down the rock ceiling as well.

Two commandos were spotted by SPETS loaders who had gone forward, right to the sheer drop-off of their cave's ledge, in order to clear rock and ice debris shaken loose by the vibration of their own firing. It was also the only place to get a draft of fresh, ice-cool air now that the ventilators that had kept the weapon bays clear of smoke weren't up to capacity due to Freeman's and Brentwood's attack on the R1 basin. But the remaining eighteen Allied commandos did the job, each man in the seven two-man teams tossing in the C-4 simultaneously. Only one missed falling, the charge exploding at the seven-hundred-foot level, sending up ice shards, some over six feet long, that caught the cloud-filtered sun before they shattered, killing two of the remaining six individual line commandos as the Delta/SAS team hauled themselves back up the cliff.

Dracheev's force, however, paid a much heavier price: seventeen of the eighteen holes or caves were hit, wiped out, AA quad mountings and SAM launchers blown off their rail mounts, inclining roofward or pointing at the ice floes at ridiculously inoperable angles. They were too heavy to manhandle back onto the rails—the latter buried in any case by collapsing rock piles and scaffolding.

From a distance it looked like a dust storm was issuing forth from the cliff, the rush of black and white rock—now gravel—pouring down the cliffs like molten waterfalls plunging to the ice floe fifteen hundred feet below, the air steaming up as if volcanic vents had been unzipped all along the cliff's base, the bodies of some of the more than fifty-three SPETS, AA, and missile crews momentarily visible in the Allied-made avalanche.

"Let me up, goddamn it!" ordered Freeman, getting up off the litter. "I'm all right."

"General, you took a bad fall. Concussion sometimes doesn't—"

"Let me up!"

It delayed the takeoff of the Apache chopper, which had been turned into an air ambulance heading back to Cape Prince of Wales. It was now sprouting two litters for wounded on either side.

At the moment when his control room shivered, photographs splintering from the enormous shock waves of the Allied charges on the cliff, Major General Dracheev knew his garrison was defeated. His SPETS would fight to the death if asked, but it would be nothing more, he told his duty officer, than a *podpolnaya boynya*—"underground abattoir."

It was impossible to get a message through the jammed hub of wounded up to R1 and so, tearing off a piece of his bed sheet, sticking it on the bayonet of an AK-74, he personally made his way through the choking dust of the tunnel leading out to the nearest AA gun emplacement.

Weaving his way carefully through the burning remnants of what had been a ZSU quad, he saw the bodies of its crew, or rather what was left of them, cast about the tunnel so violently that it only added to his resolve. The stench of human ordure mixed with the sulfurous stench of the C-4's aftermath and incinerated guano, hitherto frozen by the ice, almost overwhelmed him. Dracheev saw two Apaches, now alarmingly big, passing up then out of sight above the cliff. "Hello!" he called from the tunnel, his voice echoing out from the cliff as he disgustedly thrust out the AK-74, the white sheet slapping stiffly in the breeze.

The surrender formally took place eleven minutes later at 1411 hours, though there was sporadic fighting by groups of SPETS along the island, until Dracheev was taken aboard one of the

Apaches and, using a booster hailer to overcome the noise of the chopper, told his troops below it was all over.

"Brentwood!" It was Freeman congratulating him. "Good job, son. Damn good job."

"Thank you, sir," said Brentwood, but his mind was clearly on something else. Behind him Aussie Lewis, Choir Williams, and others were steering the SPETS to the ad hoc weapons dump in the basin. There AK-47s, 74s, even HK MP5K and rounds of nine-millimeter Parabellum along with grenades clattered on the heap. Many of the SPETS had to come up so fast they'd not had time to put on their white overlays; they were already shivering. But no one suspected for a moment that it was from fear, a strange air of equality between the two forces even in the SPETS defeat.

"Ah, General," began Brentwood, his tone betraying his unwillingness to go on, "ah, we've got a bit of a problem here, sir."

"What?"

"Sir, that CBN reporter you ordered off Little Diomede at the beginning—"

"What about him? Where's Morgan?" Freeman was looking about.

"Morgan bought it, sir," said Brentwood.

Freeman, hands on hips, stared at the pile of weapons. "Son of a bitch." He turned to Brentwood. "The news guy, too?"

"No, sir," replied Brentwood. "He's still with us."

"Well, can't kill those bastards." Someone thought he said, "Unfortunately," but this was pure speculation, the men around Freeman waiting for the general to explode on hearing that the reporter hadn't followed orders.

"Deliberate?" shot back Freeman. "Or couldn't they get him off in time?"

"Ah—deliberate, I'm afraid, sir."

"Send him to me."

The cluster of SAS men looked at one another. Normally there might have been a wink or two, relishing the reaming out of one of the "news nits," as the SAS called them; all of them hated the press. But none of the Brits were in the mood for entertainment just yet; too many of their closest friends were charred lumps, wasted by the FAE that the American general had called in.

"What's your name?" Freeman asked the CBN reporter.

"Lamonte, General—Rick Lamonte." He indicated his press card pinned to the Arctic fox collar. "CBN."

"That the Communist Broadcasting Network?"

"No, General."

Freeman grunted. "You send all your equipment to Major Brentwood here. Understand?"

"General, I'm—"

"Listen, Lamonte, I'm not having you invading America's dinner hour with your blood-and-guts footage—least not before any next-of-kin is notified. You got that?"

"I haven't got pictures of any wounded, General. Wasn't close enough—too much debris in the air."

The general said nothing, and there was an unnerving silence, broken only by the *wokka wokka wokka* of the rotors on the marine expeditionary unit's Ch- 47 transports. Most of the leathernecks were disgusted—some relieved—that they were to be used only for mop-up, or, as one sergeant put it, "roundup" duty.

On the ground everyone was waiting for Freeman to respond to Lamonte. Everyone knew that "Ratmanov Rick," as he'd already been dubbed, must have at least the FAE strikes in glorious technicolor and that the Pentagon's PR types would be scrambling for damage control.

"We'll check your tape out," Freeman told Lamonte. "Make sure you've got nobody's mug shots on there. I don't want the mother of some—"

"Fine," chipped in Lamonte.

"You got any film left in that *thing*?"

Freeman knew very well that it was a video camera and how to run it—he'd taken enough shots of his children when they were young—but he enjoyed affecting ignorance about such matters in front of the press; it gave him tactical advantage when they least expected it.

"Not much, General," said Lamonte.

"How much is that?"

"Couple of minutes."

"All right, follow me."

Lamonte, visibly relieved the commandos weren't going to confiscate his tape and equipment with it, followed Freeman toward the cliff side of the basin. The general carefully made his way over bodies, Siberian as well as British and American, till he got an angle for the video from which no faces of American dead could be seen. "All right," he told Lamonte. "Take a shot here—no further than five paces from me. Alright?"

Lamonte couldn't believe his luck: the legendary Freeman on tape, surrounded by SPETS, oily smudged air wafting across the basin from persistent pockets of FAE and smaller fires still burning, would have a dramatic effect before the lens. And that look of Freeman's—helmet on, chin strap tight. The New York anchor would flip. The son of a bitch had the pose down to a T, as if he'd practiced it before a mirror. Tough face but creased with concern, as moved by the enemy dead as his own, the cerulean blue sky and black-and-white jagged cliff behind him a perfect backdrop. Christ, he'd win an Oscar.

"Thirty-second clip," instructed Freeman, not breaking the pose. When Lamonte had finished, Freeman called Brentwood and several Delta men over. "Get in the next shot, men!" he told them.

"Big of him," said Choir Williams sarcastically, his earlier mood of high optimism now gone, wiped out when the FAE had burned the rest of his mates alive.

" 'E doesn't realize it," chimed in another Brit, "but 'e's putting himself on trial. They'll have to weigh this glory bullshit against the shots of the jelly." He meant the FAE.

"Freeman knows that," said Brentwood. "That's the point. Do we want to win or not?"

"Well, jocko," posited Choir, his familiarity with an officer nearing contempt, a tone that only the closeness of commandos could tolerate. "You weren't one of those who was cooked, were you now?"

Brentwood didn't reply, refusing to be drawn into it any further. It wasn't for him to judge; the American people, the Pentagon, every barroom "expert" would do that. All David Brentwood knew was that they were running up the Stars and Stripes and the Union Jack over Rat Island.

"You bastards!" It was one of the marine medics shouting at the SPETS prisoners while helping another marine steer Shirer toward a Medevac chopper, the first-aid bandage they'd put about his eye already soaked with blood.

CHAPTER FOURTEEN

THE PRESIDENT OF the United States was not as forgiving of his general as David Brentwood thought he would be. Mayne didn't question Freeman's decision to use FAE—after all, the White House and the Chiefs of Staff had given him the authority, and Mayne knew the burden of such responsibility.

"My congratulations, General, on your victory," said Mayne tersely over the satellite hookup between the White House and Freeman's Cape Prince of Wales HQ. "Now what in hell were you doing disobeying an order by your commander in chief?"

"Mr. President. I didn't lead the attack. I went in when I thought the situation warranted it."

"Don't dance with me, General. You may have thought the situation warranted it, but I thought I made it clear to you, what we need is your strategy, not your bravado."

"Mr. President, I understand, but if you'll forgive me, we didn't have time for a cabinet meeting on that Starlifter. Sometimes you have to know all the rules in order to break one of them." He paused. "When necessary."

President Mayne conceded the point but then, with Trainor and the Joint Chiefs of Staff listening in, he told General Freeman of the pipeline sabotage and how this meant an increased surveillance responsibility for the navy on the West Coast and substantially less naval force to protect Freeman's flank. Outside the White House the sleet was turning to rain, splattering against the windows, sweeping torrentially across the forlorn patio. "You've done the job, Douglas. You've knocked out Ratmanov and secured the shortest route to Siberia, but I have to tell you that Intelligence . . ." He paused, and Freeman could hear him conferring momentarily with Trainor and the Joint Chiefs of Staff, including General Grey.

"Douglas . . . Signal Intelligence as well as Human Intelligence confirm the Siberians have moved the Fifth Army eastward, spearheaded by their Thirty-first Motorized Division." He was referring to the famed Thirty-first "Stalingrad" Motorized Division, whose forebears had crushed the best the Wermacht had, causing Von Paulus to surrender the entire German Sixth Army.

Freeman knew that what the president was telling him was that Ratmanov had been the easy part. The hard part was about to begin.

The criticism of Freeman's use of FAE on his own troops was savage; editorial writers across the country lost no time in pointing out that he had lost 51 percent casualties, the highest in any one action since the Tet Offensive and the marines' fighting retreat from Chosin Reservoir in Korea.

"Well, Dick," said Freeman philosophically, running the fingers of one hand through his thinning gray hair while he held the offending editorials in his other, "It's a short step from hosanna to hoot!"

"Yes, sir."

"By God!" said Freeman, his ire rising, slapping the editorial. "In Europe they said the attack on Minsk was the most brilliant since Sherman wheeled and drove through to the sea. Now they're pillorying me. Those sons of bitches always root out the negative. And those powdered pricks hiding behind their goddamn cameras, criticizing us with a five-second clip. If they can't find anything to bitch about, they make it up." He looked angrily across at Norton. "I don't read anything here about that pilot of ours."

"Shirer," put in Norton.

"Yes, Shirer, that's it. Remember him from Korea. Brave man. Went in on the deck to try and protect us. No editorials about what those animals—the Siberian 'elite'—did to him, what they would have done to all of our boys if we'd lost that godforsaken rock.'' He picked up his reading glasses and walked over to the map, shaking his head, stopping, taking off his glasses, and tapping Ratmanov. "They don't think I bleed for those boys, but damn it. Seventy-four casualties, Dick, seventy-four! We lose more than that on the roads every day.'' His glasses were tapping the bunch of editorials in his other hand. "Criticism like this, it's—it's disproportionate. Fecal diatribe. First operation in history where we went in outnumbered ten to one! Yes, yes, the MEU followed, but *we* got 'em by the balls, Dick, and—''

Norton said nothing. Part of being Freeman's aide was the ability to let the general vent his spleen against "rancid reporters,'' whose ego, thundered Freeman, "is ten times as big as any general's I know.'' He paused. "Including mine.''

Norton risked a smile but knew that for the time being silence was the most prudent policy. It was still touch and go.

"For crying out loud, Schwarzkopf lost more than that!''

Norton thought it inadvisable to point out that "Stormin' Norman'' had fielded over half a million men, that Freeman's 51 percent casualty rate for Schwarzkopf would have meant a quarter of a million casualties. But he knew the general was right, too—it was comparing apples and oranges. It wasn't simply a numbers game, and he suspected that in the supposedly cool, "objective'' halls of the Pentagon there was sheer envy of Freeman's grandstand style.

"Well, General,'' hazarded Norton, "you're going to have a chance to prove them wrong about you.''

It was a sobering thought, and it stopped Freeman's outrage against the newspapers and TV editors dead in its tracks. The "opportunity,'' he knew, was Siberia. Siberia to Ratmanov was as a sea to an island, its danger far more widespread and unknown. The "tooth to tail''—logistical—problem alone would be the greatest military undertaking in history.

Freeman held the editorials over the waste bin. "One of these—'' He indicated a *Los Angeles Times* column. "—calls me 'profligate' with my troops, as if I don't—'' The clipping fell from his hand, and snatching his parka he went out into the Arctic night, swearing at a zipper that took too long to engage.

When the cold air hit him it took his breath away, and in the sheen of twilight, filled with the heavy drumming of transport planes overhead escorting the airborne sapper and engineer battalions who were clearing any remaining minefields and the ice crust off Ratmanov's summertime airfield, he saw a squiggle of water between the ice floes, and reached for his field glasses.

In the binoculars' circle he saw a seabird covered with oil, flapping and slipping helplessly on the ice in a futile effort to get airborne, exhausting itself on the floe. Another oil-soaked bird watched helplessly nearby. He thought of Doreen, and how he had not thought of her at all during the battle, of how he might never see her again, and of how many American mothers and sweethearts would think of him as a butcher. But he could not cry—not because at that moment he did not want to or would have been ashamed of it, but because he felt himself constrained by a sense of destiny, of mission. He couldn't explain it to others, but he knew it was true and would not afford him the luxury of self-pity, calling instead to his side Churchill's stirring rendition of the ancient psalm: "Arm yourselves and be ye men of valor and be in readiness for the conflict, for it is better for us to perish in battle than to look upon the outrage of our nation and our altars. As the will of God is in Heaven even so let it do."

The brief daylight of the strait was gone and across the darkness that at that moment seemed impenetrable yet across which he knew he must lead the great invasion, lay Sibir—ethereally silent and waiting, a land so vast, so used to consuming her own, that he knew she would not be loath to devour an enemy.

Back inside there were more faxes of editorial criticism. "Armchair strategists!" Freeman harrumphed. "They're all suffering from Iraqi fever, Dick—the conviction that you can go in against a dug-in enemy and suffer next to no casualties, based on the erroneous assumption that every enemy commander will be as incompetent as Saddam Insane." Freeman held up his hand as if to forestall any objection. "I'm taking nothing from Schwarzkopf. Didn't know what they'd be up against, had every right to expect major resistance. And by God, what those pilots did—our boys and those British Tornadoes going in on the deck like that. Magnificent! Brave as the Argentine flyers when they went for the warships instead of the transports in the Falklands. Course the Iraqis—most of 'em—don't want to die for a madman. But the Sibirs, Dick—'' Freeman shook his head. ''Different breed altogether.''

''General, I don't mean to interrupt, but I've got a marine captain—medical corps—wants to see you.''

''Oh, hell, I told them I'm fine. No aftereffects. Just got a bump on my head, that's all.''

''He insists on seeing you, sir.''

''All right, Dick. Send him in. Meanwhile, I want you to get the invasion book.'' It was a six-inch-thick computer printout of everything from guns to gum that American forces would need for the Siberian campaign. ''I don't want to give Novosibirsk any more time than I have to. Landings have to be made simultaneously and within three weeks. What's the SITREP on the European front? That's where the Siberians'll expect our major push.''

''You're right, General. That's why it's a stalemate. They've thrown in another ten divisions—a hundred and thirty thousand fresh troops, and they're keeping our boys and the Brits stalled. We're still over a hundred miles west of the Urals.''

But already Norton could see Freeman was thinking of the East Siberian offensive, the general telling him, ''We're going to have to make up for a fall-off in navy protection. . . .''

''Sir. The marine captain?''

''What? Oh, yes. All right, send him in. Meantime you can get a progress report for me on that Kommandorsky battle group of ours. I want the *Missouri* and *Wisconsin* pounding the bejaysus out of the air field and the sub bases there. After Ratmanov that's the one forward bastion we have to knock off. Otherwise the bastards'll harass our supply lines right across the North Pacific. *Salt Lake City*'s giving them air cover, right?''

''Yes, General.''

''And find out what the Japanese are doing—whether the president's got them off their ass to help us or whether they're doing another Gulf, sit-on-your-ass routine.''

''I'll get on to it right away, sir.''

* * *

Capt. Michael Devine was a small, stocky man with an M.D. that had given him his captain's bars. It struck Freeman, though he hadn't noticed it while he was on the chopper's stretcher litter, that the captain must have barely made the marine height requirement.

"Captain," said Freeman smiling, "now I appreciate your concern for your commanding officer. Commendable but I feel just dandy. So thank you for coming but—"

"General, that's not why I'm here."

"Oh." The diminutive captain looked even smaller as Freeman cocked his head back in surprise.

"Can I speak plainly, sir?"

"Only way, Captain. Shoot."

"Sir, you requested—ordered—my medics to take you off the stretcher."

"I did."

"I understand they—you argued with them."

Freeman was scowling. "I told them, Captain, to unstrap me from that goddamn contraption so I could get back to killing Russians. That's what I'm paid for." Freeman glowered down at Devine. "What's your beef?"

"General, it took at least forty-five seconds to get you out of that air safety harness. It takes an enemy mortar crew only thirty seconds to bracket us from the moment we land. That means from the point of touchdown to takeoff my men have thirty seconds to load four stretchers litters and to be clear for the chopper's takeoff. The kind of delay you caused us could cost me a chopper, crew, and wounded."

Freeman was reddening by the second. He walked to within a foot of the captain's face, his voice filling the room. "I've never been spoken to like that in my life, Captain. I suppose you're one of those jokers who thinks talking back to the old man gets you kudos."

"No, sir, but I'm responsible for my men out there. I can't run a MUST if half my men are killed." Devine was pasty-faced from the effort.

"Devane, I think you'd better leave. Dismissed!"

"Sir," said Devine, stepping back, saluting smartly but turning about shakily.

For a moment Freeman was speechless; then he kicked the wastebasket so violently that editorials exploded from it. Putting his glasses on he tried to concentrate on the map of Siberia. The railway, that was the key. In '45 Russkies had surprised the Japanese by being able to shift four entire armies from the western front to the far eastern theater in just eight weeks, utilizing 136,000 rail cars on the Trans-Siberian. The gall of that pipsqueak captain walking in. . . . Where the hell did he think he was? Goddamn AMA convention? He snatched the phone. "Dick!"

"Yes, General?"

"That runt of a captain you sent me tore a goddamn strip off me. *Me!* Said I was endangering his chopper crew. How d'you like that? All I wanted to do was get back in the fighting. Said I could have cost him his whole crew—medics and all. Insolent son of a bitch told me enemy only took thirty seconds to bracket."

"Yes, sir."

"Yes, sir, what?" demanded Freeman.

"He's correct, General."

"No, he isn't!" roared Freeman. "It's *twenty-five* seconds to bracket, not thirty. Dick?"

"General?"

"Second that son of a bitch from MEU to my HQ. So goddamned smart he can run all the MUSTs."

"Beg pardon, General, but not as captain. You have to be at least a colonel."

"All right, make him a colonel. Field commission. No, I don't want to hear any flak about normal channels. Remember what Von Runstedt said about normal channels, Dick."

"Have an idea I'm about to find out, General."

"A trap for officers without initiative. That Devane, he's read—"

"Devine, sir. Name's Dev*i*ne."

"Well, hell, Dick, with a name like that we'll have to make him bishop. Walked right up to me and told me I'd screwed up. We need men like that. But Dick—"

"Sir?"

"Not too many."

"No, sir."

* * *

Freeman was now studying the enlarged satellite pictures of the Kamchatka Peninsula, in particular the region about Petropavlovsk where the enemy had built bombproof sub pens in the nineteen-eighties for forward naval defense. For a moment he couldn't find his glasses and, cursing, patted his pockets, making a mental note to have one of his aides drill a hole in the magnifying glass handle. As he was shortsighted in only one eye, it would save him forever searching. No way would he wear one of those chains. He grabbed his parka and told the duty officer he'd be outside.

After the pipeline sabotage, two guards had been ordered by Norton to accompany the general wherever he went, just to be on the safe side—with the stipulation, however, that they must stay well back and make as little noise as possible. Pulling his forage cap down tightly beneath the parka hood, the general walked through snow flurries, head down against the wind and thwacking his thermal overlays with a swagger stick given him by CINCLANT—commander in chief Atlantic—at Norwood, U.K., before he'd left Europe.

Trudging through the snow he was doing what Norton and other aides referred to as his "Moses in the Desert"—meditating upon the forthcoming campaign, recalling, as was his wont, the great commanders of history; not their virtues—everyone knew those—but their defects, their mistakes. At such moments he was lost in a kind of reverie of anticipation and awesome responsibility, and now in the flurries of snow that soon gave way to a steady wind, the thought that stole quietly upon him then possessed him and would fuel all his tactics was a conviction that wherever possible *he* must choose the battleground—not the Siberians. He must force *them* to come to *him*—though it was their country—to fight on the ground of his choosing.

The trick, of course, was how to do it. It would involve doing precisely the opposite of what they would anticipate. The master plan excited him; but then, like the mournful cry of an Arctic wolf, the sound of the ice pressure ridges crushing carried the warning that the unfrozen sea to the south was both his way and his impediment to Siberia. Now that Ratmanov had been secured, marine expeditionary forces could be transported by air and air bases secured on the sparsely populated northern tundra of Siberia across the strait, bases from which U.S. air strikes could be made down the shield of Kamchatka Peninsula. But then what? He stopped suddenly in the snow, the two marine guards looking nonplussed at one another, snow now having been replaced by rain. Old "Von Freeman" was seemingly oblivious to the fact.

He had seen the burning bush. The Pentagon would think him mad, as they had thought MacArthur mad when he had decided to hit Inchon—"The worst possible choice," the experts had told him; as they had thought Hannibal mad for crossing the Alps, extending his supply line against all common sense. And so, too, Schwarzkopf's commanders had been shocked by the idea of an outflanking left hook around the Republican Guard. And there had been the great failures, too, which, as the Chiefs of Staff had said, were doomed and which had ruined many a career.

When Freeman showed it to Dick Norton, the only officer privy to his plan so far, Norton immediately saw the potential for a debacle. "In the middle of winter, General?"

"Remember Frederick the Great, Dick. *'L'audace! L'audace! Toujours l'audace!'* " It was one of the general's favorite sayings.

"Perhaps, General," said Norton, "but he won't be with us."

"Yes, he will," said Freeman, and there wasn't a trace of frivolity in the general's tone, nor in his eyes. His eyes were fixed on the map. "You know what a steeplechase rider does before the jumps, Dick?"

"No idea, General."

"Walks the course," Freeman said, indicating the map. "I've walked the course, Dick." He flashed a smile. "Metaphorically speaking, of course. But I've been with them, all right." His hand swept out over the western front. "The German campaigns, Napoleon's. But I must confess no one's been here: Far Eastern TVD. And right now, Dick, those Commies in Novosibirsk are thinking, how can they outfox *me*?" He turned to Norton once more. "You think they have any surprises, Dick?"

"Be surprised if they didn't, General."

"So would I. But what are they?"

Freeman and Norton, together with the rest of his HQ staff, pored over the myriad details for three possible amphibious landings south of the Bering Strait.

Everything was considered: special forces that might be required for beach clearance, amphibious hovercraft going in over the icebreaker-cleared channels in the thicker coastal ice, assault ships, cargo-carrying choppers, airlift Hercules, attack helicopters, landing vehicles, air cover and close ground support from subsonic to Mach 2 aircraft. Then there were engineer and sapper battalions, supertough plastic piping "fascine"—tubes that could be dumped to fill a trench and across which a sixty-ton M-1 tank could pass, as well as flail and grader tanks to clear mines, and fiberglass-hulled mine clearers for the sea lanes. One armored division alone would need 620 thousand gallons of fuel, 319 thousand gallons of water, 82 thousand meals, and 6 thousand tons of ammunition a *day*. All had to be assigned, integrated into the overall attack plans. Freeman made it his personal responsibility to talk to the catering corps commanders, eliciting individual guarantees that each man in action would receive the required 3,000 calories a day, 4,200 for troops in Arctic battle.

"Kick ass, do what you have to," Freeman told them. "But remember Napoleon: An army marches on its stomach. If any of you forget it, I'll have your hide plus a thousand-dollar fine."

"He's got no authority to fine us—least not that much," complained a cook.

"You want to find out?" asked a quartermaster.

The offended man was shaking his head, pleased to see Freeman was moving on to breathe fire over some other poor bastard. "Those SAS guys were right. It's 'Von Freeman.' "

The general had already heard a rumor about the "Von" appellation and asked Norton if it was true.

"Uh, yes, General. 'Fraid so."

Freeman made no comment and, seemingly turning to a completely different subject, informed Norton that he'd seen some of the Canadian forces personnel assigned with his command wearing beards.

"Hadn't noticed, General."

"Well, I have. I want them off. Today."

"General, Canadian Navy sort of follows Royal Navy tradition. Allows—"

"I don't give a goddamn what the Royal Navy allows. I want those beards off. And if you don't know why, Dick, you're not doing your goddamn homework."

"No, sir."

Sometimes, Norton wrote in his diary that evening, Douglas Freeman could be as ornery as a cut pig. The general, he figured, knew that, like Dracheev, Novosibirsk, in the person of Marshal Yesov, C in C Siberian Forces, had its own surprises; as yet he had no idea what they were.

Though she was thoroughly familiar with the sights and smells of a military hospital, Lana was still unprepared.

"It's not as bad as it looks," said Shirer gamely, his head completely swathed in bandages that held the compress against his left eye.

"I'm . . ." began Lana, having to compose herself after having heard from the doctor upon her arrival in Anchorage that it was possible that the optic nerve had been partially severed. She smiled bravely, spoke softly. "I'm a nurse, remember?"

"Right," said Frank. There was no point kidding one another. If the optic nerve *was* severely damaged, then it would be the end of Frank's career as a fighter pilot. The fact that it was the same eye that had been injured during his time as a presidential pilot didn't make it any easier for him to accept. He knew that Lana could live with it, preferring that he never go back into combat, but, like most of his ilk, he lived for flying. Take away that, he told her, and—

Lana said there was no point talking about it till they knew for certain, and she immediately felt guilty. If it had been any other patient she would have listened, knowing it was part of the therapy, but with the man she loved she found herself instead falling back on the bland clichés of reassurance and then just as quickly putting forth the most optimistic prognosis.

"They can do wonders now. Lasers. You know at one time when a retina became detached—remember the Rumpole man?"

Frank thought she meant the actor.

"No, Mortimer, the lawyer who wrote it. His father had both retinas detached. Slipped a few feet one day on a ladder. Blind for the rest of his life. Well, nowadays they can spot weld the retinas back with a laser. Overnight stay in hospital, that's all. Maybe even day surgery."

Frank said nothing, trying not to grimace with the pain; the Demerol was wearing off. But Lana had seen too many wounded not to have some idea of what it must have been like when the eye had been gouged, literally hanging by its optic nerve, and later when tiny fragments of foreign material had to be scraped from the eyeball. Sitting down beside his bed, she took his hand in hers and for a moment was transported back to her first casualty of the war—young William Spence—and shivered despite her resolve. She forced another smile. "Well, at least I'll be seeing more of you—when I can get leave from Dutch, that is." She tried to make it all breezy, "accentuate the positive," but could see that either Frank hadn't heard her or was momentarily overcome with the pain, or both. His hand tightened involuntarily as a spasm pierced the bloody socket of the eye, striking deep inside his skull somewhere.

"What I can't figure out," he began, shifting position in the false belief of so many patients that movement itself would relieve the pain when it was really a shift in concentration that momentarily diverted thoughts of the pain, "is why did the bastard do it? There was no point to it. I mean—" Frank forced himself up further in the bed, Lana stacking the pillows behind him, staying close to him, gently massaging his neck. He turned to her, and she could see now how swollen the purplish and dark red tissue around the eyeball was.

"No point," Frank continued, "trying to get information from me. I mean they were overrun. Under attack. Damn it! What in hell did it matter what airfield or carrier I came from? Our guys were swarming all over them."

"Vengeance," Lana said simply, her tone pregnant with the authority of experience. She was thinking of her husband, Jay. "Some people are like that."

"Doesn't make sense."

"Doesn't have to, Frank. They get a kick out of it."

"If you're under attack," continued Frank, "you do what you have to, I guess. I mean, I know what it's like in a furball— it's you or the other guy. But, hell, why would someone come back at you like he did and . . . it's . . . it's like shooting some guy in a chute."

Lana was moved by this streak of naiveté in Frank. A few years ago, before she'd been introduced to Jay and was overcome by the poise and wealth of Jay's jet-setting image, she had met Frank briefly and gone out with him a couple of times, when he was one of the "one-eyed Jacks" of the president's elite pilot list. Then *she* would have been—*was*—the naive one, not him. But with Jay she'd grown up quickly—too quickly, she thought sometimes. After La Roche, his sick sex, the beatings and the threatened tabloid smear of her parents should she even dare to leave him without his "permission," she had realized, in a rush of growing up, just how brutal life could be. And now *she* found herself explaining sheer malice to Frank, a quality that was as alien to him as the thought of being grounded for the rest of his life. He was a warrior: a reflection of her dad in his forthrightness, his assumption that bravery under fire was de rigueur and nothing exceptional.

He might be one of America's top aces, a survivor of the MiG attacks led by the celebrated Soviet who had shot him down and whom Frank had in turn downed over Korea, but about men like Jay LaRoche he would never understand. His ideal of honor, like General Freeman's, was in one sense ageless and as old, for all the high-tech machines he flew, as the dream of Camelot. Yet it was a vision that in the end sustained him as powerfully as the image of the shark held Jay in awe of sheer power unencumbered by anything "as antiquated," in Jay's words, "as principle."

It almost pained Lana more to see Frank perplexed by evil than to see him in the trauma of the pain; she couldn't bear to hear him wonder about the kind of cruelty she hoped she had left behind with Jay. She wanted to get him off the subject. "You hear about Marchenko?"

It worked, his attention immediately arrested by the mention of the Soviet top gun. Lana said it as if Marchenko were still alive, which was impossible; Frank's RIO had seen the Fulcrum burst on impact over Manchuria. Unless . . .

He felt his heart thumping. "He didn't get out?"

"That's the story," she said. "Course it could be Siberian propaganda. The rumor mill. You know how they love to—" For a split second Shirer was oblivious to his pain.

"But Anderson didn't see a silk. I mean—" He stopped, casting his mind back. Yes, they had definitely seen the Fulcrum hit. A silent orange blossom against the mountainous folds of snow. "I remember," he said. "I asked Anderson, 'Any sign of a chute?' 'Negative!' "

"Could he have missed it?" said Lana. "I mean, was it a clear day or—"

Frank felt a stabbing beat between his eyes, like someone driving a stake into his forehead above the bridge of his nose. Damn it. Lana didn't know a thing about planes—when he'd first talked to her about Mach she thought it was someone called "Mac." It had become a joke between them: "Mac the Knife!" But in her layman's ignorance of things aeronautical, she had, with the unwitting luck of people who, like his mother, chose a winner at Churchill Downs because the horse had a "nice name" instead of studying the guide to form, managed to hit the bulls-eye with her question. There *had* been cloud, and it was quite possible Anderson had missed seeing a chute. The whole wing could have missed it, high above the stratus, everyone on a high after the shoot, eyes scanning above and behind lest any more bandits should come out of the sun into their cone to even the score.

"You should ask him when you get back," proferred Lana.

"Back where?" It wasn't said in self-pity, but until the bandage came off and they'd done the tests, no one would know where he was going. That was the first problem. The second one was that the SPETS had made it impossible for Anderson to answer anything. Frank felt exhausted, the hospital gown clinging to him from perspiration. He couldn't bring himself to tell her about how Anderson had died, wondering whether they'd found his body yet on a floe. Finding your dead wasn't a high priority when you were on the eve of a major battle. Since the

Siberians were fully expecting Freeman to attack—and were probably buoyed rather than depressed by how close the Americans had come to losing Ratmanov—it was sure to be one of the bloodier battles of the war. The scuttlebutt around the hospital was that Freeman's convoys were underway even now.

"Frank?" She asked him gently, deciding that they might as well hit it head-on after all. "Have you thought what you might like to do if the tests are negative—if there isn't much they can do to restore your—"

"No," he said brusquely, "I haven't." His sudden, uncharacteristic mood change was spawned by thoughts of what he'd do if he ever caught up with the SPETS who had—maybe—blinded him in the left eye for life. He didn't like what he thought of doing and, visibly distressed, tried to evict the thoughts of sheer vengeance as swiftly as an ice hockey forward checking another. But the more he tried, the more persistent they became.

"Don't fight it," said Lana with a prescience that surprised him. "My dad always told me you can't help what you think. It's what you do that counts."

Frank shrugged. Was she talking about what he'd like to do to the SPETS or Marchenko—*if* the Soviet was still alive? Well, he told himself, he wouldn't be doing much of anything if the doc said the eye was finished. It would be home and repatriation. He knew he couldn't explain it to anyone who wasn't a flyer but quite calmly, without a trace of self-pity, Frank Shirer told himself that if he couldn't fly again, life simply wouldn't be worth it. Might as well tell a man he'd be impotent for life.

"Sorry, hon," Lana said, "but I have to go. Get my ride back to Dutch."

"Damn Dutch."

"I know, but with Freeman's—"

"Yeah," responded Frank, "you're going to be needed unfortunately."

When she kissed him she was surprised by the lack of warmth. So preoccupied was he with what the future held for him, his mind wasn't even on sex. "I've asked one of the boys flying the Medevac Hercules," she told him, "to call the hospital here. Even then I don't know when I'll be able to—"

"I know," he said. "I'll get word to you soon as I can."

She didn't trust herself to answer without getting all teary. For heaven's sake, Lana, she told herself on the army shuttle bus back to Elmendorf, he's not dead. But she'd never seen him so dispirited either; more like a small boy sent to the dugout than someone dealing realistically with his situation. Of course, it was never the same when you weren't the one it was happening to. Everyone knew how to deal with it when they weren't involved. But it was because she had loved the boy in Frank that made it so terrible. When she left him he'd looked old. Maybe after his pain subsided . . .

She closed her eyes, gripping her shoulder bag hard as the bus wound up around the ABM sites that ringed Elmendorf, praying for the return of the time during which she had believed absolutely in a benevolent and all-loving God; asking, begging, that Frank's sight not be damaged beyond repair, that he might fly again.

As rounds began for the doctors at Anchorage Hospital, the sun was shining off the Chugash Mountains, turning them a creamy pink in a breathtaking backdrop to the harbor. Over four thousand miles to the west, outside the KMK—Kuznetsky Metallurgical Kombinat—factory, in Novokuznetsk southeast of Novosibirsk, it was midnight. But there was to be no delay.

The director dismissed the argument of the works' political officer that it would be better to exact punishment in daylight, where more people would see it, the director's point being that the offense of the worker, one Dimitri Menisky, talking about the factory work through a haze of vodka among friends, was such a serious breach of security under the circumstances that Novosibirsk would simply brook no procrastination. In any case, argued the director forcefully, the execution within an hour of the man's arrest would have a salutary effect.

Accordingly Menisky, forty-three, father of two, a boy, Ivan, and a girl, Tatya, was taken outside engine shop three, well away from the pile of scrap metal lest there be any ricochet, and, despite his falling on his knees and begging for mercy, was machine-gunned to death while snow poured through the penumbra of the yellow yard light. His crumpled body was left for one hour, this being a concession to the political officer, to make the point among the other workers. It was superfluous, for within ten minutes of the execution every man and woman in the KMK already knew about the fate of Dimitri Menisky from shop three, and no one was going to say anything to anyone outside the factory about what was going on inside.

The surgeon attending Frank Shirer was twenty-nine, and with his white coat wore an air of authority that his baby face undermined. Not surprisingly he tried to compensate by wearing a no-nonsense, Gradgrind-like countenance, particularly in front of an air ace, projecting a stern preoccupation with facts. For this reason some of the older veterans among the patients called him "Detective Joe Friday"—"Just the facts, ma'am, just the facts."

"Well, Major. Fact is, the tests confirm that vision in the left eye is virtually nil. Even with our technology there's nothing much . . ."

Shirer didn't hear the rest—didn't want to. His normally rugged, handsome features took on a slate-gray pallor. While the doctor's voice seemed far off, he was nevertheless acutely aware, as in the rush of a dogfight, of every smell and color about him— a sharp smell of iodine coming from the next bed, the stench of sick from several beds to his right. Yet he looked disbelieving, his mind temporarily rejecting what he had clearly heard; this despite the "fact" that he'd been preparing for it all night. It was as if they had him up past seven G's in the centrifuge, his body clammy with the shock, feeling like a sponge being crushed by an immense, immovable weight.

"So." Detective Joe's voice was floating about the periphery of the spinning, uncontrollable world. "You'll have to be content with flying a desk from now on. Fact is . . ."

He couldn't bring himself to call Lana, the stench of defeat redolent in the hospital's pervasive and cloying antiseptic as oppressive to him as when he'd first entered. He felt his hatred of the Siberians rising and did nothing to thwart the flood of bile, sensing that if he tried to fight it now, hold it back, it would permanently poison him and make him something he did not want to be. Voodoo priests stuck pins into dolls; all he could do, knowing the improbability of ever meeting the SPETS who had gouged his eye, was envisage shooting down Marchenko, the MiG ace becoming the embodiment of all his disappointment and anger. It was unreasonable, he knew, but you had to focus on something.

When the Wave, her soft, full-bosomed perfume reminding him of Lana, removed the bandage to change the dressing, he could see only a watery, milky image of her. In the country of the blind, the one-eyed man was king, but not in the United States Air Force. The "fact," as Dr. Joe Friday had underscored with his diagnosis, was that the USAF did not, would not, entrust a one-eyed man with seventy million dollars' worth of merchandise.

A limey, one of a handful of SAS survivors from the "Rat Raid," was walking up the aisle between the beds, his face a gauze mask. "Whatcha mate? Have a fag?" He offered Shirer a Benson and Hedges. "Course you can't puff it in 'ere. Old Muvver Legree'll be onto you." The gauze mask nodded toward the head nurse at her station. "Tough old bird," commented the cockney. "Ravver fight me muvver-in-law—an' that's sayin' somethin'."

"No, thanks," said Frank to the proffered cigarettes. "Don't smoke." He wanted the man to go away; could never understand limeys properly anyhow.

"Neiver did I—till the punchup started. Miss a drag somethin' fierce when I'm in the sheep dip."

Shirer didn't know what the hell the sheep dip was and he knew the limey knew he didn't know so why the hell didn't he just bug off?

"Slit trench," explained the gauze mask. "Filled wif all kinds o' muck: sheep shit, dead rats. You name it, sport, it's there. Hard to lie in it wivout movin' for up to twelve hours. No fuckin' tea party, I can tell you that."

"Guess not," said Shirer disinterestedly.

"Still, I'd ravver a sheep dip than this lot!" He jerked a nicotine-stained thumb toward his mask. "Fuckin' Phantom of the Opera! Least you got your fuckin' face, 'aven't you?"

Frank knew that JFK had been right: Life *was* unfair, and in a world where thousands starved while you had the glorious privilege of flying, you had no cause to moan. But the limey didn't help—at least not then—with his wisecracking camouflaging his own terror beneath the British mask of self-deprecation. Yet this wounded English soldier was to have a profound effect on what would happen to Shirer.

"You a sky jockey?" asked the cockney.

"Was," said Frank.

"Ah, never say die, mate. Never say die."

The Brit reminded Frank of Eliza Doolittle's father: "Get me to the church on time!" He thought about Lana, about whether they'd ever be able to get married, whether the slimeball Jay La Roche would ever release her. Thinking of Lana, he felt himself having what the nurses called a "tent," the erection pressing against the sheet. He wanted to tell the limey to buzz off; yet he knew what the limey had said was right. You should never say die. But the prospects right then were as bleak as the Aleutians in the winter chill and, like all who are very ill, no matter for how short or long a time, he found it impossible at that moment to imagine he could ever be well again, and that fear was his real terror.

CHAPTER FIFTEEN

Northern Pacific

"QUANTITY HAS A quality of its own," said Freeman in his address to the task force commanders gathered aboard the Marines' LHD amphibious assault ship the USS *Winston Davis.* "It's a Leninist dictum the Russians have embraced ever since the Bolshevik Revolution. Their reasoning is simple: throw enough at the enemy, overwhelm him with numbers of tanks, ships, planes, and men, and some are bound to get through, enough to breach our defenses. Your job, gentlemen, now, and my job when we go ashore, is to stop them. Stop them so effectively that even if a few can get through it won't be enough to impede us. The attendant danger for us, however, is not the Siberians; it is that in stopping them we will adopt an overly defensive mode. That would be a crucial mistake. Our job is to attack, to take Irkutsk just west of Lake Baikal. Irkutsk is the key, gentlemen! If we take Irkutsk our air force will be able to radiate out into the industrial heart of Siberia. Without Irkutsk our bombers' fighter escorts would have to have in-air refueling—distances are too great. So our job is to attack the Siberian shield to get far enough in so that our fighters don't have to refuel in air and become sitting ducks.''

He paused, eyes taking in the collective brass in the ship's rigged-for-red situation room. ''There's another old adage, gentlemen, as true now as it was for Sherman: Offense is the best defense.'' His fist clenched. ''Go forward to meet them. Engage at every possible point. The entire Soviet military philosophy rests upon the necessity of the quick victory before their administrative deficiencies—their overcentralization—constipates their lines of supply. In this their navy and air force are no different from their army. They'll throw everything—everything they've got at us, but if you can hold and advance you'll turn the tide. Attack, gentlemen! Attack! That's the strategy here.''

Freeman's message to the noncommissioned officers and men throughout the Seventh Fleet's task force was much more succinct. ''Nothing in history compares with this battle. Siberia, the only country now capable of imposing its will on the rest of the world, is testing our will. Novosibirsk had a chance for peace and chose war instead. Well, we're going to give it to him—in spades. Now, you navy boys, it's your job to get us there. And I know you will, and when you do, I promise you we'll kick ass from Kamchatka to Kiev. God bless you all.''

There was a complaint from one of the female quartermasters in the task force about the exclusion of women in his address. Freeman was taken aback when Norton so advised him.

''What the hell does she mean?'' he asked Norton, the latter's grimace the first sign of seasickness as the two men made their way up from the mess deck to the open air of the 41,000-ton amphibious assault ship *Winston Davis*. It was one of scores of ships in the task force carrying supplies for Second Army, including the amphibious assault vehicles, attack and transport choppers, and AV-8 Harrier ground support fighters needed for the eighteen hundred marines aboard each ship.

"She noted, General," explained Norton, "that you didn't mention women once in your address, whereas you used the expression 'navy boys' several times."

"Oh, for Chrissake, Dick! Navy gals were the ones who flew the lead choppers into Pyongyang."

"Yes, General, I know, but in the interest of morale . . . We've got over five hundred women in the twenty-thousand-man—I mean 'person'—assault force."

"Yes, yes, all right. What's her name?"

"Quartermaster Sarah Lee."

"Goddamn cheesecake, isn't it?"

Norton could taste the bacon he'd had for breakfast. It was threatening to come straight up, and the quicker he got out to the fresh air of the flight deck, away from the combined stink of diesel oil and recycled air, the better.

"All right, relax, Dick. Won't say anything to offend the—" He paused. "—*lady*. I suppose if I call them 'ladies' I'll be on a discrimination charge."

"Will I put a call through, General?"

"Later—when we go below. But Dick?"

"Sir?"

They were passing through the "light lock," in whose chamber all illumination went out as soon as they began to spin the wheel to open the outer door leading to the deck. Although Norton could not see the general, the latter's tone had changed to one of dead seriousness. "Aren't any females in the tank divisions, are there? I told the Pentagon about that. I don't want any tank crewmen killed trying to figure out how some dame is going to piss in her helmet while everybody looks the other way. Last I heard Siberia's armored don't give the enemy time off for rest stops and I—"

"No women in the armored units, General, far as I know. Support, perhaps, but not in the tanks themselves."

Norton had lied. It had been an ongoing fight between Freeman and the Pentagon since the beginning of the war. There were several women, Norton knew, qualified as gunners, but he wasn't having the commander of Operation Arctic Front suffer a coronary before any of the first three landings they were going to make on the Kuril Islands, the opening stage of the air-land battle. Freeman was silent for a few minutes as they stood on the flight deck, cold Arctic air whistling about them, the salty tang at once invigorating and freezing, stars showing through intermittent clouds but the sky on their westward heading thickening. The sea was moderate so far, but the latest meteorological report showed the state of sea deteriorating the further westward the task force steamed.

"First few hours'll be critical, Dick. As it always is, of course, in an operation of this kind, but particularly here. We need the Kurils for air bases as well as those in Japan if we're going to make the landing on eastern Siberia proper."

Two of the three landings, unknown to anyone but battalion-level commanders, were feints, "Persian Gulfs," so-called because of the Marine feint made off the beaches of Kuwait during the Iraqi war while the Twenty-fourth made their end run around the Republican Guards. Only in this case the marine feints would be to sucker Siberian navy and air-arm elements away from the main landing. Meanwhile Freeman, as supreme commander, had designated the Petropavlovsk sub base on Kamchatka a top-priority air target, the attacks on the sub pens to be launched from Attu Island at the western end of America's Aleutian chain, which curved like a scythe toward Kamchatka, Siberia's sparsely populated protective arm.

Steaming out from Vladivostok, with Admiral Baku in command, was the center of the Soviet interdiction force, the sleek, 910-foot-long, 110-foot-wide, 43,000-ton "Kiev" class carrier *Murmansk*, her deck sprouting vertical/short takeoff Forger A and B fighter bombers together with Ka-25 Hormone and Ka-27 Helix antisubmarine helicopters. The carrier's four shafts spun effortlessly through the northwestern Pacific under the impetus of the ship's 210,000 horsepower. At thirty knots the carrier's speed eastward to meet the American force was aided by prevailing westerlies and the eastward-flowing Kuroshio Current. *Murmansk* was seven knots slower than her opposite number, the 1,040-foot-long, Nimitz class carrier USS

Acheson, under the command of Adm. Charles Burke. Her flight deck 252 feet, her displacement 91,487 tons, she was twice as big as the *Murmansk*, her two nuclear reactors giving her the 280,000-shaft horsepower with which to move her ninety-four aircraft westward. The aircraft were a "medley," as Burke referred to them, of F-14 Tomcats, F-15 Strike Eagles, F-4G Wild Weasels, Grumman Intruders, and a pride of two Stealth fighter bombers.

At first glance the core of Baku's twenty-four-ship Siberian force around the *Murmansk*—her screen including two guided-missile cruisers, fifteen missile destroyers, and six fast frigates—seemed to be outclassed by the thirty-one-ship American battle group concentrated about the USS *Acheson*, with its screen of five 9,600-ton Ticonderoga class guided-missile cruisers, five 11,000-ton Virginia class cruisers, and twenty Truxtun and Bainbridge class destroyers. And the Siberians *were* outclassed—on the surface. This despite the fact that the *Murmansk* carried something deadly in addition to aircraft—namely four twin surface-to-air launchers, twelve vertical surface-to-air N-9 launchers, and eight surface-to-surface, that is, ship-to-ship N-12—Sandbox, 340-mile-range—missiles with eight reloads.

In addition to the Baku task force, however, the Siberian commander had ordered two nuclear-powered, 24,000-ton Kirov class battle cruisers out of Pacific Fleet headquarters at Petropavlovsk. Speeding eastward at thirty-two knots, the *rang korablyna*—"first-class rated"—Kirov cruisers carried fifty-two missile launchers each and ten antisubmarine torpedo launch tubes. They sliced through the swells on their way to intercept the *Wisconsin* and *Missouri*, which were en route to shell the Kommandorsky Islands air base off Kamchatka, from which Freeman did not want to be harassed on his northern flank. The mission of the two Siberian cruisers was to dispose of the old American battle wagons, thus saving the Kommandorskys—after which the two Siberian cruisers would proceed further south to harass the American task force's northern flank. And the American advantage in number of ships over the Siberians was about to be drastically redressed by Baku's use of a piece of equipment that the Soviet admirals, true to the Leninist dictum of quantity producing its own quality, believed would overwhelm more sophisticated weaponry.

Baku, with the formidable backing of his admirals in the Red Banner Pacific Fleet in Vladivostok, had got what he wanted: flotillas of over three hundred relatively cheap, high-powered, highly efficient "littoral" craft small missile patrol and torpedo boats for regional defense. These consisted of the Sarancha class (148-foot, 60-knot attack hydrofoils carrying 60-mile-range SS-N-9 and SS-N-4 missiles with a multibarrel, thirty-millimeter gun for close-in work), the hydrofoil Matka class boats (armed with two Styx antiship missiles, a 76.2-millimeter forward gun, and a multibarrel thirty-millimeter), and Nanuchka class IIIs. The latter was in effect a thirty-thousand-horsepower-driven guided missile Corvette, which, though only 194 feet, 6 inches long, and with a draft of less than eight feet, carried SS-N-9 Siren antiship missiles in two triple launchers and also a surface-to-air N-4 antiaircraft missile. It was the same class of ship that, sprouting a 76.2-millimeter antiaircraft gun and thirty-millimeter close-in multibarrel, had been the spark that lit the fuse of war when it had attacked Ray Brentwood's USS *Blaine* off Korea.

The advantage the *gidro-samolyot*—"skimmer craft"—had, running with or without foil, was that not only did their high mobility mitigate against being hit, but because of their small size, they could weave through the wave clutter that blocked American radar. And their very presence as they attacked the Americans would cause the slower U.S. warships to expend much of their fuel and oblige the U.S. carrier to use up vital fuel in launching sorties to deal with the small, fast attack boats. Thus they would siphon off the U.S. battle group's main aerial cover, including those planes that would otherwise have been designated "strikers" as a prelude to Freeman's amphibious landings. One missile from any of these swarms of small, fast boats would be devastating against any of the modern-hulled American ships.

In all Baku had designated 212 boats to the offshore Kuril defense, and 40 to patrol in the vital Kuril Strait. The latter was crucial for the Siberians' egress out of the Sea of Japan into the Pacific. The remaining forty-eight fast attack boats were assigned to guard the other main egress passage, La Pérouse Strait, between Japan and Sakhalin Island in the event that the Japanese defense force turned offensive under U.S. arm-twisting.

But in the heavyweight division, Baku's major ships were not those like the Kiev carrier, *Murmansk*, or the two nuclear-powered Kirov class cruisers which, unlike the small hydrofoils, would show up on the Americans' radar, but his twenty-nine nuclear submarines—thirteen from Vladivostok, sixteen from Petropavlovsk on the Kamchatka Peninsula—all converging south, most of them already lying in wait, "on station." Three of these were the *Zoltaya Nyba*, or "golden fish," because of their class—revolutionary Alfa IIs.

The extraordinarily expensive liquid-metal heat exchange system of their reactor plants, superior to using the pressurized water system, allowed the 267-foot-long, 2900-ton Hunter/Killers, with a beam less than thirty-three feet and a titanium hull, to be the best HUKs in the world. At 45 knots submerged they were not only the fastest nuclear submarines in the world but the deepest-diving. The Alfa II's crush depth was four thousand feet, its armament six twenty-one-inch-diameter torpedoes fired from forward tubes and SS-N-15s which, although classified as surface-to-surface missiles, were in effect twenty-one-inch diameter, four-thousand-pound torpedo-launch rocket/depth charges with a nuclear warhead having a range of twenty nautical miles. The depth charge, attached to the solid propellant rocket, and released just above target, was capable of killing an enemy sub to a depth of up to three thousand feet as opposed to the conventional depth charge warhead, which could damage an enemy sub only within a hundred feet of detonation.

Faced with the oncoming American task force and the Americans' four-thousand-pound SUBROC sub-killing missile, capable of a longer reach than the Alfa—thirty-three miles rather than twenty-four—the Alfa's safety resided in its ability to be exceptionally silent, thanks to Toshiba Electronics having sold the KGB superior U.S. prop-tooling technology years before.

The Alfa's dilemma, however, faced by U.S. subs also, was that the sub's greatest advantage, its silence, was immediately forfeited upon firing any of its torpedoes or missiles. Once an Alfa, or any of the other Russian subs, fired, the American task force, with superior sonar both aboard its surface ships and aboard its submarines, would know precisely where they were.

Ranged against the Siberian sub packs were the American Sea Wolf IIs, including Robert Brentwood's USS *Reagan*, but as yet the two task forces, while within the 1,600-mile range of the Americans' Tomahawk cruise missiles, were still beyond the navy's "outer zone"—more than 420 miles from one another. This zone was the last in which satellite reconnaissance could be relied on, and no task force wanted to strike and betray their exact position. This was especially so while Burke was taking advantage of satellite surveillance, in particular to program his Tomahawk missiles, which needed precise target vector feed-in so long as the task force was over the horizon. And once any missile was fired it, too, showed up on the enemy's radar and could be "back-tracked" on that radar to pinpoint the position of the ship that had fired the missile, thereby putting its entire battle group at risk.

To head off the two Siberian cruisers coming down from the north, Admiral Burke, in the calming blue light of his TFCC—Tactical Flag Command Center—watched carefully the disposition of his forces coming in from the central battle group commanders to the battle watch station, or T-table. This monitored the large-screen situation display and automatic status board, and through it the old battle wagons *Missouri* and *Wisconsin* were ordered to steam due west to intercept the two Siberian cruisers as their first priority and only after—if the battleships survived—to resume course back north to shell the Kommandorskys, under whatever air cover could be provided out of Shemya Air Force Base at the tip of the Aleutians. Despite all the high tech, Burke knew that with everyone on radio silence this phase of the sea battle would essentially be the same as the battle for Midway: who would launch first?

"Watch for the Tattletale!" he told his air commander. "Once he spots us, he'll relay it to Petropavlovsk control, and all our aircraft must launch—'lock-on'—in unison. Then, gentlemen, we'll quickly have incoming missiles—Soviet style, all at once. Kamikaze. And remember, from different directions."

Burke also knew that if his own combat patrol scouts, on radio silence but using passive radar, found the oncoming Siberians, the latter would launch their aircraft immediately and, in the aerial melee that would follow, there'd be no way friendly fire from the American task force would fail to take out some of his own men.

"Tattletale yet?" Burke asked, looking up at the plastic/crayon situation board, an old-fashioned backup should all computer power be lost during an attack. The Tattletale would be the lead Soviet ship, the scout, which, with air cover and on radio silence, would be well out in front of the main task force, probing. Once he'd made contact with the Americans he would abruptly turn about, heading at full speed back toward his own fleet. The ship chosen as the Tattletale was so designed that it could fire the overwhelming number of its missiles from stern launchers. This was not only to engage the enemy with maximum firepower while hightailing it but an insurance against being confused by the oncoming waves of Siberian planes for an advance American ship. Stern salvos at the Americans were the best insurance.

"Sir!" Out of the rain-riven darkness it was the voice of an operator manning one of the battle group's E-2 Hawkeye advance warning planes, picking up a pulsating amber dot on its AN/APS 150-mile-range radar sweep.

The five crewmen aboard the E-2 Hawkeye were the first to hear radio silence broken in a squall so fierce the copilot could hear the rain that was pelting the plane's radar rotodome that extended above the fuselage, the contact between the slowly rotating dish and the rain producing halos of steam whipped away into the slipstream. It was near the end of the Hawkeye's four-hour patrol when the RIO picked up the Tattletale on the infrared scan and almost immediately heard, "Master arm on! Centering the T . . . centering the T. Bogeys eight miles . . . eight miles. Centering the dot." It was an F-14 Tomcat pilot talking to his RIO, the RIO's voice rising above the fish fry of static, yelling excitedly, "Get the tone! Get the tone!"

"Got it . . . I've got it. . . ." The Sparrow air-to-air missile was ready, its coffee-grinder growl loud in the pilot's ear. "Centering the dot—Fox One . . ." The E-2 Hawkeye radio operator heard a rush and a few seconds later the RIO's excited voice again. "Splash!"

The bogey was down.

"Good kill! Outstanding!"

They had just shot down another Tomcat, returning from combat patrol in the outer zone. It shouldn't have happened—there were "investigation friend or foe" procedures—but with so many aircraft flying and men on the razor's edge, determined not to let the enemy penetrate their defenses, Murphy's Law stalked the night.

The two downed flyers were to be the first casualties of the impending battle of the Kuril Islands. Worse, though the radar operator aboard the E-2 Hawkeye picked up a chute signal descending, there was nothing they could do this far out.

Aboard the Tattletale, a Kashin class, 3,750-ton destroyer with four single rear-firing Styx launchers, no adjustment in heading was made. Whether or not the Americans had spotted any or all of their "owl screech," "peel group," and "basstilt" radars didn't alter anything. The destroyer's job was not to run at the first sign of combat but to stay on a steady course until the Americans were sighted. So important was her function that Baku had ordered her helicopter unarmed, jettisoning machine guns and belt feeds so as to accommodate a "Big Bulge" surface-search-and-targeting radar which, with its 255-mile range, was now locating the exact position of the U.S. task group.

The USS *Acheson*'s flag data display system, or FDDS, in the carrier's tactical flag command center, began to "fuzz," the Siberians clearly dropping chaff.

"Your estimate of what's behind the clutter, Mr. Lean?" Burke asked of his chief electronics warfare officer without taking his eyes for a moment from the blue-white situation display.

"I'd estimate forgers, en masse."

"Fighter cover?"

"Fulcrums. Top of the line—C's."

"I concur. Man battle stations."

"Man battle stations!" repeated the officer of the deck, and now the rough-throated Klaxon could be heard throughout the giant ship, Prifly launching every aircraft it had, the flight deck a rough ballet of red and whitish blue exhausts, drifting steam from the four catapults, and huge shadows of ordnance men who, having pulled the safety pins from the hard-point bomb racks, were holding the pins and ribbons aloft so the pilot could see all the bombs were armed, ready to go.

With radio linkups secured among assault forces, amphibious ships, those who would be the beach masters, choppers, naval gunfire support, and the forward air control officer, Douglas Freeman and Dick Norton waited aboard the USS *Winston Davis*.

"How far are we from the Kurils, Dick?"

"Fifteen, twenty hours, sir, depending on the weather."

"Worst part—the waiting," said the general, his outline now dimly recognizable by Norton as they stood in the chilly, buffeting wind of the LHD's flight deck. Norton's face, had Freeman been able to see, was tinged a light green as the *Davis* thumped repeatedly against equally stubborn swells. "Give me the old terra firma any day," said Norton. It was getting cold on deck, even in their thermal battle fatigues, but to go back into the closed, rolling ship—to be assailed by a noxious combination of cooking odors and recycled air—was more than Norton could contemplate. He jogged feebly to get his blood warmer, but the motion, allied with the peculiar yaw and pitch of the big "fat mother," as the marines called the assault ship, only made him more nauseated.

"Well, Dick, Siberia'll be all the terra firma you'll want." The general paused for a moment or two, listening to the heavy slushing of the ship's wake, and nearby, though he could only see the phosphorescent tails of their wakes, the occasional sound of the other ships plowing through a heavy swell, throwing an incandescent spray of phytoplankton high above the bow that swept back in the darkness and disappeared. "Been sleeping well?" he asked Norton.

"Not too much, sir. You?"

"Yes, but I'm haunted, Dick, by dreams of Siberia. Maps of Siberia—all different scales. Recon photos as well. All keep crowding in on me. I feel—" His voice took on the tone of a father who, though reasonably sure he had done all he could to secure his children's safety, was yet dissatisfied, even fearful—as much as Freeman could be—that he had unwittingly ignored some aspect in the planning. Left something out. "I feel as if there's something missing. . . ."

"Siberians, I hope," said Norton.

Though he couldn't see the general, Norton knew that Freeman either hadn't heard him or was simply brushing his aide's attempt at levity aside, too preoccupied by all the concerns that assail a commander in the hours before a landing. Amphibious assaults—well, they were right up there with pilots on night carrier landings when it came to the number of things that could go wrong. He was chagrined to remember how his own designation of Ratmanov Island as "Rat," in an effort to raise morale, had also been responsible for a logistics officer in San Diego having sent several Hercules-hauled palettes of ammunition to the Rat Islands in the Aleutian chain instead of Alaska.

"I wouldn't worry too much about the dreams, General," said Norton. "Rubbish heap for nonsense, my dad used to say."

"Did he?" asked the general.

"Yes, sir."

"Well, Norton, your father was wrong. You ignore the subconscious at your peril. Remember Patton. He had Third Army poised for the final thrust into Eastern Europe, and he knew the Krauts were on their knees. Intelligence didn't—but Patton knew. You remember why?"

All Norton could think of was being stupid enough to have had a cup of coffee before coming on deck, wondering about his chances of keeping it down.

"The carts!" said Freeman. "Dream was full of goddamned carts."

Norton could sense the tension in Freeman's tone then heard the general's field holster bumping the rail. "Nazis were out of gas, Dick. They were using carts to take away their wounded. The dream told him, Dick. It was in the dream."

Norton heard Freeman's radio crackle. The general was wanted on the bridge.

As Freeman headed through the darkness toward the bridge he heard a roaring so powerful he could feel its vibration. Then he saw fiery tail of a missile, quickly followed by another, spewing up from one of the Ticonderogas' fifty-six cell-box launchers, in seven rows of eight directly forward of the guided-missile cruiser's bridge. Both he and Norton were surprised by just how close the other ships in the carrier's screen were. They watched the bright yellow V of the gas-propelled blast-offs fading into a side-venting column of white flame that soon turned to a dry-ice–like fog that covered the cruiser's deck. Now another missile erupted from the deck, forming the third arc of the triple launch, the arcs shooting heavenward, the heat momentarily creating the illusion of a summer wind. The naval battle that would last for six hours was already joined as Freeman reached the bridge of the *Winston Davis*.

Momentarily blinded by the dim red light of the ship's bridge, he was unable for an instant to pick up the radar relay trace of the Ticonderoga's three eighty-mile Mk 41 missiles whose one-thousand-pound warheads were now streaking across the night sky like fiery comets toward the Siberian task force over fifty miles away. Six minutes later as the yellow arrowhead on the Ticonderoga's Aegis screen and its target advanced toward one another on the middle vector of the triangular cone, the calm, unemotional voice of the Ticonderoga's EWO announced, "Aegis evaluates kill."

In response the *Otlichnyy*, a Sovremennyy class guided-missile destroyer, fired two solid-fuel SS-N-22, Mach 2.5 anti-ship missiles, killing range sixty-five miles. Launched from the *Otlichnyy*'s starboard quad, the missiles were more than twice as fast as the American Standard Missile salvos but were nevertheless taken out, intercepted by two five-hundred-pound-warhead Harpoons in an orange slash that could be seen by the attacking Ticonderoga's starboard lookout and by the only radar still operational on the sinking Siberian ship—the Top Steer/Top Plate combination radar mesh atop the forward mast.

One American missile hit the destroyer between the bridge and well decks, and the Siberians' thirty-millimeter Gatling guns completely disappeared, a smoking crater in their place. The other U.S. Standard struck the *Otlichnyy*'s port side midships just aft of the front dome radars, immediately knocking out most circuits and creating a fire that pinpointed the Siberian fleet's position for the American pilots about to engage a mass of Yak-38 Forger V/STOL fighter bombers. Each of the Forger A's were carrying 3,000 pounds of ordnance on four underwing hard points, including air-to-air Aphid missiles and 2,600-pound Kerry air-to-surface-7 missiles, as well as the much lighter, 550-pound, ten-mile-range AS-14.

But there was never any doubt of the outcome in the air, for even with over sixty Forgers plotted by the *Acheson* swarming toward the American task force, the F-14 pilots alone knew they would "eat them alive." The Tomcats, at Mach 2.34, were twice as fast, their service ceiling fifty thousand feet, a good ten thousand higher than what the Forgers could pull. And as if this wasn't enough, whereas the Forgers had a 150-mile-lo-lo-lo radius with maximum weapon load, the Tomcats' 1500-mile range gave the American fighters that much extra time in the air, a crucial element in the titanic battle between the carriers. But the Siberians, Admiral Burke knew, were not so naive as to believe for a second that they would all permeate the American defenses. It was the Leninist strategy again: if only ten Forgers got through, they would play havoc with the American task force—their targets not the American warships but the amphibious transports. All the American naval firepower in the world could not make a landing without live marines.

In the tactical flag command center aboard the *Acheson*, Burke was told that the Siberian fleet had apparently stopped and was turning about. No one aboard the *Acheson* or any of the other American ships thought the Siberians were withdrawing simply because their radars had lit up upon seeing the Ticonderoga's launch. Perhaps, Admiral Burke told Freeman, they were withdrawing out of the Americans' killing range. But this would only be true for the shorter-range missiles like the Harpoons; the two Ticonderogas and other American ships had twenty-seven-hundred-pound Tomahawk cruise missiles aboard with a much greater range, and the Siberians surely knew this.

The Siberian air armada was still on screen, and now the night erupted. Over ninety-three missiles were fired by the American fleet in less than forty seconds, from every kind of mount, including track-swivel "six-packs," and rows of armored vertical-launch "egg cartons" immediately below each

Ticonderoga's bridge, filling the night with a kaleidoscope of deadly pyrotechnics. So impressive was it that, despite the obvious dangers, petty officers throughout the fleet were obliged to threaten direst punishment—no shore leave—in order to keep some men, a number of cooks among them, below deck.

Aboard the USS *Acheson*, as two white dots moved toward one another on the blue screen, became one, then disappeared, the voice came once, twice, four times in fifty seconds: "Aegis evaluates kill!" There was a cheer from combat control.

"Shut up!" commanded the officer of the deck. "We've just started." From the USS *Acheson*, the last Tomcats, F-15 Eagles, and F-18 Hornets were being hurled aloft to meet the incoming bandits, but now it was recognized that the Forgers were being overtaken by thirty Fulcrum MiG-29Cs.

This changed everything. Burke, however, confident in his air commander's ability, turned his attention to blips now indicating sub-fired SS-N-15s, the thirty-three-mile-range Siberian equivalent of the American SUBROC missiles, beginning their arcs toward the American fleet. Quickly he looked up at the TMS—track management system—that was capable of processing, parsing, and correlating up to fifty-five hundred images per half hour without backlog buildup—when there were no glitches. But readouts were going haywire, and Burke had to reply on the not-so-sophisticated backup "stand-alone" ASIC—at sea independent control—tracking and targeting system. It was enough to give him the sub's approximate position, the sonar/prop recognition giving a computer image. It was a rough one but nevertheless showed a sub composite with bevelled sail sprouting a "five-stick" cluster: Park Lamp direction-finding loop, high frequency and radome masts, with search and attack periscopes. An Alfa II.

"Any change in their fleet's position?" asked Burke, as antisub control, with even its SUBROC having a range of only forty miles at best, fired off two Loral Hycor MK-36 decoys, simultaneously playing out its SLQ-25 Nixie towed torpedo decoy.

"Change in their fleet position?" demanded Burke again.

"No, sir."

"Range?"

"Thirty-five miles, sir."

It was a strange world, Freeman surmised, where, air-locked against chemical and biological as well as conventional warfare, you sat in the eerie blue combat control center, never actually seeing your enemy except for a computer image. Burke calmly tried to refine overall strategy even as his task force threw missile for missile, the Siberian fleet still retreating, its subs' positions becoming less and less certain in the din of props churning at flank speed, decoys and chaff adding to the countermeasures, the latter defending the American fleet yet also making it more difficult to locate the exact positions of the deadly Alfas. If these twenty-one-foot-long, ten-mile range, active/passive homing torpedoes, with their 1,250-pound warheads, travelling at forty-five knots, got through, the U.S. task force would be in a lot of trouble.

"Sir!" announced the OOD.

"Yes," acknowledged Burke, his right hand reaching for the message, his eyes not straying from the deceptively calm blue light of the console left of him where he pressed the "Subord" key. He was checking on the status of his CATF— commander amphibious task force—Admiral Leahy, and the CLF—commander landing force—Freeman, aboard the *Davis*.

The message he was holding told him that a Truxtun CGM— guided-missile cruiser—the USS *Prescott*, had been hit. There hadn't been any trace of a *Prescott*-bound missile either on the carrier's TFCC board or aboard the *Prescott*. The CGM lay foundering, holed at the waterline below the forward 127- millimeter gun turret where a twenty-three-foot-long, eight-foot-wide gash was taking water. Through the hole, dying sailors could see the flashes of the aerial battle, tail exhausts seen as winks of light through the cruiser's plates, peppered as though by a shotgun, on the starboard side. The fiercely burning ship soon lit up the carrier abaft of her where a roaring cacophony of blue flames and bleeding steam catapults indicated the *Acheson*'s flight deck as the last of the Strike Eagles took wing.

The *Prescott* was sinking and fast; the only ones able to leave her were those thrown into the water from the concussion, the sky above them banging, orange-white burst after burst lighting up one of the Ticonderogas like stuttering flashbulbs. The crew of the Sea King rescue chopper, hovering on station a mile off the carrier's stern for pickup should any of the takeoffs go awry, had been impatient to go help the *Prescott*'s men in the water but only now, when all planes were aloft, could the chopper move toward the few men she could spot waving on the cruiser's afterdeck and those yelling in the water in the penumbra of fire.

Most of the 575 men aboard the *Prescott* were already dead, the fires aboard her a crematorium. Those not killed by impact or suffocated by the toxic fumes from fires that had "flash-jumped" throughout the ship—twisted and buckled watertight doors offering no sanctuary—were now dying in a flaming oil slick off the starboard quarter. Others were killed as the white-hot tower supporting the air search and G-band navigation radars crumbled into itself like the skeleton of some enormous animal, sending showers of white-hot metal hissing into the sea.

The enemy aircraft were now closing, U.S. fighters engaging, the background a staccato of victors and vanquished, Fulcrums tangling with Eagles and Tomcats high above the Eagles with the added burden of trying to stop the Forgers. Burke ordered the furball chatter to be taken off PA, so that only the air commander and those immediately concerned could hear it, for fear it would interfere with the concentration of those still watching the enemy fleet. None of the Forgers had yet fired missiles, so the question was, what had gotten close enough, without being picked up either by sonar or radar, to take out the *Prescott*?

"Damn it!" said Burke, so softly not even the radar operator nearby heard it. "Patrol boats. Flares all quarters."

"Flares all quarters, sir!" responded the OOD, and within seconds they had messages, confirming Burke's suspicion, streaming in from every part of the fleet. There were swarms of patrol boats—foil-borne—reports of them closing difficult to hear above the cacophony erupting beyond the island of calm that was the USS *Acheson*'s TFCC—the sound of missiles, massed machine-gun and "pom-pom" AA fire reaching crescendos that drowned the men's voices.

"Forty plus," the OOD reported to Burke, the OOD suddenly thrusting his headset away from him, the crash of a missile hitting one of the American destroyers so loud he was deafened for several seconds and immediately ordered off the bridge, replaced by one Capt. Elias Wilkes, junior, a man whose career, although he had not come up through Annapolis, was about to take off. Realizing they were under close-quarter attack, Wilkes now hypothesized why the Siberian fleet had uncharacteristically "retreated" and why the subs, no doubt lying quiet, props stilled, had thus denied the U.S. passive-mode sonar their position. Suddenly he knew why they hadn't turned.

"Mines, sir," Wilkes told Burke.

Burke tried to suppress his alarm. Mines in choke points throughout the world—that was standard drill. Egress points, like La Pérouse between Sakhalin and Japan, were no doubt already mined by the Siberians. This was understood. The U.S. and their allies—all the world's navies—had long prepared their own egress channels for the defense of last resort. But here— hundreds of miles out from the nearest landfall of the Kuril Islands, an area well mapped and frequently patrolled by NATO's navies? If Wilkes was right—though the small patrol boats couldn't have done it, given their already-crowded decks— it certainly would explain the turning about of the fleet, suggesting that the mines had just been laid ahead of the Siberians. But no mine layers had been reported by SAT intelligence.

"The subs have been seeding them," said Wilkes.

"What?"

"Subs laid them, sir. Thousands of AMD one-thousands. The subs can't lay the AMD five-hundred." Wilkes's head inclined quizzically. "Strange that the lighter mine is more difficult for the sub. Probably the shape of its—"

"How does the AMD work?" Burke shot back. It was no time to pretend you knew everything. "What's the trigger? Magnetic? Acoustic? Pressure?" He understood why magnetic wouldn't get the hydrofoils, the latter consisting of plastic composites and the engine would be too far above the air/sea interface to trigger an acoustic mine. That left only pressure. But Wilkes shook his head.

"Pressure mine self-releases when the water column above it changes, but these hydrofoils probably don't spread their weight over a wide enough area," proffered Wilkes.

Wilkes's guess was wrong. He'd told the truth in part—that the pressure from the hydrofoil wouldn't set some of them off, though three of the fast-weaving attack boats had been sunk by others in the flotilla in the melee of the wake-streaked sea. Few men had a chance to notice the phytoplankton lit up even more beautifully by the intertwining tracer, flare light, missile explosions, and exhaust glare.

What had actually happened was that the foil-borne craft had sped through a protective channel, no more than half a mile wide, ahead of their fleet and the Tattletale, then spread out in a trumpet-shaped fountain, like angry wasps emerging from the safe, narrow channel left by the mine-laying subs. Meanwhile the subs waited in their silence should the American task force find the channel by sheer luck. The Siberians and Burke knew the chance of doing this was one in a million.

"Turn about!" Burke ordered. He had no choice, though he knew the enemy would later make great capital from the fact that the American Seventh Fleet, for the first time in its history, had turned tail and run. But to stop would imperil his ships even more, making them stationary targets for the missiles already being fired by five Forgers who had dived through under cover of an arrowhead formation of Fulcrums.

In running Burke had bought himself valuable time and fought off the foil-borne attack craft, sinking twenty-three. Another two of them were victims of their own missile fire; another was blown out of the water by an American Adams class destroyer. Even so, one of the U.S.'s Wasp class LHAs, an amphibious landing helicopter assault ship a quarter-mile to the right of Freeman's, was hit. Despite the pumps working overtime, the forty-two-thousand-ton vessel was reduced to three knots, with Marines and seamen working like navvies, the smell of their sweat mixing with the burning odors of battle as they strove to shift cargo from port to starboard to even the ship's trim before the pumps, already overheating because of "spare uniform" clogged intakes, gave up the ghost.

Watching the scene through his infrared field glasses aboard the *Davis*, Freeman said nothing. This was the navy's department, and he was too astute a commander not to know when to keep quiet. But Norton could tell the general was worried—as worried as he'd ever seen him. If the Siberians tried hard enough to stop the American force here, how much worse would it be when you tried to land on their soil and with the element of naval surprise completely lost? Two Forgers appeared, white shimmers in the rolling green sea of infrared.

"Inside!" yelled Freeman. "Quickly!"

Freeman saw one Forger disintegrate, the flash of a Tomcat—or was it a Strike Eagle?—streaking by, the Forger dropping toward the *Davis*, its "ODD Rods"—friend or foe identification antennae forward of the armored glass windscreen—glinting momentarily in the darkness, its Tumansky turbojet screaming in a seventeen-thousand-pound reverse thrust, its twin-barreled cannon spitting red tracer, before it crashed into the sea, the slap followed by a soft explosion of phosphorescent seawater that now fell like rain. But in diverting the U.S. task force away from the Kuril landing sites, the Siberian fleet only succeeded in forcing Freeman to shift the axis of his invasion force away from the Kurils south to the Sea of Japan for the main landing.

CHAPTER SIXTEEN

Khabarovsk

BENEATH THE PICTURE of the scantily clad Georgian beauty in the Khabarovsk reading room the standby Klaxon blared. The Siberian pilots, including Sergei Marchenko, looked up at the computer screen and saw a cluster of X's—enemy fighters and bombers rising up from Wakkanai out of Japan's northernmost island, Hokkaido, 370 miles east-southeast. Too far for their Fulcrums to intercept and have enough fuel to return safely. The fighters out of Cape Krilon on Sakhalin Island's southernmost tip would have to engage, but if the enemy got across the Tatarskiy Strait between Sakhalin and the mainland, the Khabarovsk wing would have to go up.

"We should have hit Japan with H-bombs on day one," Marchenko's wingman said. He knew he was talking rubbish—any nuclear exchange would be suicidal—the irony being that both sides had to fight the biggest conventional war in history. But the wingman was afraid. The American air force, though it could never win the war by itself against an enormous power like Siberia, over ten times the size of Iraq, had nevertheless already penetrated Siberia's outer, Kuril/Sakhalin defenses. The best Siberia could hope for in the air was to slow them down, knowing that the truly decisive battles would be on the ground—across the vastness of Siberian mountains, taiga, and tundra.

There was another alarm: more American planes rising from a carrier 130 miles east of the Far Eastern TVD's port of Nakhodka, just over fifty miles due east of Vladivostok. An air corridor fives miles wide and a hundred miles long from Svetlaya on the coast westward toward Khabarovsk was being blasted out by the largest air bombardment since the Iraqi war, the number of sorties in the first twelve hours—launched from air bases from Otaru to Wakkanai on Japan's Hokkaido—surpassing by 508 the 2,000 flown by the USAF in the first twenty-four hours of the Iraqi war. The fighter-protected American bombers were dropping everything from Smart bombs on the reinforced early-warning coastal radar stations to FAEs and in particular runway-destroying cluster bombs.

CHAPTER SEVENTEEN

AS THE USS *Winston Davis* rolled slightly in the swell, Norton looking the worse for wear, Freeman searched for his glasses, couldn't find them, and instead used the telescopic pointer, which he normally eschewed, to illustrate his project. Saying nothing yet to his divisional commanders gathered in the crowded helo maintenance deck, he stabbed at the lower left of Siberia on the steppes between the southernmost extremity of the Urals and the Aral Sea; the pointer then slid eastward along the fiftieth parallel, south of Novosibirsk, on through the mountainous region west of Lake Baikal, only a hundred miles now from the Mongolian border, then further east to the big 350-mile-wide horseshoe bend in the Amur River that formed the border with China. From there the tip moved abruptly up to the far northeast of the map in a right hook that took in the Pacific mountain barriers of Siberia's eastern shield. He ignored the vast central Siberian plateau and river-veined west Siberian plain that was taiga, as well as the wide crescent of treeless tundra that was northern Siberia. "Eastern Siberia, gentlemen," he told his audience, "is all we're interested in—at the moment."

He moved the pointer up and down the long Pacific flank. "Think of it as a hockey stick, the handle being the eastern mountain chain. At the bottom of the stick, in the groove, as it were, lies Khabarovsk, the gate to Lake Baikal and Irkutsk. The Siberians know the taiga is the best place for armor—ours as well as theirs. But first they have to stop us getting through this eastern shield to Khabarovsk—two hundred miles in from the coast."

Freeman's knuckles tapped out an impatient tattoo over the coastal range of the Sikhote-Alin. "Now a lot of these mountains are five thousand feet and up and we'd be nuts to try running armor through deep snow in those ravines. Next to no roads anyhow. One Siberian section with antitank rockets could hold us up for a week. What we have to do, gentlemen, is attack Khabarovsk from the south—here—from Rudnaya Pristan on the coast. Move a hundred and twenty miles inland then swing north for a hundred and twenty miles through the Malinovka River valley road to Dalnerechensk." It was then the impatience of his dreams of endless snow and ice became manifest. "Don't worry about bridges being blown—drive straight over the frozen rivers. They're your roads in Siberia. Then, gentlemen, a two-hundred-mile run north, adjacent to the Ussuri River—on the left flank, the Chinese-Soviet border—to here." His fist banged against Khabarovsk where the Ussuri met the Amur in the lowland forests and snow-covered meadows. "From there it's west, young man. Along the Trans-Siberian rail route to Baikal and Irkutsk."

Norton moved uneasily in his seat. When it was all added up, Lake Baikal was over a thousand miles to the west, and despite the valleys that formed the Trans-Siberian route, the last two hundred and fifty miles would be through high country like the Khamar Daban Range. But Freeman, as if reading Norton's mind, had anticipated his aide's question. "ATO," (air task order), said Freeman, "will be to secure total air superiority from our beachhead at Rudnaya Pristan to Irkutsk forty-five miles from Baikal's western shore." Freeman turned to Miller, general of the air forces in Japan. "Bill, can your boys handle that? Or are they too fat from eating all that damn sushi in Tokyo?"

"What's in it for me, General?" asked Miller cheekily.

"A medal if you do," replied Freeman unhesitatingly. "A kick in the ass if you don't! Have you got what you need?" Freeman asked Miller.

"Well, sir, Intelligence reports that Lake Baikal is surrounded by the most intense ABM and AA defenses we've ever seen. Denser than they were around Hanoi. Compared to what they've got around Baikal, Baghdad was just a bunch of firecrackers."

Norton could see Freeman was getting impatient, smacking the pointer against his right leg. He didn't want to hear all the problems; he already knew them. But Norton knew that Miller was building his case, giving the air force some leeway.

"How long?" asked Freeman, the levity of his earlier comments gone.

"Three weeks, General. Two if you can secure the beachhead at Rudnaya Pristan so the engineers can lay enough matting for an airfield. And we'll have to have airfield perimeter defense."

"Patriots."

There was a cheer, the Patriot still enjoying its legendary status from the Iraqi war. But not with Freeman. He'd pored over the reports and understood that it was the Israeli defense forces who, not sticking to standard firing procedures, had in-

troduced shortcuts that were responsible for the Patriots over
Israel taking out most of the Scuds. But not the warheads. You
could end up technically "knocking out" a Scud but causing
more carnage on the ground when an unexploded warhead came
down with the rest of the scrap metal.

Freeman had ordered in the armored-vehicle-mounted
Oerlikon-Buhrie ADATs. The eight high-velocity ADAT missiles, equally effective against armor and aircraft, had only a
commander/gunner crew and were air portable by chopper or
C-130. With a twelve-mile radar scan, the ADATs had laser-
beam ranging (up to five miles) and optical radar track with
FLIR—forward-looking infrared—TV tracking. And ADATs
could operate while the vehicle was on the move, the wingless
missiles shooting out from the eight-container turret at two thousand miles per hour, target acquisition and aim taking less than
one second.

For further perimeter air defense, Freeman also preferred the
ninety-pound British Rapier—eight tracked missiles on an en-
closed two-man vehicle—because the Rapier's warhead was
made to explode *internally*, not outside the target. An internal
explosion meant you didn't simply knock the incoming enemy
missile off trajectory but actually blew up the warhead in the
air.

Freeman sensed a current of opposition running through the
American units who had been long used to the U.S. Patriot and
Nike-Hercules and the West German Roland. Yet he understood
that it wasn't simply a matter of national pride. Hell, half the
electronic components in the F-18s and Eagles were dependent
on the Japanese electronics industry. No, what the Americans
objected to was that they wouldn't have time to retrain crews.
But Freeman had thought of that, too, and had requested Canadian units from the joint Canadian/U.S. NORAD units. For
once the Canadian Parliament did not debate the issue ad nau-
seam, and the Canadian ADATs team, along with a British-
manned Rapier regiment, was already en route, taking the long
flight from the U.S. west coast to Hawaii and then to Okinawa,
skirting the still-unsecured sea lanes off the Kuril Islands.

"Gentlemen, I want this operation ready to roll in seventy-
two hours. The carrier force that will make the Vladivostok feint

south of Rudnaya Pristan is already underway out of Yokohama. Now I want to reiterate, for those of you who haven't already heard it, that the great Communist weakness is their overdependence on centralization. *Overcentralization*. It grows naturally from suspicious minds, gentlemen. No one trusts anyone else—haven't done so since nineteen seventeen. Why the hell should they change now? That's why it took them so long to shoot that KAL airliner down. MiG pilots had to keep checking with central command so Far Eastern TVD wouldn't think the sons of bitches were defecting to Japan.''

There was a ripple of laughter in the audience as they watched Freeman getting wound up. ''Overcentralization doesn't only play havoc with tactical decisions, gentlemen. It is death to any self-sustaining tooth-to-tail logistical system. You've got to understand that in a Communist system—and I don't give a shit where it is or who's running it—goddamn Stalinists, Marxists, Leninists, and Maoists are all the same when it comes to administration. Everybody's so busy covering their ass, signing forms in quadruplicate, that nothing ever gets done fast enough. Course in war, things speed up, but the *disease*, gentlemen, is in the body politic. On occasion it administers some self-help medicine, but they can't cure it. You've all heard the stories about the factory making ten thousand left shoes and no right ones just to fulfill the five-year plan quota. Well, it's not much of an exaggeration, I can tell you. Now I don't know whether you realize it or not—and every one of you above the rank of colonel should—but no one below a Soviet sergeant is allowed to carry a goddamn map. That should tell you something right there. These are the telling details, gentlemen. . . .''

Norton was watching the officers watching Freeman. It was the general at his best. He had what the troops called his ''George C. Scott look.'' He turned and thumped the map at Khabarovsk so hard that the entire Far Eastern TVD shook, several red pins marking the positions of Siberian divisions popping out, toppling over the Siberian/Chinese border into the vastness of Outer and Inner Mongolia and then to the floor. ''The *details*, gentlemen. Such details are going to win the war for us—if we stay alert to them. But—'' He hesitated. ''That's my job. Yours is to remember only one thing. . . .''

"L'audace, l'audace," murmured a lieutenant colonel of artillery in the back row. *"Toujours l'audace."*

"Speed!" thundered Freeman. "I don't want to get any SITREPS whining about anyone being 'pinned down.' You get yourselves unpinned—and fast—and get on the move again. And keep moving! Is that clear?"

There was the silence of assent.

"I'm not going to pump sunshine up your ass and tell you that there won't be substantial opposition. There'll be plenty of it. This is their land, their home, and they'll fight for it as hard as you would. They've got the numbers—in equipment and men—but I know we have the quality in equipment and men to stop them!" He paused, hands on his hips, looking out at the divisional and corps commanders. "Any questions?"

There were plenty, and Freeman knew it, but they were the kind that could be answered only in the coming battles.

"What do you think, Dick?" asked Freeman as the last of the officers shuffled out. Norton said it all depended on how many troops the Siberians could manage to move east to the coast.

Freeman was searching for his glasses again, patting his battle dress pockets. "Damn it! I can never find those goddamn reading things. Only need one of 'em anyway. Have one of the boys in med corps make me up a single lens."

"A pince-nez?" said Norton, surprised.

"Jesus, no. Look like a goddamn fairy. No, just one lens with something to clip it onto so I don't lose the damn thing."

"A monocle?" said Norton, amused by the idea.

"Fine. Now look here, Dick. Only way we're going to get the jokers on the run is to stay mobile. We've got to keep moving. Keep 'em off balance. Don't give 'em a chance to stabilize anything, from their big guns and armor to their airfields. Bill Miller's boys'll pound anything that looks as if it's big enough for a mosquito to take off from. That'll keep their PVO—air force—occupied. Meanwhile we've got to keep their ground forces off balance. Do the unexpected. Go around them."

Freeman's right hand made a sweeping movement west then south of the BAM—the northern Baikal-Amur mainline loop—

to Irkutsk, just west of Baikal. "Get Airborne. SAS/Delta, air mobile artillery and armored units behind them. Light tanks, APCs, M-1s, multiple rocket launchers, and some concentrated rocket artillery barrages as well. Scatter them to hell, Dick— isolate them. If it's too sticky in one area, then we'll do a Mac-Arthur island hop. Bypass the bastards, attack another unit. Keep them so damned occupied in their rear they'll find themselves fighting on *three* fronts." He pointed all the way west on the map four thousand miles to the north-south spine of the Urals. "British and American forces pressing east from Minsk. Our boys here heading west from Khabarovsk, and our special forces driving them crazy in the center." The general, hands on his hips again, was nodding, satisfied with the plan. "You know about the fruit seller?"

"No."

"Iraq," explained Freeman. "Special forces. Our boys and the Brits. An Arab goes up to an Iraqi HQ with a basket of fresh fruit." Freeman looked at Norton. "He's a Brit in mufti—hadn't washed for weeks. Son of a bitch *argues*, Dick, with the Iraqi commander over how many dinar for the fruit. I couldn't do that. Hate goddamn haggling. Son of a bitch in Carmel tried to sell me a car like that once. It was beautiful. Forty-two Packard. Impeccable condition. Big hubcaps. Anyway, the Iraqi finally agrees on the price. While he's in getting the money, this Brit pushes an infrared stick into the sand. Thirty minutes later, an F-18 attack. Thousand-pound Smart bomb. Not only got the commander but the whole goddamned HQ."

Freeman stood back from the map, a myriad of details running through his head. "Sow havoc behind the lines, Dick. That's what we have to do here. Like those SPETS bastards did to us in the Dortmund-Bielefeld pocket." Whether or not it was the mention of the Dortmund-Bielefeld pocket or the long day the general had put in, Norton noticed Freeman's hands had moved from his hips to his lower back, massaging it, a grimace of pain in his face. Norton wondered if the injury the general had sustained when being thrown out of the Humvee during the breakout was flaring up again. But he knew better than to mention it.

The general picked up the pointer stick, collapsed its telescoped sections to ballpoint-pen size, and clipped it in his battle dress pocket. "Be the biggest air drop in history, Dick. Bigger than Crete. Bigger than Arnhem, and we won't make the mistake Montgomery did. There won't be a bridge too far in this lot." He turned to Norton. "Know why?"

Every general's aide understands that part of his role is to be a constant sounding board for his commanding officer's ideas, but now and then it was nice to be able to outguess them. "You're not going to try to capture all of them?" proffered Norton. "Just enough to screw up their supply line here and there."

The tone of Freeman's voice changed. It was quiet, measured, as if his public persona had fled him and he was talking to his inner self, to his own memory, which he absolutely believed transcended his own lifetime, belonging to another time, to history. He turned away from the map, leaning against the edge of the Khabarovsk/Baikal model, gazing over the now-vacant seats. "Jung," he told Norton, "tells the story of the Yucca moth. 'Flowers of the Yucca plant open for one night only, and the moth takes pollen from one of the flowers, kneads it to a pellet, flies to another flower, slices open the pistil, lays eggs between the ovules, then stuffs the pellet into the funnelled opening of the pistil.' " He turned, his face barely a foot from Norton's. "It does this, Dick, this complicated ritual. Then dies."

Norton looked back at the general, utterly bewildered.

"How do you explain it, Dick? No learning involved. Yucca flower's open for only one night. One night, Dick." He looked back over the empty seats. "Can't have been learned, you see. We call it intuition, by which we mean it is innate—already there, already known, in the brain of the moth. We have that same kind of pre-knowledge, Dick, but we don't know what to call it exactly, so we take a stab at it and say it's instinct." He turned to Norton again. "You see what I'm saying. The moth has the image of the flower already in its brain. Before it's even born. Remember what the poet said, Dick. 'Trailing clouds of glory do we come from God who is our home.' We've already been there. The moth already knows. We know. I know. It was in the dream—the map of Siberia. Something missing, Dick." He eased himself away from the model, stretching, his hands again kneading the small of his back. "It came to me at break-fast. I was going over the dream—damn thing had kept me awake half the night, felt like I'd been on the rack." He turned about to face the huge wall map. "Can you see it?"

"This 'Wheel of Fortune,' General?"

Freeman gave a rough smile, his right hand extended, moving from the Urals east across the west Siberian plain, the central plateau, and then the eastern mountains. "All their communi-cations—all their topographical communications, Dick. Auto-mobile enthusiast like myself should have spotted it right away. Different from any other map in the civilized world. No roads. No goddamn roads, Dick!" Freeman was visibly excited. "You see in the south, from Sverdlovsk in the Urals through Novosi-birsk, Irkutsk, and on to Khabarovsk—no main roads. It's all goddamn rivers, Dick. That's the secret. The bridges. We forget about everything else but the bridges. We blow their bridges not to stop their road traffic but their river traffic. Their rivers are their roads—their lifelines—Dick. Frozen in the winter. Like Lake Lagoda."

For once Norton, too, felt victorious. "You mean the Rus-sians resupplying Leningrad in World War Two. By road from Murmansk and then across the frozen lake."

"Goddamn it, Dick! You win the Toyota and the trip to Dis-neyland."

"Well, I'll be—"

"We collapse those bridges on them, Dick, and it'll be like the Ventura Freeway at peak hour. Nothing'll move."

Norton looked more closely at the maps. Freeman was right on the money. It was so simple once you saw it. Three hundred miles or so east of Chita, itself three hundred miles east of Baikal, there was absolutely no main road into the Far Eastern TVD. "What about the Trans-Siberian Railway?" he asked Freeman.

"With our superiority we'll cut it, too."

That night both men went to sleep more easily than at any time during the previous two weeks. Freeman became somno-lent recalling Churchill's summons to Buckingham Palace after

the Munich crisis of 1939. Finally called to be leader of the
nation in its darkest hours, after having been out in *his* wil-
derness, Churchill had later said he had gone to bed peace-
fully that night, having no fears of the morrow and confident
that "facts are better than dreams."

"I'll take both, Winston," said Freeman, switching off his
bed lamp. "I'll take both."

It had not occurred to the commander in chief of Operation
Arctic Front that dreams are but often one step from night-
mares and that the Siberians had dreams of their own and that
these no less than those of the American commanders' were
rooted solidly in the recognition of certain indisputable facts—
which they would soon give him ample evidence of.

CHAPTER EIGHTEEN

Rudnaya Pristan

THE YAK VERTICAL takeoff fighter bomber diving on the
landing helicopter assault ship *Winston Davis* got off one Acrid
radar homing missile before being taken out by saturation fire
from the ship's two "pope miters," the high-domed, six-
barrelled, twenty-millimeter Vulcan Phalanx Mark 15's that fired
one hundred rounds a second and enveloped the Siberian fighter
in a dense hail of depleted uranium. The fireball that a moment
ago had been the Yak now hit the LHD, the Yak's starboard
wing's Koliesov/Rybinak vertical takeoff lift jets slamming into
one of the forty-thousand-ton ship's five antisurface guns, sending
white-hot shrapnel whooshing through the air, killing the bridge's
port lookout, and raising fears among the two thousand marines
below that if the twelve thousand tons of aviation fuel were hit

they'd all be incinerated within a matter of minutes. As the shock of the impact continued to reverberate deafeningly through the jam-packed half-deck hangars below, a fully equipped battalion, gathered about its palletized supplies, which took up 150,000 cubic feet of the ship's huge interior, waited anxiously for the landings that might or might not happen depending on the outcome of the great naval battle now swirling and crashing about them.

What Admiral Burke feared most was the Siberian fleet's two ultramodern guided-missile cruisers, now still over two hundred miles away but racing south at flank speed to intercept him on his right flank. His only hope was that the two old Iowa class battle wagons, the *Missouri* and the *Wisconsin*, would stop them. But it was seen by Burke's commander as a forlorn hope. And indeed because of the two ships' age, despite weapons modernization, most of the officers in Burke's fleet had serious doubts about the behemoths of another age being of any use in the high-tech war.

There were those, like Adm. John Brentwood, who, joined by others in the U.S. DOD—Department of Defense—and the British MOD—Ministry of Defence—were preoccupied by an unanswered question: Would the Tomahawk missiles aboard the Iowa class battleships be more than a match going up against the Kirov guided-missile cruisers' SS-N-19, three-hundred-mile-range, four-thousand-pound missile? The latter, as well as being over a thousand pounds heavier than the Tomahawk, was more than three times as fast. The American cruise missile's speed, at a subsonic 520 miles per hour, made it a slowpoke compared to the over-1700-miles per-hour Siberian missile. It was a difference that UK Liaison Officer Brigadier Soames at the White House referred to, with typical British understatement, as "a slight advantage for the Sibirs."

The undeniable advantage of the Siberian's speed allowed the Kirov cruisers to wait until the *Missouri* and *Wisconsin* had fired two Tomahawks apiece, two for each of the Siberian cruisers; they had ample time, even in the split-second world of over-the-horizon electronic warfare, to respond. It was a luxurious five seconds in all after each Tomahawk, in a feral roar and with its peculiar "ass-dragging" motion, skidded out from one of the eight armored box launchers like a huge, vertical cigar moving sideways, the missile arcing high enough to afford Siberian radar a glimpse and to get a back-track vector, before the American missile dropped in altitude.

At wave-skimming height, the Tomahawk's cigar-tube shape began its metamorphosis, its tail unfolding, stubby wings extending and air intake popping up to gulp air, allowing the missile's own engine to take over as the rocket booster finished. Looking now more like the V-1 buzz bomb from which it had been derived, the missile's 1,000-pound conventional warhead, replacing a 450-pound nuclear tip, followed its preprogrammed terrain-matching contour guide which afforded the Tomahawk a CEP—circular error of probability—of only 250 feet. This was normally not critical for most large land targets, but for a moving target at sea it raised the odds considerably.

The captain of the nuclear-powered Frunze IV had personally picked up on the Tomahawks' firing, receiving details of the Tomahawk's trajectory from a Bear recon aircraft out of the Kommandorsky Islands to the north. In response the Frunze IV and the other Siberian cruiser had each launched five SS-19 missiles from hatches forward of the cruiser's Gatling gun turret and from both port and starboard stations.

In all, ten missiles were now streaking toward the *starye amerikanskie sufi*—"old American bitches"—as the *Missouri* and *Wisconsin* were contemptuously referred to. The sinking of either one—or hopefully both—would only add to the impression in Novosibirsk of an overwhelming American naval defeat, the Americans still withdrawing south, one of the battle group's foam-filled minesweepers already sunk. While her weight and nonmetallic fiberglass hull had not set off any pressure or magnetic mines, the sound of her props had triggered acoustic mines that had literally blown her clear of the water, her spine snapped, her foam-filled interior giving off a thick, oily, and highly toxic smoke, the two halves of the sweeper taking longer to go down than they would have without the foam that kept them floating about like some ancient fire ships sent among an enemy fleet to sow confusion and break up its order of battle.

By now the *Missouri*'s two Tomahawk cruise missiles were locked onto by the Frunze IV's "Top Pair" three-dimensional, long-range radar scanner. They were intercepted eleven miles out by a cluster of type 4, 6, and 9 missiles fired by the Frunze.

It was impossible to say what type had downed one of the two American missiles, so many target and antitarget vectors were converging in the general area; so many Siberian missiles, in fact, that it was likely, given their inferior guidance system, that it had been a case of "fratricide"—debris and shock waves from one missile altering another's course, preventing it from making a direct hit. Either way, one of the Tomahawks was down.

The second Tomahawk hit the Frunze IV starboard midships, the explosion shattering all glass on the bridge, decapitating two officers on watch, while a great hole, over ten feet in diameter, now gaped at the waterline. The dark, inky sea turned to a frothing cauldron as it churned into the cruiser, the enormous intake of water causing the ship to roll sharply starboard and capsize—sinking in less than eleven minutes, all 794 hands lost. Most drowned in the first five minutes or so; others swam through the ice-cold sea of oil and flotsam to a few inflatable rafts where they hauled themselves aboard only to die shortly of pneumonia, coughing unceasingly, lungs coated in oil—in effect, drowning in their own fuel.

Of the ten surface-to-surface SS-19s that the cruisers had fired at the *Missouri* and *Wisconsin*, two struck *Missouri* and three the *Wisconsin*. Three of the others were shot down by American Harpoon and Vulcan AA fire; the remaining two exploded in the sea, sending enormous spumes of white into the tracer-streaked night. And now the argument that had raged for years over the advisability of keeping the old battle wagons was answered.

Both had seen active service, particularly the *Missouri* in the Iraqi war, but not ship-to-ship confrontations, and the moment the two battleships were struck, there was in the Pentagon an almost unseemly rush to hear what had happened. What happened was that of the two missiles that hit the *Missouri*, one exploded starboard side against the bridge, the other made a wide-angle hit on the stern deck that took out two of the battleship's four SH60-Lamps helos; the other two helicopters were aloft on antisub watch.

When the first missile hit the bridge it killed two men in number two turret from sheer concussion, its fireball so intense that the explosion took out four of the five-inch guns on that side, killing twenty-six men while engulfing one of the stern-facing five-inch guns, sending a sheet of dense, curdling fire rushing along the starboard side as if some enormous flame-thrower had belched, the smoke and flame spilling over the stern's triple sixteen-inch turret.

It did not destroy it but, because of the heat, made the turret, even with its air conditioning, uninhabitable for the next half hour as fire hoses crisscrossed in dense smoke to get the deck fire under control. But the main concern was the missile that had hit the starboard side of the bridge, nearer the ship's combat control center. It was known that no air-to-surface missile, such as the Exocet, which could smash through any of the lighter-armored modern ships, could penetrate the battleship's armor belt, but now the surface-to-surface Siberian missile, striking the seventeen and a half inches of thick class A steel that girded the bridge, failed to penetrate.

Inside the bridge two officers would lose their hearing forever from the impact, and several others would also be repatriated, suffering permanent inner-ear damage. But no one in combat control was killed, and while the navigation electronics were knocked out, the "stand-alone" fire control for the two forward turrets, with three guns apiece, and the fire control for the three guns in the lone stern turret were unaffected, despite the fact that the latter was still not visible because of the thick, choking, white smoke that had replaced the black as the fires were being doused; the urgent *thump, thump, thump,* of the pumps was audible to the *Wisconsin* several miles off the *Missouri*'s starboard quarter.

The *Wisconsin* sustained damage to two of her four shafts from the missile that had hit the stern's solid 12.5-inch-thick steel armor belt, causing spider fractures. But here, as aboard the *Missouri*, bulkheads had held. The "old" battle wagons, once so disparaged by the "bottom line" accounting experts as outmoded "floating nostalgia," had more than once proved their resilience to enemy missiles, their armor belts far thicker than the thinly skinned, higher-tech cruisers and destroyers of more recent years.

As if this weren't enough, they were now about to do what no other ship in the fleet could. In addition to its array of Tomahawk missiles, Vulcan twenty-millimeter Gatling guns, and five-inch, dual-purpose guns, the old ladies' nine sixteen-inch guns administered the coup de grace to the USAF's bombing assault out of Attu against the Kommandorsky Islands. Each of the eighteen 16-inch guns of the two battleships hurled a 2,700-pound shell, the equivalent of throwing a Volkswagen Beetle twenty-three miles. And they did it thirty-six times a minute. The crews of the twenty-four smaller five-inch guns had to wait until the battle wagons got closer to the islands. The five-inch guns were only able to throw seventy-pound shells fourteen miles, by which time *Missouri*'s Harpoon missiles had dealt with three of the hydrofoils sent out from the Kommandorskys; the *Wisconsin* took out six.

The Siberians' mistake in having concentrated all their available air power from Kamchatka south against the American battle carrier group and losing the fight for air superiority was now compounded by the terrible punishment the two American battleships were meting out to the Kommandorsky airfields, killing any hope in Novosibirsk of using the Kommandorsky Islands as an advance carrier for the MiG-29s, the inferior V/STOL Forgers in Baku's fleet unable to stop Burke's task force from protecting Freeman's landing.

Worse still for the Siberian TVD, Far Eastern Military District HQ in Khabarovsk, was the dilemma now confronting them. Should they concentrate their forces south nearer the Sea of Japan—Japan being the Americans' carrier in the far east, particularly the island of Hokkaido; or should they move those forces already in the south north to reinforce the Kuril garrisons? But this would be in vain if Freeman decided, in light of the terrible air offensive now underway against Sakhalin, to bypass the Kurils and Sakhalin and actually invade the mainland.

Splitting their forces violated fundamental military doctrine, and particularly Soviet military doctrine, of concentrating all your forces, of amassing overwhelming strength before attacking. Even now, Novosibirsk was receiving information from the four Kuril Island Strait monitoring stations that the enemy—most likely the American navy's Seals—was probing the straits, possibly readying to detonate the mines in one or all of the vital gateway channels between the Pacific and the Sea of Okhotsk.

But in Novosibirsk, Marshal Yesov knew that if the Americans' activity around the straits was a feint and they kept moving south, the Siberian garrisons on the Kurils and Sakhalin might simply be bypassed. Yet if the garrisons weren't maintained, the Americans might decide to land there as a springboard for an attack on the mainland.

General Ilya Stavkin, C in C Fifth Army's shock artillery division on the Pacific border, which included regiments of tactical missiles, self-propelled artillery, and massed *Katyusha*—mobile barrage rockets—approved of Yesov's strategy, favoring "scorched earth" from the coast inland as far as it took to make what the Americans called their LOTS—logistics over the shore—supply problems as critical as possible. It had worked against Napoleon and the Wermacht—why not against Freeman? Better to *obmanut amerikantsev*—"suck the Americans in"—and give them what their whole national psyche was worst prepared for: not a quick campaign but a long, drawn-out one. Soviets could wait. The usually somber Yesov told his staff a joke to illustrate the point. "You won't be able to get your new car for ten years," the Moscow salesman tells a buyer.

"When will it be delivered?" asks the buyer. "Morning or afternoon?"

"Are you crazy?" says the salesman. "You have to wait ten years for your car and you want to know whether it will be delivered in the morning or afternoon? What's the difference?"

"Well, the plumber's coming in the morning."

The Americans couldn't wait for anything, Yesov told them; they like "drive-in, drive-out" wars. No, the strategy was, let their bombers out of Japan and the Seventh Fleet level the docks and sub pens of Vladivostok. Let their troops land where they wanted now that Baku had failed to stop them. Besides, Novosibirsk didn't know where they were headed and so couldn't do much about it. Suck them in and let the Russian winter and Chernko's surprise do their job. And harass them all the time as Giap did in Vietnam. The Siberian army had many more soldiers and much better equipment that Giap ever had. And he won.

It was during this conference of Yesov's that the Siberian Fifth's Stavkin, a man not easily excited, was first told of Chernko's secret.

"Bozhe Moy!"—"My God!" Stavkin said, leaning toward his colleague, a general who commanded the Chinghan Sixth Guards Tank Army. "The Arctic Foxes'll be well fed this winter." He meant fat with American dead.

"Da!" agreed the Chinghan commander, whose titanium-capped teeth looked as tough as his T-90s. "This Chernko business will finish them."

Stavkin listened to Yesov outline his plans for the withdrawal in detail, stressing the importance to Khabarovsk and Chita HQ—further west of Khabarovsk—of coordinating the tactical withdrawals. But Stavkin had difficulty concentrating on the details, his excitement at being one of those who would defeat the legendary Freeman, the Freeman of Minsk and Ratmanov fame, making it difficult for him to sit still. Yesov, a thickset, bullish-looking man, his face, as the saying went, always the color of the party, was now pounding it into them that the Americans had an obsession with high ground. "If the Americans do not gain the high ground," he said, "they immediately become depressed and need tranquilizers!"

This was cause for great laughter throughout the Siberian officer corps.

"Unopposed?"

"Unopposed, sir," reported Norton, his face flushed with the effort of having run up the stairs to the LHA's bridge to confirm what the marines had been reporting from the LCTs as they went into Rudnaya Pristan. Norton's face was slack from the sense of relief.

"No fire at all?" pressed Freeman.

"Oh, a little," Norton conceded, "but small arms, General. Looks like Buryat militia. Local units. And our UAV (unmanned air reconnaissance vehicle) has spotted only six 122-millimeter howitzers. They're in firing position—high on their swivel trailer mounts but no trucks anywhere. And they're not self-propelled. Firing's sporadic, too."

"By God!" said Freeman, his mood suddenly the opposite of all those around him on the LHA's bridge, his eyes narrowing as he took off his helmet, running his hand through the gray shock of hair. "I smell a big fat Commie rat here, Dick. What's

Yesov up to?'' He turned around to the LHA's captain and the marine commander. ''Yesov's a crafty son of a bitch. Saw some of his work in western Europe before he joined Siberian command.''

''General,'' said Dick Norton, ''has it occurred to you that after Ratmanov and the beating they've taken trying to stop Burke's task force that they might be having second thoughts?''

Freeman glowered at him, as a coach might a player who'd opined that the other team looked like they'd had enough.

''What the hell's the matter with you, Dick? Some of those goddamned Aphids hitting us softened your brain? If this is a retreat, it's tactical.'' Freeman took up his field glasses, scanning the shoreline. ''The one thing I want to make damn sure of is that there are no more mines around here. We wasted enough time on that bullshit already. Talking to some of those Seals who went in off of a Sea Wolf_sub when we thought we might try the Kuril Straits. They told me the Siberians had every mine down there you could think of—magnetic, pressure, acoustic. One of the guys told me he figures the sons of bitches have probably got hamburger-sniffing mines.''

''They got any general sniffers down there, sir?''

It was an inappropriate remark, and Norton knew it the moment he'd said it; but it was too late—out before he could stop himself, so buoyant was his mood at the news of the landings being virtually unopposed.

''So what's a general sniffer?'' asked Freeman, still scanning the shoreline with his binoculars.

There was an awkward silence, the marine battalion commander winking at his second in command to ease the tension. Everyone was relieved; it was the kind of reverie that overtakes men who one minute are convinced they're facing death and the next find out they are not, or at least that it has been postponed.

''Well?'' pressed Freeman, turning the binoculars further down the beachhead. ''How do you sniff a general?''

''Ah—hot air, sir,'' Norton replied sheepishly.

Barely lowering the binoculars, Freeman glanced down at the map. ''Yesov could have mined the road leading inland.''

''Pretty deserted beach out here, General. Unless they knew your exact plans they wouldn't have time for that. First they'd have to get the mines down here. Your point about centralization and . . ."

"Yes, yes," said Freeman impatiently, still unnerved by the lack of opposition. "Subs?" he said suddenly.

"Still outside, sir. That's one thing we're sure of. MAD overflights from the P-3s have shown they're still outside. No way they want to get trapped up in here with us commanding the Kuril entrances and our air force ready to hit them if they try to run through the Japanese Strait. No, sir, they're outside—waiting to hit our supply lines, especially the Alaska-California oil runs."

"What are our POL reserves in Nippon, Dick?"

Norton, fortunately, had the petrol, oil, and lubricant figures in his head. "Three months, with severe rationing in Japan and depending on our rate of advance."

"Well, the Japs've done a good job of burying their oil reserves. Less, o' course, the Siberians have another Sorge who knows where they are."

Norton was alarmed. Richard Sorge had been the German Communist agent who, posing as a Nazi newspaper man in Tokyo during the Second World War, had thrown flamboyant parties for the Japanese VIP's on his yacht in Tokyo Bay while down below he was sending messages to Moscow, the most important one being that he had discovered that the Japanese weren't going to attack Siberia's flank after all but were heading south to take Hong Kong, Malaya, and on to Australia. This single piece of information allowed the Siberian reserves, a million fresh troops, to be withdrawn from Siberia and sent into Stalingrad where they turned the tide against Von Paulus's Sixth Army. Even so, it wasn't the mention of Sorge that worried Norton but the general's lackadaisical use of "Japs" instead of "Japanese." Lord, if the Japanese press got hold of that, outrage would rain down on the Americans like fléchettes.

"Japanese, sir," Norton reminded him.

"What? Oh, right. Well, let's hope their depot sites are secret."

Unfortunately the hopes of a general do not carry any more weight than those of the humblest private. Every single depot, from the two within thirty miles of Tokyo's sacred bridge across to the emperor's palace to the four depots on the west coast, had been known to Chernko's agents for years. If the Siberian air force could not penetrate the Eagles and Falcons of the U.S. in Japan then SPETS-recruited Communist agents from the Japanese underground "Red Army" could and did penetrate the POL dumps' defenses. Within the next seventy-six hours, as Freeman's troops poured ashore virtually unopposed at Rudnaya Pristan, already stretching their supply line, four of the six Japanese POL depots were hit. Only two of the attacks succeeded due to a vigorous, some said fanatical, defense by the Japanese defense force, which paid the price with twenty-nine dead and another sixteen wounded. Even so, the SPETS attacks reduced Freeman's POL supply to six weeks.

In New York oil prices set an all-time high, with a ten-dollar increase per barrel. Also, fears that the Siberians might use chemical weapons as a last resort drove up the price of Fuller's earth, used in decontamination field hospitals, while shares in Mediclean 2000 water-spray-vacuum decontamination MASH units and in activated charcoal dressings rose dramatically, many of the companies owned by Jay La Roche Pharmaceuticals. ABC's "Nightline" charged that the rumors of impending use of CBW—chemical biological warfare—by the Siberians were false, planted by unscrupulous war profiteers to drive up their shares, not only in America but abroad.

The allegations were false, however, and because of this, subsequent rumors that nerve-gas–resistant bromide pills had been laced with cyanide by KGB sleepers were vigorously denied. They were proven true, however—Freeman's first casualties on the beachhead at Rudnaya Pristan being a marine platoon who, mistaking colored tear gas fired by the Yakut militia as a possible CBW attack, swallowed the bromide pills and died agonizing deaths as their central nervous systems went into spasm, their ordeal end with defecation and suffocation. Bromide company shares collapsed, but for Jay La Roche it was like a shark sniffing blood. Through conduits on the Shanghai Free Trading Area stock exchange, he bought all available shares of Chinese companies licensed by the Chinese government— seventeen in all—concentrating only on those who made cherry food coloring, used for everything from cherry candy to cherry-flavored fruit pies for export. The cherry flavoring also contained an essential ingredient for the making of lethal BZ gas, which the Soviets had already used to kill many of the rioters in dissident republics.

The news report in the morning was followed by an FBI announcement that "invoking the president's suspension of civil rights, a full counterintelligence investigation was being made of the bromide scandal." By breakfast time the following morning, now 9:00 P.M. in eastern Siberia, the bromide pill incident had been overshadowed by the shock that a General Dynamics factory in California, manufacturing the F-16, had been attacked. No guards were killed, but in the sheds on which the mortars had landed, eleven damaged F-16s were write-offs. The cost of testing even marginally damaged planes and the intricate microchip circuitry of the war planes was considered to be both ethically and financially unacceptable.

Meanwhile the La Roche tabloids had hit the streets, screaming, BROMIDE BARRAGE KILLS OUR BOYS!

Jay La Roche loved the headline. Circulation of his tabloids would skyrocket in every supermarket in the country, and he was making a killing on the stock market, both from toxic chemicals used in the war and their antidotes.

Freeman had been badly shaken by the poisoned-pill disaster and although pressing on, leading the marine column in his Humvee along the road from Rudnaya Pristan, he was waiting for the Siberian tiger to bite. But so far Second Army's spearhead column of thirty M-1 A-1 sixty-ton battle tanks rolled unmolested.

Then, approaching Dalnegorsk, twenty miles inland and northwest of the beachhead, the men in Able Company, Second Battalion of the seventeen-thousand-man MEF First Division heard five or six muffled explosions on the mountains on either side of the Rudnaya River road, the steepest mountain on their left. Then they saw the mountainsides begin to move as thousands of tons of snow avalanched down, smashing into and covering the middle of the column, burying over fifty marines.

Freeman immediately ordered air strikes in from the carriers standing off in the Sea of Japan, but the pilots could not bomb for fear of setting off more avalanches—one of the first lessons of the Siberian campaign. Besides which there were no targets. If there had been any Siberian sappers around, left behind to detonate the avalanches, they were now gone.

It took four hours to dig all the men out, Marine Corps tradition demanding that they try, as far as humanly possible, to bring out their own dead. But not all could be recovered, and Freeman ordered the column on to Dalnegorsk, which the pilots found easy to locate, using the thousand-foot smokestacks as a reference point. By now engineering corps officers had radioed Freeman that there had apparently been no enemy units on the mountainsides, the charges having been set off by pressure-triggered circuits when the M-1 tanks rolled over them. By the time Dalnegorsk and the road to Krasnorechensk and Zavetnoye, on the way to Bikin and Khabarovsk, had been secured, it was discovered by the advance marine patrols, covered by low-flying Falcons and tank-killing A-10s, that the towns had been abandoned. Not a living soul was left, all livestock had been butchered and the towns set afire in the last few hours. Freeman looked at Norton worriedly. "In Normandy, twenty miles in six hours would have been a miracle. Here, with these distances, it's nothing. It's worse than nothing, Dick. It's disastrous!"

Norton remained silent.

"This isn't a Siberian feint," declared Freeman, pulling his collar up against the bitter cold, steam rising from the lead tank behind his Humvee. "This is our fuckup. A monumental, Grade A, mega-sized fuckup! And damn it!" Freeman was standing up in the back of the Humvee, left hand resting on the .50 caliber machine gun, right hand crunching and flinging ice disgustedly away. "It's my damn fault!"

The cold was so intense that it made Norton's throat sore just to try to speak, but in all fairness he felt he should point out that much of it, the weather, for example, was beyond any general's control. Behind the Humvee the stationary M-1 was idling, keeping up the revs, the gas turbine's purring remarkably low for such a powerful engine. Even so it was eerily unsettling in the great white valley, the high ground far above them, Norton unable to shake the conviction that the mountains were waiting, biding their time to fall in on them once more.

"At this rate," said Freeman, "we'll be old as Canadians in Florida before we get to Bikin, goddamn it! Dick, we've got to get out of this hole. We're not on first base yet, and we're huffing and puffing like—" It was then that the Apache strike choppers appeared, over thirty of them, swarming up the valley like angry gnats, going on ahead to secure the road as far as possible while engineers sent a remote-controlled "sniffer" vehicle ahead.

The sniffer slowed the advance further but was safer. And then Freeman got his surprise. It came from a marine intelligence officer in the advance patrol who was bright enough to note the sight of hastily left meals and some livestock not slaughtered but peering out dolefully from the elaborately carved white window shutters of their barns, which looked better than most of the ramshackle houses nearby. What this told the marine, and thus Freeman, was that the Siberian withdrawal had been so rushed that even the traditional Siberian scorched-earth policy had been abandoned in their flight, a few militia men probably being the only ones who had had time to rig up a set of avalanche charges. Even so Freeman sent demolition teams ahead, suspecting that the hurried evacuation itself might be a Siberian bluff, though he also had a hunch that the marine lieutenant's observation, given that they'd landed in such a sparsely populated area, was correct.

There were no more demolition charges found for several hours, and as suddenly as they'd been halted earlier, the marine tank column and mobile infantry leading Second Army picked up the pace. Freeman, the bit between his teeth, ordered full speed, the armored personnel carriers and supply trucks finding themselves on hard, tank-packed snow, the M-1s cruising at thirty-five miles per hour, Freeman holding them back from their maximum of fifty miles per hour only in order to get maximum mileage for minimum fuel spent. When demolition charges were sniffed out, the engineers quickly laid pipe charges, and the column had only to stop for a matter of minutes before speeding on again.

Within four days, while he had not equalled the rapid advance attained by McCaffrey's Twenty-fourth Mechanized Infantry Division in Iraq or got anywhere near equalling Rommel's armored run in France of two hundred miles in one day, he *was* in Bikin, pausing only to refuel, a blizzard swirling about him making for an anxious time but giving the U.S. pilots, with their more sophisticated electronics, the edge in instrument flying. Though if the Siberians' night-fighting equipment wasn't as good as the Americans' there was nothing lacking in their courage. While the refueling was in process, the armored column could hear a distant thunder high overhead, massive B-52 raids out of Okinawa, the planes still within Khabarovsk's AA missile envelope but protected by Eagles and Falcons as they pounded the city with more ordnance, including Smart bombs from lower-flying F-111s preceding them and dumb bombs, than was dropped on Baghdad in the opening hours of the Iraqi war.

"However," warned Freeman in his first press conference since the landing, "Khabarovsk could be a major battle."

When he got to Khabarovsk there was no major battle: the military was gone; only the population, confused and worried, left behind for the Americans to feed. Only some of them, mostly Jews, were happy to see the Americans. The regular army had vanished, and only the militia remained. They were no match for the American marines. The civilians, who hid in terror for the first few hours, were now venturing out, soon forming a sea around the tank columns. The tanks were warm, and all heat and electricity to the city and the sparsely populated coast had been cut off by the retreating regulars. The American pilots commented on how it reminded them of flying over Alaska and the Canadian north: utter darkness, not even lights of outlying settlements visible.

Norton was already looking exhausted; they'd been on the road for almost twenty-four hours without a break. "Sir, far as we can make out, no civilians were allowed to leave. Shops were stripped bare by the army, the crowds left for us to feed."

"Yes," confirmed the marine commander. "Only civilians to get out were prisoners. Apparently they were taken out by the KGB on the Trans-Siberian."

Within twenty minutes of the Americans having entered Khabarovsk there was a series of enormous explosions in a rough semicircle east of the city center as far out as seventeen miles.

Soon there was the glow of fires everywhere over the frozen salt marsh as fuel depots blew along with ammunition dumps. Anything the Siberians could not take with them they had destroyed, including the city's four airfields. The brutish smokestacks, most of them in the northern sector of the city, stood in the flickering light, visible only to the four-hundred-foot level. They came in and out of view amid the choking, soot-colored smoke that rained black on the snow.

"Where's the battle, General?" asked a CBN reporter.

Freeman grumpily ignored him, turning to Norton instead. "How about the Trans-Siberian?"

"G-2 says it's ripped up from here to Birobidzhan."

"Blown up?" asked Freeman irritably. "Or ripped up?"

Norton didn't know.

"Goddamn it!" shouted Freeman. "Find out!"

"Yes, sir."

From Khabarovsk west over the hundred miles of frozen salt marshes to Birobidzhan, then three hundred miles to Belogorsk, all the while following the Trans-Siberian Railway around the big, 250-mile-wide, right-to-left horseshoe bend in the Amur River—at times less than twenty miles from the Manchurian border, the U.S. Air Force having taken out Zavitinsk airfield fourteen hours before—the tooth of Freeman's Second Army, its M-1 A-1s gulping, even at cruise speed, three gallons per mile, was fast outrunning the tail of its supply line.

The quarter-mile-wide ribbon of ice of the south-north Zeya River took on the look of burnished gold at Svobodnyy before more snow began falling and was, Freeman predicted, the perfect place for the Siberians to have blown the bridges. A few miles on and he found he was right. The enormous twisted steel of the railroad span was caught in the ice, a crippled skeleton of steel, the bridge's pylons left standing naked, the fresh snow pillows atop them affording the pylons a symmetry and beauty amid the collapsed spans. But the Siberians' scorched-earth policy, at least here, was of little account, holding Freeman up only for as long as it took his M-1 A-1s with plough blades and the engineers' rocket-propelled pipeline charges to clear the ice of mines. Most mine positions were immediately obvious from the frozen mounds of scraped ice that stood out like pimples of broken glass amid the new snow that was not yet deep enough to obscure the detritus. Self-propelled howitzers could be seen here and there in the forest, intact, their crews blue and bloated if they could be picked out at all from the shattered timber and decapitated trees that marked where infrared Smart bomb attacks by the U.S. air force had been made from the captured airfields.

Where tarmacs had been blown up, the U.S. engineers simply hosed in hot water under pressure from the water trucks, the water-filled craters instantly freezing, after which the graders topped them off as one would level off a filled-in posthole, and the Marsden matting was laid. U.S. planes were using the fields within an hour of their completion.

The railway was another story. The Siberians, having sacrificed much of their heavy fighter cover—mainly MiG-29s—to protect sacrificial MiG-27 Flogger-D ground attack aircraft, had dropped each Flogger's 6,600-pound ordnance on the multiple track west of the Zeya River between Shimanovsk and Mukhino. This meant that the pea-colored *Rossiya*, or "Train Number One," which ran from Vladivostok to Moscow, was unable to proceed because of the downed transmission lines. The Siberians, however, quickly hitched the carriages carrying evacuees from Khabarovsk to three steam engines, drawn into service from the dozens of such locomotives which had previously been disbanded beside the line with the coming of the electric engines.

Moving slowly through the dense, fogged-in and snow-draped taiga of larch, pine, and fir, the train approached the top of the horseshoe hump of the Amur. Instead of the usual caboose, the train dragged an enormous hook-shaped, stump-jump plough behind it, ripping up the ties like matchsticks, the splayed rail now pushed uselessly to the side on this eastern section of the forty-eight-hundred-mile railway. The guards at each tunnel entrance and bridge gratefully hopped aboard the last passenger carriage, the carriages alternating with AA quads mounted on flatbeds, every fourth flatbed in the car train sprouting SA-6 AA missiles. The "Mukhino Express," as it had been wryly described by the American pilots who had come down through the heavy cloud layer only to have their infrared signature detectors thwarted for a time by the thick bone-chilling fog, was finally stopped in a river of high explosives before it could reach the station at Mukhino. The pale blue station disintegrated in a spectacular explosion that sent ancient pine planks, black earth, and fire-streaked snow, together with iron heating-stove plates and the woodpile, whirling in a minitornado a quarter mile high before it came down in a crashing hail.

Meanwhile Freeman and his commanders welcomed the pause necessitated by having to clear the minefields across the Zeya, for it gave the vitally needed tank and POL resupply trucks time to catch up. Freeman was asked by his chief of logistics, Gen. Malcolm Wain, whether they should go to blivets. Wain had been impressed by the way in which the blivets, or flexi–plastic bags containing thousands of gallons of fuel, had proved so useful in the Iraqi desert to store gas. But here he didn't have in mind the huge, depot-sized bags that could be buried out of sight of aerial reconnaissance by the roadside but rather the tank-sized bags which, providing a tank was not in action but in transit, could be carried piggyback, an extra jerry can, as it were, one which could be jettisoned before getting the call to go into action or at the first sign of Second Army's spearhead being attacked.

Freeman spread out the map, slipping in the single-lens monocle that had caused the name "Von Freeman" to stick among those who bore him ill will for his decision to use the fuel air explosive bombs to break the Ratmanov deadlock. The monocle was impatiently tapping sector twenty-one, northwest of Mukhino, and beyond twenty-one to sectors thirty-three and thirty-seven where the Amur reached the apogee of the hump. "I like it," he told Wain. "Our rate of progress—soon be doing better than Erwin."

Wain looked across at Norton without the general seeing. Whenever Freeman was making good time, the heroes of his military pantheon were referred to by their first names. If he got held up, it would quickly be that "bastard Rommel."

"But," Freeman sighed, "I don't like it. Scorched-earth policy is one thing. I understand that. But this is—this is a turkey shoot. After Ratmanov I expected a fight."

Wain disagreed. "I don't see it that way, General. After Ratmanov they're going to avoid a close-in fight if they can. Especially with our air superiority."

"Maybe," said Freeman, unconvinced. "But they're not going to give up the whole damn country. They've got to stop—stand and fight somewhere. They've got to counterattack." Freeman folded the map case and slipped it into the Humvee's back seat, smacking his gloves together. "God, it's cold!" He looked about unhappily at the column stopped for refueling.

It was against everything in Freeman's book to halt. He'd built a career on movement. Movement! Movement! Movement! as against the Siberians' obsession with refusing to attack until they had overwhelming numbers in men and matériel. If Freeman stopped, Norton knew, it would make everyone down the line happy—give them a chance to catch their breath and allow the supply tail to thicken. But, Freeman was asking himself as well as Norton and Wain, what was that crafty son of a bitch Yesov up to? Freeman was nodding to himself, concluding that Yesov would be gambling on his, Freeman's, lifelong commitment to movement, the Siberians sucking him in deeper and deeper, the American supply line becoming ever more overextended.

"Mal."

"Sir?"

"We'll pause here. Twenty-four hours. Dick, give the order to establish defensive perimeter. Air task order—saturation fighter cover and attack gunships ready to go."

"Yes, sir."

"We're in 'overreach' with our fighters. I realize that. We're already heavily committed to in-air refueling." It was as if he was trying to justify his uncharacteristic decision to stop. "But we need to consolidate here. Get another airstrip going. Must remember the aim, gentlemen—to capture Irkutsk. From there our fighter-bomber radius can hit the industrial underbelly. We're now at a critical stage, however. We can't pause for too long for resupply. I'll bet that's what Yesov's counting on—hoping his scorched-earth policy'll force us to drag our ass. But, gentlemen, his scorched-earth policy is outmoded. Takes no account of the American genius for resupply. He obviously hasn't learned anything from Iraq. Well, let him withdraw. By the time he's got his big battalions ready on the ramparts, we'll be knocking the ramparts out from under him.''

Freeman held up his hand to silence any protest that his stopping was perhaps unwise for the same reasons that he was criticizing his Siberian counterpart, for stopping created a stationary target, and it was a maxim of Freeman's military strategy that a stationary target in modern warfare has no chance. But neither Norton nor Wain had been about to protest, and Freeman holding up his hand seemed to them more a gesture of doubt than confidence, something they'd not seen in him before. Perhaps the terrible casualty rate on Ratmanov had affected the general more than they thought. At odd moments Norton had seen Freeman, when he thought no one was looking, leaning back, his hands massaging his lower back, still in pain. But for Norton there was no doubt—Freeman had made a sound military decision, right from the textbook. To go on without having consolidated your supply line was always a risky proposition.

CHAPTER NINETEEN

MARSHAL YESOV'S AIDE was in a hurry, his chauffeur-driven Zil swishing past the great, snow-crowned dome of Novosibirsk's opera and ballet theater. The statue of Lenin, his noble vision fixed on the future, was even more impressive in the strange, pinkish-brown light of the pollution-colored dusk. The soldier, sailor, and airman on Lenin's right flanked him proudly; the heroic worker and torchbearer to his left were dusted by snow but looked equally heroic. It added to the aide's excitement when, arriving at the Akademgorodok or "Science City" apartment block, he ran up the six flights—the elevator wasn't working—to the apartment of Professor Leonid Grigorenko, the head of the KMK project. But when the door opened it was to Marshal Yesov that the aide blurted out, *"On ostanovilsya!"*— "He's stopped! The American has stopped!"

Yesov showed no emotion, his blunt facial features unmoved as he walked back to the apartment's window looking out on the frozen expanse that was the Ob Sea, where the River Ob had been dammed, and which in summer provided excellent sailing for the privileged ones in Akademgorodok and the party elite. He saw two guards in greatcoats and fur caps trudging as smartly as the snow would allow them along the ice-sheathed concrete slabs that inclined down to the frozen Ob, which in summer, by which time he would beat the American, would serve as a beach for those sunbathing to watch the colorful sailboat races.

He was not so worried about the Allied armies to the west— tired and busy administering Moscow and its environs, they had not yet breached the Urals. He turned from the window, and now that the lights in the city were coming on, pulled the blackout curtains shut, though there was little danger of air raids. To the east Freeman's forces were further away than those in the west, over fifteen hundred miles from Novosibirsk. Still, it was Freeman's forces that Marshal Yesov was most concerned about, for while the English Channel, across which the Allies in the west had been resupplied, had effectively been closed by Siberian submarines in the Arctic, Freeman's supply line from Japan was uninterrupted, Freeman's troops fresher, and Freeman himself more daring than the more conservative threat faced to the west. *"On upryamy"*—"He is a tractor," said Yesov, looking out toward where the Trans-Siberian crossed the frozen expanse of the Ob. "He keeps on. This pause of his will not last long."

"We will stop him," said Grigorenko, calmly smoking his thin cigar as he went over the final plans of Chernko's KMK project. "I hope there have been no more security leaks, however."

"None," Yesov assured him, explaining that even the man from engine shop three who had been shot knew only part of the project. Yesov was as confident as Grigorenko that Chernko's plan would work. But he, Yesov, had had more experience than the scientist who had overseen the design and manufacturing process, and said nothing. Scientists could afford to say what they wanted. They were important to the state, particularly in a modern war, but the general had to be more circumspect; and when the Americans were defeated, Yesov had aspirations to be the president of the United Siberian Soviet Republics. Grigorenko, however, mistook Yesov's silence for undue concern. "You mustn't worry, General. Everything is in place, I assure you. The Americans will be demolished—utterly!" As he said this, Grigorenko sat back, stroking his goatee, his piercing gray eyes looking first at the general then his aide. "You know, of course, the supreme irony of the situation."

The aide guessed it was the Iraqis who had been training in Poland before the Iraqi war for just such a project as Chernko's—but he wasn't going to do anything to steal the Akademician's thunder.

"The Iraqis!" proclaimed Grigorenko, pleased with himself, leaning back and taking a bottle of Smirnoff vodka—the best, something that the average Russian hadn't seen for months, the aide thought. Everything from nylon stockings to toy production had been conscripted for war materials.

"Yes," Grigorenko said, pouring the three vodkas, a little extra for himself, the aide noticed. "It will add insult to injury for the Americans, comrades, that half of the attacking force will be Iraqi."

The aide was trying to look surprised, a difficult thing to do when he knew by heart the story of how Hussein had sent Iraqis to the eastern bloc to train for just such a project in the Gulf war but how, because of Gorbachev's stupid bungling, and against the advice of his military, the Iraqis were not permitted to carry out such an attack in the Iraqi war. Unable to get back home because of the UN boycott and U.S. intelligence on the lookout for them, the Iraqis, all members of Hussein's dreaded *Mukhabarat*—his secret police—were still in Siberia and as expert as their Russian instructors. Grigorenko passed around the glasses and proposed a toast: *"Za porazhenie amerikantsev!"*— "To the American defeat!"

Yesov lifted the shot glass and allowed a thin smile to crease his otherwise bullish face. *"Za unizhenie amerikantsev!"*—"To the Americans' humiliation!"

"Na mnogo luchshe!"—"Much better!" added Grigorenko. The aide was not a believer in psychic phenomena or anything else he called "mind rubbish," but he could not deny the fact that within seconds of the general having proposed the toast, the call came in from Kultuk, 850 miles east of them at the southwestern end of Lake Baikal and only 76 miles from the Mongolian border, that everything for Chernko's KMK project was *gotov*—"ready to go."

Grigorenko looked across at the commander in chief of all United Siberian Soviet Republic forces like an expectant father, waiting for the general to give the word. The American, Freeman, had stopped at Mukhino, and though it was almost a thousand miles further east of Kultuk, well away from Novosibirsk, the scientist's expression of pained expectation said it all, that every day Yesov waited—every hour—the Americans got closer to reaching Lake Baikal and Irkutsk. And from Irkutsk their aircraft could strike Novosibirsk. But Yesov refused to be hurried, holding his glass out for another drink. Using it as a pointer, he moved it east to Baikal to the hump of the Amur that formed the Siberian-Chinese border. "Let him reach the very top of the hump, comrades. Then we're in the clear."

The aide nodded and glanced knowingly at the general, his look clearly saying that while Grigorenko might be one of the world's greatest scientists and engineers, his political *um*—"savvy"—was about as sophisticated as a yak's. Chita HQ, halfway in the crescent of mountains and forest between Baikal and the top of the hump, had repeatedly *advised* Novosibirsk, Yesov specifically, not to act too close to the Chinese border, particularly not anywhere along the Amur where there had been border clashes since time immemorial between the two countries.

"No," said Yesov, in answer to Grigorenko's silent plea. "Not yet. The Chinese don't like the Americans any more than we do, Doctor, but they are very touchy about their border. No, we cannot fire across the hump for fear we may drop short into Chinese territory." He meant inside the hump. "No, we'll wait until he is at the top.'' Yesov used the rim of the oily vodka glass to indicate the area where he would spring his trap. "Here, between Never and—" The general required his reading glasses. "—Skovorodino." The seven-and-a-half-mile road between the two towns was 170 miles west of where Freeman had stopped.

"He'll be reassured, resupplied," said Yesov. "Tanks topped up."

"Da," said Grigorenko approvingly, "all the better. His humiliation will be all the worse."

The cruise missiles came in so low that neither Freeman in his advance command Humvee nor the radars of the helicopters flying cover saw them, the eight 672-pound missiles visible only five miles from target along the Never-Skovorodino Road. The first thing that the fifty M-1 tanks and six M-3 Bradley fighting vehicles and six mobile heavy mortars that formed the spearhead of Second Army's II Corps lead tank battalion saw was the sudden appearance of the low-flying lead missile making a tight, right-hand turn before roaring overhead and exploding further down the line.

At the angle they saw it from it appeared to have detonated over the trees, but the CBN reporter with a tripod and zoom lens saw that it was exploding right over the midsection of the four-mile-long spearhead even as Second Army advance reconnaissance units looked back disbelievingly at the missile as it veered through the clear blue sky over the tip of the spearhead toward the center of the column. The CBN cameraman, too, was in awe, transfixed by the abrupt turn that another of the subsonic missiles made to avoid power lines. Rising no more than ten feet above them before descending again, its belly opening even as AA fire stuttered toward it, the missile exuded a hail of smaller missiles that buzzed in the air—antipersonnel fléchettes and antitank bomblets. American tanks, the best in the world, were disintegrating, most of them still moving as if driven by ghosts, the screams of their dying crews soon lost amid the technicolor phantasm of light as the tanks spewed fountains of red and white rain as if being welded from the inside, a rain of sparks and flame oozing from the penetrated seals over the sloping glacis plate.

HEAT rounds exploded through the cupolas with a jetlike roar, and several tanks slewed broadside, ramming others, which were in turn struck by tanks coming from behind. The series of explosions from the fuel bladders sent sheets of orange-black flame billowing over the armored personnel carriers behind the tanks. The APCs' crews and the twelve troopers inside each died agonizingly, the APCs becoming nothing more than ovens.

Those who made a run for it from the APCs' rear doors were cut down by the buzzing bees of the fléchettes, the darts not killing all but inflicting such terrible wounds that the medics and, as the CBN reporter would soon see, the MASH units to the rear were overwhelmed.

Chopper accidents added to the chaos as two air-sea rescue Blackhawks collided with four Cobra and Apache gunships in the thick battlefield smoke. One chopper, a Bell OH-58C Scout, slammed into one of the last incoming missiles. Chips of the heavy 350-millimeter, blocklike Chobham armor packs from the tanks whistled through the air, still intact, their resin-sandwiched steel, ceramic, and aluminum layers unpenetrated but blown in toto away from the tanks when the M-1s' fifty APFDS—armor-piercing fin-stabilized discarding Sabot rounds—reached their flash points and exploded internally, ripping the tank cupolas apart. The mechanized battalion's tanks and the APCs of Freeman's II Corps were further victims of the "bolt from the blue" Siberian attack against Freeman's seven-corps, 379,000-man Second Army.

In addition to the sixty-six tanks destroyed, the Siberian cruise missiles had laid waste to and/or incapacitated over forty twelve-ton M-113 armored personnel carriers and twenty-three Marine Corps expeditionary force AAV-7A1 armed amphibious troop carriers and seventeen fourteen-ton light armored assault vehicles of the marines' second expeditionary brigade, the vehicles now either gutted completely or burning.

In all 493 men were killed, over 600 wounded. Freeman's Second Army spearhead was not much more than a smoking ruin. As suddenly as it had begun, the Siberian attack ceased, but not the suffering, as men, tearing open their CFA—combat first aid—kits sprinkled spore-contaminated antiseptic powder on wounds, which immediately turned the blood septic. In fact, only a few of the hundreds of the CFA kits were so contaminated, but the fear instigated by the certain knowledge that some had been tampered with meant that hundreds of men were loathe to use the packs. Consequently dozens more died, despite the exemplary efforts of medics and Medevac choppers.

The CBN reporter had not seen anything like it since the American A-10 Thunderbolts had come in with their cannon and chopped up the retreating Iraqi columns in the Gulf war. Though not immediately evident, it soon became clear, at least to Freeman's G-2, that the Siberian cruise missiles' TERCOM—terrain contour mapping—computers had been finely tuned and programmed not only to hit the tanks in the Second Army spearhead but to avoid the most forward, and hence far more lightly armed, Humvee scout cars.

Freeman was shattered, his hopes of a home run dashed, but he had no time to feel sorry for himself even if he had felt disposed to it, for now the ADATs and quickly deployed Patriot batteries were in position, or at least in the best position they could manage, given that some could not get out of the rubble of gutted vehicles, burning bodies and equipment. The anti-missile Patriots' box launchers were left where they were, their crews sent out to put the pole radar on higher ground. Now Freeman was receiving reports that there were massive troop movements heading east from Baikal toward Chita to the east, the troops identified as the Thirty-first "Stalingrad" Motorized Division. It was the army of Stalingrad fame.

"Son of a bitch!" said Jesus Valdez, called "Juan" by the other marines in his ten-man squad. "That's all we need, man. Fucking Thirty-first."

Another marine, hunkered down in the foxhole of ice, made so by the snow having been instantly melted in the heat of the missile attack after which the melt had refrozen, looked disbelievingly at the junkyard of burning tires, drooping guns, shattered armor, smoldering hulks of APCs, and the high, thick, black smoke churning from burning tires, red flames licking softly in the eerie blue twilight. Some of the marines gathered around the flames, warming themselves, until a marine lieutenant told them to douse the fires.

"Yeah," said Jesus Valdez, "they might see where we are!" He'd lost three buddies in the missile onslaught and hadn't found a trace of them. It was so terrible it didn't seem real. The attack had lasted less than seven minutes—hardly a shot fired back, the Patriot launcher support units not then deployed, with the column being on the move. The marine lieutenant didn't chew out Valdez for his sarcasm; the lieutenant, too, was still reeling inside at the carnage. He, too, had lost friends, and it took all his willpower to deploy the remaining seventeen of what only minutes before had been his thirty-man platoon to defensive positions off the road to take the radar aerials to the summit of the two-thousand-foot-high hills that ringed the death road between Never and Skovorodino.

Freeman's first order after the attack was to keep out of the townships, attractive to tired, cold troops but a perfect setup, he believed, for another cruise attack. A townsite was perfect for terrain contour imaging, sticking out, in his words, "like a nun in a whorehouse." Forward patrols reported that the railway had been ripped up from Never on and the pipeline running parallel to the Trans-Siberian shut down.

"How far away is their Thirty-first?" Freeman asked Dick Norton, momentarily too ashamed to look his aide in the face, a thing he normally detested in a man. Instead he was gazing at the wreckage, the acrid stench of defeat burning his nostrils. Mixed in with the oily reek of destroyed equipment and vehicles there came the sweet, sickly smell of burnt bodies.

"They're coming from Chita," said Norton. "Now as the crow flies it's about—"

"Never mind the goddamn crow! How long till they can attack?"

Stunned by the general's outburst, Norton stepped back. "Ah—they're motorized. Five—four days. If they travel at night, maybe three."

"Forty-eight hours," declared Freeman, his left hand pulling so hard on the cuff of his right glove that Norton could see the general's fingers straining against the white Gore-Tex. "Toughest outfit in their army—except for the SPETS. They'll attack in forty-eight hours." He was staring at the clump of smoking debris and a bloody, bone-pierced stump that had once been a man's head. Freeman's voice was tremulous. He coughed, swore, his tone steadier now but heavy with anger. "Can you tell me," he turned to Norton, "can anyone in this godforsaken place tell me why I lost so many fine young men? Why those satellite intelligence outfits can tell me the Siberian Thirty-first—a whole goddamn army—is on the move and yet they can't give us any warning of a multiple cruise launch? Even if radar contact missed 'em because the bastards were coming in so low, how was it that our satellites didn't see launch plumes? Or are their infrared spotters on goddamn holiday?"

A major, his head in a blood-splattered bandage, handed Freeman the updated casualty report. Those killed now numbered over five hundred, several of the most recent having died of fléchette wounds either on the way to the MASH unit at Mukhino or after arriving.

Norton relayed the general's question, keeping his voice low from force of habit, the speaker close to his ear.

"General," he told Freeman, "marine G-2 says the Siberians started a whole bunch of fires in the forests around the suspected launch area. SATINT can't distinguish between natural hot spots and exhaust plumes. Both give off heat signatures." Freeman was walking away from the ruins of his advanced armored column. "So they lit fires to confuse satellite IR pickups, but they must have spotted trajectories?"

"No, sir. We've still got a big low that's come down from the Kara Sea. We'll have to wait until it clears a bit before—" Freeman was pulling out the map. "Before we can use the K-14," Norton continued, referring to the intelligence satellite. "But it has to be in the right orbit when they take pics."

"My God, Dick, if there is a next time, we're going to be ready. Where the hell are those Starstreaks?"

Starstreak was the state-of-the-art, three-dart-headed successor to Stinger, an intercept missile that could, if necessary, be mounted on the back of a Humvee and which provided Mach six "blanket target" protection against air tactical missiles.

"In transit, sir. Siberian Backfire bomber out of Sakhalin—before we took out its airfield—got lucky over one of the convoys from Japan."

"You sure more are coming?" Freeman asked, his face flushed despite the cold.

"Yes, sir."

"Well, that's something. Meantime I want ADATs up ahead, Patriots—have the box launchers down here stick the pole radars high."

"I'm doing that now, sir."

"Good." The general looked up at the cloud-shrouded summits, visible for a moment then gone. To others in the column, the deployment of what AA batteries had not been taken out by the missiles would afford a measure of security, a circling of the AA wagons, as it were, until the road was cleared for the column to move—anywhere but where they were. But Norton knew how bad it was for the general. Freeman had never exulted over the Patriot as others had after the Iraqi war. It bothered him that a Patriot had missed the Scud that killed the marines in Riyadh during the Iraqi war and that if the body of an incoming missile was hit, but not the actual warhead, the missile could end up wreaking the same kind of damage as occurred in Riyadh.

Dick Norton was making a quick call to Malcolm Wain to order in as many batteries of Starstreaks from Japan—from anywhere—as they could lay their hands on.

"How many are coming across now?" asked Wain.

"None," said Norton. "Just get 'em on choppers—C-5s, anything, but get them here. Any way you can."

"By Christ!" said Freeman, coming up behind him. "I'd like to find the son of a bitch who engineered this."

To do this, however, as he would soon discover for himself, would be impossible unless he was prepared to visit an Italian graveyard. But if he was not to meet the genius behind the Siberian missile assault, he soon experienced another assault—a cruise bombardment. Patriots, ADATs, and finally some Starstreaks were able to thin it out; nevertheless, it continued to pound Second Army so that Freeman was trapped. At the top of the Amur hump, unable to go either forward or back for fear of risking the disassembling of his AA defensive ring, he remained hemmed in by the high, snow-covered ridges, as he waited for clear weather so that the trajectories of the Siberian missiles could be more accurately traced. Casualties after the second attack were over two and a half thousand killed, sixteen hundred wounded.

To the public back home the mess from the Siberian front was bad enough, but they sought solace in the fact that the U.S. navy, thanks to the effectiveness of battle-wise skippers such as Robert Brentwood, commander of the nuclear sub USS *Reagan*, had been punishing the Siberian navy at an ever-increasing rate, protecting the vital sea lift resupply route from the American west coast to Japan.

Freeman prayed for good weather with all the energy his belief could muster. The bad weather didn't clear; only a few gaps opened up as a new front howled malevolently down from the Laptev Sea over the tundra into the taiga, as if determined to take up where the previous front left off and continue making life as miserable as possible for Second Army. Meanwhile, news had come in via Japan that the British/American force approaching the Urals in much calmer conditions had come under fierce Siberian armored attack and was reeling southwest of Sverdlovsk. There were rumors of the Siberians having used sarin, a nerve gas whose "persistence" rating in cold, calm weather was high.

When Norton suggested to the general that he should carry his atropine injector—a self-contained hypodermic whose jab would penetrate a CBW suit—Freeman pretended not to hear him. He didn't believe in doctors or any other medical assistance—until he was hurt. The general was more preoccupied with the report received moments before that yet another Siberian cruise missile attack was underway. This time SATINT and SIGINT would hopefully get much better trajectories. Freeman's AA defenses opened fire, the roar of Patriots and the high scream of Starstreaks filling the hills about Never-Skovorodino, causing minor avalanches, one of these burying a scissor-folding mobile bridge span. The general was receiving SATINT from a fighter-protected E-3A Sentry early warning radar and control rotodome aircraft that the enemy cruise trajectories were definitely originating from around the Lake Baikal area.

"What in hell do they mean?" pressed Freeman, pulling out

the Hershey bar from the MRE—meal ready to eat—tray, ignoring the rest. "From Lake Baikal?"

"Frozen lakes make as good a launch area as any other, I suppose," said Norton. "Sure as heck not many trees around."

"Yes, well," said Freeman, chomping on the Hershey bar as if it were a cigar, "they're about to get an education. Get out an ATO and tell them we want as many aircraft as possible flying against the Siberian cruise missile launch positions around or on Lake Baikal. They won't be able to hide under cloud cover now."

He was correct about the cloud cover, but there weren't any launch sites on the ice. Instead, SATINT was suggesting that trajectories indicated mobile sites in the heavily forested areas around the northwestern edge of the 390-mile-long lake.

The F-15 and F-18 pilots, after passing through the heaviest antiaircraft gun and missile fire any of them had seen since the war began, including Ratmanov Island, lost fifteen American planes. Only six pilots bailed out. The remaining American fighters mixed it with a swarm of Fulcrums coming out of the superhardened concrete shelters hidden in the taiga, the bases circling the lake from Ulan-Ude in the southeast, barely a hundred miles north of the Mongolian border, to Kalakan northeast of the lake, back down through the Zima pipeline and rail junction on the Trans-Siberian west of the lake to Irkutsk on the Angara River, the lake's only outflowing river.

For the next two days the Americans, despite increasing air losses, dropped more bombs on the infrared-spotted, cruciform-shaped cruise missile launch site clearings, while A-10 Thunderbolts covered Freeman's column with their deadly thirty-millimeter antitank cannon as Second Army, refueled and resupplied, got on the move again through the taiga to Urusha and Yerofey Pavlovich, two towns over a hundred miles west. With the Thunderbolts looking for targets of opportunity and finding them, the lead air controller broke radio silence only once to give the grid reference of "massed armor" twenty-five miles west of Yerofey Pavlovich. The tanks, he reported, were in camouflaged revetments but detectable because the snow-weighted netting created unusual shadow patterns.

More up-gunned T-90s were reported lying in wait to ambush Second Army's spearhead around Chichatka Station just a little further west, the tanks detectable through ID signature, heat given off by motors kept idling in the cold. Their exhaust was piped through flexihoses into snow berms—antitank ditches whose walls of ice were ten feet thick—but still heat patches showed up on infrared. The resulting air bombardment, a combination of A-10s, Eagles, Falcons, and F-111Fs, refueled midair from the coast, was as formidable an air strike as Freeman had ever seen, unloading more ordnance on the enemy's newfound positions than was dropped on Hussein's Republican Guard units in the first six days of that war.

Even so, Freeman, while exhorting his men, nevertheless cautioned them not to be "damned foolhardy," adding, "when you attack, you are to assume that not one, I repeat, not *one*, of the enemy's T-90s—or any other of his tanks—has been destroyed by the aerial bombardment. And I don't give a damn about what reports we get from Air Command. They're doing a great job—absolutely superb—but they're not on the ground. We are. I don't want you taking your tank platoons in there thinking that all we've got to do is mop up. The Russians taught the Iraqis how to revet their armor, remember—dug 'em in so deep even our bombers couldn't get at them until they decided to come out and make a run for it. Well, I can tell you one thing—those Siberian sons of bitches aren't working for Hussein. They're working for themselves. When they come out—if they're not coming at us already—they're not going to run away. That you can bank on.

"Another thing—you can't expect our air superiority to help much once we engage. You've seen it enough at Fort Hood, and the fact that this is snow, not sand, doesn't make one whit of difference. Once the fighting starts, it'll all be weasel shit and pebbles flying—identification friend or foe hard enough for us, let alone for our boys in the air. They'll have enough work cut out looking after themselves. But remember, each of your tanks has infrared-visible ID marks. Last thing—" Freeman paused, taking off his battlefield Kevlar infantry helmet, putting it squarely on the briefing table, pulling a tank commander's helmet to him. "Remember à la the Israelites?" He expected an

answer, for it wasn't a Biblical injunction but one passed down
by the Israeli tank commanders in the Arab wars. The men
roared in unison. "Keep moving!"

"Didn't hear you."

"Keep *moving*!"

"Right. Now, remember your buddies you left back there on
that never-never road. Cream these jokers!" With that Freeman
put on the new helmet, adjusting the throat mike and slicking
his hair down under the rim. The interior of an Abrams M-1 A-
1 was a high-tech marvel, but it was so cramped that a strand
of hair loose over a laser sight could cost you the battle.

Norton told Freeman straight: if the general insisted on leading one of the front two command tanks of the twenty-two-tank
battalion spearhead, then the colonel was going to make his
protest official. Bravery was fine, but "damn foolhardiness,"
to use Freeman's own words, was something else. What would
happen if Freeman was—

"General Wain'd take over," responded Freeman. He turned,
the front of the wide firing-control helmet almost touching Norton's, his voice lowered. "Goddamn it, Dick, I appreciate your
position. Respect it. But after that—" His thumb jerked back to
the bloodied road whence they'd come, or rather inched over,
in the last few hours. Several marine companies had been dec-
imated, other Americans were dead, their bodies vanished, va-
porized in the horror of modern explosives, the only memorial
to them now bloodstained snow and a small white cross hammered into the hard Siberian soil. "I couldn't live with myself
after that if I didn't lead," he told Norton. "My God, Dick,
'Skovorodino.' " He was looking into the distance—not into
Siberia or any other place he'd known but to his field of glory.
"Skovorodino! God, what a beautiful name. Even sounds victorious." His mood suddenly darkened. "It should have been
our victory." He turned and climbed aboard the first of the two
command M-1 tanks of the twenty-two-tank echelon that would
lead the two-hundred-tank spearhead.

"No secret to the strategy, Dick. If anything happens to me,
just keep pressing west—whichever way'll get you to the east
bank of Baikal and Irkutsk. Then we'd be far enough in to bomb
the shit out of anything we like—far as the Kara Sea if we have

to. Remember, the carriers can't do it. Despite what the public thought, the flat tops accounted for less than five percent of all sorties flown in Iraq. We have to have land bases in deep.''

"Yes, General.''

"Don't look so worried, Colonel,'' said Freeman, grinning down at him. ''We're going to make ground round of 'em!''

"Can I quote you, General?'' It was the CBN reporter, hopping out of a Humvee, its driver looking apologetically nonplussed at Freeman.

"Sure!'' said Freeman and, still standing up in the cupola, rapped on the tank. ''Radio silence. Let's go!''

Norton turned to the CBN newsman. ''I thought it was made clear to you people that we're running this by media pool and that none of you were allowed forward of Skovorodino.''

The reporter was shooting off the end of a roll of four hundred ASA at the general, snow flying up in clumps from the M-1's tracks, the tank's aerial leaning back as the war machine, for all of its sixty tons, shot forward from zero to twenty-five miles an hour in less than seven seconds, still nowhere near its forty-five-miles-per-hour cruising speed. It looked great. Freeman brought up his binoculars.

"Marvelous!'' said the reporter. ''He should be in the movies.''

"Listen!'' insisted Norton. ''I asked you what the hell are you doing up—''

"Got urgent news for the general,'' said the reporter without even turning around. ''His wife died.'' The reporter was switching to another camera, Voightlander Vito B—older, simpler but with a good lens. ''Didn't think I should let him know before he goes into battle.''

Norton jerked the reporter around by the Voightlander's strap. ''You quote him, you set him up before this thing's settled, and I'll shoot you, you son of a bitch! You'll be out of the pool, *Dan*! 'Friendly fire.' Got it?''

"Hey, hey. What the—''

"Shut up! Listen, big shot. While you're beaming your videos back home he's carrying over a thousand dead on his conscience. Nothing he could do about it then, but now he can. So don't you report anything until the thing's done. You get it? We don't want any Baghdad Pete shit from you swinging your god-damned camera around so any Commie intelligence asshole can—''

"Hey. Easy, man.''

"You got it?'' Norton was still holding him by the collar; an MP moved in to lend a hand.

"Wait until we're done!'' repeated Norton. The MP had never seen the colonel so mad.

The reporter put up his hands and backed away toward the Humvee, the cameras bashing against one another. The clouds were parting now, the sun turning the snow and endless taiga blindingly white, surface snow turning to ice. "Till you win, huh?'' said the reporter sneeringly. "Christ, I'll be an old man.''

Norton was moving menacingly toward the Humvee. "Get him out of here!'' he yelled at the driver. The Humvee spun around in its own axis, splattering Norton head to foot with freezing, oil-stained slush.

Freeman's tanks, though their gas turbines were the quietest of any main battle tank in the world, were still emitting a deep rumble through the taiga as arrowhead formations of A-10s came up to support high-flying B-52s. Navy carriers and cruisers in the Sea of Japan had already fired Tomahawk cruise missiles, programmed to hit the launch sites reported to be in the taiga around Lake Baikal far to the west.

"The boss runs over that Siberian armor up ahead and our cruise missiles flatten those launch sites, Colonel,'' said Wain, "the general'll sweep a double header.''

Dick Norton looked at his watch. He figured they wouldn't have long to wait.

He was half right. The U.S. cruise-missile strike against SATINT-identified launch sites would take one hour and fifty-two minutes to reach the targets in the Baikal area, the U.S. cruises traveling at a ground-hugging five hundred miles per hour. Freeman's armor should engage the enemy around Chichatka Station at about the same time.

It would be a decisive battle, Norton believed, because while there were thousands of Siberian main battle tanks and over fifty divisions within the Far Eastern TVD, Freeman's master stroke had been in landing, like MacArthur had at Inchon, where no one thought he should or ought to land—on a remote part of the Southern TVD coastline. But like most master strokes it would be recognized as such only if Freeman won.

Despite the heavy armor reported to be concentrating around Chichatka, which Freeman was about to engage, U.S. air superiority meant that it was taking time for the Siberians to bring up troops and more tanks from the flatlands of the Siberian plain. The Siberians had few roads to do it, relying on relatively few rail lines together with the multiple track of the Trans-Siberian. If Freeman could inflict a decisive defeat here at Chichatka and move forward quickly, he might be able to take Irkutsk before the full weight of the Siberian divisions could be brought to bear on Second Army.

Back further in the marine expeditionary unit, Jesus Valdez was getting the news, passed up from the coast quicker than a blizzard, that back home the pounding they had taken on the Never-Skovorodino Road was being reported by the La Roche tabloid chain as the "Second Army Stuck in Neverland." The more respectable media, it was said, had begun its reporting of the effect of the Siberian missile attacks in a more dignified manner, but once the La Roche papers had taken the low road, "market forces," as they were saying on "Washington Week in Review," had moved even the more "responsible" papers to follow La Roche's sensationalism. The cruel truth for Freeman's troops was that Second Army was becoming something of a joke; already there were not-so-subtle suggestions in Congress that Freeman ought to be replaced. Valdez was flicking the safety catch of his squad automatic weapon back and forth until Private First Class Joe Kim told him to knock it off.

"I was just thinkin'," said Valdez, "that if I saw that CBN son of a bitch, I'd blow his friggin' head off."

"Easy, Juan," cautioned Kim, who in the past had been the butt himself of jokes about his surname, it being the same as General Kim of the North Korean army, whom Freeman had defeated decisively in the raid on Pyongyang. "Don't get all het up about it, man. Save it for the Thirty-first."

"Yeah," said Valdez. "Where the hell are they?"

"Don' worry," said Pirelli, who hailed from Brooklyn. "They'll get here, I guarantee."

"Not if Freeman takes out those wagons up ahead," said another marine. "His M-1s'll own the road."

"That's right, man," said Kim, who as a boy—before his family emigrated to the United States—had fed himself on movies from the sixties and still put "man" at the end of everything he said, believing it made him as American as baseball. "Hey, hey," he said excitedly, looking overhead. "You see that, man?"

An American cruise missile was passing over them, just above the top of the hills that spread north of the Amur, its white speckle camouflage making it difficult to spot but its stubby, squarish wings cutting the cold, Arctic air and making a sound like cars whipping past one another, the subdued growl of its motor coming to them only after it had passed overhead. Then there was another, and another.

"Holy cow," said Valdez. "Ain't that somethin'!" The effect on morale of finally striking back, now that the Siberian trajectories had been back-tracked, was electric, sending a surge of badly needed confidence through the forward units of Second Army.

CHAPTER TWENTY

APACHE AND COBRA gunships flying NOE—nap of the earth—missions following the contours of the taiga ahead of Freeman's armored column were so close to the treetops, it was regarded as inevitable that some would be lost to wind sheer. The gunships skimmed the up and down of air currents over the white, rolling sea of forest. A sudden unexpected drop of a few feet, and the trees would reach up and take you down. But none were lost—at least not on the way in, the pilots long used to such tactics in western Europe, the steady stream of information needed to assist in NOE fed back from the twenty-five-inch-diameter combination thermal imaging sensor, laser, TV, and boresight system through a .1-inch-diameter tube to video displays in the cockpit. Each pilot, in symbiotic relationship with the cyclic control column, was ready to touch-alter forward, backward blade, pitch, and yaw controls in response to the main computer display.

The cockpit of the lead chopper of the thirty sharp-nosed, 140-mile-per-hour AH-1S Cobras was suddenly invaded by a loud buzzing noise and flashing red light. The rate of climb had fallen precipitously in a downdraft; the craft's pod load of eight TOW, or tube-launched, optically tracked, wire-guided, antitank missiles, and two pods of nineteen 2.75-inch rockets for softer targets—should infantry be sighted—were abnormally buffeted. In addition there was the weight of the universal-swivel, turret-mounted, thirty-millimeter machine gun and its ammunition belt under the nose with which to contend. The pilot instantly altered the pitch, the rotors responding quickly in the colder Siberian air, giving more lift than in the warmer climes of western Europe and Southeast Asia.

Still, it was hair-raising flying, heartbeat and blade beat alarmingly out of synch at times, the first tanks in sight either T-72s or 80s; it was difficult to tell because of the camouflage netting. Adding to his anxiety, the pilot was already depressed after having received the news that morning that his brother in the navy had been killed, sucked overboard by the enormous vacuum created when the *Missouri* had fired one of its salvoes against the Kommandorsky Islands.

But in the split second of sighting the target a half mile away and racing toward him, the pilot forgot all the questions he wanted answered about his brother's death—such as why the hell he was out on deck when the guns were fired? He felt the adrenaline taking over as he shot off a TOW missile equipped with the latest warhead, upgraded to penetrate—he hoped—the layered reactive armor of the Siberian tanks, the armor that could explode an incoming round, diffusing its impact.

The Cobras, now joined by Apaches, made a force of sixty

choppers in all. They swarmed over the taiga that erupted beneath them with streaks of orange light, pale against the snow but thunderous in their explosions. Shrapnel screamed as camouflaged "cold"—therefore not infrared-detectable—antiaircraft quads of rapid machine-gun fire opened up. For all their sophistication and versatility in the air—an aspect constantly celebrated by Hollywood—the truth, as every chopper pilot knew, was that his craft, flying at plus or minus 150 miles per hour, was a slow combatant in the modern world of high-subsonic and supersonic warfare, and low to the trees they were terribly vulnerable.

The Siberian quads continued to unleash a terrible and concentrated fire by means of the single most important antihelicopter defense of modern warfare: the Soviet-developed high-velocity AIRDEM, or air defense mines. The weapon was really misnamed as it was not, strictly speaking, an antiaircraft mine at all, having no effect on faster, fixed-wing aircraft. Rather it was specifically an antihelicopter weapon. But misnamed or not, the Siberian radar-and-heat-sensor-equipped mines exploded in V-shaped cones of shrapnel four hundred feet high and over a hundred yards in diameter.

The mine, triggered either by the approaching rotor slap or engine heat, proved devastating to the U.S. helicopter strike force, knocking out fifteen of the sixty choppers, three of these lost in midair collisions as a direct result of confusion and equipment gone awry in an air whistling with fuselage-smashing metal bits.

At first the younger reporters assigned to Second Army's media pool back in Khabarovsk had difficulty understanding the seriousness of what had happened. To their inexperienced eyes, while fifteen downed out of sixty was bad news, it still left forty-five choppers fully operational. But older hands pointed out that if Freeman had lost 25 percent of all his choppers in one action, very soon he'd have none left. And as serious as the loss of 180 million dollars of sophisticated technology was, the loss of thirty pilots was far more serious.

The remaining forty-five U.S. choppers did not flinch, despite the losses. Most of their pilots were veterans of NOE flying in Europe and Iraq, and they exhibited all the deftness that was required in hugging rolling terrain at treetop level.

The instant a target was spotted, the chopper would dip down in the nearest fold, hovering, its mast sight extended high above the rotors, the sight's small TV, invisible to the enemy, providing a clear video of the enemy tank or gun position. Then, with the target fix gained within seconds, the chopper would pop up, fire, pop down, wait for the explosion, and move on. The Apaches had an advantage over the Cobras as the latter, because of logistical priorities, had been assigned TOW missiles whose 447-pound electronic firing control box was much heavier than the Hellfire antitank control box used aboard the Apaches. The difference in control-box weight allowed the heavier Apaches to carry much more ordnance than the smaller, ten-thousand-pound Cobras.

It was not only the Siberian AIRDEMs that plagued the Apache/Cobra strike force but the mobile remote-controlled ZSU-23 sixty-five-round-per-minute AA quads that had already gained a reputation in the air defense of Ratmanov Island.

At Chichatka it wasn't Freeman in the lead M-1 A-1 who realized what had happened but one of the model-airplane-sized Pioneer UAVs—unmanned aerial reconnaissance vehicles—launched from the column's midsection.

Heading into the cacophony of fire, snow-laden trees shattering and splitting on either side of it, snow, fire, and dirt sweeping across the road from the AIRDEMs' explosions, Freeman's tank in the first four-tank platoon was a thousand yards from the summit of the hill before Chichatka Station. Sitting higher, behind the gunner, who was encased by solid steel beneath the base of the 120-millimeter cannon, Freeman moved his right thumb and depressed the M-1 A-1 cupola's traverse and laying control, his eyes flicking over the nine observation periscopes he had available to him, ready in an instant to go to "override" control should he glimpse the hull or any other part of an enemy tank or its camouflage net.

On either side of the road, fire breaks ran through the taiga, but as yet he saw neither tank tracks, though these would have been covered by the recent snowfall, nor any other sign of troop concentrations. Though he could see nothing of the enemy, Freeman, like the loader on his left and the gunner and driver in front of him, was sweating with concentration, the sour odor filling the tank. And despite the fact that the Abrams' superb torsion-bar suspension made it the smoothest tank ride in the world, allowing the gun to traverse and remain stabilized regardless of the degree of buck and yaw even at full speed over rough ground, the fact was that a tank was still a tank, not a convertible.

The sheer volume of noise within the tank—an echo chamber for the fifteen-hundred-horsepower gas turbine, the nerve-rasping whine of the turret moving, and the heavy thumping of tread-compressed clumps of snow thrown up against the tank's belly, all combined together with the four men's intercom phone—added to the tension made worse by the knowledge that snow seeping back was reducing the infrared and laser-ranging sight capability.

Like every other tank commander, Freeman knew he would have only a split second to get a bead through the sighting scope. The "watch" was split between Freeman, taking the front 180-degree traverse, the loader, responsible for left flank to rear, and the gunner, right flank to rear. All the while Freeman was ready to plug into the intertank Bradley infantry fighting vehicle and armored personnel carrier radio network in the event that any of the tank crews spotted infantry that, he suspected, even now could be moving through the trees on either flank, waiting until enough tanks had passed before launching antitank rockets against the American armor.

A rock hit the glacis, the front-sloped armor, and Freeman saw the loader start. Mindful of the beating he'd taken on the Never-Skovorodino Road, Freeman wondered for a second whether it might have been better to wait for the self-propelled, eleven-mile-range, 155-millimeter howitzers and seventeen-mile-range M-110 A-2 artillery. But everything was a judgment call, and by the time the Never-Skovorodino road behind him would be cleared of the burned-out hulks caused by the Siberian cruise missile attack, and so clear enough for the howitzers to pass through, the Siberian armor would have time to position itself.

"Dolly Parton, three o'clock!" shouted the gunner, and in the half second it took Freeman to spot the outline of the busty armor of what looked to be a four-hundred-millimeter-thick T-72 turret, the gunner, having seen the target hidden down a firebreak on the right flank, had already got off a HESH—high-explosive squash head—round, the cold, clean air in the tank immediately replaced by a gush of hot, acrid-smelling smoke, the rush of the air conditioners' antigas overpressure system automatically cutting in. Freeman immediately spotted another angular shape, its hull down but just visible above a snow berm about a thousand meters down the road. Going to override he got the fix and, hearing the roar of a gunship overhead, squeezed the trigger, sending off another HESH round at over a thousand meters a second to the target, and saw another M-1 tank right aft of him firing. He fired again; the muffled "crump" he heard, octane exploding. The first target already burned fiercely, nothing visible but a wall of orange flame licking into the white-green forest on either side of the firebreak, snow from previously heavily laden branches sliding to the ground like sugar.

In 2.3 minutes Freeman's M-1 A-1 fired ten rounds. At this rate he knew they'd be out of ammunition in just under ten minutes. It was well within the M-1's rate of fire, the midbarrel fume extractor capable of handling the rapid passage of the fifty-six-pound HEAT round down the smooth bore, but it also meant the logistics of resupply quickly loomed as a major consideration.

So far no M-1s had been hit, to Freeman's knowledge, though in the confusion of battle, including the noise of choppers overhead, no one would really know what had happened until after. His M-1 still advancing, the low hum of the computers making constant adjustments for barrel bend, wind drift, and outside temperature audible between the heavy thumps of other M-1s firing, Freeman broke into the intertank radio circuit, ordering any tank with more than thirty of its fifty rounds expended to withdraw for rearming. Tanks further back were told to go to battle speed and to close the gap wherever the more open ground around Chichatka Station would allow. Freeman hated ordering any kind of withdrawal of tanks who still had ten rounds, but he was suspicious now because of the apparent absence of infantry.

The forests beyond the clear area were ideal for infantry antitank positions; he didn't want to be the man who led his armor into a trap. But he already had.

For the gunships it had been an unmitigated disaster, and Freeman's realization that, albeit unwittingly, he'd delivered his air cavalry into the snare of quads and AIRDEM mines set by Yesov came via a radio message from his G-2. It was short and blunt and immediately explained to the gunner in Freeman's tank and in many other M-1s how it was that Freeman's armor had been so successful so far, the only casualty being a bad eject of a spent shell that seriously burned a loader. The message sent in plain language from Freeman's G-2, its conclusion verified by the unmanned reconnaissance aircraft, was: "Enemy tanks fake."

Worse was to come. With his choppers withdrawing, his tank crews knowing they'd been had, even if the helicopters had taken out some of the remote control quads in the forest, Freeman, the recon pics now rushed to him by dispatch rider, stood there in the cupola looking at the blowups. The caption over them bore the euphemistic title: "Simulated armored vehicles. French made." The hastily typed G-2 report added the French manufacturer's name, Lancelin-Barracuda, misspelled with a single "r."

The fake tanks that had deceived the aerial reconnaissance were of fiberglass/plywood construction, their hollow interior containing a ten-gallon drum of gasoline, a four-cubic-foot box of junk metal—ample supplies of this available from the many disbanded old steam engines along the Trans-Siberian—and a clear-burning, Japanese-made kerosene lamp. The lamp produced the heat source for IF sensors aboard either the UAV reconnaissance craft or helicopters, such as those that had been flown by the thirty American helicopter pilots who were now dead. G-2 also informed Freeman that a Pentagon file matchup just received indicated that the cost to the Siberians of just one T-80 equalled the purchase price of at least sixty fake tanks. To add insult to injury, it was less subtly pointed out that C in C Second Army should also "be advised" that Allied intelligence "has known for some time that ZSU-23 quads could be tripped by the pulse of approaching aircraft engines,'' which would ''clearly explain the lack of troops.''

HEAVY CASUALTIES IN SECOND ARMY was the headline of *The New York Times*. The La Roche paper, in funereal tones that belied its brutally flippant headline, FREEMAN FOILED AGAIN, suggested it was time ''to ask serious questions about General Freeman's leadership.'' This time there was not even a reference to the Pyongyang raid or the breakout of the Dortmund-Bielefeld pocket and only an ambivalent reference to the ''heavily won'' victory on Ratmanov. Dick Norton and everyone else in Second Army now knew that Freeman had not swept a double header; what he had instead was a double humiliation. How Yesov must be laughing in Novosibirsk.

No one but Norton had the courage, when Freeman returned through the pall of still-burning helicopters, to tell Freeman the news of his wife's death. And at this moment, on the worst day of his life, General Douglas Freeman was also informed by the E-3A Sentry advance warning reconnaissance that another Siberian cruise missile offensive was on its way from Baikal. Freeman wanted to be alone with his grief for the one person who had shared his innermost ambitions and fears and all the joys and disappointments of their life together. And so did many others who had seen their closest friends literally torn asunder. But mourning was a luxury no war indulged, and the stars he wore on his collar dictated unequivocally that he give all his attention to, and husband whatever energy he had for, the welfare of his men in Second Army's most perilous hours.

Though Second Army moved forward through Chichatka, its pace was sullen, the air of defeat heavy as skunk cabbage. On one level the problem was as simple as it was critical; the U.S. Tomahawk cruise missiles had reached Baikal and taken out their designated targets, but more Siberian cruise missiles kept coming. Of course the launch sites had to be fake—only convincing enough, like the fake T-80s, in heat emission, size, and shape, to sucker the Americans into wasting precious cruise missiles of their own in the same way Freeman had lost fifteen of his prime antitank weapons in the downed Apaches and Cobras. It was evident now, G-2 had told him, that the Siberians must be using mobile sites, somehow covering their tracks, which the satellites weren't picking up.

"Maybe they're dragging a bush behind them," said a junior officer jokingly. But no one was laughing, especially not the commander of the marine expeditionary force, who had lost another fifty-six men and forty-three wounded to the latest Siberian cruise attack.

Freeman, Norton, and the G-2 colonel were poring over the latest satellite reconnaissance pictures of the Baikal area, the colonel having circled the four Ushkanyi Islands jutting up like pimples in the photograph. Next to the satellite pics he put four tatty amateur photographs of the islands, slightly out of focus, the islands looking like tiny white stones encrusted by the ice. "What are these splotches?" asked Freeman in as desultory a tone as Norton had ever heard. The general was putting on his long white camouflage winter coat, preparing to go for one of his walks, and Norton couldn't blame him. It was bad enough to lose a game without having to suffer replays in the dugout.

"Splotches?" said the colonel. "Well, most of it, I think, is overexposure—especially on these amateur shots we were sent. Some of it, of course, is varying thicknesses in the ice." He tapped the amateur photographs, brought to them by one of the Buryat underground who'd nearly got shot by a jittery marine and who "claimed," the colonel said suspiciously, that he'd gotten them from some Jewish underground.

Freeman grunted, picked up his helmet, and, as he always did before he went out, checked that his belt revolver was fully loaded, ready to go.

"Want me to come along, General?" asked Norton.

"No. Thanks all the same, Dick." He forced a grin, trying to belie his mood to the others. "Have to nut a few things out," he said, and was gone, flurries of snow bursting in unceremoniously just before the door closed. Outside the wind was moaning through the taiga.

"Some congressmen," said one of the G-2 officers, "are pressing for his recall."

"Where the hell are they coming from?" asked Norton, refusing to be drawn into any speculation about Freeman's fitness for command. But his interjection was taken by the others as one that any duty-bound aide would have to make when his superior had his back against the wall. But if they thought that Freeman was venturing out alone to lick his wounds, they were wrong. As the general moved along the edge of the road, trucks rolling by him in the darkness, the drivers wearing infrared goggles and guided by MPs stamping their feet in the bitter cold as they kept a convoy of Second Army inching along wherever the road's shoulder was too narrow, Freeman asked himself one question: Would he have replaced any commander who had experienced the defeats he had in the last few days? The answer was an unequivocal yes—*if* the commander had had sound intelligence about a possible sucker ploy. And "No," if he hadn't had reliable information of what the Siberians were up to.

For the remainder of his walk, hands behind his back, head down against the bitter cold, Freeman thought of his index files, of all the notes he'd made about all the possible campaigns he might be called upon to fight, just as Schwarzkopf had predicted and readied himself for a desert war. He recalled the history of the Russias, of the Transbaikal, which he had read as assiduously as the chronicles of Sherman and Grant; and he thought, too, of Nolan Ryan of the Texas Rangers on that unforgettable day in '91 when, before the game against Toronto, Ryan confessed to his coach, "My back hurts, my heel hurts, and I've been pounding Advil all day. I don't feel good. I feel old today. Watch me." They had watched him, and after he performed the miracle, he proclaimed, "I never had command of all three pitches like I did tonight. . . . It was my most overpowering no-hitter."

"By God," Freeman told himself, "watch me, you bastards!" He walked for another half hour and on the way back to the G-2 hut availed himself of the MEF's satellite hookup, ordering a call to the Pentagon on scrambler after which, without a word, he put down the phone and made his way back to the G-2.

In the intelligence hut the colonel in charge was alarmed when he saw Freeman, the ice crust on the general's eyebrows making him appear particularly despondent and grim. The colonel rose, forcing a smile, being as cheery as you could be with a man who had just lost his wife and who was now in the blackest hole of his career.

"Coffee, sir?" asked a corporal.

"Potemkin!" said Freeman. Norton, who'd been hunched over a pile of SITREPS that chronicled the disastrous day's action, pushed himself away from the fold-up desk and walked over to where the general, snowflakes now melting and dripping from his coat, was taking off his gloves, rubbing his hands vigorously, and nodding his thanks. He took the coffee, gratefully cupping it with both hands, letting the steam clear his sinuses. "*Sibir*. Know what it means, Colonel?" he asked the intelligence chief without taking his eyes off the laid-out satellite photos. "Sleeping land," Freeman answered for him. "That's what we've been doing. Goddamn sleepwalking. Well, I've had enough!" Other officers in the hut stopped what they were doing and watched him. "Potemkin," repeated Freeman. "Prince in the time of Catherine the Great. Whenever he heard she was leaving the Winter Palace to have a look-see among her subjects, Potemkin would have fake villages built all along her route, neat façades, so she wouldn't know what the real situation was." He looked around at the assembled officers. "Fake tanks, gentlemen. Fake launch sites—all of 'em."

"But," responded the intelligence colonel, "those cruise missiles they fired were real—"

"Yes, but not from there." Freeman was using the monocle to circle the lake. "Not around Baikal. Or from the islands—too obvious. *In* it."

It was said so calmly, matter-of-factly, yet almost casually, that for a second no one saw it, and when they did there were a few unsettling looks among the intelligence group. It wasn't the first commander some of them had seen crack up. One of the junior officers laughed—perhaps it was the general's idea of light relief.

"Ah, yes," put in a major. "Only one problem with that, sir." The officer was astounded that no one saw the objection; it was so obvious.

"The ice," said Freeman, anticipating him, still looking at the photographs. "These photographs. Something bothered me about them earlier this evening." The monocle was moving from one of the satellite photos to the amateur pictures report-edly taken by a member of the Jewish underground. "How thick is the ice on the lake?"

"Two to four feet," shrugged the colonel.

"Exactly!" said Freeman. "And why is that?"

One of the junior officers toward the back turned to whisper to his colleague, "Because it's friggin' winter."

Freeman surprised and alarmed the young lieutenant by hav-ing overheard the remark. As the general turned, the monocle caught a glint of light, giving him an unbalanced, even mad look even as he concurred. "Precisely, Lieutenant. Winter. But why does the ice cover vary? That's the question."

The monocle popped out into Von Freeman's hand, and he gathered the men in closer. "Look here!" The monocle was tapping the photos again. "These amateur shots which you got from the Jewish underground. Fuzzy, bit out of focus." And then he turned to the K-14 satellite pictures. These were much sharper, but they had one thing in common—apart from being in black and white. The monocle moved from the southwestern end near Port Baikal to the far north of the 390-mile-long lake. "Some of the ice is whiter-looking than the rest. The amateur shots, taken from the southern shore, show the same thing." The officers crowding around the table saw the splotchy effect easily enough. "You said, Colonel," continued Freeman, "that the ice thickness varies from two to four feet."

"Yes, sir." The colonel saw the general's point. "That would explain why some areas are whiter, more dense, than others."

"But why?" Freeman asked, and again answered his own question. "Spring water escaping from fissures in the bottom of the lake. Happens in all lakes, gentlemen. I'm something of an authority on ice."

"Jesus!" the junior lieutenant said, but this time he spoke so softly that Freeman didn't hear it.

"Met boys call it upwelling," continued Freeman. "Com-mon enough. Same thing happens at sea. Springs bubble up and spread out. Reflects the light differently." Freeman let them wait. He wasn't the most flamboyant general in the U.S. army for nothing. Substance, yes, but he knew the value of style. And this is where the training, the reading—the Patton-like attention to detail—paid off. "Subs," he said. "They're using subs, gentlemen. Lake is more than twice the size of the Grand Canyon. And deeper, over six thousand feet. They've been doing a Potemkin on us, gentlemen. Fake launch sites like fake tanks. We've been firing off cruise missiles at over a million bucks a pop for sweet fuck all. They're imitating the nerpa!"

Norton thought it was the name of a ship.

"Seal!" explained Freeman. "I remember it because it was mentioned in the chronicles of Genghis Khan." Freeman's monocle slid southeast of Baikal. "Genghis Khan was born here. Ruled from Vladivostok to Moscow." Freeman was shaking his head in admiration. "Magnificent son of a bitch. Then his descendants were swept out by the Cossacks. Cossack cavalry was like our M-1s—went through 'em like crap through a goose. But even then the Mongols—they thought Baikal was holy—knew about the nerpa. Only freshwater seal in the world."

The G-2 was looking across at Norton, visibly alarmed, the general's rambling, seemingly unconnected soliloquy a symptom of crackup. But the G-2 officer was mistaken, and Norton knew they were in the midst of a Freeman brainstorm.

"For the life of me," said Freeman, "while I was out there tonight walking I couldn't understand why that damn seal was on my mind." He turned to Norton. "Like the rivers, Dick. Kept at me. Soon as I heard our Tomahawks had hit their marks but the missiles kept coming. There was only one answer. Missiles were there but they weren't. Submarines. But how could they transport something as big as a submarine to Baikal? And there's no shipbuilding on Baikal. Nothing. Anyway you need an enormous infrastructure." Freeman looked about his audience. "The nerpa seal, gentlemen." The monocle in his right hand was tapping his temple. "The seal. Has to breathe. Spends its winter in the water using a dozen or so air holes—has to keep them open so he picks the thin ice. That's how the subs do it, gentlemen. Pop up through the thin ice, fire, and go back down." There was a stunned silence of admiration broken by Freeman. "Problem is, gentlemen, what to do?"

"Hit the ice?" said the junior lieutenant eagerly. "With our cruise missiles. Or have our subs launch ICBMs—conventional warheads."

Freeman shook his head. "Thinking in the right direction, son, but you're missing a few things. No good hitting the ice. Warhead explodes, expends all its energy on impact. Remember how far Baikal is from the coast, from here. We've been dropping them by air. From our subs—even one close to the coast— a cruise missile, travelling at five hundred miles per hour, even if it could reach the lake from the coast, which it can't, would take hours. By that time their sub would be long gone from its firing position."

"But," cut in the colonel, "General, you just finished saying you can't transport a submarine to a lake. And their very length—"

"Midgets," said Freeman. "That's all I can think of. It has to be." He turned to Norton. "Dick—young David Brentwood?"

"SAS?"

"Yes. His brother. Crackerjack sub skipper—"

"Pacific Fleet, sir."

"Yes. Where the hell is he?"

"Haven't got a clue, General."

"Find out. Immediately. I need expert advice. And Dick?"

"Sir?"

"David Brentwood. Where's he?"

Norton shrugged. "Far as I know, he's still on Ratmanov. Or at one of the Alaskan—"

"Get him, too. No reason why we can't make this a family affair."

"Sir," proffered Norton, "if it's information about midget subs, I suggest we save time and call the Pentagon. They'll—"

"No, no. I've already done that," said Freeman, his irritability rising in direct proportion to his excitement, the men around him watching with the awe of beginning violinists realizing they were watching a maestro conducting and composing at the same time. "I've already got the information on that." He seemed grumpy that Norton hadn't made the connection. "Goddamn it! Nerpa's a small seal, you see. Only four and a half feet long. A midget.

"Most likely candidate, the Pentagon says," Freeman announced, "is this thing. A GST—standing for gaseous storage in a toroidal hull.'' He flattened a crumpled fax. The GST was an ugly thing to look at.

"Designed,'' Freeman informed his listeners, ''by some Italian joker called Guinio Santi.''

The picture of the sub looked like what the Pentagon and others had described as a ''Michelin tire man lying on his side.'' This was before the outer, more streamlined hull, was added on. It made the GST look like a huge egg, the multiple bicycle-tube ring effect under the superstructure created by three-inch-diameter piping that, wound around and around the hull, allowed engineers to overcome the problems of making a simple, relatively cheap, nonnuclear, quiet submarine. This also meant it was a much less detectable submarine. Because of the wraparound piping, the GST, unlike the other nonnuclear subs, did not have to come up for air so often and risk disclosing its position either by showing a snorkel or by creating thermal patching, which put regular nuclear and diesel-electric subs in danger from aerial and satellite surveillance.

And so, ironically, its plans stolen from the Italian designer by Chernko's agents, the fat, egg-shaped GST, using a constantly reusable, nonnuclear chemical-exchange-powered engine—originally scheduled by its manufacturer, the Kuznetsky Metallurgical Kombinat, or KMK works in Novokuznetsk, 180 miles southeast of Novosibirsk, to create chaos among the Allied blue water fleets—was now, following the loss of Vladivostok and other Siberian naval bases on the coast, being used not in the Pacific or Atlantic but in the inland Sea of Baikal.

But if this much was known about the midget sub, it took Captain Robert Brentwood, USN, after a gruelling ten-hour flight by chopper and jet to Hokkaido and Second Army HQ, to fully explain to Freeman and the rest of the officers in G-2 exactly why the toroidal hull was so dangerous. With a total displacement of only 250 tons against the Soviet-made Alfa's 4,200 tons and the U.S. Sea Wolf's 10,000 tons, the toroidal-shaped hull would occupy less than 6 percent of regular attack-size submarines. Only fifty feet long, it was designed specifically to defeat the superior sound-detection technology of the United States and her allies, its exhaust gases being constantly stored and scrubbed rather than being expelled into the water. With a burst speed of twenty-five knots submerged, faster than most full-size diesel-electric subs, and a cruising speed of plus or minus fifteen knots, it could range 230 miles without coming to the surface. Except, as Brentwood pointed out, to fire its missiles. And even these would be fired subsurface, after its "pic" and/or small float-drum charges had blown a hole in the thinner ice.

"It's a formidable weapon," conceded Brentwood. "Compared to our subs, a GST of this type would look like a speck of fly dirt. The Iraqis were being trained for midget subs in Poland, but when the Gulf war came Hussein never got a chance to use them. Couldn't get them through the embargo."

"Why the hell didn't *we* go for it?" asked Freeman.

"Because," said Brentwood, with elegant simplicity, "we thought we had the best."

"How big a crew?" Freeman asked.

"Six to eight, sir," replied Brentwood. "Essentially same controls as for any submarine. Long shifts. Probably twelve hours on, twelve off, three to four men each shift. Minimum would be captain, engineer, electronics warfare officer, and CPO or enlisted man on the rudder control. General, asked Brentwood, "do we have any wreckage of the cruise missiles used against Second Army? Any that didn't go off?"

"They all went off," said Freeman grimly. "Why?"

"Well, I'd guess they were using SS-21Ds—sub-launched, converted land-attack missiles. Twenty-one feet long, two-thousand-mile range. It's so much like our Tomahawk, we call it the Tomahawski."

The junior lieutenant thought it was amusing. Freeman didn't. He was figuring that with each salvo fired on Second Army being a minimum of twenty missiles, there wasn't just one GST out there that they had entrained to Port Baikal from wherever the hell they were making them—there were more. He put it to Brentwood.

"Once clear of the water," said Brentwood, "missile's jackknife fins extend, reach Mach 1.2 in two minutes. And I'd say with ripple launch, General, and given their length, we're looking at maybe four missiles apiece."

"What's this ripple launch?"

"Well, sir, you fire one missile from your starboard forward tube, the second, port aft, to counteract the rocking effect of the first missile. Then you fire port forward, then port aft."

"How long would you say to launch?" Freeman put to him.

"Two minutes. Four minutes and they're loafing."

"Holy dooly!" said the young lieutenant, with a high whistle.

Freeman glowered at him then looked at Brentwood. "So how many subs do they have?"

"I think we're looking at five, General. If I'm right about four missiles apiece. That we can't be sure of. But if we're talking twenty missiles a salvo, then that's just about—"

"Yes, yes," said Freeman impatiently.

"I should add, General, it depends on the thickness of the ice or if there's an open space due to upwelling. They could probably launch in less time. Same thing happens when you're in the polar ice. You can get wafer thickness or—"

"Yes, yes," cut in Freeman, again impatiently, his mood reflecting his and G-2's realization that if he could not take out the subs—and he couldn't by air or missile attack because of the ice roof—he'd lose the war. "They have to be taken out," he said, looking steadily at Brentwood, who felt his stomach roll over like an ice-encrusted ship, capsizing, top-heavy in the polar pack.

When Freeman outlined his plan, he didn't make it an order but a request, adding, "Besides, your brother's experienced in these matters. He'll be a great help." Freeman paused. "You're the oldest, aren't you?" Freeman made his question about Brentwood being the eldest sound like small talk at a cocktail party.

"Yes, sir," said Brentwood evenly. "I'm the oldest."

"I hope I don't embarrass you, Captain, but damn, your father must be proud of you boys."

"I wouldn't know," Brentwood parried. "I haven't seen him in over a year. I've been at sea for so long—"

"Good! Good!" said Freeman, slapping Brentwood affectionately on the back as he steered him over to the map table. "And when this is over, we'll see you two get special leave. Fair enough?"

Robert Brentwood looked across at General Freeman. "Fairest thing I've heard all day, General."

"By God, Brentwood, that's the spirit." He turned to Norton. "I wish that old limey fart—" He paused. "What's his name, Dick? At the White House?"

"Soames, sir. Brigadier Soames."

"Yes, well I wish he was here. We'd show him American know-how. Eh, Dick?"

"General, that lake is heavily defended. Now that railhead at Port Baikal is bound to be heavily defended. Only place in the south where they could have slid a midget down slips direct from the rail tracks."

"Defended by AA batteries, yes," responded Freeman, "but they're expecting fighters, bombers, Dick. Not a commando raid."

Norton was confused. "But sir, the risk of a drop through all that AA—"

"Drop?" said Freeman, surprised. "Who the hell said anything about a drop?" He thrust his monocle at the map. "I'm not going to send brave men to drop on top of AA fire. You've got it ass backwards, Dick. We'll fly them in. Can leave in the dark, but it'll have to be a daylight raid, given our scanty intelligence on the layout of Port Baikal." He was talking to Brentwood now. "Your brother'll lead an SAS/Delta troop. Twelve men." Without a pause he told Norton to make the preparations. "Now, Brentwood, you tell me what you need. I suggest seven more men from our navy base in Hokkaido to bring your strength to eight. Or do you want to pick your own outfit?"

"My own crew, sir."

Freeman, his left hand pressed hard against his forehead like a sunshade, right hand with the monocle pumping time, was walking back and forth in the G-2 hut, giving orders left and right, including the minutiae of equipment needed by the small but mobile force. Norton and the G-2 officers took notes, looking like overworked waiters at a fast-food takeout.

"How long to get them here, Dick?"

"Took me ten hours," said Brentwood, not quite yet believing that he was actually volunteering for the mission.

"Outstanding!" said Freeman. He looked at his watch to put

the mission's ETD on Zulu time. "Oh three hundred hours tomorrow." Freeman was now talking to his logistics officer, Malcolm Wain. "Mal, I want you to oversee chopper preparation. Suggestions?"

Wain took the roll-rule and punched in the numbers on his calculator. "Five hundred miles with extra tanks—yes, sir. NOE flying. It'll be risky, General. They'll be under the radar screen of course, travelling that low, but there's always the unexpected and—"

Freeman swung about from the map. "What the hell's the matter with you? I picked you because you were a man with initiative. You can't handle it, Mal, I'll get someone who can." There was silence in the G-2 hut, broken only by the steady hum of the computers.

"Yes, sir."

"All right," said Freeman. "Can you get them there?"

"Yes, sir. Four hours flying. Reach there by dawn. Return after dark. Two Cobras riding shotgun for two Super Sea Stallion choppers carrying the strike team. Six SAS/Delta troops, four of Brentwood's crew and four collapsible Snowcat 'Arrow' vehicles in each Stallion. With a Stallion crew of three, that makes thirteen men apiece. One chopper goes down, we still have one team—albeit a skeleton one—intact."

"Anyone superstitious about thirteen?" asked Freeman. He gave no one an opportunity to answer. "I'm not." He paused, hands on his hips, shaking his head and looking up at the man he'd chosen because he was reputedly the best of the finest in the service whose promise was *"Venio non videor"*—"I come unseen." "By God, Brentwood, I envy you. I wish I was going with you, but I don't know beans about driving a submersible."

"Too bad, sir," said Brentwood in as neutral a tone as he could manage. Norton coughed, turning away. The G-2 duty officer was handing Freeman an urgent decode. After reading the message, the general shook hands with Robert Brentwood. "You and Dick work out the fine-tuning here with Wain." With that the general turned abruptly and walked over to the far corner of the hut where a terrain map had been spread out on one of the large folding tables.

Brentwood looked across at Norton, feeling as if he'd just

been through a squall, suddenly realizing that the "fine-tuning" would have to include some way of getting back—after they'd got to Port Baikal and highjacked a GST. "Maybe," he said to Dick Norton, "they'll all be asleep."

"It's very sparsely populated," said Norton. It was the only thing he could think of that might be remotely comforting. "Port Baikal—from the aerials—is just a bit of a village. I don't think you'll have trouble getting in there. Our chopper guys are the best in the world—flew special operations in the Iraqi desert."

"Bit colder, I guess," said Brentwood.

"Minus thirty. Good for the choppers, though. Gives 'em more lift."

"Great," said Brentwood who, though facing the hazards of the deep every day of a submarine patrol, had always been of the mind, unlike his kid brother, that anything that flew was inherently unsafe. He was still watching the general who had now, it seemed, turned his attention to some other matter. The G-2 duty officer came up and gave Norton a copy of the decode.

"Sure would like to talk to him about some of those 'finer details' he mentioned," said Robert Brentwood. "Like what the SAS/Delta boys'll do if we make it to Port Baikal. They spend a few days hiking in the woods, waiting for us?"

"Oh," said Norton, moving under the light to better read the message, "they're trained to survive for days, even weeks, in—" He didn't finish what he was going to say, falling silent, jaws clenched, realizing now why Freeman had abruptly ended the conversation with Brentwood to go to the maps. Norton showed the message to Brentwood. The Thirty-first "Stalingrad" Motorized Division, leading the Fifth Siberian Army, was only two hundred miles away. Robert Brentwood was a naval, not a military, tactician, but it was as obvious as the nose on his face that if he couldn't kill the cruise threat from Baikal, Freeman wouldn't stand a chance.

Two hours later, as they were going over the supplies needed, from every piece of winter clothing to the hand-held Magellan GPS—global positioning system—that gives a soldier his position within fifteen meters anywhere in the world, the young G-2 lieutenant came in with full kit for Brentwood, which included a small capsule called the "L" pill. "It's optional," explained the lieutenant with an apologetic smile. "We've had reports that in the Urals, when our boys from Ten Corps were cut off, well—"

"Siberians don't take prisoners," said Norton. "They figure looking after POWs is a drain on resources."

There was an awkward silence, which Brentwood himself broke by a game attempt at humor. "I take it 'L' isn't for love."

"Lethal," said the lieutenant. Norton said nothing. There was absolutely no point in telling Brentwood that the Siberians wouldn't even waste a bullet on prisoners. In the Urals they'd used their rifle butts on a company of Ten Corps POWs. It saved ammunition—even if it took a little longer.

"You'd better get some sleep," the lieutenant ingenuously suggested, then looked about conspiratorially. "I can get you a fifth of sake. Not as good as whiskey, but—"

"Sake'll be fine. Thanks, Lieutenant." Brentwood was a stickler for running a dry submarine and rarely drank, even when he was ashore. Last time he could remember having done so was having a beer with Rosemary on his last leave. But right now a fifth of anything would suit him just fine.

CHAPTER TWENTY-ONE

COLONEL NEFSKI, RECENTLY of Khabarovsk, had already learned that Marshal Yesov had arrived in Irkutsk, forty miles west of Lake Baikal. Yesov had come not simply to finalize the attack but to use the cruise missiles aboard the *miniaturnye podvodnye lodki*—"midget submarines"—to produce a total *ognevoy udar*—"fire shock"—and *udar voisk*—"troop shock"— against the American Second Army before Freeman could reach beyond the Amur hump and split his forces in a two-pronged offensive, one southwest to Irkutsk, the other swinging north to Yakutsk. If either—or worse, both—was ever captured by the Americans, it would afford them non-air-refueling radii to pound the Siberian army's arsenals and factories.

The political officer, the *Zampolit*, of the Siberian Thirty-first, was screaming at Nefski. Advance SPETS scouts, dropped ahead of the Thirty-first with their BMD fighting vehicles at the tip of the Stalingrad Division's spearhead, had rounded up several civilians near Kultuk at the southernmost end of Lake Baikal. One of the prisoners, a Jew suspected of working for the *yevreyskoe podpolie*—"Jewish underground"—had been "persuaded" after his fingernails had been torn out to reveal that the camera he possessed had indeed been used for sabotage; that photographs of the lake had been passed on via the *Rossiya* express to contacts at Irkutsk further west. The KGB knew there was an active Jewish underground working from Irkutsk all along the Trans-Siberian to Krasnoyarsk railhead 530 miles west of Baikal then northeast on the BAM—the Baikal-Amur mainline loop—from which it could find its way through to Allied lines. Nevertheless, despite what might be the seriousness of the situation, Nefski refused to be cowed. Who did this *Zampolit* think he was—Chernko? Nefski asked him coolly how it was that he assumed it was one of Nefski's prisoners who had received the photos of the lake or whatever from the old Jew.

"I *told* you!" shouted the political officer. "The old man confessed. He gave it to someone on the *Rossiya*. By the time the SPETS got the old fool to talk, the photos had already been passed."

"To whom?"

"The old Jew had no names. It's a rule—they never give one another their real names. All the SPETS got from him was that it was a Jewess on the Khabarovsk carriage."

"Was she pretty?" enquired Nefski.

The *Zampolit*'s face was creased with worry. "If the Americans suspect we're slipping the midgets under the ice from Port Baikal at the southern end of the lake they'll try to bomb the rail line and—"

"Why?" said Nefski, not minding his insolent tone. "What

good would bombing Port Baikal do? The submarines are already safe—deep in the lake.''

"Yes, but they must come in for armament resupply.''

"Ah,'' said Nefski, trying to reduce the consequences for both of them, because he had suddenly realized who it might be. "I don't think the Americans know, Comrade. And if they did try to bomb Port Baikal and got through the heavy antiaircraft ring we have all about the lake, so what? If they hit one or two subs in the dock that were in for ammunition resupply, the other subs would still be at large in the lake. Plus they would be warned off by the explosions.''

"Ah!'' said the *Zampolit*, mocking Nefski's own tone. "You don't understand the Americans, comrade. Haven't you heard? They can be ingenious. They will try something.''

"Then,'' shrugged Nefski, "put everyone around the lake on extra alert.''

The political officer conceded the point. "Nevertheless, you must try to find this woman and stop any other messages that might be—''

"Oh,'' said Nefski, lighting a cigarette, "there is no mystery there, Comrade. There's only one pretty Jewess that was sent from Khabarovsk to Irkutsk. I have interrogated her before. Her whole family is rotten.''

"Then I suggest you question her again. Get as much information from her as you can before you get rid of her.''

Nefski took a long drag on his cigarette—a Winston, the *Zampolit* noted enviously. Imported from Japan, no doubt. "That might be difficult,'' Nefski was saying. "To eliminate her.'' The political officer looked angrily at the KGB colonel. "Why? You shoot people every day. It's your job.''

"A pilot,'' said Nefski, "transferred to Irkutsk PVO with all the others from Khabarovsk station—he fancies her.''

"I don't care what some pilot fancies,'' began the political officer.

"This pilot is the son of a high party official, Comrade. Kiril Marchenko.''

"He's in Moscow!'' said the *Zampolit* defiantly.

"Ah, yes, but who knows who else is in Moscow? Perhaps he's helping us.''

"I don't care. Interrogate her then have her shot. Moscow's finished. Novosibirsk is what counts now, Comrade."

"The pilot is one of our aces," Nefski informed him.

The *Zampolit* sneered contemptuously. "Never heard of him. Eliminate her."

Nefski rose and saluted. "As you wish, Comrade."

Nefski told himself he wasn't afraid of the political officer, but nor was he a fool. You did what political officers told you or you would be eliminated.

CHAPTER TWENTY-TWO

"CHRIST! IT'S COLDER'N a fish's tit!" These were the first words that Aussie Lewis said as he stepped off the C-5 after the long haul from Alaska via Japan to the Never-Skovorodino road. "There a whorehouse 'round here, Yank?"

The marine assigned to drive the twelve SAS/Delta Force troops to Freeman's HQ was busy chipping ice from the Humvee truck's windscreen. "Nearest cathouse around here, buddy, is Japan. Thataway!"

"Oh, lovely!" said Aussie. "You hear that, Davey boy? You're gonna have to play with yourself for the duration."

"Better than being on Rat," responded David Brentwood, saluting and shaking hands with the marine colonel who, though senior in rank to David Brentwood, was awed by the presence of a Congressional Medal of Honor winner.

"Take no notice of him, sir," David told the colonel. "He's an Aussie. They all talk like that. Good man in a firefight, though."

The colonel grinned. "Yes, I knew a few in 'Nam around Da

Nan—'' The Humvee's radio crackled loudly in the frigid air. "Incoming! Incoming!"

Aussie Lewis hadn't heard any heavy artillery. Where were the Russian guns? The Commies didn't fire any artillery unless they had at least a hundred of them.

"Cruise missiles!" yelled a marine. "Let's get outta here!"

"Beautiful," said Aussie, heaving his eighty-pound pack into the back of the Humvee. "Hear that, Choir?" he called out to Williams. "No fucking class, these Sibirs. Can't wait till a man's unpacked." Williams, the last man in, pulled the door shut. "Well, with you yabbering away, Aussie, they'll have no trouble knowing where we are."

"Now, don't get shirty!" said Aussie and, either oblivious to or uncaring of a colonel of marines being present, adopted Choir Williams's accent, explaining to all in the truck, "He's a fucking Welshman. Take him out of the Estedford and he gets terrible cranky. He'd rather be singing in chapel you see. Tenor—'Men of Harlech' and all that shit!"

David Brentwood, in the front with the colonel and driver, turned around. "You pack those Norsheets?" He was anxious that the Norwegian tent segments, which could be used to make various sizes of small tents, had been brought along.

"Planning on using them, are you?" asked Aussie.

"Did you pack them?"

"Yeah. Course I did. But we won't need 'em with our cold-weather garb," he added. Beneath each man's Gore-Tex parka and overpants there were three other layers: fiber pile, quilted jacket and pants, and polypropylene underwear. "She'll be right, mate."

"Thought you were cold?" said Choir good-naturedly.

"Not for long, Choir, not for long. Girls all say that I'm one hot—"

There was a scream of air, an enormous flash of light over the next rise. They saw a Humvee thrown at least forty feet into the air, its doors flying off, the black silhouettes of the marines flung from it.

The colonel and the SAS/Delta troopers felt the sudden jerk of acceleration as the driver put his foot down, and while Aussie might have been one of the toughest of the twelve commandos, he had never been under cruise salvo fire before, and wondered what the hell the driver was doing. But the marine wasn't listening to advice; his helmet hard up against the windscreen, he peered through a tiny hole in the ice, picking up the infrared headlight beam.

"They land a quarter-mile apart," explained the marine colonel. "Like running a traffic light. Provided you can—" Suddenly he stopped. Night was day, and they felt a warm wind actually push the Humvee forward as the vehicle hit fifty-five miles an hour on the hard snow road, started to skid, and righted in a rain of dirt, snow, and God knew what else falling on the vehicle's roof as it continued on to Freeman's HQ. No one said anything until the vehicle came to a shuddering stop, an MP swearing and jumping out of the way just in time, his weapon raised, momentarily fearing it was some kind of terrorist attack. The driver sat there shaking, the MP bawling him out. The colonel toned everything down, and while the SAS/Delta team moved into Freeman's HQ to be briefed on what the general called the "game plan," Choir Williams, tongue in cheek, blithely asked, "You making book on this mission, Aussie?"

Aussie didn't answer until after the briefing, which lasted a half hour.

"Well?" asked Choir Williams. "What odds are you giving now?"

Aussie was checking his ammo pack. "Why don't you take a flying fuck at a doughnut?"

"Oh, how kind," said Choir, turning to David Brentwood. "You hear that, Captain? Is that any way to talk to a tenor? I ask you now."

Aussie saw ice was already forming on his magazine pouches, and as he replied to Choir Williams his breath looked like a fiery dragon's. "Why don't you take a flying—"

"All right," cut in Brentwood. "Six hours sleep—then it's off to the lake resort."

"*Resort?* Oh, spare me!" moaned Aussie. "*Two* fucking comedians. I can't stand it."

"Don't worry, Aussie," said O'Reilly, one of the four Americans, including David Brentwood, in the team. "Least you don't have to hoof it."

"I don't like those friggin' Snowcat 'Arrows,' " said Aussie. "Make more noise'n a bloody chopper."

"Not to worry," responded Choir. "Snow'll muffle the sound, Aussie."

"I'd still rather hike in."

"Not enough time," commented David Brentwood. "You heard the general."

"Too bad," said Aussie, shifting his attention to his nose, one of the most insidious dangers of a winter campaign being that the flesh could freeze so fast you didn't even notice it. "Least my prick is still warm."

"You're hopeless," proclaimed Choir. "Get in the truck, you horrible man."

David Brentwood was glad of the repartee among members of the team. Without high spirits, not even the best equipment in the world would be enough on such a mission as this. As the Humvee drove away, David Brentwood went back in the HQ to see his eldest brother. The briefing of the mission had been so detailed and required so much attention that apart from a handshake they'd not had the opportunity to say much to one another. David felt badly about it, but the fact was he hesitated going in to see his brother. They'd never been that close, the age gap between them much wider than it was between Robert and Ray, the second oldest. Besides, having stayed alive during the war so far without having seen that much of one another, David harbored what he knew was an irrational but powerful conviction that seeing one another now and being on the same mission would be—well, just plain bad luck.

He had no idea that Robert, now opening the door, holding up a fifth of Vodka, felt exactly the same.

CHAPTER TWENTY-THREE

NEFSKI DREW THE blackout curtains but not because of any imminent threat of an air raid on Port Baikal. The blizzard sweeping down the 390-mile-long lake, though abating, was still wrapping Irkutsk, further west from Port Baikal at the mouth of the outflowing Angara River, in thick, protective sheets of white. It would make even instrument flying for the Americans difficult, if they were so foolhardy as to try anything—particularly over the heavily defended eastern perimeter of the lake.

In any event, Nefski welcomed the overcast for another reason: the room assigned him by the local authorities for the interrogation was on the ground floor of the old Port Baikal library, and, as such, anyone passing by could see in unless the drapes were closed. And the room was stuffy, overheated, the result of the ample electricity produced by the hydroelectric dam further up the ice-free stretch of river that flowed westward toward Irkutsk. He wanted a cold room, for cold, hunger, isolation had, in Nefski's long experience of interrogating prisoners, been the most reliable trinity when it came to extracting information. Given his choice, he'd choose isolation above everything else, and for this reason he'd regretted having put her among the other prisoners during the withdrawal from Khabarovsk; it had broken her weeks of solitary. While she hadn't been allowed to speak to the other prisoners on the train, their very presence and the fact that the Siberians were retreating from Khabarovsk had given her new hope, her wild, defiant eyes fiercer than ever on the edge of starvation, stoking her fire of resistance.

Nefski pushed away the gooseneck lamp the corporal here at Port Baikal had turned on Alexsandra in his usual inept attempt to equal Nefski's record for "confessions." Not wanting to show she was grateful in any way, she shifted her head only slightly, as if the bright light had not been at all uncomfortable. Nefski waited—he had no intention of hurrying it. That was the problem with so many interrogators, like the buffoon of a corporal who was now ogling the Jewess from his post by the closed door. The younger KGB recruits wanted everything done yesterday—all the information to come at once, in a torrent. On the other hand, the *Zampolit* had a point: time *was* pressing.

Though he knew she didn't smoke, Nefski offered her a cigarette to demonstrate goodwill—the fact that he was willing to be civil about it. Or else. He was determined not to let a woman—a Jew at that—put it over him, for though he was a full colonel, having distinguished himself in the regular army's *Maskirovka*, or camouflage, units from which he'd gone on to KGB border-troop rank and then to Khabarovsk, he was laughed at behind his back because of his wife. He knew the corporal and other junior NCOs enjoyed their jokes at his expense around their samovar of a morning. They called her the "T-85." There was no such tank, the eighty-five centimeters, or thirty-four inches, said to be the size of her neck. With a neck like that, it was said that she was worth two 152-millimeter howitzers. Just let her loose in the Thirty-first's spearhead and let her run at tanks. It would be the end of the Americans.

It wasn't funny to Nefski. In his late fifties, his sexual appetite hadn't abated, but his wife's had. She had become more interested, it seemed, in the Japanese and Chinese delicacies that he had been able to "acquire" from ship's captains whose vessels had docked at Vladivostok. He had thought of using the promise of the expensive clothes and other bric-a-brac he could weasel or threaten from the merchantmen of the ports in his old jurisdiction, and it might have bought him her favor. But she was so enormous, so off-putting, he had ceased trying, encouraging the worst of the rumors he'd overheard, namely that he couldn't do it anymore because he'd lost it—that search parties had failed to find it in her taiga.

Nefski's face reddened at the very thought of the humiliation he was suffering. No one, of course, would dare hint at his nickname of "Limp Dick" to his face. If they had, he would have had them shot on "corruption" charges—he had enough evidence among his "forbidden imports." Or he could have sent them to one of the *perms*, the far-flung Siberian labor camps that had been reopened after Gorbachev's idiot regime.

He drew heavily on his Winston, the thought of having his detractors put in a *shizo*, the four-by-eight punishment cell, more and more appealing. No blankets, with a hard fir plank for a bed and the steel-grated light that was left on twenty-four hours a day. If they broke the forty-watt bulb—another month. Then let them joke about Colonel "Limp Dick." He felt his erection throbbing. Like him and the corporal, the Jewess was perspiring heavily in the overheated room, her sackcloth prison dress sticking to her like wet brown paper, her nipples tantalizingly outlined but not clearly visible, sweat trickling down the alabaster whiteness of her throat, disappearing between her breasts, her dress also clinging to her thighs. The comparison between her and his wife was like that between two entirely different species. "Whom," he asked her quietly, "did you give the photographs to at Irkutsk?" He was staring at her, the bluish-gray cigarette smoke wafting idly above him before being caught in the sultry currents of the stuffy room.

"What photos?" she shot back innocently.

"Not their actual name," he said amicably. "I don't expect that. A description of who it was. Man? Woman? How old?"

"I don't know anything about photographs."

Nefski indicated the small, narrow, black bench by the door, where overdue borrowers of state-approved books had once sat obediently before being summoned by the librarian to give good reasons why they should not be fined. "Tie her down," he told the corporal. "On her back."

She sat up rigidly, the hatred in her eyes shot through with fear.

Nefski called in two more guards. It was astonishing how strong even half-starved prisoners were when their fear overtook them. Besides his subaltern needing help, Nefski reasoned that with three other men as witnesses, it would put an end to Colonel "Limp Dick" talk.

She fought violently as they tussled with her. She didn't scream, not once, but was huffing and puffing like a dumb animal who knew instinctively it was destined for the chopping block.

"No," said Nefski, "leave her head free." He would pull her long, black hair down behind her with one hand, kissing her neck and squeezing her breasts with the other. Suck them.

After they tied her down, her breathing became even more rapid as she made futile attempts to loosen the binding tape. Nefski took the long pair of scissors from a plastic stand on the blotter and, walking over, straddled the bench. Looking down at her, he took the scissors and slit the dress open. The three other KGB men were fixed where they stood by her saturnine beauty, the subaltern so aroused he was squeezing his tongue hard between his nicotine-blackened teeth. Nefski tossed the scissors back on the desk, spat into his right hand, and wiped his hand between her legs, then did it again and again until he thought she would be wet enough. He undid his belt and unzipped his fly, letting his trousers fall down to the bench as he lowered himself onto her. She started to whimper, and he slapped her hard, snapped his fingers for one of the men's handkerchiefs, and stuffed it in her mouth. As he entered her they saw her stiffen, but Nefski only pushed harder, and the subaltern, trembling with envy, saw his chief's eyes close in ecstasy, one hand clasping one of her breasts, the other wrapped in her hair, jerking her head down hard on the bench.

After, breathless, exhausted, he stepped back, almost stumbling, telling the others it was their turn for *sverkhurochnye chasy*—"overtime." It was a good joke, he thought, and, more importantly, it would assure their silence.

None of them knew the rape would change the course of the war.

CHAPTER TWENTY-FOUR

PULLING ON SIBERIAN uniforms taken by Freeman's forces from Siberian militiamen captured in Khabarovsk, the twelve-member S/D, as the SAS/Delta team was designated in Freeman's HQ, were lost in clouds of steam rising from the long-nozzled de-icing hoses spraying the rotors of the two Super Sea Stallion choppers. The Stallions, their crews also in Siberian uniforms, would carry the team seven hundred miles, skimming over the vast taiga, in a nap-of-the-earth flying mission that would take them to Tankhoy on the southeastern shore of the lake, twenty-seven miles across from Port Baikal, the latter situated on the ice-free outflow of the Angara River.

The rotors of the two escorting Cobra attack helicopters—dwarfed by the Super Stallions, much larger at 99 feet long—were already cutting into the softly falling snow. David Brentwood would have preferred a smaller-silhouette chopper, but the big Stallions had a range of 480 nautical miles, each powered by three T64-GE-416 turboshaft engines. Strong enough to lift a 150-millimeter howitzer and the gun's five-ton truck, each of them could certainly carry four of the three-man Arrow vehicles Freeman had insisted on for the mission; above all the big choppers could carry hefty extra fuel tanks.

As important as any of its other attributes, the Stallion could be refueled in flight from a KC-130 tanker so that by using additional drop tanks for the seven-hundred-mile run in and partway out, it would be able to be refueled in the air on its way back, beyond the deadly AA missile and gun batteries around the lake. In addition, the chopper had a remarkable 27,900-foot

ceiling and also had two .50 caliber machine guns mounted
starboard and port beneath the engines' cowling, which two of
the S/D could handle if necessary.

Though it wasn't snowing heavily, the snow was bothering
the pilots of the two attack Cobras more than the Sea Stallion
crews, who had already done a lot of bad-weather flying in
"pickup and deposit" rescue missions after, and sometimes
during, the Baikal-launched missile attacks, taking litters of
wounded to MASH units, and in some cases flying them as far
back east as Khabarovsk. One of the Cobra pilots in particular
seemed spooked, grumpily ordering his weapons officer/copilot
to double-check that all red tapers had been taken from the
sixteen Hellfire antitank missiles. The copilot had already done
so, but the pilot thought the de-icing steam had momentarily
obscured the ground crew who in turn might not have seen his
thumbs-up signal. Meanwhile the seven crew members flown in
from the USS *Reagan* to join Robert Brentwood, bringing the
team up to twenty men, were adjusting their S/D-issued,
extremely-cold-weather gear.

Freeman shook hands with every man, including the four
chopper crews who were going on the mission.

"Remember now, engineers have assured us that the noise of
the Snowcat Arrows is similar to the kind of engines the Sibirs
use on their snowmobiles, so the noise in itself shouldn't draw
undue attention. And as you can see, we've spent all night paint-
ing your transport in snow/gray Siberian camouflage pattern. So
what more could you want?"

If anyone laughed, no one could hear it over the rotors of the
Sea Stallion coughing to life. "If for any reason," Freeman
continued, his voice in competition with the choppers, "you
can't rendezvous after—" He meant if the choppers were unable
to fly. "—remember, just keep heading northeast. Once you're
in the taiga on the east side of the lake, we'll lock on to your
location transmitters. That'll tell us where you are within a thousand meters. And if, God forbid, you should go down, going in
or coming out, deploy away from the craft. We'll home in on
the 'bipper' as fast as we can but I repeat, don't stay with the
chopper, no matter how tempting."

Freeman looked up into the falling snow. "And as I told you

last night, your pilots will exit our area by flying due south, then east toward Tankhoy on the east side of the lake in order to avoid any more antichopper mines the bastards might have sown directly ahead of Second Army. We're sweeping and grading for them now, but it'll take twenty-four hours.'' The general paused. "Anyway, all this is purely academic at this stage, gentlemen. I've every confidence you're not going to be spotted. Good luck!''

Aussie Lewis's tone was easy, typical of SAS/Delta veterans who, while not contemptuous of authority, were certainly not intimidated by it. "General, you think this newly painted red star'll get us in more trouble than it's worth?'' He gestured toward the nearest Sea Stallion. "Attract friendly fire?''

"All forward observers—including air and ground units—have been ordered not to fire on any chopper in our area for the next half hour. You'll be out of our fire zone after that.''

"Siberians don't have anything that looks like a Sea Stallion, do they?'' asked Aussie.

"No,'' admitted Freeman, "but the Cobras'll be out front, and their silhouettes are second cousin to the Siberians' Havoc attack helos. By the time any of 'em spot you, the Cobras will already have spotted them.''

"Right,'' said Aussie enigmatically as he grasped the cold, stiff handle of the Haskins M-500 sniper rifle case and boarded the first Sea Stallion. "Duck hunting is it, Aussie?'' asked Choir as they buckled up.

"Yeah,'' answered Lewis, his mood more buoyant after a night's sleep, and reassured by the fact that the falling snow would help screw up the enemy radar.

David Brentwood and his brother were silent, both knowing they were sharing responsibility, not only for the men under their command, but for a mission that, like Freeman, they understood could turn the tide for the U.S. Second Army and win the Siberian war.

From now on the choppers were on radio silence.

"S'truth,'' said Aussie, his mood changing abruptly, "these bloody things make a racket.''

No one among the other five S/D men aboard Stallion One—David Brentwood, Choir, and the three Delta men, O'Reilly,

Lawson, and Salvini—or the four submariners, including Robert Brentwood, said anything, all occupied by their own thoughts.

"Jesus!" said Aussie. "We're not going to a bloody funeral, you blokes. Lighten up! Anybody want a fag?" he asked. He offered a packet of filterless cigarettes.

"Bad for your lungs," said Choir disinterestedly.

"Oh, spare me," rejoined Aussie. "Where the hell you think you're—" He stopped, nudging David Brentwood and nodding toward one of the four submariners, the sonarman called Rogers from the *Reagan*. The man had his eyes closed tightly, head down, lips moving in prayer. "Say one for me, sport," said Aussie.

"Hush," said Choir with an edge that David Brentwood hadn't heard in a long time, S/D volunteers being chosen for their ability to get on with one another in situations that would have other men at one another's throats.

"Sorry, mate!" said Lewis, lighting his cigarette. "Sure you don't want a fag?"

Rogers smiled and said something, but beneath the rumbling roar of the Sea Stallion's three engines, Aussie couldn't hear him.

After flying thirty miles south-southwest of the Second Army for a distance of seventy miles above the frozen Shilka River, where the outside temperature was minus forty degrees Centigrade, the four choppers swung southeast for the five-hour run over the vast, white landscape of birch, pine, and beech taiga to Tankhoy on the southeastern side of the 390-mile-long, banana-shaped lake. Here they would deplane for the final forty-five-mile east-west run from the southernmost tip of the lake around to Port Baikal situated on the southwestern end.

They were two hours into the flight, the taiga a whitish blur beneath the haze of the falling snow, when Choir heard the high-toned alarm sounding, the weapons officer saying something that ended with ". . . locked on." Stallion One pitched so violently that Aussie almost lost his grip on the sniper rifle case. One of the submariners, walking back from having relieved himself, was thrown to the floor, sliding as the Stallion yawed hard to port. They heard a soft thump, barely discernible beneath the roar of the turboshaft.

"Splash one Havoc!" said the copilot on the internal radio. "Way to go!"

"What's going on?" asked a sickly-faced Rogers. Robert Brentwood handed him another brown paper bag.

"One of our Cobras got the bastard!" announced the Stallion's copilot excitedly.

"Hey! Hey!" two of the four submariners said, celebrating, as if suddenly brought to life by the information, their hands meeting in high fives.

"Brilliant!" said Aussie, lighting another cigarette, his tone killing any excitement in the cabin as surely as any missile. "So much for our fucking camouflage."

"They don't know where we're going," said David Brentwood, trying to reassure the submariners. "We could be reconnaissance choppers out looking for the forward units of their Thirty-first. Anyway, target's a long way off."

"That's what worries me, sport," said Aussie, electing to take the most negative implication of David's observation.

"Not like you, Aussie, is it?" said Choir, surprised. "To be fretting so."

"Hey, why don't you take a flying—"

"Knock it off!" said David. "We'll be okay. We're all a bit edgy. Only natural."

"Like All-Bran!" said Aussie, winking at Robert Brentwood and Rogers. "You blokes got all the Russki stuff down pat?" He meant the instructions above the various dials in the midget subs that would be written in the Cyrillic alphabet.

"Yes," answered Rogers, head back hard against the fuselage now, eyes half open, a drooling, seasick look about him.

"More than we need," said another submariner. "You get us to one of those GSTs, and we'll take her down."

"No problem," said Aussie easily, his mood swing uncharacteristic of him and something David Brentwood didn't like. "Hey, Brentwood!" Aussie shouted across at Robert. "You know Russki?"

"Some," said Robert. "Enough to make sense of an intelligence report. Technical specs, that sort of thing."

"We," began Rogers, finding it difficult to get enough spittle to talk, "if you can get us to one—we can take her down."

"Yeah, yeah!" said Aussie. "So you told me." But now the phrase "take her" had shifted Aussie's attention—he was thinking of a "bird" he said he'd had once in Wales. Yelling at them through the trembling of Stallion One as it dipped and rose over the contours of the taiga, more like a frigate in a rough sea, he was describing his good fortune to the submariners. "Jugs on her like this!" His palms cupped as he made an up-and-down motion. "I swear, biggest nungas you ever saw."

Choir shook his head at the submariners.

Back at Second Army headquarters east of Yerofey Pavlovich, an eager young PR lieutenant came in and requested he be allowed to speak to Gen. Douglas Freeman on an important matter, refusing to tell Dick Norton what it was about. Freeman had come out, exhausted from giving his undivided attention to the minutiae of logistics that would be required to break out southwest toward Irkutsk and north to Yakutsk if the "Brentwood boys" succeeded.

"What's on your mind, son?" asked Freeman. Norton, sensing the general's mood, made a tactical retreat toward the coffee urn at the far end of the HQ hut.

"Sir, I'm Lieutenant Simpson, sir, and I'm responsible for your PR in the media pool in Khaba—"

"Don't waste time," Freeman ordered. "Spit it out." This, with astonishing courage, the lieutenant proceeded to do. "Sir, the La Roche papers are murdering you. Not only back home but in Japan, the U.K.—all over the world, sir. And—" The lieutenant paused but then got right to it. "And the monocle doesn't help—sir."

"*What?*"

"The monocle, sir. Well, sir, it—it looks ridiculous, General." He hurried on. "They're calling you 'Von Freeman'— the La Roche papers—and the Siberian propaganda radio is calling you a Nazi."

Norton, seeing the general's hand drop to his waist, thought that Freeman—fatigued from having been on his feet for over forty-eight hours without a break—might actually draw his revolver and put an end to the lieutenant.

Freeman stared at the lieutenant who, having said his piece, was leaning back at an impossible angle as Freeman advanced on him. "You cheeky son of a bitch! I oughta have you—*NORTON!*"

"General?"

"Is he correct?"

"Ah—well, that's what they're telling me, General."

"Who?"

"The press."

"Goddamn fairies!" Freeman exploded, rounding on Norton. "It's your goddamned fault!" With that Freeman tore the monocle from its cord and threw it to the ground, crunching it under his boot. "You see that?" he bellowed at the lieutenant.

"Yes, sir."

"Tell those fairies that that's what I'm going to do to the Siberian Thirty-first." He turned about to get the attention of everyone in the hut. He already had it. "Or they will do it to us. We beat them or we die. Here—in Siberia. Every one of us. The U.S. Second Army does *not* retreat. Is that clear?" There was silence. "Norton, get me a WAM here immediately." It was an Xm93 wide-area mine.

"Yes, General," said Norton. When Freeman had disappeared through the green curtains that separated his war room from the rest of the hut, someone manning the radar said in low tones, "Is he going to blow us all up?"

"Shut up!" commanded Norton. "If I hear any more smart-ass—" The cruise alarm began its familiar howl. "Incoming!" came the warning over the PA. "Incoming!"

There was a shuffling noise outside the headquarters hut, for even though the cruise was still 150 miles—seventeen minutes—away, many of the men were already heading for the sandbagged shelters.

Mine clearance was still going on up ahead so that soon the Second Army would be on the move again, but so long as the missiles kept coming from Baikal, Freeman knew he couldn't advance in any meaningful military sense of the word. And yet retreat would not only mean a triple humiliation for Second

Army but the Siberians, smelling blood, their supplies building up along the Transbaikal for Yesov's attack, would be content with nothing less than the destruction of the entire army.

CHAPTER TWENTY-FIVE

THE SNOW HAD stopped falling. Beyond them, under the steady roar of the choppers' engines, lay the enormous folds of snow-covered Siberian cedar, larch, black spruce, and pine, broken here and there by clear, low-lying areas of *oleniy mokh*— "reindeer moss"—in reality flat areas of snow-covered lichens—and beyond this the five-thousand-foot barrier of the Khamar Daban Range. The effect of their sudden exit from the falling snow of the predawn light caused ambivalent feelings. For the two Cobras' crews, clear weather meant good tank-killing conditions, but the S/D strike force and pilots aboard Stallions One and Two following the Cobras were not so joyful. The choppers might very well be like "needles in a haystack" against the vastness of the taiga, but even needles caught reflective sunlight that could be seen for miles beneath patches in the overcast but clear subarctic sky.

"Oh, isn't this nice!" yelled out Aussie, jerking his head toward the panorama of forest and sky. "Just what the doctor ordered." David Brentwood mustered as tough a look as he could, for even though he knew Lewis was one of the hardest men he'd ever served with, he doubted whether the newcomers aboard would be able to ignore the Australian's inverted sense of humor. His brother and the other submariners, though David wouldn't have had their job for the world, must, he thought, feel particularly vulnerable—quite literally fish out of water.

There was a "white out." It was a phenomenon the pilots

knew about but, contrary to widespread belief, the condition wasn't something that occurred in a roaring blizzard. Rather, the sudden and, for those who had never experienced it, terrifying loss of perception could only be likened to that lightning-like anxiety suffered by panic attack victims. It occurred most often in clear albeit overcast conditions because of the contrast between the different whites of old and fresh snow.

The mistake of Stallion Two's pilot was that in the moment of exhilarated relief during the exit from the falling snow to clear weather, he went off instrument flying to visual assist too quickly. In that split second he lost all depth perception, thinking he was far too high above the taiga when in fact he was far too close—only sixty feet above the blur of spear-shaped firs. His copilot realized it the moment the nose went down and pulled the stick, his feet jabbing the rudder control for uplift; but a rotor caught, and they were gone in a single somersault, rotors still spinning but upside down, cutting and slashing into the timber. The self-closing gas tank, built to absorb fifty-millimeter armor-piercing shells, imploded like a collapsed drum, spewing gas over red-hot bearings. The chopper disappeared below Cobra Two in a silent ball of saffron flame and snow, the latter rising like talc, coming down in a fine shower of rain that did nothing to extinguish the twenty-foot-high flame now licking the pines. There was a bang that everyone on the remaining Stallion and two Cobras heard.

"Holy mother of—" began Choir, but then, like the rest, he fell silent beneath the high whine of their Sea Stallion's three General Electric turboshaft engines, its pilot instinctively going for height after the crash of the other Stallion before settling down again to the dangerous NOE flying. The submariners' grim-lipped sonarman, Rogers, was sweating, praying again.

"Do as I tell you, damn it!" barked Cobra One's pilot at his copilot/weapons officer. "We can't go back. Endangers the whole mission. You know the fucking rules."

The pilot was back on instrument flying and put on his sunglasses; not that this would be any protection against white out, but it might reduce the equally hazardous risk of ice blink, once they negotiated the passes of the range. In ice blink mirages of something twenty or more miles away across a vast sheet of ice could loom up with stunning clarity as if they were only a few hundred yards ahead.

"Relax, fellas!" It was Aussie. "Not as bad as you think. It helped us in a way."

"What the shit d'you mean?" asked Rogers, uncharacteristic anger momentarily overcoming his air sickness and fear.

Aussie was lighting another cigarette. "Won't be able to tell what it was—wreckage'll look like a scrap yard. And same paint as their own, red star and all. And the guys—in Siberian uniforms." Aussie looked at his watch. Freeman had even taken care to make sure *they* were of Russian make. "What are we, Davey?" Aussie asked Brentwood. " 'Bout a hundred miles from the lake? Twenty minutes from touchdown? Hell, it'd take 'em fifteen minutes or so just to send out a search party—even if anyone did see the explosion. By then we'll be down, or close enough. What we've gotta do now is head south for a while, out of sight of any pain-in-the-ass search party."

"Yeah," said one of the submariners, "but what if they've already spotted us?"

Aussie smiled. Choir and Davey had already seen it, Choir explaining it to the submariner. "Well, laddie, if anyone sees us, they'll think we're part of the rescue party. Same paint job— from any distance at all it'd be hard to tell. We're too far inside enemy territory for them to think we might be—"

"You hope," said the submariner.

"Ah, that's not all," said Aussie confidently. "You see, mate, when we start up those noisy Arrows anyone within cooee distance'll think it's one of their damned snowmobiles joining the search for the downed chopper."

David Brentwood clicked on his throat mike. "Captain?"

"Go ahead."

"This is Captain Brentwood. Suggest we divert south for a while—avoid any search party coming out of Port Baikal."

"No problem."

It took two minutes for the Stallion pilot to signal the two Cobras—intercraft radio silence being strictly enforced and requiring either hand or "craft maneuver" signalling before the three remaining choppers swung south on the last leg through or, if necessary, up over the six-thousand-foot Khamar Daban range before they could take a fix on Tankhoy, twenty-seven miles across the ice from Port Baikal.

Fifteen miles from where the Stallion had gone down, an argument was building between the ten members of a SPETS squad standing by a Hind helo.

"Idite za nimi"—"I say follow them in," said the SPETS leader, referring to the three dots they could see heading for the Khamar Daban Range.

"Zachem?"—"Why?" asked the *serzhant*. "They're probably ours. Big one's probably a Hind, like ours. Other two are probably Havocs."

"Hinds, Havocs!" shouted the SPETS leader. "You can't tell from here even with binoculars. They were more than a mile off."

"Whatever you say, Comrade," replied the sergeant. "But I say we're wasting time. Let's go on to Ulan-Ude. Our orders are to relieve one of the sections at the head of the Thirty-first's spearhead."

"There are already two thousand of us at the Thirty-first's spearhead," said the leader. "I say let's follow those three choppers."

"Make up your mind, comrades," advised the Hind captain assigned to transport the ten SPETS. "Personally I think we should go on to Ulan-Ude, as the sergeant says. We're getting low on gas anyway."

"Did you see them?" snapped the SPETS leader, a big man, well over six feet and broad but not an ounce of flab on him.

"No," admitted the Hind pilot.

"You?" the leader asked the gunner.

"Too far off, sir," said the gunner, and, quickly trying for compromise, added, "Why don't we call Irkutsk, leave it up to them?"

The nine other SPETS waited for their captain to bawl out the air force pilot for forgetting they were on strict SPETS operational procedure—no radio contact allowed in the event it might be picked up by distant American AWACs. Tightening the sling of his AK-74, the SPETS leader then lifted his right fist, waving it in a circular motion. The Hind coughed, sputtered, and snow swirled about the SPETS as they clambered aboard. The Hind's nose gunner, immediately in front of and beneath the pilot, was cursing, strapping himself in behind the twin 12.7-millimeter machine guns in his armor-plated cubbyhole. He had a girl, a Buryat, waiting for him in Ulan-Ude.

"Polnym khodom!"—"Dash speed!" ordered the SPETS captain. This should take it to 180 miles per hour—but a few miles would be lost because of the extra weight of the ten SPETS and the helo's four "Swatter" antitank missiles.

The pilot went visual as he could not put on his radar; otherwise he would run the risk of setting off every AA gun and missile battery that was strung along Baikal's lakeshore, camouflaged in the forests.

He barely managed to get a fix on the three distant helos; they looked like dots of pepper against the white pallet of the western sky. He was watching the gas needle—soon they'd have to be refueled, the nearest POL depot at Port Baikal. Damn the SPETS—they should have gone on to Ulan-Ude. He banked the gunship in the direction of the dots, doubting he'd catch them unless they suddenly jinxed due west and he could take the hypotenuse vector between them. If it was a Hind and two Havocs on patrol out of Port Baikal or Irkutsk further west, it would make him and the SPETS look real *idioty*. Well, it was the SPETS leader's decision, not his. The pilot swung the Hind's gun-sprouting nose up, climbing, going for "high ground" from which he could see better across the taiga. Even so, he lost sight of them for a moment, the three dots heading into one of the passes through the mountain range toward the frozen inland Sea of Baikal.

By now the lead Cobra was looking for muskeg, hoping for an open patch in the forest, no more than a mile or two from the shore, using Tankhoy as a general heading but keeping well away from any sign of habitation. It was the copilot who spotted a promising site, and within seconds the Cobra began a "sway," signalling the Super Stallion and the other Cobra that he'd found a landing. The air was so clear now he could see a thin wisp of smoke from what had to be Port Baikal across the lake, the smoke rising to the right of creamy white cliffs of the Trans-Siberian Railway's spur line from Kultuk at the southern end of the lake to Port Baikal. He told his copilot he didn't know which was best for the commandos: clear weather, which would make it much easier and therefore quicker for them to reach their target, or snowy conditions, which, while slowing them down, would have provided them with more cover.

"They got clear weather, man," said the copilot/weapons officer. "You can see for miles. They ain't got no choice."

"True."

The Snowcat "Arrow," technical designation UH-19P, was based on another American air-cushion vehicle speed record-holder, the UH-15. Like the UH-15 hovercraft, the Snowcat was triangular or, as seen from above, arrowhead-shaped, a mid-placed cockpit seating three, the military version placing the driver slightly higher and behind the other two.

Nineteen feet long and seven and a half feet wide, the triangular Snowcat, with an eight-inch clearance, was powered by an 1100cc Toyota car engine, its speed the same as the old record-setting UH-15: eighty miles per hour over water, ninety miles per hour over ice or snow, with a maximum gradient tolerance of thirty to forty degrees, depending on the condition of snow or ice pack. Its payload was a thousand pounds, which could easily handle three commandos and their equipment. In the lead Arrow this included a heavy, swivel-mounted, forty-millimeter M-19 machine gun in front of the cockpit as well as the gun's box-contained belt feed ammunition—the gun's forty-inch barrel having a theoretical 180-degree traverse. In practice, as Aussie had discovered on a dry-run assembly, the safest maximum arc of fire was 90 degrees, consisting of a 45-degree swing left or right. The noise that bothered him was, ironically, not the main thrust engine but the air cushion's lift system, powered by an 1800-horsepower, 1600cc Briggs and Stratton vertical-shaft lawnmower engine, which drove an axial fan, the latter's six-foot-diameter blade mounted at the back, or widest part of the arrowhead.

Delivery of the three-man crafts, ordered much earlier in the campaign by Freeman, had been delayed not because of any mechanical malfunction but because of the general's insistence that the usual black skirting for the air cushion be painted white. The delay in delivery meant that the eight "designated drivers," as David Brentwood had called them, had had only an hour or so to practice the previous evening. Now, with one Stallion gone, he had only four drivers. But the controls were simple, even if Aussie complained of their "bloody Sunday" lawnmower noise and the rough ride, which frankly had surprised all of them except Robert Brentwood who, as part of his naval training in combined ops amphibious training, was already familiar with the gut-shuddering motion of ACVs, in particular the monstrous, barge-sized marine hovercrafts.

As the four craft from the remaining Stallion slid effortlessly down the rollers of the Stallion's ramp door, guided by the six-man S/D and four-man sub crew team, the crews of the three choppers, zipping up their thick thermal jackets, were already busy spreading out the camouflage nets over the lone Stallion and two Cobras.

"Did you know the men on the Stallion well?" Robert Brentwood asked his younger brother, in an effort to share his loss of the four submariners.

"No." It was said almost rudely, but David, as commander of the land part of the mission, was too preoccupied with its details for any sentiment to intrude. Besides, there was a nagging, albeit childish, determination on his part not to show any weakness to his older brother. As if reading his mind, Robert immediately deferred to his younger brother's authority on the timing of the mission now that there had been the complication of the Havoc attack. "Wait till nightfall?"

"No," answered David, adjusting his ammo pouch pack. "We go now."

"You worried about that Havoc?"

"Yes. Maybe they'll send out a search party. Better we push off soon as the birds are covered."

Aussie looked around at the mention of "birds," obviously thinking of making a crack, but he didn't. There was too much to do helping Choir who, with David and Aussie, would man the lead Arrow; the sub crew of four and the other three Delta men would spread out in the other three Arrows. Some weapons, including a Stinger, a LAW antitank tube, and Aussie's long sniper rifle, had to be strapped to the fuselage before they left. Choir was checking the front of the Arrow, making sure the protective plastic barrel cap was tight enough to withstand the rapid vibration of the air cushion.

Robert Brentwood called the other three submariners over. He would be driving one of the Arrows, Rogers another. "Remember, we'll go in single file—S/D One leading, S/D Two covering our rear. Literally." A couple of men smiled. "They're the ones with experience in this kind of operation. Rogers—"

"Sir?"

"You'll be right behind their lead Arrow. I'll be behind you. Remember, single line formation for as long as we can—hopefully the whole way. But if anything goes wrong and we're fired on from the flanks, then we move to abreast position."

"Whose breast?" interjected Aussie nearby. The submariners ignored him. Robert reassured them. "Your part'll start on the sub." They all knew he meant *if* they reached Port Baikal and could take a GST without being killed first. But Brentwood knew it wasn't time to kindle the doubt in everyone's mind.

"What are they going to do after?" asked Rogers. He meant what would happen to the S/D team.

"They'll come back to the choppers, wait till darkness or a snowstorm, whichever comes first, and take off with the Cobras and the Stallion. Look, don't worry. Once we get a sub we'll be the safest of all." Only Rogers understood immediately, the point being that, once they were below, the sub would be the same as any other of the three or four GSTs they figured were operating in the lake.

"It'll be a lookalike masked ball," Robert Brentwood joked. "All look the same; nobody'll be able to see us anyway. All done by sound, remember, fellas."

"Quiet!" It was Aussie Lewis, and through the ear-ringing silence of the forest they could hear the distant chopping sound of helicopters. "Sure as hell's not ours," pronounced one of the Cobra pilots.

"Get those Arrows out of the open!" ordered Aussie.

With everyone but Aussie Lewis lending a hand, the four

Arrows were pushed back up the rollers into the Stallion beneath the camouflage net.

Aussie broke off into the cover of the forest, whipping off the canvas cover from the Haskins rifle, and, without flipping open the bipod, rested the ice-cold, twenty-three-pound weapon against a fir, turning the scope's "bullet" impact screw. Withdrawing the bolt—this being necessary before loading each 1.5-ounce bullet, whose combination incendiary/HE/high temperature, super-hardened penetrator head was capable of smashing through a plane engine or passing through an APC—he waited. Either way, Lewis figured if the Siberians spotted something and hovered over them even for a second, he'd cost them a pilot, gunner, or the "whole mother," as the three Delta men called an enemy chopper. The noise was louder now; the rotor slap, while not overhead, was coming much closer. He glimpsed Rogers, the submariner, only about ten feet from him, under one of the Cobra's nets, eyes closed. Another prayer. Aussie preferred to trust in his Kevlar bullet-proof vest. He saw movement—Choir Williams kneeling beneath the camouflage net of the Stallion, ready with his squad automatic weapon, and Salvini, one of the Delta men, his M-60 resting on his knee, right hand on the grip.

In Port Baikal, the overtime midnight-to-eight shift over, Nefski's subaltern came home to his small, drab apartment block, one of the largest buildings in the town. Taking off his greatcoat, he kissed his wife, her Buryat face lined with the travail of being a garrison wife. He told her that she looked tired.

"Kak vsegda"—"Like always," she replied, surprised by the kiss.

Hanging up his coat in their apartment's tiny hallway, he glanced at the laundry bag that hung from the knob on their bedroom door and announced generously that he'd take it down the hallway to the communal laundry for her.

"I'll do it," she said. She always had.

"Rest," he said.

"Rest?" She hadn't heard him tell her to rest in twenty-two years. Not even when their second child, now a KGB border guard like his father, had been born did he tell her to rest. Whenever he was off guard duty she was expected to be his servant—

the only thing he'd do would be to take his boots off, then it was "You have the samovar going?" And always, like this evening, it was going. Except tonight there was no question about the samovar—His Royal Highness had become Comrade Highness. Peeling one of the onions she'd had in the line of glass jars she kept in the window to catch what winter sun she could, Tanya's eyes began to water and, taking the kitchen rag from its rack by the old age-veined porcelain sink, she wiped her eyes. Seeing the rag was ready for washing, she took it out into the hallway. "Ivan!" she called. The moment he looked back at her from the front door, he was a picture of guilt, a thief running away with the laundry bag. Another peculiar thing—he'd changed into his best weekend trousers.

"What's the matter with you?" she asked.

"Nothing. Can't a man offer to help his wife now and then?" he shot back defensively. "All the time we hear about Siberian women complaining they are slaves, you never get help. Well? I'm giving you help, woman."

"In your Sunday clothes?"

"Ah! I spilled coffee on them," he said, meaning his uniform.

It was a dim, sickly, thirty-watt bulb in the hallway, but even so she could see he was blushing. Immediately she suspected another woman and grabbed the bag from him.

"Ah—" he uttered disgustedly, snatching his greatcoat from the hallway and jerking open the door.

"Where are you going? Ivan, where—"

"Out!" It meant he was going to the Port Baikal Hotel to get blind drunk.

Tanya was convinced it was another woman now. And when, her heart beating in panic, she inspected the trousers, she found the evidence. He'd tried to sponge it off, but the edge of the stain was stiff, as if it had been starched. She sat in the hallway for half an hour without moving, but all that time a volcanic rage was welling within. Finally she made her way to the kitchen, the soup nearly burnt dry, where she took one of the onions from the jars, laid it on the countertop, and sat waiting for him.

The moment he came in she screamed and threw the jar, aiming for his head. He recoiled, getting an arm up in time, the jar hitting him below the left eye. Closing, raining blows against him, she told him she'd never let him touch her again, shouting that he was to get out and never come back. She didn't care if he died in the snow.

"Touch *you*!"-he shouted back drunkenly. "Who'd want to touch *you*, you fat slob?" She threw another onion bottle at him, the onion's long shoot trailing like a taper, but all her strength had gone in her rage, and the jar missed, hitting her anorak instead, falling harmlessly to the floor, rolling along the worn linoleum. He stuck his head back inside to say that it was his apartment, too. She tried to throw the laundry bag at him but fell.

The KGB duty officer told him there was no way he could come in on his shift tomorrow afternoon looking like that. He could lie and tell Nefski he'd fallen or something, but Nefski would never believe such a story and suspect he'd been drunk and fighting again, for which Nefski would give him a punishment.

"You'd better stay here," the duty officer told him. "Take guard duty at the dock. Easy work, but don't go taking a snooze."

Ivan didn't like the idea of guard duty at thirty below, in Port Baikal or anywhere else, but in truth he rather relished having told his comrades just what had happened. A man whose wife suspected him of seeing another woman—well, his reputation rose among the boys.

"Colonel Nefski's back on duty later today," warned the duty officer. "In case he visits the dock you'd better have a good explanation ready. Tell him you were hit by an icicle or something." It was a good story, Ivan having seen a number of soldiers who had been injured, some of them seriously, when a huge icicle, having built up after successive snowstorms, thawed a little and fell from a roof's eave like a club.

The pilot of the SPETS chopper that had been following the three fly-size specks had now lost sight of his quarry. They had disappeared somewhere in the taiga, but the taiga was a sea of snow-covered forest, clearings like those he'd already flown over as numerous as troughs in a sea, and all looking more or less the same. He could spend weeks in a futile search. "Turn back?" he asked the SPETS captain.

"No, go around to the end of the lake. See if they came down there. Maintain radio silence in case they are enemy choppers."

"Tak tochno"—"Yes, sir," answered the pilot, taking the Hind out over the edge of the forest. The Hind was now above the southern end of the mirror-finish expanse of ice that was twenty-five miles wide and almost four hundred miles long.

David Brentwood saw the blob of the SPETS chopper looking for them, passing within a quarter mile, and glanced at his watch. The Stallion pilot told him the Hind would probably be doing around 150 knots.

"So," estimated David, "they should be across the lake in fifteen to twenty minutes."

"Yeah."

"Do we still go across in daylight?" asked Robert Brentwood.

"Affirmative," said David. "If they do report any possible enemy activity to Irkutsk or Port Baikal, then we might as well hit 'em sooner rather than later. Give them less time to prepare."

"There's another consideration," put in Robert. "You don't load on your torpedoes and missiles at night if you can help it."

"Good thinking, Bob!" said Aussie approvingly, Robert Brentwood more surprised than offended by the Australian's easy familiarity with rank.

"Okay," said David, "then we go now. Synchronize oh eight one zero hours . . . now! We leave at eight-thirty." He glanced across at Aussie. "Hope you and Choir made sure that these jobs—" He indicated the four Arrows. "—are properly winterized?"

"Yes, sir," said Aussie with exaggerated bonhomie. "Oil in those suckers'd lubricate a desert whore."

One of the submariners asked Aussie, "You ever think of anything but sex?"

"Sure."

"Oh, yeah? What?"

"Beer! Lordy, what I'd give for a schooner of Foster's right now."

"Freeze your guts out," said Choir. "I can't feel my toes."

"Then wriggle them, sweetheart," said one of the Delta men. "You never have winter training?"

"What for?" asked Aussie facetiously, despite the fact that the SAS winter training had been a top priority. "That's only for ski bums."

"Keep quiet!" said David.

From then on all they could hear was the soft moaning of the taiga, as lonely a sound as any of them had ever heard. For the next twenty minutes it was time for every soldier in the ten-man team and the Stallion's and Cobras' crews, who would stay behind, to be with himself, to go over what he had to do—to meditate upon the need for speed and surprise. David smelled the clean fragrance of winter pine that not even deep snow could suffocate, and momentarily he thought of Georgina, of what she was doing at this very moment. In England it would be 11:15 in the evening. A clump of snow fell from a branch, jolting him back to the taiga. He went over the satellite pics again, noting that what looked like it could be a slipway was left of the town near one of the railway tunnels they'd had to build on the cliffs coming around the lake's southwestern end.

At 8:30 they started the four Arrows, the rattling roar of the engines alarming.

"Christ!" said Choir, usually the quietest of the three SAS men. "They'll hear us clear to the Pole."

"Ah, rats," said Aussie, climbing into the front seat, strapping himself in next to Choir. "Don't sweat it, mate." He patted the SPETS shoulder patch on the otherwise all-white winter garb. "They'll just think it's a few comrades coming across."

Choir said something about Aussie being the one who'd been going on so much about the noise, but it was lost to the roar of the four engines. Aussie and Choir found it a squeeze. Although normally there was plenty of room for two, they were both in bulky winter uniforms. And while the case containing Aussie's sniper rifle was lashed to the fuselage, Aussie, on David Brentwood's order, had to hold the Stinger's AA tube like a cylindrical map case between his legs, eliciting an obscene comment from the Delta man with the M-60 light machine gun in the fourth and last Arrow. Choir checked the first few exposed rounds of the forty-millimeter box/belt ammo feed for the M-19 heavy machine gun mounted on the front of the lead Arrow. Each six-ounce round, both ends looking like round lollipops, was in effect a six-ounce grenade, capable of piercing sixty millimeters of armor plate at three miles, the rate of fire in "cooler barrel" Arctic conditions being 350 rather than 320 rounds a minute. Though it could be either electrically or mechanically operated, Choir didn't like the "beast"; the M-19, for all its firepower, had a bad habit of jamming every twenty-nine hundred rounds or so.

"Not to worry, sport!" yelled Aussie. "If you can't kill what you gotta kill in nine minutes, Choir, you ain't never gonna do it."

As they moved off, throttles closed down to just above stall, the heavy snow and trees absorbing the noise much more than they had anticipated, they made their way cautiously through the trees and light underbrush to the lake's edge. Choir was still tugging the forty-millimeter belt worriedly. "Don't worry, mate," Aussie told him. "Hopefully you won't have to use it."

"Right."

"You mean 'bullshit'!" laughed Aussie.

"Right."

The lake hurt their eyes. Though overcast the glare was intense, and within seconds every one of the ten men in the S/D/ sub team had pulled down his sunglasses which, again on Freeman's insistence, were all Soviet issue, captured on the way to Khabarovsk.

The SPETS chopper saw them.

Following David Brentwood's lead in the first Arrow, the drivers in the other three Arrows behind opened up the throttles so wide their wrists ached, the midpoint between the railway tunnel up left a hundred yards or so above the lakeshore and the town's small library and hotel a few hundred yards to the right.

Sonarman Rogers, driving the second Arrow with Delta trooper O'Reilly, swung left to avoid the exhaust from the first vehicle, his Arrow shuddering over small, swollen ice ridges on the otherwise mirror-glass-smooth lake. Rogers glanced ahead for a second to get a quick bearing on the terrain. Someone yelled, then someone else, but it was too late. They hit a ridge—only a foot high. The Arrow upended, skittering across the ice, leaving at first a thin but then ever-widening wake of frothing arterial blood.

In the third Arrow, the Delta driver, Lou Salvini, caught a glance, but despite what he saw he didn't hesitate and closed the gap, the three of them now heading straight for Port Baikal.

The submariner in Robert Brentwood's Arrow, the man who would have to take over Rogers's sonar job if they made it, did all he could not to throw up when he spotted what looked like a sodden black-red mop: Rogers's head, rolling obscenely across the ice, a gray spaghettilike substance trailing it. O'Reilly was still, his neck broken.

David was waving to the Hind coming to investigate, its bug eyes growing by the second. They were all waving. The Hind made a low pass and went into a left turn for another look-see.

"Smile, you Welsh bastard!" Aussie yelled at Choir above the roar of the Arrow. "Smile at the fucking comrades." Choir waved, forcing a dour Welsh grin into something more gregarious looking while flipping the safety off the M-19 that he didn't like. "What's the bloody vertical on this?" he shouted at Aussie, his smile widening.

" 'Bout thirty degrees," said David.

"That's a lot of—" He waved at the comrades again as the chopper passed overhead. Port Baikal, now six miles away, was clearly visible, a mirage of it looming out on the ice far to their right. They were bucking a head wind now, flowing southward in advance of the forecasted blizzard over four hundred miles due north. David Brentwood glanced at his watch, the speedometer needle quivering between fifty-five and sixty. The Port Baikal old dock was clearly visible, but they wouldn't reach it for another seven to ten minutes. The most important thing was to go straight to the railway tunnel that was two hundred yards to the left of the hotel and library.

Aussie tried to get a bead on the tunnel and dock, but the vibration against the Stinger tube was giving him a headache. He passed it to Choir who had spotted the slipway—a concave, smooth but definitely gutterlike depression, about ten to fifteen feet wide, that led, like a gradual slide from the mouth of the tunnel to the spread of ice-free water by the dock where the Angara River began its exit from the lake.

Nefski's subordinate wasn't the first to see the approaching snow vehicles, which he thought were some kind of *snegovoy traktor*—"snowmobile"—but rather he was the one the guard called over, wondering what they were. Ivan went to the big stand holding Schneider 11 x 80 power binoculars by the tunnel's entrance, morosely pulled the canvas cover up, and bent forward to adjust the focus. A blur of dots snapped into sharp relief against the ice.

"Ours, I guess," he said disinterestedly, without taking a second look, still nursing the bitter fight he'd had with his wife and generally feeling pretty sorry for himself. "Haven't seen snowmobiles like that before, though." Then again, he told the other guard, they certainly made as much racket. It wasn't until another three minutes had passed that, his mind off his wife for a moment, he told his comrade grumpily, "Better tell the duty officer. Who's on?"

"Nefski."

"Shit! You tell 'im. I don't want him to see this." He pointed to his black eye. "Bastard'll put me on punishment."

The other man slung his rifle and walked over the hard-crusted snow, his breath going before him like steam as he made his way toward Nefski's office in the old library.

"Colonel, sir. There looks like a patrol coming in."

Nefski was alarmed. Despite the fact that they were hundreds of miles from the most forward troops of the U.S. Second Army, he was immediately suspicious. He didn't know of any patrols supposed to be coming in. "Call out the squad!"

"Yes, sir," said the guard, walking outside to start the siren. *"Begi!"*—"Run!" ordered Nefski. "There are two subs in, you idiot!" Before the Klaxon began its long wail, Nefski had grabbed the phone from its cradle and was pushing the red button for the dock. "How long till you leave?"

"We're almost ready now, Colonel. Be about another—"

"Get them into the water—now! Move!" shouted Nefski.

"But, sir, some of the men are over in the hotel. . . ."

"I don't care. We don't have the time. Get the winches moving. I'll call the ho—" The library wall was disappearing in front of his eyes, forty-millimeter grenades ripping, tearing it open like a pull-tab on a beer carton, debris flying everywhere.

"Bogomater!"—"Mother of God!" He fell to the floor, the phone banging beside him, its Bakelite cracked beyond repair, his nose bleeding. Luckily through the dangling earpiece he could hear the phone in the hotel ringing three times.

"Hotel—"

"Colonel Nefski. Tell all the submariners to get back to the tunnel immediately. You understand?"

"What's going on?"

"Tell them!" he screamed. The next moment the line was hissing like a samovar.

In the tunnel a skeleton crew of four men worked like navvies at the winches that would let down one of the fifty-foot-long by fifteen-foot-wide toroidal subs, its eight "anti-lake-access" torpedoes looking for all the world like stovepipes attached to its superstructure, the bulges of the four cruise missiles wider but shorter on the outer casing.

The first sub was a quarter of the way down the hundred-yard ice slipway; retractable wing vanes extended from either side of the black, egg-shaped sub like the outriggers of a canoe to stop the midget from rolling before it reached the water. The four Siberians working the winch, not realizing that it wasn't the sub that was under fire but rather the library and hotel, frantically redoubled their efforts—a line of twenty to thirty KGB border guards racing toward the slipway. Behind them came the squeak of a tank heading down from its defilade position on the steep forested slope along the narrow road leading westward from the town.

There were screams of men hit, one flung backward like a rag doll under the impact of the forty-millimeter, while at the far end of the tunnel, the two-man Goryonov 7.62-millimeter machine-gun crew were dead, one slumped over the gun, the other, his face missing, flung back over the sandbags by the rail tracks that had carried the midget submarines the last few miles to the slipway. There was more screaming now, mixed with a sound like wasps swarming as the three Arrows surged up the incline from the lake, stopping about twenty yards abreast, close to a heavy ice bank that formed the eastern wall of the slipway. The line of border guards fifty yards ahead across the slipway and now slightly above them poured fire in their general direction. David Brentwood, hard up against the ice wall, smacked Choir's shoulder hard so that he'd feel it through the Kevlar vest. "Get the M-19 off the Arrow and on its bipod. Aussie, three o'clock high!"

Aussie Lewis looked up, squinting despite the shades, and saw the twin bubble nose of the Hind rising from behind the hotel into the sun, its pilot now realizing it had been an enemy force they'd seen on the lake.

The chopper, relying on the glare to blind its opponents, was in Aussie's line of sight for only three seconds—the time it took him to fire the Stinger from two hundred yards, which was virtually point-blank range. The explosion was crimson, spilling fiery fuel down around the hotel, some of the gasoline sweeping across four or five of its defenders, sending them screaming, rolling into the trench behind the border guards' ice wall, distracting their comrades and kicking up so much ice and snow in their efforts to douse themselves that two of the three Delta men had no difficulty lobbing six grenades in as many seconds, the grenades' flashes lost in the sunlight but going off deep in the trench, killing at least another three defenders.

The sub, passing down the slipway between them and the defenders, was nearing the water.

"Stop those bastards!" yelled Aussie, swinging the Stinger to his left at the men working the winch and executing his own command before any of the other S/D men needed to. Two of the winchmen simply disappeared under the rocket's impact; what was left of them splattered over the remaining submarine. Aussie reloaded, got a bead on the second sub in the tunnel, and heard Robert Brentwood shouting, "No! Let's be sure of the first one before we—"

"Roger!" said Aussie and, turning right, fired the Stinger round into the hotel, a hundred yards front right, just to keep things moving. The next instant he heard a "thwack!" and one of the Delta men, a moment before spread-eagled atop the ice wall for a better shot, was tumbling backward, grabbing at his throat, but there was no hope. The jugular severed, he was spurting blood in jets, tumbling into the slipway, sliding all the way down, smashing into the midget sub's keel. But by now the defenders, thoroughly demoralized, were retreating to the library as David Brentwood, attaching three "bread rolls"—balls of plastique—on the cable leading from the winch to the sub, pushed in a pencil-size detonator and flicked the fuse selector to "three minutes."

"Off you go!" he told Robert and, without a look backward, Robert Brentwood and the two remaining submariners slithered down the gutter-shaped slipway, using their boots to brake themselves against the keel, one of them already with a hand on the right side vane to haul himself up to the six-foot, oil-drum-shaped conning tower.

"Not yet!" Robert Brentwood ordered the seaman. "Not till the charge goes. Get forward of midships. Otherwise when that cable blows it'll—" It blew, the sudden release of tension recoiling one half of the wire back to the winch, making a high, singing noise, the other half whipping toward the sub but catching Lawson, one of the Delta men, and almost severing his right foot. For a second or so he felt absolutely no pain, only astonishment, realizing that in breaking the impact of the wire, he'd saved the life of one of the two submariners with Robert Brentwood. The cable smacked the keel, flopping to the icy slipway and finally lying still, like a dead snake.

The sub was now afloat with Robert Brentwood and the two submariners already down the conning tower. The powerful whiff of sweat assaulted Brentwood's nose, and for a split second he thought one of the winchmen was hiding in the sub; but there was no one, the sub simply not having had enough time to be aerated by the cold pine smell of the taiga.

By now Choir and the remaining Delta man, Salvini, had the M-19 on its stand and were pouring a terrible fire into the library and hotel. Aussie rested the Stinger tube across the Arrow's cockpit for a good shot at the second sub. There was a "swoosh" of back blast from the Stinger, a crimson explosion in the tunnel, and a ringing of scrap metal. That GST was gone.

Once inside the midget submarine it was easier than Robert Brentwood and his two crewmen thought it would be. They didn't need to know anything about the Cyrillic alphabet, the dials self-explanatory to any submariner. The three men moved automatically to the stations they'd have to operate as a skeleton crew. For them, the sensation was very much like moving from a fully automatic automobile to a VW Beetle with standard shift. It was all more or less clear at a glance, the only real difference being the pipes that went round and round the toroidal hull, which allowed for the storage of recycled gaseous oxygen for them to breathe; it also ran the GST's closed-circuit diesel engine.

The immediate concern was to submerge as quickly as possible. "Hatch closed!" said Johnson, one of the two remaining submariners. The other man, Lopez, stood by the diesel motor control and steerage levers that would allow him to work the relatively primitive yet effective horizontal hydroplanes that would govern their "up" and "down" angles, and the vertical rudder, half above, half below the horizontal plane, to control the yaw, or left-right movement.

"Very well," Brentwood responded to Johnson. Turning to Lopez, he ordered, "Stand by to discharge."

"Stand by to discharge, sir."

Brentwood switched on the small sonar screen by the narrow twin day and nighttime periscopes column, no bigger than six inches in diameter, and checked there was no obstruction ahead or below registered by the "passive" radar sensors that were built into the GST's hull.

"Dive! Dive! Dive! Open all vents!" he commanded.

"Opening all vents, aye, sir!" responded Johnson, and they could hear the water rushing and gurgling in, its noise transmitted through the pressure hull. Lopez immediately put her nose into a sharp dive, Brentwood wrapping an arm around the scope column as the GST went down on a twenty-degree incline.

"Twenty feet . . . thirty feet . . . forty feet . . ." announced Johnson unhurriedly, rhythmically, multiplying the readout in meters by three, already getting the feel of her.

"Level at one hundred," ordered Brentwood.

"Level at one hundred, aye, sir. . . . Forty feet . . . forty-five . . ." They could hear the icy growl above them as huge plates shifted. The slight movement was unnoticeable to the naked eye, but it was in part a response to the enormous struggle, the pulling apart of tectonic plates far below the five-thousand-foot lake which caused fissures that accounted for the temperature inversions throughout the lake and gave rise often to the fast, warm, upstreaming currents that created thin ice here and there.

"Seventy feet . . . eighty feet . . ."

"Stand by to declutch."

"Stand by to—" began Lopez.

"Declutch!" ordered Brentwood, and within three seconds Lopez had levelled the tiny sub, though it was rocking slightly, and disengaged the generating power from the diesel that had been charging up the batteries, shifting the power to propulsion charge. All three of them were surprised by the lack of any forward sensation other than levelling out. It was an extraordinarily quiet vessel.

"Steer one one two," ordered Brentwood.

"One one two, sir."

"Half ahead," ordered Brentwood.

"Half ahead, sir." Within five seconds they were running at eight knots. Brentwood, for the first time in the mission, relaxed slightly, nodding his head in admiration at the other two, his mood taken up by Johnson, who, watching the pressure gauges, announced, "That old Italian, Santi, designed it good, eh, Captain?"

"The Siberians built it," said Brentwood, "but you're right. We have us a good craft, gentlemen. Even so, 'fraid it's going to be hard going with only three of us. At the most only one of us can catch a nap now and then."

"No sweat, sir," answered Johnson. Lopez gave a diplomatic smile.

"How deep's this lake again, sir?" asked Johnson.

"Goes to six thousand," answered Brentwood. "Eight thousand square miles of ice above us, gentlemen—eight thousand square miles of mud—accumulated silt—beneath us." They could hear a popping and then a crackling sound—the battle, not abating, still going on at dockside. The noises of the odd grenade or round striking the ice-free entrance—the outflow of the Angara River—sped through the frigid water at over four times the speed they would in the air.

"Sir?" It was Johnson up forward.

"What is it?"

"I've just noticed there's a second hatch here. We were in such a hurry getting down I just automatically—"

"That's all right," said Brentwood, but he was puzzled, even as he told Johnson to secure the second hatch. Before it closed, however, he spied a small pressure gauge, the size of an alarm clock, on the side of the five-foot-wide, six-foot-high conning tower and realized it was an airlock that could be flooded and pumped out, if need be.

"Well, good old Santi!" said Johnson. "Escape hatch and all, eh, Skipper?"

"Yes," said Brentwood, about to bring up the painfully obvious fact that—in his opinion at least—building an escape hatch, taking up extra space in the already-crowded midget, had been a waste of good material. If a torpedo hit the midget submarine anywhere, he doubted there'd be enough time for anyone to make the airlock. Besides which it would take awhile, once the bottom hatch was secured, to bleed in water through the top hatch, allowing the escaping submariner to pop out and close the hatch so that it could then be pumped empty for the next man—providing you had at least one of the three pumps working after a torpedo attack. By that time the sub would be below its crush depth of around two thousand feet. The slightest hairline fracture then would create an aerosol inside the sub coming in at over a thousand pounds per square inch, such a force imploding the sub flatter than a sumo wrestler sitting on a paper cup.

The passive sonar sensors were operating at full strength, their nine green lights on without a flicker. It was the first moment of silence that they'd had in the mission; Johnson only now had time to look around for the toilet. After the sheer fright of the firefight on the shore, he felt like his bladder was going to burst. "Where's the head?"

"Right under me," said Lopez, pointing to the waste chamber. "They thought of everything, Captain. Guy on steerage doesn't have to go far to take a leak."

"No one has far to go in here," said Johnson, looking about the instrument-cluttered sub, so jam-packed with equipment that it was virtually impossible for two men to pass at once. There were only two six-foot-long, two-foot-wide, fold-down plank bunks, whose mattresses were made up of two spread-out SCUBA "Arctic escape" diving suits, the two SCUBA helmets and relatively small, champagne-bottle-size oxygen tanks fixed to the bulkhead only four inches from the nose of whoever used the top bunk for a nap. "Everything in this damn thing's so small," complained Johnson, looking at the small O_2 tanks.

"Well, don't worry," said Brentwood. "Hopefully we won't have to use them."

The temperature in the sub was sixty degrees Fahrenheit, but with each man wearing four layers of winter-battle uniform, it felt like a sauna bath. Brentwood set the lead by stripping down to his long johns; the problem was where to stow even the tightly rolled, sleeping-bag-size bundles of uniform. Lopez sat on one, and they jury-rigged the other two forward and aft of the scope column, Brentwood inspecting the lashings to make sure there was no possibility that the six-inch-diameter day scope, or smaller three-inch night scope, would have any chance of being snagged. The first thing they found out was that while the heat exchange and scrubbing system above the GST took good care of the oxygen, it did what Johnson called "sweet FA" for human sweat. He only hoped it would deal better with the human waste tank under Lopez. They couldn't risk venting it for fear the sound might give their position away as they began their search for the three other submarines, whose four cruise missile salvos had brought Freeman's Second Army to a standstill.

One of the nine thimble-size sonar sensor lights was blinking amber, and on the screen they could see "a little dancing," as Rogers would have called it. Johnson turned up the magnification, giving Brentwood the scale. But even on maximum enlarge, the "dancing" was too small to signify any threat, and Brentwood guessed they were getting tiny "flits" of sound from the *golomianka*—"fish"—that were indigenous to the lake and whose eyes, taking up a third of their nine-inch body, could give off a signal. Each female gave birth to around seventeen hundred small ones each fall, and their schools were capable of giving off a boat-size "echo." The "dancing" had disappeared.

"Wonder how the boys are doin' up there?" asked Johnson.

"Hope they're out by now," said Lopez. "I sure as hell wouldn't—" He stopped, in deference to Robert Brentwood. Brentwood looked at his watch. "If they can get back in the taiga around there, around Port Baikal, and wait it out till dark, which should be around three P.M. at this latitude, they'll have a good chance, I think."

"Yeah," said Lopez, nodding in agreement, but it was more wishful thinking than conviction.

"They'll be fine," said Johnson.

"Yeah." It was a small thing, Robert Brentwood hardly ever saying "yeah," but in the close confines of the midget submarine such informality came much more naturally, and was almost necessary, in his view, if they were to work well as a team.

"One of us should take an hour's nap at a time," he told Johnson and Lopez, "so that—"

On the sonar screen there was a large blip that had appeared very suddenly, the magnification showing that it was moving at over thirty knots. It was heading straight for the GST.

"Bearing?" asked Brentwood.

"Zero three three, sir," answered Johnson.

It was on their left quarter.

"Range," added Johnson, "three thousand yards and closing."

Lopez was tense at the steerage position, keeping an eye on the sonar screen which he couldn't see clearly for Brentwood.

"Speed," announced Johnson, "we got . . . Jesus! Thirty-two knots!"

Robert Brentwood glanced at the knot meter. The GST had a maximum of only sixteen knots submerged. It couldn't be one of the three GSTs—had to be a torpedo. The sonar lights were blinking red.

"Two thousand yards and closing. Time to impact . . ." Johnson began.

"Bring the ship to zero zero niner," ordered Brentwood,

adding, "Firing point procedures. Master zero one four. Tube one."

"Firing point procedures, master one four. Tube one," came Johnson's confirmation immediately, followed by, "Solution ready, sir. Weapon ready. Ship ready."

There was no panic; this was their "line of country."

Brentwood watched the bearing, corrected the heading, and announced, "Final bearing and shoot. Master one five."

CHAPTER TWENTY-SIX

THE T-80 SQUEAKING its way noisily on the narrow road that crossed the tracks leading to the dock couldn't see the Americans firing from beneath the high ice bank that led up sharply from the shoreline. One second there was a burst of submachine gun fire far left at the tank, then at ten yards farther right the tank gunner saw the fiery tongue of the heavy American M-19 machine gun. It was the M-19 that the T-80 driver took a precise bead on: 203.1 meters, just over two hundred yards away, but the next moment the tank's laser sight was knocked out by a burst of the bullet-grenades from the American M-19.

The T-80 emitted a cantankerous, bearlike growl, its turret slewing as it backed up a few feet for a better defilade position, lowering its bulk for a slighter silhouette, the laser sighting gone. But at two hundred yards the Siberians in the tank, manning the 12.7-millimeter and 7.62-millimeter machine guns and the main 125-millimeter cannon, knew that if they couldn't knock out the American weapon they ought to be sent back to Novosibirsk gunnery school. The tank belched, the shell's explosion throwing earth-rooted ice blocks high into the air, creating a wide, jagged, U-shaped gap in the ice wall. But Aussie, Choir, and

David Brentwood, knowing what would happen the moment the T-80's turret had stopped and hearing the whine of the barrel depressing, had abandoned the heavy M-19 machine gun.

They had rejoined Salvini, who was fighting by the three parked Arrows, the latter's noses hidden by the ice bank. The other wounded Delta commando, Lawson, had dragged himself into the cockpit of one of the Arrows where Salvini was now hurriedly giving him a second shot of morphine, not realizing Aussie had already given him one a few seconds after the wire had sliced into his ankle. Lawson's leg, elevated to help staunch the bleeding, was now sticking out of the Arrow's open cockpit, the plastic bubble having been detached to accommodate him, the leg looking like a short log with the four layers of thermal clothing and the ankle now swollen to three times its size.

As they looked down at the gap in the ice wall, the five remaining members of the SAS/Delta team saw that the M-19 and the Arrow it had been mounted on were no more. The crash of a 125-millimeter shell from the T-80 was still smoking and remnants of the M-19 were still skittering across the ice near the frozen lake's edge. The Arrow was completely gone, except for its skirting, which was wobbling across the ice like a drunken punctured tire from some enormous bicycle.

By now Salvini had lined up his LAW 80—light antitank launcher—and fired it, the round hitting the tank's sloped composite armor a glancing blow. Nevertheless, the relatively slow-velocity HEAT round did damage, its molten jet of white-hot steel squirting a tadpole-shape inside the tank. They could hear one of the Siberians screaming inside, saw the slewing turret suddenly stop, and waited for the explosions from the rounds stored by the gunner even as they kept the remainder of the Port Baikal KGB border troops from raising their heads or taking too much comfort from the arrival of the T-80.

Salvini was loading another LAW round as David ordered the withdrawal, sure now that the midget sub under his brother's command must be well and truly away under the protection of the thick ice. "Choir, you drive the first Arrow with Lawson aboard. We can't get anyone in next to him with that leg of his. Aussie, you and Salvini in the second Arrow with me. I'll—"

They ducked, the whistle of mortars going overhead, crashing on the lake, splinters of ice shrapnel raining down on their helmets, a shard slicing through three layers of Aussie's winter uniform, barely missing his carotid artery.

"I'll drive," continued David. "You ride shotgun," he told Salvini. "Aussie, bring the Stinger."

"Yes, ma'am," shouted Salvini. He fired off another LAW round. This time it hit the glacis plate in front of the driver, penetrating the armor. At first there was only a short jet of flame from the hole but then, with David yelling for Salvini to "run," David already in the cockpit starting the Arrow, the tank resounded with a cacophony of small-arms fire, its machine gun ammunition exploding like firecrackers. This time they heard murderous screams from the tank crew and saw the cupola flung open, a cloud of thick, white smoke issuing forth as a gunner, trying to escape, was engulfed in flame, the bulging earpieces of his Soviet-style leather tank helmet melting even as he struggled to get free. David fired a long burst from his HK submachine gun; the man was flung back. David dropped the HK into the Arrow's cockpit beside him, his shoulder bruised and aching from the punishing recoil of the gun having been on full automatic; but it kept the Siberians' heads down.

Aussie scrambled into the front of David's Arrow as Choir, heading for the second Arrow, tossed his last two grenades toward the Siberian trench.

"Give 'em a good-bye shot!" David called to Salvini who, having dumped the M-60 light machine gun into the Arrow, snatched up the LAW and fired a round at the Siberian trench. It hit the far side of the trench but in doing so threw up a thunderous, exploding wall of powder snow and ice over the entire trench. The Americans used the curtain of falling debris to head for the lake, the two Arrows hitting forty-five miles an hour as they reached its shore. One skidded slightly before righting itself in their race away from Port Baikal, the two vehicles already executing a medley of zigzags, two hundred yards apart, the crack of small-arms fire and hastily ranged mortars chipping and denting the ice behind them.

* * *

The torpedo Robert Brentwood had fired had hit nothing, running its two-mile maximum range then losing speed, sinking, disappearing into the black abyss of the lake. Renowned for its clarity, the lake gave up all light after a hundred meters or so. The torpedo soon gained momentum under the accumulating PSI, the pressure on it soon so great that it was speeding, aided by its streamlined shape, deeper and deeper. Imploding at four thousand meters, it was still heading for the bottom at over eighty miles an hour, to be lost forever somewhere in the five thousand feet of accumulated silt.

Robert Brentwood had made a mistake, one that might be excused by others as an error made under stress, but a mistake nevertheless, in firing at what he now believed must have been some kind of fish or mammal—it would have to be a seal, given its speed—its curiosity aroused and coming straight for the GST like an enemy torpedo.

"Damn! It'll mean our torpedo's launch will have shown up on the other three GSTs' sonar."

"Yeah," said Johnson, "but, sir, there's been no voice communication in the sound channel. We would've seen that on sonar. At least they're not contacting one another, whether they heard it or not. Besides, they'd have to go to the surface to trail an aerial. For all they know, it could have been an ice charge pack—you know, one of the charges we figure they must be using to expand the thin ice patches before they launch the missiles."

"So?" asked Lopez. "They'll still know where we are. No way their sonar could've missed picking up our launch."

Robert Brentwood now had hold of a new possibility born of Johnson's suggestion. "Could have been an ice charge, I suppose," he said, trying to think like the other captains aboard the three enemy GSTs. "Anyway, there's no reason to think it was aimed at them. I mean, seeing there's been no voice communication, they probably don't know we're in the lake. At least not yet."

"We'll soon find out," said Johnson, pointing to the sonar scope. A blip larger than the one that had been made by what Robert Brentwood was sure must have been a seal was showing up five thousand yards off, just over two miles away.

"Might be coming to see if we need help," said Robert

Brentwood. "Firing point procedures . . ." But even as he gave the order he knew that should he fire this second torpedo and it hit the oncoming sub, the other two, probably much farther away in the northern sector of the lake, would pick up the explosions on their sonar, unless they were so far away that their sonar mikes were being blanketed by ice growl. What worried him was the possibility that Port Baikal might have gotten the message out on its radio about a sub being taken.

In fact, Port Baikal, even had it not been totally preoccupied with its self-defense, had been incapable of sending out any radio messages, the microwave dish on the top of the two-story library having shattered, crashing to the ground following one of Aussie's Stinger rounds. The demolition had so alarmed Nefski that, afraid he might lose his prisoners before he had a chance to interrogate them, he'd ordered them removed quickly from the library across to the hotel. However, in the murderous fire that the Americans were pouring toward the library and hotel, as well as at the KGB border troop defenders, several guards and prisoners had been hit. Some, like Alexsandra Malof, were not injured at all, as prisoners and several guards broke and ran toward the woods to avoid the commandos' fire.

Shouting through the linoleum-ripping sound of machine-gun fire, the crash of grenades, and the crack of half-a-dozen different kinds of small arms, the pilot of a Hind that had been parked behind the hotel, out of view of the S/D team, was now shouting at Nefski, asking that he be allowed to take off immediately to alert Irkutsk HQ from where, just possibly, some ad hoc underwater communication link might be rigged somewhere along the western shore of Baikal, seeing that Port Baikal's communications had literally been shot to pieces. "Maybe they can get the message to the subs' trailing aerials."

The pilot could see Nefski didn't have a clue what he meant. "The subs trail VLF—very low frequency—aerials. It's one way to—"

"*Stop* them!" Nefski screamed, pointing out at the ice, his finger trembling in the direction of the escaping commandos. "*Stop* them, you fool, before they reach the other side of the lake!"

"It's them or Irkutsk!" pressed the pilot resolutely, impatient with Nefski's vengeful streak. "I can't do both, Colonel."

"Yes, you can!" Nefski shouted back. "It'll only take you a few minutes to get them. Then go to Irkutsk for all I care. Get them and then break radio silence!" raged Nefski. "So what if you draw U.S. fighters to you through our AA screen."

"Their AWACs'll jam my message," said the pilot angrily, seeing Nefski wouldn't give way. "Come on then," the pilot shouted to one of the ground crew members. "Haven't you finished?"

"There you are, sir," said the ground crew foreman, hastily extracting the hose and snapping the armored lid shut on the self-seal tank. "It's full."

"About time."

Lifting off, he was only fifteen feet above the ground, behind the KGB troop trench. At least eleven KGB were dead or wounded, one sitting—difficult to tell whether he was actually dead or merely stunned from the concussion—not moving as the Hind passed over him, nosing higher. The pilot could now clearly see the two white triangles, twelve to fourteen miles away, heading for the other side of the lake nine miles beyond them. *"Oni umnitsy"*—"They're crafty," he told his weapons officer below, seeing that the two Arrows—the bruised sky of the approaching blizzard racing southward—had separated well abreast of one another. There was at least a mile between them, virtually making an attack on both at precisely the same time an impossibility. "Well, we won't play cat and mouse, Oleg," the pilot told his weapons officer. "We've got lots of time. We'll take them one by one."

On the ice Aussie saw a fine, foglike vapor streaming behind them, but since the temperature was well below freezing he knew it couldn't be fog. Then he got a whiff of it. "Hell! We're leaking fuel."

"I know," shouted David, his eyebrows and the edges of his sunglasses caked in ice.

"What're our chances of the Arrow reaching the other side?" called out Aussie, his voice quickly whipped away in the slipstream.

" 'Bout fifty-fifty," said David. "I'll try to take her on as straight a line as I can, use less—" There was a flapping noise, then the vapor became a cloud, the engine coughing.

"For Chrissakes!" yelled Salvini. "Gimme a break!" The Arrow's speedometer needle quavered between fifty and forty-five, then fell to twenty, ten; then the Arrow conked out, only the air cushion sustaining it. The Arrow slid a hundred yards farther, with a snuffling noise, under the residual momentum of the now-dead fan. As they came to a stop, David Brentwood, Aussie, and Salvini saw Choir's Arrow, with the wounded Lawson aboard, slowly pulling away from them, off to their far left. Whether or not Choir or the Delta commando looked back, they couldn't tell, but it didn't matter, for there was only one rule in this situation and that was that Choir had to keep going. He couldn't break radio silence to call for help either from the Cobras or the Stallion who, as Wain had pointed out before the mission, wouldn't take off before nightfall.

"Blizzard might help us," said David as he saw the purplish-black sky gathering power and moving rapidly southward toward them. As they alighted from the Arrow, Salvini, out of habit, took out his foot-long, saw-edged ranger knife and did a proper job on the fuel tank so the gasoline could be dispersed away from them by the wind whipping up in front of the blizzard.

"I dunno," said Aussie, breathing hard on his gloved fingers, swearing at the frozen zipper of the Haskins case, breathing on it, then quickly extracting the rifle, and flicking out its bipod legs. "He's gonna get one pass over us at least." He moved left of the Arrow, Salvini using the vehicle as a rest for the M-60 light machine gun, which he swivelled so that the Arrow would give him as much protection as possible.

David had already moved out to the right, south of the Arrow, but turned west now in the direction of the oncoming blip of the Hind, the Stinger in hand, his HK submachine gun slung across his shoulder. He prayed for a "hover" shot. If he got it, it would be the Fourth of July. The chopper, however, didn't come at them at all. Nose down, skimming the ice like an unstoppable bird of prey, it was heading instead toward the other Arrow farther on.

"Smart fucker!" Aussie called out across the ice. "He's leaving us for friggin' seconds."

David had a bead on the chopper. Anticipating the track, moving the Stinger's barrel with the missile, he fired—missing the chopper by a good one hundred yards, the round landing farther up the lake with the sound of a brown paper bag exploding. The sudden "boomp" registered on the sonar screens of Robert Brentwood's GST and the three other submarines, two in the far north, one closing in to investigate the first sonar blip, caused by Robert Brentwood firing at the seal minutes earlier.

The sub now closed on Brentwood's GST, its skipper assuming that the second chrysanthemum pattern on his screen—coming from close to the surface—might mean that some American armored force had reached the eastern shore of the lake. Alarmed by such a possibility but unable to find out without going to the surface for a thin ice hole, after which he'd have to trail the long VLF aerial, the captain warned the other GSTs by reverting to one of the oldest methods of communication in the world—tapping out a Morse message through the hull, the sound racing through the sound channel.

"Thank you! Thank you! Thank you!" Johnson said in celebration, the message itself unintelligible, but the sine waves of the message and its source clearly identified on the sonar screen. When the other two subs answered, Johnson transferred the sonar blips onto the superimposed E7 ONC—operation navigation chart. Two were in the northern section of the lake in the southwestern corner of the navigation chart's "8⁵" grid, one of the subs at latitude 54 degrees, 11 minutes north, longitude 109 degrees, 03 minutes west, the other twenty miles farther north.

But there was still a serious problem for Brentwood. While he now knew the exact position of the two northern subs, as well as the one heading for him, the information narrowing his search area by over 70 percent, he knew that if he fired the torpedo at the oncoming GST the two northern subs could break out of their quadrant on battery power—silent running—and come looking for him. Then it was pure mathematics: one would fire and in order to protect himself he would have to fire back, and the second would immediately have the vector, its torpedo getting him in the cross fire.

"Johnson."

"Yes, Captain?"

"We're not going to fire the fish."

"We aren't, sir?" said Johnson, looking painfully confused.

"No. We wait. How far away is our Snoop?"

"Ten minutes."

Choir waited till he saw the Hind spitting orange, then he turned hard right and hard right again and applied the brakes. A mistake—the Arrow spun uncontrollably on the skating-rink surface of the ice so fast that it threatened to throw the wounded Lawson out of the cockpit had it not been for the fact that he was strapped in. But it did throw the chopper's aim off as the Hind swept low, a twin path of machine-gun bullets chopping up the ice to Choir's left. The chopper went into a sharp climb, banking hard left in a tight turn to come back at Choir. It was only in semihover for two seconds, but it gave Aussie the time he needed, the chopper centered perfectly in the Haskins' ten-power scope, its belly filling the cross hairs as Aussie squeezed off the armor-piercing, HE/incendiary bullet toward the Hind over a mile away. The noise of the sniper rifle was a mere pop in Choir's ear as he pulled the throttle wide open again, heading for the tree line growing bigger by the second.

The Haskins could hit a ten-gallon drum at over a mile with the ten-power scope, but the Hind was a much bigger target. The HE/incendiary tore into the chopper's starboard gas tank like a poker through foil, the explosion barely visible to any of the SAS/Delta crew. The first squall of the blizzard had enveloped the southern end of the lake, completely swallowing Choir's Arrow and, with the downed Hind, any hope of Irkutsk finding out about the American-crewed sub in the lake.

Once in the cover of the taiga, Choir immediately reduced speed; even so he almost wiped out the Arrow against a snow-covered stump. Driving more slowly now, the noise much decreased, absorbed by the snow-thick forest, he stopped the engine and listened for the other Arrow. There was no sound but the mounting fury of the blizzard. This was where, Choir knew, their SAS/Delta training paid off, a regular soldier's forced march merely a morning run for them.

Choir took off his sunglasses and looked at his compass. "Six miles to the choppers," he said. "How you holdin' up, boyo?"

Lawson didn't answer.

"Hey," said Choir, "you all right?" There was still no answer. Choir unbuckled, leaned forward over the driver's column, and felt for the Delta man's carotid artery. It was beating, slowly but steadily. Lawson had a babylike expression on his face.

"You bastard!" said the normally polite Choir. With Aussie's second morphine shot in him, Lawson had been blissfully out of it all the way across the ice.

It didn't take him long, but by the time Robert Brentwood got into the SCUBA suit that was the fold-down bunk's mattress, his face was glistening with perspiration and the approaching blip of the other sub was much larger on the screen, now being only nine hundred yards—a half mile—away. Brentwood spat into the SCUBA helmet's face mask, rubbing the spittle around on it so as to prevent condensation.

"Nice shooting!" David told Aussie, watching the faint glimmer of the Hind's debris burning as he helped Salvini lift the M-60 from the Arrow's nose.

"Thanks, mate," Aussie told David. "Wasn't a bad shot at that. Now all we have to do is walk to the choppers."

"What d'you say?" asked Salvini. "Must be eleven to twelve miles?"

"Nearer eleven," said Aussie, "as the crow flies. Everybody up to it?"

"No worries, mate," said Salvini, borrowing the Aussie's accent.

" 'Sat a fact, mate? A dozen Foster's you're the first to beg—*beg* for tiffin."

"Is she any good?"

"*Tea* break!" responded Aussie. "Tiffin's a tea break. Fuck a duck! Don't you Yanks know anything?" Aussie zipped up the Haskins case and gave his boot to the Stinger's sight, rendering it virtually useless. They could carry only so much.

"Hey," said Salvini, "you're travelin' light. This M-60 weighs a ton, man. Plus I've got the two oh three," he added, slapping the grenade-launcher barrel on his personnel M-16.

"Oh, tell me about it, Salvini," said Aussie, shouldering the sniper rifle case.

"Knock it off, you two," said David Brentwood. "We're not into the woods yet and we've got—"

"Shush!" It was Aussie. "You hear that?"

All Brentwood and Salvini could hear was the blizzard, its cold dropping the temperature another ten degrees to minus forty, turning their perspiration to ice—a major danger, even to the Arctic-trained commandos. You had to keep moving, cool off gradually, otherwise the perspiration could encase you, despite the layers, in a sheath of ice. Hypothermia could set in without you knowing it. You'd start to feel peculiarly warm, slow, and comfortable, the agony of frost nip passing through frostbite and then—to nothingness.

"Can't be anything," said David to Aussie's inquiry, though he was conscious his ears were still ringing from the battle.

"A motor?" proffered Salvini, still hearing only the blizzard.

"Nah," said Aussie. " 'S gone now." They started off, Aussie pulling back his parka's Velcro mouth guard then ripping the wrapper from a Hershey bar. As far as he was concerned, it was the only good part of the rations. "Thought I heard a dog."

"Sure you didn't fart?" asked Salvini.

"Oh, very droll. Very fucking—"

"Shut up!" ordered David. "Save your energy." They had a minimum of eleven miles with heavy pack. They should make it in less than two hours, providing they kept a strict east-northeast heading. David slipped the compass string about his neck, not standard marching procedure but he didn't want to veer off the 22.5-degree heading by even a few yards. He would need to glance at the compass often without having to dig into his pockets, letting in the frigid air.

As Robert Brentwood sat in the pitch darkness of the five-foot-diameter, six-foot-high escape hatch, the luminescent glow of the pressure gauge became visible only when the escape chamber was already half full of water. The surge was less violent now than the initial rush of water, but he was still uncomfortable. Compared to his last semiannual "submarine survival" update course in the Norfolk, Virginia, water tank, the claustrophobia he was suffering now was markedly more severe. He hadn't suffered from it when he first joined the navy—it had crept up on him over the years, the fear kept at bay in the much larger nuclear subs. But even there it had become exacerbated after he had lost the USS *Roosevelt* off Iceland. Now, six hundred feet below the two-to-four-feet-thick ice roof, the sense of claustrophobia was pressing in on him.

The temperature of the water swirling about his neck was only two degrees or so above freezing, shocking his system until the microslim water layer between the Arctic SCUBA suit and his skin could steady the heat exchange ratio. His body's thermostat adjusted as he kept clenching and unclenching his fingers in the tight yet spongy rubber gloves. He told himself, forced himself, to be calm, feeling only an inch or so away from sheer terror as the water level reached the base of the SCUBA helmet and began creeping up, covering the visor. He counted slowly, as he had habitually done during the yearly prostate examination, the naval doctor impatiently ordering otherwise imperturbably calm officers not to stiffen up. "Relax the sphincter, man. Relax, damn it!"

Then the gauge, as well as the cessation of the rushing water, told him he could now open the top hatch. The moment he'd done so he felt his body rising effortlessly, the flippers grazing the hatch edge, his breathing still too fast—the visor, despite the spittle precaution, suddenly misting at the shock of seeing the other GST only sixty feet away. While stilled in neutral buoyancy, its bow had a slight up angle, its fat teardrop shape outlined in the blackness by beads of phosphorescent freshwater plankton, first cousins of the kind that gave sea waves their luminescence even on the darkest night. Unhesitatingly looping the basket he'd made from his T-shirt under the knife scabbard so as to prevent its sinking should he be buffeted by an upwelling, he swam, arms by his side, straight for the GST, struck by the irony that, though he would show up on the enemy's sonar as a very discernible blip, his shape like the seal he'd fired upon, they would be as confused as he had been.

It was only then that he saw what could only be a raft, its outline, for some inexplicable reason, only partially delineated here and there by phytoplankton. It looked to be about thirty feet square, half as long as the GST itself, its neutral buoyancy assured by what must obviously be depth-sensitive floats.

Exhilarated by the discovery of how it was that the midget subs were in effect hauling their own torpedo and cruise missile resupply, the raft probably holding eight missiles at least—two salvos' worth, in addition to the four already on the GST—it took him only a minute to swim to the raft.

About to place a lump of C-4 plastique from the T-shirt basket, he felt a U shackle, about five-eighths inch in diameter, he guessed, connecting the cables between the enemy GST and its raft. Using the handle spike on the end of his knife he unscrewed it and immediately felt the raft moving away from him. Now it could not act as a flotation platform for the GST. Next Brentwood turned his attention to the GST.

Within ten feet of the sub, he noticed the curved phosphorescent outline of the GST break, as if a string of pearls had been cut, most of the microscopic creatures disappearing as quickly as they must have alighted on the midget submarine. Without their guiding light he slowed, not wanting to bump into the hull but rather stand off it. Feeling the long, horizontal, stovepipe shape of one of the cruise missiles, he looped the T-shirt basket about its twenty-one-inch-diameter mouth, tying the basket tightly. Next, he pushed the basket's "goodies," as Johnson had referred to the centrex plastique, hard between the mouth of the cruise and the algae-slicked metal of the V-weld that connected the cruise tube to the pressure hull.

Making sure, purely by feel, that the six-inch-long detonator was firmly embedded in the plastique, he turned the timer knob sharply counterclockwise, feeling the soft click. Glancing back, he saw his own sub clearly outlined by the phosphorescent phytoplankton. He turned and, kicking hard, started back to the sub, then felt a vibration behind him to his right. He turned to see a spume of luminescent bubbles erupting behind him from the hatch of the enemy GST. The trail of bubbles then abruptly changed from the vertical to the horizontal as the attacker, his knife trailing a secondary stream of bubbles, came straight at him.

It was all confusion, but instinctively Brentwood's left arm shot for the thinner trail to grab the knife arm. Somehow he missed and felt a warm sensation deep in his left shoulder where the blade had sliced open his SCUBA suit, cutting him deeply. Quickly he thrust his left hand forward again, felt something solid, and drove his knife forward, feeling it go into something soft then hard, the blade rebounding on bone. He gripped his knife's handle harder, ripping hard left, opening the attacker's stomach.

Brentwood felt himself being dragged down, the attacker's body limp, jerking spasmodically now and then. The grasp on Brentwood's left arm was like steel. With nine minutes left on the ten-minute detonator, his mind's eye filled with a vision of being pulled down into the countless layers of diarrhea-like mud. He pulled his knife back and thrust forward again. But there was no need; as suddenly as it had taken hold, the Siberian's grip relaxed, the life drained out of him.

Breaststroking and kicking with all his might, Brentwood made his way back to his GST's hatch and three minutes later was inside the escape chamber, rapping the top of the bottom hatch with his right hand as he began turning the wheel of the top hatch with his left. But now his left hand cramped as he squatted there, his body crouched monkeylike. He switched to the right hand to close the top hatch, his left arm simply refusing to obey his brain, the nerves of the shoulder numb.

He heard and felt the quiet whirr of the GST's battery going for "burst" speed of seventeen knots which, in the next five minutes, would have them just over a mile and a half away. Brentwood had to stay cramped in the water-filled cubbyhole of the conning tower, as any siphoning of power from the battery to pump out the water would be power taken from the prop. He would have to wait until Johnson figured they were far enough away from the impending explosion before he could start the pump to vent the water in the escape hatch. In severe pain now, Brentwood remained crouched, sincerely hoping that neither

Lopez nor Johnson would accidentally bump the "up scope" switch.

As the GST slowed and the venting of the escape chamber began, the water level dropped rapidly, and Brentwood almost drowned, knocked unconscious for a moment, his head lolling dangerously as the midget sub itself trembled violently from he shock wave of the detonation over a mile away.

The explosion, as Brentwood hoped it would, had set off a cruise warhead on the enemy sub, the resulting "Varoomph!" heard for miles, sending an enormous spume of ice shards skyward above the broken surface of the lake, as well as shattering the Siberian GST into thousands of pieces, the noise reaching Brentwood's GST two seconds later. It stunned the three men; Lopez, though he'd plugged his ears, was unable to hear Johnson's order for him to disengage battery power and go to diesel, heading at 15.9 knots for the northern quadrant a hundred and ninety miles away, their ETA depending on the currents and the time taken to intercept the loose raft—the latter, clearly visible on the sonar screen, having deflected some of the explosion's sound waves.

"Why do we need it, sir?" asked Johnson, who believed, correctly, that now his skipper was wounded he, Johnson, would have to be the one to go out through the hole and attach the raft to them.

"We can reload our empty torpedo tubes," explained Brentwood, his voice heavy, slow—still groggy from his ordeal, now and then grimacing from Lopez's inexpert dressing of his wound. "Easy enough to do with two of you," continued Brentwood. Lopez looked alarmed. "Subsurface float buoy's," added Brentwood, "on the raft. Just push her over to our sub and shackle her to the ring bolt."

At one point Brentwood almost passed out from the pain and only then, albeit reluctantly, agreed to lie down on the lower bunk.

"You think the other two GSTs up north'll still be there?" asked Johnson.

"No reason why they shouldn't be," answered Brentwood. "All they've seen is an explosion on their sonar screen," he explained. "They'll figure one of their GSTs has fallen victim to a malfunction—internally caused explosion. There'll be no sign of an external attack. Anyway, even if they suspect there was and come looking for us, all the better for us. Either way, we'll find one another."

CHAPTER TWENTY-SEVEN

THOUGH HE KNEW precisely where they were by virtue of his GPS unit, Choir couldn't help the wounded Lawson get any closer to the chopper camp unless he was willing to go the last mile by Arrow—something that David Brentwood had forbidden anyone to do for fear that, no matter how small the possibility, it might draw an enemy patrol to the hidden choppers. As a safety precaution, the last mile was to be on foot. This being impossible for Lawson, despite the lingering effect of the morphine shots, he and Choir decided it would be quicker and safer for Choir to go on ahead to the choppers and on the way out, the Stallion, on infrared, could lower a harness for Lawson. Brentwood, Aussie, and Salvini would, if they'd made it across the ice, find their own way through the taiga to the helos.

Before Choir left, he slit open Lawson's vapor-barrier boot. The Delta commando's foot was in bad shape from the deep slash of the cable, a piece of rusted, grotesquely twisted wire that had passed through the soft calf into his ankle still in place, scraping against the bone. With the morphine wearing off, Choir knew that what the doctors and nurses back in Dutch Harbor would call "discomfort" would soon set in with a vengeance. It meant that without another shot of morphine, Lawson, despite his Delta training and all the will in the world, would be unable to keep quiet, let alone put any weight on the foot. Choir pulled

out the white/green winter camouflage net from beneath the
Arrow's seat and tossed it over the vehicle, propping Lawson up
so that the butt of the M-60 rested in his lap with another shot
of morphine by his side and an MRE with its regulation 4,200
calories for winter conditions also within easy reach. "Enjoy
your picnic," joked Choir, tapping Lawson encouragingly on
the shoulder. "And remember, boyo, drink your four liters."

"How'll I piss?"

"Aim high," said Choir, smiling for the first time that day.
"Listen, boyo, if I don't make it back to you, take the chance
and go active with your finder beeper, but give me two hours.
Don't want the Sibirs homing in on the beep if we can help it."

"I'll wait," said Lawson. "You'll be back."

Choir, with one last glance at his GPS, started off for the
choppers, which he knew were now a mile away. He didn't go
in a straight line, using instead SAS "rabbit" zigzags and back
tracks, crouching, absolutely still, listening to detect the slightest
untoward noise within the rushing-river sound of the blizzard in
the high timber as fresh powder snow started to fall. Passing
down through the heavy drifts on the bank of a snaking frozen
river, Choir scanned left to right for signs of any footprints or
vehicle tracks and took another GPS fix. The choppers should
now be no more than a hundred yards ahead, but damned if he
could see them, his vision obliterated by either trees or the camouflage nets or—

Then he spotted the nose of one of the Cobras, and as he got
nearer, experienced the pleasant fright of recognition as the bigger, almost brutish, shape of the Super Stallion became distin-
guishable under the snow-dusted net. At twenty yards he stopped
and knelt down to make sure no one was following him. Nothing
stirred but the blizzard.

He waited a full five minutes, watching. Something was
wrong. He couldn't smell it or see it, but his sixth sense told
him. As sure as a mother detects the slightest change of rhythm
in her baby's sleep in an otherwise noisy house, he knew that
something was amiss. For a start there should have been some
sign of movement around the choppers, their crews surely as
anxious, hearing the distant gunfire, to see the returning SAS/

Delta men as they would be to see the chopper crews. Yet, peculiarly, he didn't sense a trap.

Silently, his slow movements completely muffled by the blizzard, he eased forward a few yards and stopped again, noticing what looked like a patch of oil, its coloration and form different from the folds of snow about him. Then he saw it was a canteen shape. He was in a minefield.

Without moving an inch, without blinking, he stared at the choppers, knowing that everyone inside had either been taken prisoner or killed. Whatever an enemy patrol had done, securing the open area by circling it with a ring of antipersonnel mines, they had now gone, not staying with the choppers when they had heard the firing down by the lake, and obviously not having blown the choppers up for fear of drawing attention to themselves. Turning, retracing his footsteps precisely, Choir made his way back through the trees, his earlier footsteps still visible enough that he could avoid stamping on any new ground. After a quarter mile or so he paused, waited, and, sensing no danger, moved on, till, to his immense relief, he spotted the Arrow.

Lawson's throat had been cut, his snow-veiled stare silent testimony to the utter surprise and horror with which it had happened, so much blood around the Arrow that it looked like a spill of pink algae, the snowfall diluting the dark red.

His jaw tight with anger, senses bristling, Choir saw the footsteps of the Siberian patrol. There had been three—possibly four—no doubt coming round in a circle from the choppers after hearing the Arrow making its way through the woods. The Arrow's gas tank was punctured in three or four places, the gas gone.

Choir switched the safety off his HK-11 then began the "lope" run, the kind that, because of the high adrenaline energy it consumed—eyes, ears, trigger finger on the edge—could exhaust even the fittest commando in half an hour in the heavy snow. He heard a dog, its panting downwind of him. As it turned, one man in the group of four turned with it, but by then Choir had fired three long, rattling bursts, downing the dog and the two SPETS nearest it, the other two quickly dashing behind tall firs.

Choir, still running, suddenly tripped on hidden roots, his vest taking the brunt of the fall, bullets whistling above where a moment before he'd stood. Now rolling over, he performed the minimum requirement of the SAS, its calling card: changing the magazine in midroll, returning fire within three seconds, not hitting either of the SPETS but keeping them behind the trees, as he also took cover behind an ice-cream-domed stump.

One SPETS was firing, only the barrel of his AK-47 visible. Choir could hear the other moving twenty feet to his right, going down on his knees. Choir was lifting his weapon when, as if in slow motion, he glimpsed the other man's face and the white toque he was wearing becoming one, suddenly blurring, the man's face and scalp separating from him like torn paper as David Brentwood's Heckler and Koch nine-millimeter Parabellum punched into him from behind, bark flying everywhere. There was another shot. This, in its singularity, was much louder, more of a "thwack" than the outraged chatter of David Brentwood's machine gun. Aussie's Haskins, firmly braced by the best Siberian pine, spoke only once, its HE/incendiary literally blowing the remaining SPETS' head off, Salvini covering the rear.

No one spoke for several minutes, all frozen in attitude, braced for the counterattack—if there was to be one—making sure that absolutely nothing else was moving. Softly Aussie told Salvini, "Told you I heard a fucking mutt!"

They took Lawson's dog tags but had no time to bury him. It was hardest on Choir, but it was necessary and, with only one backward glance, he moved off with the other three, telling them briefly about the choppers and the vanished crew who were no doubt dead inside them. It was up to David whether to go on and destroy the choppers but there would be the mines to negotiate—too time-consuming in itself and besides, any noise would only attract further enemy patrols. Plus the SPETS patrol could have already reported the position of the chopper to an HQ.

"We hike," he said simply to Choir, Aussie, and Salvini. "East-nor'east."

"Just what I felt like," said Aussie somberly. "Bloody four-hundred-mile walk."

They never doubted they'd make it. If an SAS/Delta man couldn't make fifty miles a day, he was loafing. It would be eight days to the forward units of Second Army who, given the GST the team had taken out in the tunnel and the explosions from the lake, must be mightily relieved at having at least the cruise salvos already cut by more than half. Besides, the four men had their weapons, two MRE's apiece, and after what they'd been through during winter—survival course at Brecon Beacons for the SAS, the High Sierras for Salvini—they had no fears except how cold it might become, already minus forty as it was growing dark.

But here, too, they had two outstanding allies: their physical condition—the ability to go beyond fifty miles a day with their much-lightened packs—and, just as important, the small Nu-wick 120-hour candle in their kit. Weighing fourteen ounces, looking like a can of tuna, the light/heat candle came with six small and, according to Aussie, obscene-looking movable candles: one candle for light, two for cooking and, as two troopers slept under their Norway flap tents, two on guard, three candles for heat.

The deaths of Lawson and the others on the mission weighed heavily on David during the next seventy-two hours, more so as there was no opportunity to talk—each man refraining from speaking unless it was absolutely necessary. They were conserving energy, all communication done by hand signal, the four of them moving in a diamond firefight pattern, just far enough from one another to have arcs of interlocking fire should it be required. David had to force himself, especially when he was on the point, to stop thinking about the choppers they'd had to abandon; it irked him that even some of their equipment would fall into enemy hands.

As they got closer to the north end of the lake, his mood began to improve, however, with the expectation of meeting up with Freeman's advance forces. The mood was shattered when they heard, though they couldn't see, another salvo of four cruise missiles passing overhead toward Second Army. David's anxiety increased, too, for his brother's safety; but then on their satellite bounce shortwave radio they picked up a static-riven BBC over-seas service broadcast announcing "reduced enemy cruise activity" and a substantial victory for Second Army east of Yerofey

Pavlovich, which meant Freeman was on the march. Though it was a cause for celebration, they still couldn't make any noise, and indeed the news only alerted them to another danger, namely that in their SPETS uniform any advance American patrols probing southwestward to Baikal would shoot first and ask questions later. They ripped off the SPETS shoulder insignia, but even so the Siberian white coveralls had a baggy form with a distinctive belt, unlike the Americans' white overlays.

CHAPTER TWENTY-EIGHT

ROBERT FINALLY HAD to sleep. But it wasn't for long, and waking from his turn on the "plank," one of the GST's fold-down bunks, he felt sick from the suffocating smell of diesel. He was in a hellish red light, Johnson informing him triumphantly that he'd found the "rigged for red" switch while he, Brentwood, was asleep. In the event that they might have to go topside, through thin ice into the pitch-black Arctic night, the ruby glow would be easier on their eyes, allowing them to adjust to the darkness. "Do we still have them—" Brentwood almost passed out with the pain, a persistent hammer blow radiating from his shoulder through his neck and head muscles down into his lower back and buttocks. "Do we still have them in the northern quadrant?"

"Yes, sir," answered Johnson. "One of 'em moved a few hundred yards or so but not far. They've come up close to the surface—just fired off another salvo. Means they're still pretty close to the ice hole—only about a hundred feet below. Guess they're going to pop off another few. I figure they must be near some upwelling—thin crust—so why move? Probably don't even have to use any 'charge-pick' through the thinner ice now they've fired.''

Robert Brentwood didn't respond, for as he sat up he felt his head was literally going to fall off, consciousness having torn him brutally from a dream. He'd been with Rosemary and his little boy—would it be a boy or would it be a girl?—in a sylvan glade in Oxshott, the embracing, cool calm of a huge oak tree above them as they'd picnicked—chicken—with one of those wicker baskets so beloved by the English with everything in its right place, and his child smiling at him, eyes wide with wonder, and then David and Lana were there with her pilot boyfriend, the one she wanted to have as a fiancé if La Roche ever condescended to agree to a divorce, and the pilot's head, which had somehow become Robert, was bandaged, sore, eyes covered as Lana had described in a letter.

"We're going to fire our missiles," he told Johnson and Lopez, easing himself off the bunk. "Convince 'em we're still one of them." He paused then pointed at the ONC E-8 chart, the position of the two subs, from which they hadn't moved, marked with red crosses. "They'll think we're hitting Second Army." He tried to smile at his own brilliance, but even the effort emitted a fiery pain deep inside his skull.

"All *right*!" said Johnson, his enthusiasm echoing throughout the tiny sub, pummeling Brentwood's head some more. Such enthusiasm was something that Robert Brentwood himself hadn't been able to regain, however much he wished, after the shock of the knife wound. At forty-three he was still a relatively young man, but he was growing old for submarines.

"Way to go, Skipper!" echoed Lopez.

"You okay?" Brentwood asked, squinting in the redded-out light. "You look like hell."

"A bit whacked, sir."

"After we shoot off the missiles, you hit that bunk."

"Sir, I'll be all—"

"Do as I say."

"Yes, sir."

To Lopez's utter amazement Robert Brentwood chewed two aspirin without water as he punched in the coordinate vectors for the attack arcs, double-checking the distances and remembering the forty-mile-an-hour winds expected in the blizzard they'd seen racing south down the lake as they'd egressed Port Baikal. In any event Brentwood knew that with the two enemy subs' exact "quadrant 8^5" position known and the two subs being close to the surface, a direct hit wouldn't be necessary. A half mile either way, even across the 8^5 line into nearby 6^5 or 5^6 quadrants, would do the job. "I'd say that after that last salvo at Second Army they're either into quadrant six five or just moving into five six. Here, southeast of—" He couldn't pronounce it and spelled it, "S-B-E-G-A. How'd *you* say that, Johnson?"

"Asshole country, sir."

Then Lopez had a suggestion. "Sir?"

"Yes?"

"Sir, could we pop one on Irkutsk?"

"*Pop* one?" In the fatigue that gives rise to silly laughter, even in the most introverted souls, during moments of high tension, Johnson and Robert Brentwood, a world apart in rank, broke up in common cause, Brentwood shaking his head, Johnson, tears in his eyes, looking across at Lopez. "*Pop* one! You dork!"

"Well, I'm telling you, Lopez," said Robert Brentwood, right hand holding his head as if it were a basket of eggs, "I'm not gunning for civilians—nor is Freeman—but I like your idea. Matter of fact, I like it so much, if we get out of this I'm gonna see you get promoted."

"Hell no, sir."

"Only let's spread the good news around a little, Lopez," said Brentwood. "On behalf of Second Army and—" A stab of needlelike pain forced Brentwood to sit down abruptly on the bunk.

"You okay, sir?" asked Johnson anxiously.

"No. Son of a—" The pain passed but left him nauseated and dizzy for a few minutes. Johnson was trying not to look worried, but he was scared. As a Sea Wolf captain Brentwood had all the Soviet firing procedures down pat. Without him, Johnson doubted he could handle it—*knew* he couldn't handle it.

Brentwood had Lopez strap his left arm against his chest, moved to the computer, triple-checked the coordinates, then stopped. Without looking around he announced, "Lopez, I'm gonna promote you whether you damn well like it or not." He looked around at Lopez, on steerage, then forward a few feet to Johnson. "We *are* going to spread it around, boys. Johnson, how many cruise missiles on that raft?

"Eight, sir."

"Right! With the four we already have that makes twelve. We'll clobber the Stalingrad Division from behind with six. Won't know what the hell hit them. Confusion'll be worth as much to us as the casualties we inflict. And, gentlemen, let's not be mean about this. We'll split the other six with two for the KMK factory at Novokuznetsk, which we'll fire first, and two we'll donate to Akademgorodok, near Novosibirsk. The KMK factory," he explained to Lopez, who hadn't picked up on the name, "is where they make their tanks as well as these GSTs. And that leaves two for our two friends up north. Seeing they stole our technology, let's demonstrate its accuracy, gentlemen. All right?"

"All *right*."

"Okay. Let's have a sonar ping," ordered Brentwood, and the easy tone of a second ago was now replaced by his professional demeanor. "Come on, hurry it up."

"Yes, sir." Now they were on active sonar, Brentwood explaining, "Might as well be brazen about it. What's that old man Freeman always says? *L'audace, l'audace, toujours l'audace!*"

"He stole it from Patton," said Johnson.

"Who stole it from Frederick the Great," said Brentwood. "Well, it's ours now."

The active's "pings" were now bouncing, or "bonging," back, telling them that they had a relatively thin ice roof no more than half a mile three degrees starboard.

"No problem, sir," Johnson pronounced. "Looks as thin as a virgin's—"

"Yes, yes, all right," said Robert Brentwood, notoriously prudish about such matters, even in front of his sister Lana who, as a nurse had seen it all and had "done time," as young David put it, with "Scumbag" La Roche.

Reaching the area of the thin ice, Brentwood ordered Johnson to take the sub to a depth of two thousand feet, approaching the sub's crush depth, and at an off angle to the targeted ice patch. He then pulled the lever to release float charge. Two minutes later there was a gut-wrenching thud, and Brentwood immediately ordered the GST to fifty feet.

"Fifty feet, aye, sir," came Johnson's confirmation. At fifty feet he levelled the sub out, still surprised at how quickly the tiny GST, a seal compared to a whale in size, responded. The problem was not to let it get ahead of you and slam into the ice.

"Half speed," Brentwood instructed Lopez, then to Johnson, "Twenty-five feet."

"Twenty-five feet, sir. . . . Levelling at twenty-five."

"Very well. Man battle stations missile. Set condition one!"

"Condition one, aye, sir," responded Johnson.

"Departments ready?" asked Brentwood. There were only two departments, Lopez's and Johnson's, but Brentwood knew that this was a time for tried and true procedures to steady their nerves.

"Steerage ready, sir," reported Lopez, followed by Johnson's, "Sonar ready."

"Very well," acknowledged Brentwood. "Neutral trim."

Johnson made a slight adjustment to starboard. "Neutral trim, sir."

"Stand by to flood tubes one and two," ordered Brentwood, it being standard procedure on any missile submarine to be ready to fire torpedoes in defense of the ship should an enemy vessel try to interfere with the missile launch. "Completing spin up," Brentwood advised them as he entered the final salinity and current corrections that would affect the missiles' trajectories. "Spin up complete. Prepare for ripple fire."

"Prepare for ripple fire," responded Johnson.

"Fire one," ordered Brentwood.

"Fire one. One fired." There was a hiss of compressed air and a rasping noise, the sub rolling ten degrees port before regaining neutral trim.

"Fire two."

"Fire two. Two fired."

In less than three and half minutes all four cruise missiles had passed through their nose cones' protective membranes, exited the ice-free hole, booster rockets engaged, and were en route to their targets. Lopez and Johnson exited the sub for the reloads, while Brentwood made copious notes on the GST's performance as he prepared a course to take the sub toward thinner ice at the eastern shore after all salvos had been fired.

"In the spring, General," said Professor Leonid Grigorenko, looking out on the frozen Ob Sea that was Akademgorodok's private lake, "I hope you'll find time to come out sailing with me and Irena."

The gruff, heavy-browed Yesov shook his head. "*Nyet*, thank you all the same, Professor. I am no sailor. Besides, there will still be ice in the spring."

"Oh, come now, Comrade. It adds to the adventure, yes?"

"*Nyet.*" Yesov looked about so that none of his aides at the professor's cocktail party, to celebrate the success of the GST offensive, heard that he was leery of anything to do with water—including bathing, some had said. "I get sick in the Jacuzzi, Professor."

"Ah, Marshal!" said Chernko, his familiarity claiming Yesov, marshal of all Siberian forces, as if he were a long-lost friend. "How goes the Thirty-first?"

"Well," said Yesov curtly—he didn't like Chernko, even if he was hailed in Novosibirsk for his GST plan. Yesov was willing to accept the general's help, but to Yesov it had been too conditional altogether—Chernko telling them, insisting on what pleasures and luxuries, including dachas, he would get in return. Yesov despised him. Here was the Russian, a former KGB chief, now sucking up to the Western alliance in Moscow while slipping Novosibirsk vital information via his spies, information that Yesov had to grudgingly admit had served them well in stopping the Allies at the Urals, pummeling the Allies in fact. Still, he disliked the man's opportunism. As far as he was concerned Chernko was little more than the old bourgeois "Communist"—as ideologically unsound and, at root, as uncommitted to the military as Gorbachev had been.

"*I'm* well satisfied," said Chernko. "If the Thirty-first does as well in the east against this Freeman as we have in the west, eh, it'll be over soon. A cease-fire, and then we go for American aid. The Americans are suckers. Once the Thirty-first mauls Freeman's soft Second Ar—''

The apartment building shook, everyone thinking it was an earthquake, broken glass, whole windows popping out and whizzing through the air, expensive dresses of the elite slashed, many of the generals' wives screaming from the minor cuts and abrasions created by the first shock wave. Yesov had moved under the mahogany dining table with all the finesse of a charging T-80, sending two colonels' wives splaying on the plush Persian carpet. As people were getting up off the floor, his beeper was set off by the pressure of his folding gut.

''*Machinu!*''—''Stop that thing!'' one of the women screamed hysterically.

''*Tishe!*''—''Be quiet!'' Yesov replied, red-faced, lumbering up with the help of an aide, whom he quickly shook off like an offending mullet. The marshal was in the throes of regaining his ruffled dignity. It was seven minutes, the phone lines being down, before he heard that the KMK works in Novokuznetsk had been badly hit, as well as the Institute of Defense Science in Akademgorodok.

The damage—over 192 killed, several hundred wounded, was not of particular concern to the marshal even though it abruptly ended the cocktail party. Whatever his faults might be, Yesov had been the first in that room, or in Novosibirsk's Central Committee, to realize that the Americans had suddenly and dramatically demonstrated that they had the ability to reach deep into Sibir. It could only mean that the Americans must now have established forward air bases, despite the Thirty-first's advance, from which to fire off their air-launch cruise missiles which, skimming at tree level across the taiga and steppe, had hit both the political heart and a vital industrial organ of Siberia. It was clearly a warning of the terrible danger that the vital Siberian oil fields at Mirnyy, in the very center of Siberia and without which she could not continue the war, were at immediate risk. The same would then be true of Siberia's vital defense industries all the way from Mirnyy, believed to be invulnerable to all U.S. tactical missiles, to the oil field, barely two hundred miles north of Novosibirsk, at Belyy Yar. Everything was now within Freeman's reach.

"You know what this means?" Professor Grigorenko demanded, rather than informing Yesov. But the marshal already knew. He might be slow afoot, but his brain was in excellent condition. Still the professor, shakily pouring himself a large vodka and ignoring the general's glass, went on, "It's brutally simple, Marshal. If they want to they can turn this into another Kuwait. On fire!"

"Do you really believe they'd do that?" asked an aide.

"Are you senile?" growled Yesov. "They're not playing baseball, Comrade!"

"No, sir."

In fact, Sonarman First Class Johnson aboard the GST was thinking in precisely those terms. They had stolen first base (the KMK works at Novokuznetsk), the second (Akademgorodok near Novosibirsk), and the third—he looked at his watch. Right about now.

Five hundred miles east of them the six one-thousand-pound cruise warheads came "shuffling" through the air over train tracks and a pipeline only yards apart in quadrant 5^6 just west of Sbega. When he heard them coming in, a *praporschika*—a warrant officer—in the Siberian Thirty-first knew as well as anyone else in the Stalingrad division that if the explosions of the incoming subsonic missiles—loaded with armor-piercing bomblets—blew out the pipe or rail tracks, 90 percent of the Thirty-first's supplies would be cut off, only 10 percent able to make it on the poor road system. They simply did not have the kind of airlift capacity of the Americans.

The first missile took out a copse of snow-laden birch trees and did no harm to speak of. The second missile, however, tore up more than thirty feet of track; the remaining four missiles tore up even more, and their rain of armor-piercing bomblets sliced through the Thirty-first Stalingrad Division trucks in showers of white-hot steel, hitting over fifty fully loaded troop trucks in the 2,300-vehicle convoy, most of the casualties—over nine hundred—caused not only from the detonation but from the hornetlike swarms of fléchettes.

Far more serious was the severing of the pipeline by the thousands of bomblets from missiles four and five. The oil line running adjacent to the road erupted in flame, the fire speeding along the ruptured pipe like a quick fuse.

The oil, already under pressure, jetted out like water from a long, punctured hose along a snaking, forty-mile section that, like the rest of the line, ran close to the road. The long, spurting tongues of fire set trucks, armor, troops, and self-propelled 120-millimeter howitzer haulers ablaze, and consumed another hundred vehicles, including BMDs—armored personnel carriers—in the most devastating single loss—over four thousand killed or injured—suffered by Russian arms in the past year.

The fire alone attracted American fighters in the overcast. Although they paid heavily, losing over twenty-three to the Fulcrums, they had such overwhelming numerical and instrument-flying superiority, they delivered what the Thirty-first commanders and those few still alive in the column were calling a "Kuwaiti highway" massacre. A-10 Thunderbolts were coming in, their seven-barrelled, thirty-millimeter Avenger cannons blazing, picking off the Siberians' T-80 tanks at will.

Streams of tracer poured down so fast that they created the illusion that the tanks were actually sucking the fire from the planes, the tanks exploding, providing more target identification for the American air force. They created such a massive traffic jam on the second-rate road, hemmed in by the taiga and snow banks, that Freeman, seeing his chance, issued orders that the carnage continue unabated and that he would personally court-martial anyone who let up attacking in the next twenty-four hours for any other reason than to refuel and rearm.

The Thirty-first Stalingrad was taking a terrible pummelling, its morale as savaged by the belief that it was now surrounded as by the actual punishment it was taking. So savage was the American counterattack that, despite the thick white overlay of cumulonimbus, the battle became visible as a pulsating, red vein to satellite reconnaissance.

As suddenly as it had seemed an overwhelming threat, the Thirty-first was now in full retreat. Freeman, the Baikal threat against him now removed, ordered his armored divisions into the "fishhook" configuration he'd been waiting for. One column of over a thousand tanks with close air support arced left, southward, heading for Irkutsk on any side roads and rivers they could find. Some roads had been literally bombed and napalmed out of the taiga by U.S. engineers. The right curve of the fishhook turned northward, heading for Yakutsk. Freeman's Shermanlike breakout *around* the flanks of the smashed-Thirty-first became a rout, the Siberian division finally pocketed, unable to move, its GST backup, as Freeman announced in a message to the president, "no longer in service." The greatest strain on the American supply line was surrendering Siberians, most of them wounded. U.S. Medevac facilities were stretched to the limit.

For the crews aboard the two GSTs in quadrant 6⁵ there was no warning, no gradual foreboding of ice growl or increase in subsurface turbidity. There was only the world coming to an end, the explosions of the two cruise missiles hitting them, so cataclysmic as to shock each man's nervous system into instant, irreparable crisis, as surely as the subs' hatches were buckled, preventing escape. The two GSTs, squashed like molten bottles, plummeted to over five thousand feet below into the primeval silt of the boreal forest.

"What can we do?" asked civilian members of the Novosibirsk Central Committee in panic. Yesov looked at each one of them in turn, then at all of them contemptuously. "Arrange a cease-fire, you fools!" He was a soldier first, he told them, but also a realist.

The American public, led by La Roche's tabloids, were overwhelmingly in favor.

Freeman was appalled, Dick Norton handing him a faxed copy of the *New York Times* editorial which, like the La Roche papers, joined in heartily for an immediate cease-fire as offered by the Siberians, warning only that a cease-fire should not "extract unreasonable demands and sacrifices" from the Siberian people, "as did the Treaty of Versailles of the German nation, thereby assuring continued bitterness in the rebuilding that would have to be done."

Outside his victorious forward headquarters at Sbega, west of the Chinese/Siberian hump, Freeman strode up a snow-dazzling embankment, the sky the bluest he'd ever seen. Smacking the *New York Times* headline, he thrust the newspaper back at Norton. "By God, this is, this is treachery, Norton."

Norton looked stunned.

"They talk about the Treaty of Versailles," thundered Freeman, frightening a bird from a nearby perch, the bird startling Norton, who reached for his sidearm. "Remember what Churchill said about the Treaty of Versailles?" said Freeman. "It was an armistice, he said, for twenty years. It's the same here, goddamn it! Dick, if we don't run with the bit while we have it between our teeth, we'll have to fight these jokers again. Didn't we learn anything from that bastard Hussein?" Freeman was beside himself, right glove smashing into his left. "Why don't they let me do it, Dick? What the hell's the matter with them back there at the White House?"

"President's under an awful lot of pressure, General, for this cease-fire. Nobody wants any more fighting."

"Neither do I, damn it! But can't you see? Can't anybody see that if we don't finish it now, we'll have to finish it somewhere else—forced into a rematch at a time and place of *their* choosing?"

Norton, quite frankly, didn't have the courage to show the general the copies of the other newspapers' headlines. "BRING OUR BOYS HOME!" the La Roche papers cried. "ENOUGH IS ENOUGH!"

"They're praising you a lot, General. Saying if it hadn't been for your brilliance, your planning—"

Freeman wasn't listening. "They must be made to understand, Dick. I want you to send a message to the president. Immediate. 'Strongly suggest we finish the job. Do not trust Siberian offer, which I see as merely an opportunity to regroup—especially given their strong position on the western front. Please let my views be known to the Joint Chiefs. Sincerely, General Douglas Freeman.' "

It was of no avail. President Mayne agreed with the American public: it was time to bring the boys home.

"YOU ARE ORDERED," President Mayne's reply message read, "TO CEASE ALL MILITARY OPERATIONS AT A MUTUALLY AGREED-UPON TIME WITHIN THE NEXT TWENTY-FOUR HOURS. REPEAT TWENTY-FOUR

HOURS. THE NATION IS GRATEFUL FOR YOUR BRIL-
LIANT LEADERSHIP. NOW IS THE TIME TO LEAD THE
PEACE.''

Norton received the response from the White House and immediately went out to give it to the general. Freeman read it,
crumpled it, and thrust it deep into his greatcoat pocket. He
looked down the snow bank on the gaggle of press types trying
to negotiate the slope in their frantic eagerness to interview
"Dogged Doug," a sobriquet he abhorred as much as he disliked the unwillingness of the press pool to go back to Khabarovsk now and interview some of the individuals—everyone from
supply officers to grunts—who had made it possible. No, now
they all wanted to be up at the front, now that it was all quiet.

"Look at 'em!" Freeman told Norton. "By God, I'd like to
bulldoze all of them into Baikal! You see, Dick? That's how
short a step it is from hosanna to hoot.''

"General, if you don't feel up to it, perhaps we can arrange
another—''

"Don't fret, Dick. I won't disgrace Second Army. Let the
bastards come up and take their pretty pictures. Look good
against the skyline, don't I?''

"Yes, sir. It's terrific.''

"All right then. Send 'em up.''

The first of the press corps to make it was a woman reporter
from Detroit who, barely able to get her breath, asked the general, "It's said, General, you wanted to drive on once you'd
turned the battle. Is that true?''

"I did.''

Norton looked skyward in exasperation.

"However,'' continued Freeman, looking as happy as a father who's been told his daughter has just become engaged to a
parolee, "the U.S. Second Army is an instrument of national
policy. I do what I am told. That is all.''

"But General—'' Freeman walked through the rapturous ac-
claim back into his headquarters, urgent messages already coming through from the Joint Chiefs that he was, as soon as it could
be arranged after the cease-fire, to make himself "available" to
return to Washington for consultation.

"Ah,'' he told Norton disgustedly. "Clear as the nose on my

face. Far as the White House is concerned, the war is over. By God, they think it's finished, Dick.''

At the signing of the cease-fire at Irkutsk, a dour Freeman shook hands with a dour Yesov, both flashing a smile for the cameras, Norton careful to keep Freeman out of mike range, which was just as well. "I tell you, Norton, there's not one of them," he said, smiling icily across the table at the Siberians, "you can stand near. Breath stinks like a goddamn—"

"General."

Yesov was smiling again, this time for the French press.

"I don't trust those Frogs either," said Freeman. "They let us down when we wanted to overfly France—get that son of a bitch Khaddafy."

"They helped us in the Iraqi war, General," Norton whispered.

"At the last goddamn minute. Not like the Brits."

"It's over, General. In a few days we'll be flying back to Khabarovsk and—" He was interrupted by applause as Yesov was acclaimed by the Siberian press—the marshal's grin at the camera so transparently insincere, Norton thought, that it would need drastic touching up if the Siberian propaganda ministry was going to use it.

"It's over," Lana told Frank Shirer.

"I know," he said, holding her, trying to feel good again. "You know that young cockney guy—all the facial burns and—"

"Yes," she said, trying to hold her impatience, wanting to put any talk of wounds and hospitals—her work—behind her. It was time to celebrate.

"He says," continued Shirer, stroking her hair but his mind clearly elsewhere, "that I should try for a transplant."

She knew he could. One grisly fact about the war and the abilities of the Americans to get their wounded back more quickly than anyone else was that organ donor banks—and most servicemen were donors—were full of spare parts.

"Well, tell him you don't want to—not now. Your fighting days are over, mister. Everyone's fighting days are over, thank

God," she said, her hand holding his, guiding it to where she wanted it. It was the only magic that could overcome his depression at the prospect of no longer being a pilot.

"God, I love you," he said.

"You, too."

"Problem is, not everyone's compatible." For an instant she thought he was talking about them, but then realized his preoccupation about losing the eye—and a transplant—was still with him.

"All depends," she said, "on whether you're a candidate in the first place. Priorities." She hesitated, then thought she might as well say it. "Some people can't even see, honey." But for all Shirer's maturity, it was about as effective as telling a child to eat his broccoli because thousands were starving in Ethiopia. But for the moment, with the help of her professional knowledge of anatomy, the admonition was working, and soon she felt the hardness growing. "Nothing wrong with this," she said, looking up, giving him the sweet, full smile that had first attracted him to her.

"No," he said. "It's ready for takeoff."

"Looking for somewhere to land?" she asked, snuggling in closer.

"Have to do some maneuvering first," he answered with a grin, and she knew that for the time being the horror of what they had done to him would abate.

"God, I love you," he told her.

"You, too. Oh now, sweetie, we can have time for each other instead of this damn war."

"Yes," he said. It was almost disappointment.

"Hold me," she said. He took her in his arms.

CHAPTER TWENTY-NINE

IT WAS THE sixth day. Salvini was on point, David left of him in the diamond, Choir and Aussie, right flank, when Salvini gave them the "freeze" signal. To have gone down would have kicked up the powder snow and made too much noise. The patrol coming toward them through the trees, about ten men, hadn't seen them yet but soon would. It was up to Salvini; he could see the most. The other three had all gone off "safety." Simultaneously Salvini waved the diamond down and took a chance. "American!"

There was a roar of submachine gun fire and men shouting. Then a white flag—an overlay held aloft, its bearer growing as he rose unsteadily to his feet, advancing now, waving the white overlay side to side. All the others, nine of them, were walking forward now, hands raised. They were Siberian regulars—hungry, tired, wearing the patch showing a bear with a lightning rod in his paws, the insignia of the Siberian Thirty-first Stalingrad Division. As the clatter of their surrendered weapons seemed to fill the forest with sound, Aussie noticed one of their weapons was an American-issue .45.

"Where'd you get that, Ivan?"

The Siberian affected ignorance, signifying he didn't speak English. Aussie flipped open the Siberian's holster flap and saw the "US Navy" stamp—Lieutenant R.C. Simpson.

"One of the Stallion crew," said Salvini.

"You sure?" asked David.

"I'm sure. Helped him load the Arrows."

Aussie drew his boot knife. "Where are they?" he asked the Siberian coldly.

"Easy, Aussie," cautioned David.

"Where the fuck are they?" repeated Aussie, the blade under the Siberian's chin.

A captain, hands still up, marched forward. "I speak little English."

"Yeah?" said Aussie, without taking his eyes off the man in front of him. "Where are the helicopter soldiers?"

The captain shrugged. "We find on way to front, yes?" he said, indicating the .45. "All kaput in helicopters. Everyone dead." He imitated a machine gun so well that Choir swung about and almost blew his head off.

"Sorry," said the Siberian quickly. "Sorry, but everyone kaput." He made a slashing motion across his throat. "SPETS-NAZ. You understand. Ah—"

"We understand," said David.

"I don't believe the bastard," said Aussie.

"I do," said David.

"Then how come they're heading back this way if they're on their way to the fucking front?"

"Excuse me, please," said the Siberian captain. "War is all finished."

"Bullshit!" said Aussie. "I oughta—"

"Knock it off, Lewis," warned David. "Back off. And that's an order."

Aussie sheathed the knife reluctantly without taking his eye off the Siberian. "If I find you're lying, Ivan, I'll hang you out to dry."

The Siberian was utterly unafraid. "You have radio? You hear war is over?"

"When was it over?" Aussie shot back.

"This last night."

It was three hours before they could pick up the BBC overseas broadcast, a mood of unhappy suspicion hanging over the S/D team as well as the hapless prisoners, their hands tied in a rope chain as they sat glumly in a circle.

When the S/D team heard the news of the cease-fire, the mood was more relief than exhilaration. Now they could break silence and call for pickup.

Aussie threw the Siberian captain a packet of cigarettes, but he was still morose. He'd never know for sure, but for now he believed the captain's story. They sure as hell weren't SPETS—no blue-and-white striped T-shirts to start with. And they didn't have the look. He only really hated the SPETS.

David made the call for pickup, and after waiting for an hour they started the purple smoke flares. David, seeing Aussie was still grumpy, embarrassed now by his outburst with the knife, looked over at Choir Williams. "Hey, Choir. How long you think it'll be till pickup?"

"An hour," said Choir.

"Salvini?" asked David.

"The same I reckon," answered Salvini, somewhat non-plussed.

"Gimme the map!" said Aussie. David let him study it for a moment or two, then asked casually, "Well, Aussie? How long do you say?"

"Forty-five minutes. Maximum."

"Ah, too soon," said David confidently.

"All right, Nostradamus," challenged Aussie. "Put some money on it. Ten to one?"

"Rubles?" inquired Choir.

"Fuck rubles," said Aussie. "Dollars—U.S." He looked around, indelible pencil in hand. "Who's in?"

CHAPTER THIRTY

WHEN COLONEL NEFSKI surveyed the rubble that had been the old library and hotel at Port Baikal, it was a wonder to him that any of them had survived the SAS/Delta commando attack. Half the prisoners had gone, vanished in the taiga, but he had little doubt that most, if not all, would be rounded up again. Top priority, he told his subaltern, was to be given to finding Alexsandra Malof. It was possible that the Jewish underground, using her as exhibit A, would try to reach the Americans, moaning again about "civil-rights abuses" and starting some damned UN investigation.

"We won't take a chance with that," Nefski told the corporal. "Shoot her on sight."

"What about the Jewish underground? She can still give us information—"

"If you find her, shoot her," snapped Nefski. "Where'd you get that bruise?"

"Ah, bit of wood, I think. Ricochet."

"Better get it seen to," advised Nefski, an unusual moment of concern for the well-being of the junior ranks. He felt more magnanimous now he'd cheated death, and more emboldened, determined to root out the undesirable elements now his efforts could turn away from what had been the wartime concerns to those of the cease-fire, to getting back to his old haunts in Khabarovsk.

As he walked toward the entrance to the hotel, its fairy-tale dome of snow sparkling in the sunlike sugar icing, he glanced at its ruined façade, shot through by SAS/Delta Force small-arms fire and the odd LAW round. But even among the ruins, the golden glints of sunlight off the ice along the eaves gave beauty to the place. He took it as a good omen; already he was thinking about hopes of promotion in the spring, though he would have to greatly increase the estimated number of American commandos that had attacked Port Baikal so as to further enhance the report of his vigorous defense.

His first step on the snow-laden steps of the hotel crunched in the warm winter sunshine. It was the vibration of his second step that proved too much for the fifty-pound icicle. Its stem snapped—and its long needle plummeted, smashing Nefski's skull like an eggshell. As he lay crumpled on the snow, *"bez priznakov zhizni"*—"dead as a doornail," as his subaltern said, everybody was already blaming everyone else for not having cleared the icicles, all and sundry later telling Novosibirsk HQ that under attack they'd had better things to do than look after the eaves.

Aussie lost sixty dollars—U.S.—because the Chinook helo, having spotted three figures moving north along the edge of the lake—Robert Brentwood and his two crewmen—had gone out to pick them up. It made the Chinook over an hour late. Aussie argued that "crook helicopters" rendered the bets null and void but he was howled down by his three compatriots whom he delicately called "fucking Ned Kellys," after the infamous Australian highwayman.

CHAPTER THIRTY-ONE

Two weeks later

GEORGINA HAD CHOSEN Lake Louise in the Canadian Rockies because as a child she had fallen in love with the grand, unabashed magnificence of the Canadian Pacific Hotel, the stolid, imposing holdout of what was commonly, if erroneously, thought to have been an easier and gentler age. David, to be truthful, didn't care where they got married—it was the marriage that counted. As it turned out, the small and cozy snow-covered Episcopalian—or, as Georgina called it, Anglican—church of St. George's in the Pines in Banff was perfect. And if Georgina's parents were prevented from attending because of the combination of cost and uneasy skies between Europe and North America, then at least David's mother and father were able to attend.

Standing ramrod straight, as became his rank, Admiral John Brentwood, Retired, said little during the ceremony except to advise his wife, "For Heaven's sake, Catherine, it's not a funeral.

Keep on like this, and we'll have to start the bilge pumps!''Catherine took no notice and was smiling beneath the intermittent tears. The admiral snuffled a lot, complaining later that the air was "too damn dry up here. Plays hell with my sinuses." When he shook David's hand he mumbled an advisory—no one knew exactly what, except it had something to do with "decks" and "heading into the wind." To Georgina he was positively grandfatherly and endearing, having decided in their brief meeting that her being a student of the London School of Economics and Political Science did not pose any immediate threat to the North American Alliance. What made his day complete, however, was the news, broadcast to his great satisfaction by the CBN network, which he detested, that his youngest son, along with several others, had been awarded the Silver Star for "action above and beyond the call of duty" around Lake Baikal.

During the fifty-mile drive from the small, private reception at the Banff Springs Hotel to Lake Louise for their honeymoon, they were as moved as a million tourists before them had been by the majestic sweep of blue sky and towering, snow-covered mountains. Mount Eisenhower was particularly impressive with its ramparts thrusting heavenward from the forests girding it around the frozen course of the Bow River.

"Another medal?" Georgina said it to David in that insouciant English way that admires the very thing it pretends to be mocking.

David shrugged bashfully, folding his pants neatly, SAS inspection-style, knifelike edges carefully aligned, before he draped them over the plush recliner set before a window that looked out on the dazzling turquoise edge of the Victoria glacier, astonishingly beautiful in the twilight. Georgina, fully clothed, keeping her coat on despite the heat of the room, watched him against the Rocky Mountain vista. "Stunning, isn't it?" she said.

"Sure is."

"That's why I chose it."

"Must have cost your dad a packet," said David, shaking his head in awe. "I chose the right father-in-law!" He turned from the awesome glacier—intent now on another view and just as impressed. It was going to take some time—longer than the brief wedding ceremony in Banff. Or could he wait? He reached for the cord to close the drapes. "Leave them open," said Georgina cheekily. "I'm sure the glacier won't mind."

"Tourists will."

"There are none, silly. Not this time of year. It's not exactly spring yet."

"I'd rather them closed," he said, pulling the cord, walking toward her, unbuttoning his shirt. "I'm going to do terrible things to you."

"*David!* You promise?"

"Yes, ma'am."

Apart from the obligatory wedding peck in Banff——he didn't like making it a public spectacle—it was the first time they'd kissed, really kissed, since he'd left for the Ratmanov mission that now seemed so long ago. They lingered as long as breath would allow and then some, his hand slipping beneath her dress, sliding along the firmness of her thigh, pulling down the panty hose slowly. She pressed against him, his arm sliding between her legs, then his hand cupping, lifting her up and onto the bed, her soft murmur enticing him, her rose perfume washing over him, the tight, smooth V of her panties now moist, she feeling for him, squeezing him, her nipples engorged. He could restrain himself no longer, her sudden gasp one of pleasure, the feel of her gripping him, pulling him, engulfing him, filling him with a happiness he'd dreamt of in the past few months but doubted he'd ever experience again. She arched, her head moving from side to side, lips insistent, auburn hair a sheen in the soft, peach glow. She stopped—dead still. Waiting.

"What's wrong?" asked David, alarmed.

She was trying to speak, her throat parched, her smile the most beautiful he'd ever seen. "I want to start all over again."

"Holy dooley!" he said, the cornseed expression making her chuckle, making her even more desirable. They began again, and all he could hear was her whispering with terrible, loving urgency, "Harder, David—harder!" and he, wanting to make it last, to draw out the ecstasy, switched his thoughts to something distant—to Lake Baikal and the men who were gone and would never feel the pleasure he was feeling. Away from her for a moment, when he returned it was as if they were together for the first time, ready now to let go utterly.

CHAPTER THIRTY-TWO

"OH, THAT'S LOVELY, that is!" proclaimed Aussie to the British liaison officer in Freeman's Khabarovsk HQ. "Very bloody nice. You mean we've gotta stay in this burg for another six weeks. Bloody Brentwood, he's home. Probably dippin' his wick for all I know."

"Your papers haven't come through," said the British liaison office sergeant coolly. "That's all."

"That's all! This bloody Welshman here—" He turned, his thumb jerking at an amused Choir Williams. "He's on his way home. On one of your plurry Hercules, and here's me—the bloody hero of Baikal—don't even get my picture in the local rag."

"Stars and Stripes," corrected the sergeant. "Anyway, they've got bigger news than you. Bigshot La Roche is up on stock market charges. Inside trading for army supplies."

"Who the hell's La Roche?" said Aussie disinterestedly.

"You carryin' any aspirin?" the sergeant asked him.

"What?"

"Well, if you are, he probably sold 'em to the army. Supplied everything from chemicals to shoelaces. Could be put away in the slammer for ten years."

"Hey, hey," interrupted Aussie. "I don't give a fig about La Roach or who the hell he is. What I'm worried about is while Williams here is about to shove off back to friggin' Wales, I'm stuck here on friggin' cease-fire duty."

"Not to worry, Aussie," said Choir. "Salvini's pulled the same duty. They'll have you back in Wales soon enough, boyo."

"This might surprise you, *boyo*," said Aussie, "but I don't like bloody Wales."

"You volunteered, boyo."

"Yeah, so I'm a mug."

"Ah, don't fret, lad," said Choir, winking at the duty sergeant, without Aussie seeing it. "You'll probably be here in time for the Amur caper."

"What the hell's that?"

"Come spring, summer," explained Choir, "lot of nude sunbathing on the banks of the Amur, I'm told."

"Yeah?" said Aussie.

"Isn't that right, sergeant?" Choir asked.

"That's right. Tits from here to the sea."

"Camping sites," added Choir, "all along the river."

"You lyin' bastard!" charged Aussie.

"No, no," said Choir seriously. "True, boyo. Siberians love the sun. Now, you could get a Humvee from the car pool. . . . That a possibility, Sarge?"

"I suppose," said the sergeant, "it could be arranged for the 'Hero of Baikal.' "

"Fair dinkum?" asked Aussie, meaning, was it true or were they pulling his leg. "They go topless?"

"No!" said the sergeant, going over a "lost property" report. "They take it *all* off, old son. That's what I'm told."

"Yeah?"

"Absolutely."

"Well, I might stay, then," said Aussie.

"Course," added Choir, "you don't have to go to the river beaches to find it, I'm told. Place in Khabarovsk—'Bear' Restaurant. KGB used to use it, so they say. Lot of crumpet there now, I'm told."

"Hey, I'm loaded for Bear, fellas!"

"I know," said Choir.

The sergeant wasn't listening any more. The quartermaster in one of the Second Army's supply battalions had sent a fax saying that enough American artillery uniforms had been stolen to equip a whole battery of 155 howitzers. Someone said the uniforms had probably ended up being flogged on the black market south of the Siberian-Outer Mongolian border, in Ulan Bator. The Mongolian party officials, always much closer to the Soviets than the Chinese, whom they hated, were apparently allowing a lot of free enterprise these days—or at least what they thought was a lot of it.

"Hell," one sergeant said, looking at the fax, "we're selling army surplus stuff all the time anyway."

"Yeah, but not stolen stuff. Anyway, it's the wrong time of year to be flogging off winter gear—soon be spring. Strange."

An hour before he was to leave Irkutsk, after three days of having to perform what he called one of the most distasteful duties "of my career," shaking hands with Siberians and officers from the Outer Mongolian garrisons, Freeman took time off, sightseeing, with Norton accompanying him.

From the frozen onion dome of Irkutsk's Church of the Crucifixion, they gazed out over the ancient city of the Transbaikal city. The church from which they were admiring the sight, Freeman informed Norton, had been the administrative center for all the Russian Orthodox churches in *Russkaya Amerika*—"Russia-America."

"Irkutsk," he told Norton, "was also the most important trading center on Baikal on the way to Russia-America-Alaska. That is, before some congressman, who everyone thought was nuts, bought Alaska."

Freeman was squinting against the brilliant white light of the snow-covered chimneys idly issuing curlicues of smoke into the pristine winter air.

"You know where the Alaskans would be if we hadn't bought it?" Freeman answered his own question. "In the silver mines of Nerchinsk—slaves of the tsar. Huh. Tsars were almost as bad as Stalin when it came to slave labor in the mines. Usual flogging was a hundred strokes with the *plet*—three-strand rawhide. You had to walk there from here—Irkutsk—and if you faltered and fell, you died where you fell. Hell, in the mines they didn't even note a prisoner's death. In World War Two we sent Wallace, the vice president, over to Magadan in the northeast to have a look at their gold mines there.

"Well, of course they did a Potemkin village on him—all the prisoners were well fed, looking great. They should have been. Bastards were members of the NKVD—secret police before they changed the name to KGB." Freeman shook his head disbelievingly. "Unbeknown to the vice president, it was the head thug of the camp, the director—and his wife, as much a thug as he was—who had shown them around. It was pathetic. The VP's sidekick, a *professor*, went back to Washington, said the head of the camp they'd toured was a man who had 'a deep sense of civic responsibility.' Thug had another job—people's representative of Birobidzhan. Jewish autonomous region. Some of the Jews figured it was time to leave." Freeman turned eastward and from the tower looked over the taiga beyond the city in the direction of Lake Baikal. "Can't imagine why, can you?

"You see," Freeman's voice echoed as he walked down the steeple's stairwell, "that's what continues to amaze me, Dick. They send over intellectuals with the naiveté of a four-year-old to assess the situation. No wonder we have to end up fighting them. It's the four-year-olds who are dictating the cease-fire."

Norton didn't answer. Politics was deep water in the army, something the general was blindly naive about, for all his sophistication in matters military. It wasn't until they were out of the church, walking toward the general's staff car, four U.S. outriders starting up their motorcycles, that Freeman, seeing trucks of the Siberian Fifth Army rolling past the Cathedral, said, "To think we came so far, Dick. Over a thousand miles in from the Siberian coast, damned near past Baikal, which," he added, "we wouldn't have if I hadn't authorized that FAE strike on Ratmanov."

Norton nodded his assent.

"And," continued Freeman, "had it not been for those Brentwoods and other men . . ." It was then that Norton saw tears in Freeman's eyes. "Freedom," he told Norton, "sometimes exacts a terrible price but in my heart of hearts, in this Freeman that only Freeman sees, Dick—I believe that ultimately we have to pay for it, buy it in blood." He exhaled wearily. "So that bloodless gentlemen can call me a 'warmonger' without me shooting the sons of bitches."

On the way out to the airport, U.S. MPs flanking him, their

motorcycles throwing up fine trails of snow, Freeman glanced back and pointed out the frozen fountain in front of the Angara Hotel. "In spring, they tell me they swim in that fountain." He turned back to Norton. "I was struck by that fact, because it shows how they use everything they have. Tough, too, swimming so early in the thaw."

The general fell into a deep, reflective mood. Finally when he spoke, his tone was one of mellow speculation laced with warning. "Come spring I don't know where the hell I'll be. Those clowns in Foggy Bottom are regrouping to get me home as soon as they can. Well, home is where my war is, Dick, and I want to know the moment the first lake cracks—the moment the melt starts."

Norton was jolted by the implication. "You think they'll try something, General?"

"Spring thaw's very bad for armor, Dick. Floods, mud. If I was that son of a bitch Yesov, that's when I'd counterattack. Catch us with our pants down."

"Lord, General, I hope you're wrong."

"It's a cease-fire, Dick. Not a surrender."

"Well," said Norton confidently, "we've got the Russian president, Chernko, on our side. He should keep them in line. Did good work for us in Moscow."

"We'll see," said Freeman, watching a hawk hovering high toward Lake Baikal.

In Anchorage Lana, sitting and talking with Frank earlier, had now been overtaken by a combination of exhaustion and relief at the news of the cease-fire and was dozing, resting her head on the edge of the bed.

Gingerly, not wanting to wake her, Frank reached for the newspaper cutting the limey had left him on the bedside table. It was a clipping from a six-month-old *Stars and Stripes* Backgrounder column talking about how Soviet air ace Sergei Marchenko, before he had gone missing over North Korea, had clashed with Soviet air officialdom. Apparently his vision had been deficient in one eye—below the standard required by the Air Force Academy—and he had tried, unsuccessfully, to invoke the case of General Adolf Gallind, Germany's top air ace and head of the Luftwaffe Fighter Command, who had flown not only the prop-driven Messerschmitt but also the first jet fighter, the Messerschmitt 262. He had done it with only one eye, the other being glass.

Quickly Shirer flipped over the clipping for more details, but all he saw was an ad for Coca Cola—"the real thing." He waited for the limey to reappear, but it was a full twenty minutes before he showed up, ambling through the ward. Lana sighed in her sleep and snuggled further into Frank, who was anxiously waving the limey over.

"What's up, mate?"

Shirer spoke softly but urgently. "How'd he pull it off?"

"Who?"

Shirer indicated the news clipping. "Galland."

The limey shrugged. "Dunno, mate. Might've memorized the old eye chart."

"I've thought of that," said Shirer, his voice low, "but they make you close one eye."

"Yah," said the limey, "guess you're right. I dunno."

"You're a great help," said Frank. "He must've thought of some—"

"Tell you what, sunshine," said the cockney, his tone markedly at odds with the grotesque burn mask he was obliged to wear. "I'll ask the professor—mate o' mine—when I get 'ome."

"That'll be months," said Frank, not meaning to be unkind but clearly anxious.

"Yeah, but what's the big 'urry? Cease-fire, mate."

"Yes," responded Frank. "Well, if you find out, let me know."

"Not to worry, sport. Ta ta!"

"Frank?" asked Hana, looking drowsy.

"Yes?"

"What's up?"

"I am," he replied. "New flight plan."

"The war's finished," she said, yawning.

"Maybe, but I'm not, babe. Not yet."

ABOUT THE AUTHOR

Canadian Ian Slater, a veteran of the Australian Joint Intelligence Bureau, has a Ph.D. in political science. He teaches at the University of British Columbia and is managing editor of *Pacific Affairs*. He has written numerous thrillers, most recently WORLD WAR III, WORLD WAR III: RAGE OF BATTLE, and WORLD WAR III: WORLD IN FLAMES. He lives in Vancouver with his wife and two children.

IAN SLATER